"An effortlessly charming d___ us great comedy in the form of feuding-family shenanigans, along with swoony romance . . . and huskies. What more could you want? This is an engrossing read that will take you on a trip to small-town Alaska and make you fall in love."   —Jen DeLuca, author of *Well Played*

"*Heart On A Leash* had my heart from page one. . . . Whether you're a dog lover, cat lover, or romance lover, you're sure to fall head over heels for this book."
                        —Sarah Smith, author of *Simmer Down*

"With two charming leads, three irresistible pups, and a small town unlike any I've read before, *Heart on a Leash* tugged at my emotions and warmed my soul. The perfect book to snuggle up with and savor."
                —Rachel Lynn Solomon, author of *The Ex-Talk*

"A small-town romance that defies cliché. Complex family rivalries, swoon-worthy romance, and (of course!) adorable dogs make this a heart-melting love story."
                —Michelle Hazen, author of *Breathe the Sky*

"A heartwarming contemporary romance that puts a new spin on the enemies-to-lovers trope, *Heart on a Leash* takes us on an insightful journey of falling in love without the support of family. Sexy and sensitive: the undeniable chemistry between the heroine and hero (and a pack of adorable huskies) drive the story to its charming conclusion—tail wags and HEA included."
                        —Samantha Vérant, author of
                The Secret French Recipes of Sophie Valroux

TITLES BY ALANNA MARTIN

....

The Hearts of Alaska Novels
Heart on a Leash
Paws and Prejudice
Love and Let Bark

LOVE
AND
LET BARK

Alanna Martin

JOVE
New York

A JOVE BOOK
Published by Berkley
An imprint of Penguin Random House LLC
penguinrandomhouse.com

Copyright © 2021 by Tracey Martin
Excerpt from *Heart on a Leash* by Alanna Martin copyright © 2021 by Tracey Martin
Penguin Random House supports copyright. Copyright fuels creativity, encourages
diverse voices, promotes free speech, and creates a vibrant culture. Thank you for buying
an authorized edition of this book and for complying with copyright laws by not
reproducing, scanning, or distributing any part of it in any form without permission.
You are supporting writers and allowing Penguin Random House to continue to
publish books for every reader.

A JOVE BOOK, BERKLEY, and the BERKLEY & B colophon
are registered trademarks of Penguin Random House LLC.

ISBN: 9780593198872

First Edition: November 2021

Printed in the United States of America
1 3 5 7 9 10 8 6 4 2

Cover design by Farjana Yasmin
Book design by Alison Cnockaert

To Al, who knows why

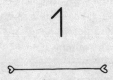

1

IF THE WEDDING didn't kill everyone, Lydia Lipin might have to do it herself. Surely no judge would convict her, not when they learned about the circumstances. Her younger sister wasn't even getting married for another nine months, but already the strain Lydia felt was bone deep.

Actually, make that premeditated murder deep.

Her hometown of Helen, Alaska, had been torn apart by the Lipin-Porter family feud for over a century, and while it didn't make being a member of either family fun, it was something everyone was accustomed to. Like tourists, and rain, and mosquitoes—if you lived in Helen, you accepted that the feud was life. But Lydia's sister was engaged to a Porter, and Taylor and Josh exchanging kisses—never mind vows—was not something either family was ready to accept. Lydia wasn't sure how the planned nuptials hadn't exploded into true violence yet, although to be fair to both families' ingenuity, it had come close. In the meantime, Lydia was waiting and getting exhausted.

Nine more months had become her litany. Nine more months before the happy, troublemaking couple said *I do*. Nine more months before there was a chance of the animosity between the families dying down. And most important, nine more months before Lydia no longer had to shield her sister from the relatives who were furious about her engagement.

Then, who knew how long she'd be serving as a shield between those family members and the married couple? Possibly the rest of her life.

Yup, homicide almost seemed like a benign option at this point, and a half-decent defense attorney had to be cheaper than Lydia's ballooning wine budget. If only she dealt with the stress in a healthier manner—say, exercise—she'd probably be in top physical condition.

There were a lot of *if only*s in Lydia's life. Most of them could trace a line straight back to *if only* there weren't a feud.

But there was, and one of its most ardent supporters was standing on the other side of the desk in Lydia's cramped office, holding a cream-colored piece of card stock between her thumb and index finger as though it were covered in cooties. Lydia didn't have to ask what it was. Her own wedding invitation was sitting on her kitchen table.

"The venue Taylor and the man have chosen for the wedding is entirely inappropriate," Theresa Lipin said.

"Taylor and the man" was how her grandmother had taken to referring to her sister and Josh. Lydia had heard the phrase enough times over the last few months that it was starting to sound catchy. Derek and the Dominos, Siouxsie and the Banshees, Florence and the Machine. Taylor and the Man.

Lydia stifled a giggle. God, she was tired, but laughing in front of her grandmother would be a terrible way to defuse the situation, and defusing the situation was the best wedding present she could give to her sister. Lydia loved Taylor even if she kind of wanted to strangle her for creating this mess. Of all the men Taylor could have fallen in love with, she had to pick a Porter. It was just like Taylor, causing trouble without even trying. Lydia, on the other hand, wouldn't know where to start.

"What's wrong with the venue?" she asked, not really caring to hear the answer since it would only be an excuse. Nothing needed to be wrong with the venue when the wedding was simply wrong enough in the family's eyes.

"I attended a wedding there several years ago," her grandmother said. "The building is drafty, the ballroom's decor is outdated, the food was mediocre at best . . ." And on it went.

Lydia kept her face impassive, although she'd gone from wanting to laugh to wanting to scream at a faster than usual speed. The irony was that Lydia and Taylor ran a hotel that had earned accolades for being one of the best places to get married in the state.

The Bay Song Inn was as much her family's legacy as the feud. Her grandparents had opened it decades ago when tourism in their coastal town was starting to take off. What had allegedly begun as Theresa dreaming about owning a bed-and-breakfast had morphed into them opening a boutique hotel with over thirty guest rooms, a multipurpose function room, and a detached restaurant—the Tavern—that catered to guests and non-guests alike. Never let it be said that her grandmother didn't dream big.

When her grandparents had given up the day-to-day running of the hotel, it had passed to Lydia's father and mother. But rather than either of them running it until retirement age, her father had slowly abdicated the responsibility as he got involved in town government. Then last summer, her mother had announced she'd had enough of being forced into a profession she'd never wanted and had run off to Anchorage, and Taylor returned to Helen to help out after years of living in Los Angeles. The end result of all this upheaval was that Lydia was currently in charge of the Bay Song with Taylor working as her hospitality manager. When Taylor wasn't cavorting with the Lipins' sworn enemy, that is.

But at least Taylor had someone to keep her bed warm while she wreaked havoc over everyone's life. All Lydia had was her cat, cheap wine, and a lot of headaches.

The computer screen in front of her showed a mock-up for the hotel's new website, taunting her with visions for how they could advertise their wedding facilities. But no matter how much sense it made to have her sister's wedding at the Bay Song, that was not happening. If there was any chance of the event not ending like a scene in *Game of Thrones*, it had to take place in neutral territory.

Lost in worries of a blood-soaked reception, it took Lydia a second to realize her grandmother had stopped ranting.

"Taylor handles all things wedding-related here," Lydia said, trying to be both sensible and conciliatory. "I'm sure she knew exactly what to look for when choosing a venue."

Lydia was more than sure because she and Taylor had spent hours discussing the various options, but part of being a shield meant downplaying how much she was helping her sister. She couldn't be a buffer if the more aggressive members of the family realized how much she sided with Taylor. They would ignore her then, and there would be no one to soothe the savage beasts or prevent them from getting near Taylor, something Lydia did on a regular basis when they came by the hotel during business hours.

And Lydia did side with Taylor, despite the grief her sister caused. Lydia envied her finding the (would-have-been) perfect guy, but just as much, she envied her sister's bravery and determination for trying to make her relationship with Josh work out.

She also couldn't imagine being that reckless herself, but whatever. Taylor and her grandmother might not get along these days, but there was no denying Taylor had the feud's fighting spirit in her blood. Lydia, not so much. Even in appearance, Lydia favored her mother's side of the family.

That was never more evident than when watching her grandmother now. Theresa might be a widow in her early seventies, but she looked a decade younger with her short gray hair and steely eyes. She was a rock, hard and immovable. Lydia usually felt like driftwood, dragged along by the current and trying to hold herself together.

"I no longer trust that Taylor knows anything about what she's doing." Theresa crossed her arms, glaring at the photos of her beloved hotel hanging behind Lydia's head.

Clearly, her grandmother assumed Taylor was going to ruin the place, and Lydia spun her chair around so Theresa wouldn't see her roll her eyes. Lord, with all the tension she was carrying in her shoulders, she could use a massage. A hot, wealthy man to sweep her off her feet and make this mess go away wouldn't hurt either. But she'd settle for a massage.

"Where is she?" Theresa asked. "I want to talk to her. Is she by the kitchen?"

Probably, yes, but this was the part when Lydia did her best to become a barrier between an irate family member and her sister. She reached for her phone, preparing to text Taylor as soon her grandmother left the office so Taylor would have a chance to run.

Before Lydia could neither confirm nor deny Taylor's whereabouts, however, the front desk buzzed her. "Hey, Ms. Lipin?"

Perfect. Just the distraction Lydia needed. "Hi, Shawn."

"I've got a guest checking in who says he was a friend of yours, and he asked if you were around?" Shawn sounded uncertain, and he kept his voice low, suggesting whoever this friend was, he might still be hanging around the lobby.

Theresa made a disapproving face. "You're in a meeting. It's not appropriate for the staff to be bothering you if it's not an emergency."

Shawn, who was on speaker, likely heard the comment, and Lydia gritted her teeth. "Did he leave a name?" she asked, ignoring her grandmother. Damn it, this was her hotel now. She'd run it how she liked, and she was meeting with family, not a client or a guest. Which Shawn knew.

Shawn also knew that whenever Theresa Lipin stormed into the hotel, searching for one or the other of her granddaughters, Lydia hung an invisible "Please Disturb" sign on her door.

Shawn lowered his voice further, but some excitement crept in. "It's Cody Miller. Isn't he the Hitched guy?"

Lydia froze for a second as her brain processed this information. Cody Miller, friend, and Hitched were not three things that were meant to go together. Yes, she'd been friends with Cody in school. More than friends at times, actually. And yes, Cody was the guy who'd built Hitched—a travel and ride-share app. But super-wealthy, tech darling Cody and friend Cody had always been two different people in Lydia's mind, even though logically she understood that they were one and the same. Probably it had something to do with the fact that she hadn't seen Cody since before college, and they'd lost touch completely soon after.

So how was it that Cody was in her hotel and asking after her? Cody might be from Helen, but the town was not the sort of location that was likely to draw tech magnates. The only explanation that made sense was that Cody was visiting family, but Lydia could have sworn his family no longer lived here.

Regardless, Cody was here, he was an old friend, and perhaps just as importantly, he was an ideal distraction.

"I'll be right out," Lydia told Shawn, and she ended the call.

"Hitched?" her grandmother asked. "That's an app, correct?"

Lydia was only mildly surprised that Theresa was familiar with the app. Her grandmother might dislike most technology, but she wasn't precisely a Luddite. She simply preferred face-to-face interactions. It was easier to turn a critical eye on someone that way.

"Yes." Lydia stood, slipping her phone in her back pocket. Most days she tried to dress in a style that Taylor referred to as *Alaskan professional*, a snarkism that proved you could take the sister out of L.A. but you couldn't take the L.A. entirely out of the sister. But today was a Friday, and Lydia hadn't dressed to impress— jeans and a simple cowl-necked sweater would have to do for meeting a billionaire. After all, tech darlings got away with wearing whatever they wanted, so why not her? Lydia had never seen a magazine or news photo of Cody wearing anything other than jeans.

"Cody is the boy you went to your prom with, isn't he?" her grandmother continued.

That was much more surprising than Theresa knowing what Hitched was. But then, she and Cody had been an on-again, off-again thing for years. "Yes."

Theresa nodded thoughtfully, the savage anti-wedding beast soothed, her invitation forgotten about on Lydia's desk. "He was a nice boy. Smart."

Cody had been smart, no doubt. He'd beaten out Lydia for valedictorian. Yet Lydia assumed her grandmother's praise had more to do with Cody's family being firmly pro-Lipin in the feud.

"Rich now, too, I'm guessing," Theresa said. "Interesting that he came by to see you."

It *was* interesting, but that was Lydia's cue to make a hasty retreat for the lobby. The next sentence out of her grandmother's mouth would likely involve the state of Lydia's ovaries. Her grandmother had been determined to get Lydia married to the right sort of guy—that was, one of her choosing—for years. While Theresa and the rest of the family might not approve of Taylor's choice of husband, her younger sister getting married had only made the nonsense Lydia had to deal with worse.

Late January was not a typical time for people to visit Helen, although true outdoor recreation enthusiasts were never deterred by the weather or lack of sunlight. As such, the hotel was one-quarter booked, but that didn't mean corners had been cut. Flames crackled happily in the oversize fireplace, casting flickering light over the rustic wood decor, and the air smelled faintly of pine thanks to the scented candles lit at the reception desk.

The inn's complimentary homemade cookies and coffee sat out near the glass doors that overlooked the patio. It was almost time for Taylor to bring out the evening wine, which meant Lydia had to shake their grandmother soon. Cody had distracted her, but for how long?

Speaking of Cody, it took Lydia a second to recognize him sitting in one of the armchairs by the fire. For some reason, she'd expected him to be surrounded by an entourage, like a rock star, but he sat by himself, playing with his phone in one hand and holding a peanut butter cookie in the other. He looked totally at home and was dressed to Taylor's exacting *Alaskan professional* standards—rugged khaki pants, thick sweater, and durable boots. Lydia suspected those clothing items were made by a brand that the average Helen resident couldn't afford, but for the first time, her brain was able to reconcile the two Codys it carried around.

He jumped up as she strode over to him. "Lydia! It's so good to see you." Cody pulled her into a hug that she hadn't been anticipating, and she had to course correct before smacking her nose into his shoulder.

Well, that was unexpected, but they had been close during school. Lydia decided to shrug it off and follow his lead. "It's good to see you too."

Cody beamed at her, holding her hands while he assessed her. "You look fantastic. Haven't changed a bit."

Okay. Although she was trying to follow his lead, that might have been a touch over the top. Lydia cracked a questioning smile. "I can't decide whether that's too sweet or just hilarious. But you look exactly like you do in all your press."

Which was to say Cody looked more like Hollywood than Silicon Valley, though Lydia figured it was wisest to keep that to herself, since Cody's ego likely didn't need the boost. Creating a hugely successful product would get you only so much publicity. Creating a hugely successful product while looking like a charmingly boyish blond god got you a lot more, even in the tech industry.

"What brings you here?" Lydia asked. "A family visit?" And why now? Cody must have visited his family previously, but he'd never stopped by to see her.

"Actually my family moved a few years ago," Cody said, finally releasing her hands. "I got them a nice place down south." *Down south* could mean anywhere in the Lower 48, but Cody continued before Lydia could ask. "I missed this place, though, you know? I bought a little vacation spot just outside of town. I'm having it renovated, so I'm here to meet with the architects and discuss what needs to be done."

With the architects, plural. Somehow Lydia doubted the spot was all that small. "Are you staying here, then?"

She tried to hide it, but a note of bewilderment crept into her voice. Cody had to be staying somewhere, but the Bay Song, while upscale for Helen, didn't seem like it was upscale enough for someone with Cody's money. For all she knew, he flew in and out of town daily on a private plane.

"Absolutely." Cody grinned. It was the smile that had turned him from a simple tech darling into a tech darling heartthrob, and yet Lydia's heart didn't skip a beat.

That was also interesting. Whatever she'd once felt for him had evaporated over the years, and that was disappointing. Hadn't she just been thinking that she could use a hot, rich man to sweep her off her feet? Cody showing up on her doorstep had, for a second, felt like the answer to a prayer. Yet her feet remained firmly planted on the inn's floor.

Of course, if Lydia were being honest, she'd admit to

herself that her feelings for Cody had diminished months before high school graduation. It wasn't time that had made her realize she'd always been tepid about him; it had been feelings for someone else. It had been discovering what it was like to kiss a boy who made her insides feel like they were burning up beneath her skin.

But that had also been a long time ago. So, practically speaking, there was no point in such honesty, and Lydia dismissed the memory.

"The Bay Song was always the dream," Cody said, chuckling at her surprised face. "Growing up here, I used to think if you could afford to stay at the Bay Song, you'd made it. I had to stay here."

Lydia smiled but she felt like her face might crack. No pressure there. "I hope we don't disappoint."

"Not possible." His gaze was heavy as it roamed from her feet to the top of her head, giving Lydia the sense that he wasn't referring to the room amenities.

"You always did have a silver tongue." She needed a distraction from her distraction. If she'd still been attracted to him, Lydia would have been flattered. As it was, she mostly felt unsure of herself. "Let me know if there's anything we can do for you."

"How about getting together?" Cody glanced at his phone. "I've got a few projects I'm working on that need my attention while I'm in town, but I can always fit you into my schedule."

"That sounds great." Rather, that *would* sound great, except for her distinct impression that Cody's motivation for getting together was different from hers. But she could figure that out later. And besides, it wouldn't be terrible to give the man a chance if her interpretation of his motives was correct. Her dating life wasn't exactly overflowing with possibilities.

"Great. Let's catch up later. I've got to go return a call." Cody squeezed her hand and leaned closer. "It's really good to see you."

"You too." Lydia's smile drooped, and she breathed easier as he strode toward the elevator.

"I like him." Her grandmother's voice startled Lydia, and she turned around. Theresa leaned against the reception desk, discreetly out of the way but with an unimpeded view of everything that had just taken place.

"You always did," she reminded her grandmother.

"Yes, but I like him still." Theresa pulled on her coat, which meant the Taylor crisis might be adverted. "And he seemed to like you."

"I picked up on that."

"Good." Her grandmother was actually smiling. "Sometimes I wonder, based on the way you turn your nose up at every suitable man you meet."

The level of wine in Lydia's future glass rose another half inch. It was her reward for holding her tongue.

"But that one." Theresa pointed a finger in the direction Cody had disappeared in. "He's attractive, he's rich, he's smart, and he's famous. I knew of his app, but I didn't realize how well known he was himself. Shawn was showing me articles on his phone."

Apparently her grandmother had been spying and researching at the same time, such impressive multitasking. "I know."

"I'm sure you do." Her grandmother kissed her cheek. "You're too smart to have missed the possibility here. And too beautiful and too good of a granddaughter to deserve anything less."

Lydia put her well-practiced smile back on her face, hugged her grandmother, and didn't relax her shoulders until the older woman had disappeared into the dark, chilly air. Her grandmother's bias aside, Theresa wasn't wrong to dream big. Cody wasn't just a good catch; he was a next-to-impossible one.

So while Lydia didn't feel the slightest uptick in her pulse despite all that close contact, she knew she'd do exactly as her grandmother wanted. She'd keep an open mind. Even if nothing came of it, spending time with Cody would make her family happy, and making them happy right now was no small accomplishment. Plus, a happy family would make life more pleasant overall, which would make Lydia happy.

Since no man had yet to manage that, she'd take the victories she could get.

2

⚬————————⚬

A HORRIBLE NOISE jolted Nate Porter awake, and it took him a second to realize it was coming from his phone. It was a long second, because being jolted set off waves of pain that made it impossible to think clearly. They started as a dull throb radiating outward from his left shoulder before crystallizing into something that felt like a hot knife. Then that, too, melted away, leaving him with an overall unpleasant sensation somewhere in between.

The phone rang a second time as Nate contemplated whether it was too soon to take another painkiller. In the corner of his living room, his two young puppies barked excitedly at the sound. The little monsters were adorable but also the reason he was napping at seven in the evening. Little dogs had little bladders. He needed to work on getting them to pee on his schedule, not theirs. Having just survived a collision with a tractor trailer, it would be a shame to end up dying from sleep deprivation.

Blinking wearily, Nate reached for his phone. "Hi, Kels."

"Did I wake you?" His younger sister sounded amused.

"Maybe." He yawned as the puppies began tussling on the floor. Why had he thought it was a good idea to adopt two hyper husky puppies last month? He was so weak, but the brother-and-sister pair had been rescued as newborns, and they'd clung to him as soon as he'd met them, and . . . Yeah, he was weak.

He was also utterly lacking in logic. Nate didn't know what he was going to do with the pair once fire season started. Adopting them had been an impulsive decision, but at the age of thirty-one, he was realizing he needed something to unconditionally love and to love him unconditionally in return. It wasn't like he had any other prospects—a circumstance that was largely due to his own choices, but that didn't fill the occasional emptiness inside.

"Sleeping at six?" Kelsey asked. "When did you get to be so old?"

"It's seven here," Nate reminded her. "When did you forget I'm in Washington?"

"Whatever. It's only a one-hour difference. Why were you sleeping? Oh." Her tone changed, the snark mellowing into concern. "Is it the drugs?"

Nate smiled, though he was glad Kelsey couldn't see his expression. His sister reminded him of this Yorkshire terrier one of his friends used to have. She'd been an adorable ball of fluff with a vicious bark, but also a fiercely loyal sweetheart to those she loved. Much like Kelsey.

Of course, Nate would never tell his sister this. Family bonds and loyalty meant only so much, and although he was pretty sure he could take Kelsey's five-foot-nothing punch, he was in no condition to try at the moment. As a firefighter, Nate took risks for a living, but even he had his limits.

"No, it's not the drugs." Bracing himself, Nate maneuvered into a more upright position, setting off fresh pain, this time in his torso. To be fair to the puppies, they weren't the only things keeping him up at night. One fractured clavicle plus multiple bruised ribs didn't exactly make for restful sleep. The pain had lessened over the past week, but lessened was a far cry from him feeling comfortable.

It was wisest to say nothing of this to Kelsey, however. Their mother had just flown back home after parking herself in his house for the past several days to help, for which Nate had been grateful. But five days of being nursed by his mother was enough. She'd wanted him to return home, to Alaska, so she could continue to dote on him while he recovered, and she wasn't the only one. Kelsey made the pitch as well each time she called to check up on him.

Like he didn't have people here who could help? Okay, fine, his friends were more apt to laugh at his condition than to express concern, but that was just what happened with guys. In the end, they came through. It was impossible not to form close bonds when working his kind of job, so Nate had people in his life whom he could count on. They simply weren't family people or a girlfriend. And that was fine. He didn't need the latter, and he sure didn't need to return home to listen to his mother chide him (again) for this great failing.

"It's Dolly and Spark," Nate said, watching the pair zip around the room like black-and-white rockets. "I'm still getting them trained."

"And how's that working out with your injuries?"

Not great, but manageable. As long as he had one good arm, he could keep them under control. "I'll be fine."

"Will they?"

"Oh, now I get it." Nate propelled himself off the sofa, trying to get the move over quickly to minimize the way his ribs screamed their displeasure. "You don't care about me. You want to play with my puppies."

"Took you long enough to figure that out."

"Doesn't Kevin have a puppy for you to play with?" Nate asked, referring to Kelsey's twin brother. For that matter, Kelsey had three adult huskies of her own. It wasn't like she was dog-deprived.

Kelsey sighed. "He does, but Neptune is more teenish these days. It's not the same."

"Hey, knock it off." Nate ignored his sister for a second as he attempted to stop Spark from chewing one of his sneakers. With his left arm in a sling, he had to put the phone down, and he winced as he lowered himself to the floor.

Yeah, things were definitely not great, but manageable.

"I am worried about you." Kelsey sounded serious, almost as though she could see through the phone and knew what had transpired.

"I told you—it's fine." He set the phone on speaker, using his good arm to close the blinds. His driveway sat empty, the spot where his car should have been was another reminder of how his life had been turned upside down one week ago.

Nate had always assumed if he were going to be injured, it would be on the job. Firefighting was a dangerous profession, and as part of a Hotshot team for the Forest Service, he frequently pushed his body to its limits each fire season. But it wasn't burns or smoke inhalation that had sent Nate to the hospital. It was that damned tractor trailer.

In the off-season, Nate volunteered with the Humane

Society's Animal Emergency Services team. According to Kelsey, this was the result of him not being able to sit still, and she wasn't entirely wrong. But it was also because, like her, his bleeding heart tended to get the best of him. Animals were vulnerable creatures; since Nate *could* protect them, he felt compelled to do so. That was why he'd found himself on the road before dawn last week, heading out on an assignment, when out of the misty fog had come a tractor trailer barreling down the wrong side of the highway. Nate had vague memories of thinking he was about to die, vaguer ones of EMTs loading him into an ambulance, and then not much else until his head had cleared in the ER.

Between his off-season job as an EMT and his years working as a firefighter in Helen, Nate had responded to more accidents than he had actual fires. He knew they were unpredictable and that he'd gotten relatively lucky. Still, his two-year-old car was wrecked; his shoulder was broken; it hurt to breathe (although that was improving); and if he didn't heal well, his career . . .

Nate shook off the thought. Raging fires didn't make him panic, but worries about his future could. It was good that he had puppies to play with.

"All right, if you say so." Kelsey didn't bother to hide her doubts. "But if you don't want to come home, do you want to know who did grace us with his presence?"

Nate wasn't sure he cared. He'd left the local gossip—most of which had to deal with the absurd feud between his family and the Lipins—behind. But Kelsey was clearly eager to share. Despite his intention to stay put, Nate missed her and the way she relished telling him stories.

"Who?" The puppies followed him into the kitchen. He'd slept through feeding them dinner, and he was surprised they'd let him get away with it.

"Cody Miller."

Nate dropped the scoop filled with puppy food, and pieces rolled across his kitchen floor. Dolly and Spark dived on them with barks of delight. Food on the floor was apparently much more exciting than food in a bowl.

"The guy behind Hitched?" Kelsey said, filling in the silence on his end.

"Yeah, yeah, I know what Cody's done." Nate scowled at his own reaction and finished dishing out the dogs' dinners.

Although he was surprised, news about Cody didn't interest him. Nate cared about technology to the extent that his devices worked and didn't cost half a year's salary. Of course he knew what Cody had accomplished. Everyone from his hometown did. But growing up, Nate had never liked Cody, so he did his best to ignore the guy.

"I wonder what drove him back to Helen." Nate stared into his cabinets. His mother had made him a lasagna before she left, but after eating it three days in a row, he could still taste tomato sauce and garlic on his tongue. He needed a change, so Honey Nut Cheerios it was. Dinner of wounded champions.

"Apparently he's building or renovating a vacation house," Kelsey said. "More interesting is that he's staying at the Bay Song while in town."

The emphasis Kelsey put on the hotel's name was not missed. He'd been busted, even though Nate was certain his sister remained in the dark about why he so often asked about it. "Even smarmy rich guys have to stay somewhere, Kels."

"True." Kelsey sounded bummed by his lack of response to the Bay Song's name. "I also heard from Josh, who heard it from Taylor, that Cody was hitting on Lydia Lipin. Maybe that explains it."

Cody was hitting on Lydia? Nate's grip on his spoon tightened. Now, that was actually interesting.

No, wait, it wasn't. Cody and Lydia had done the on-again, off-again routine throughout high school, which meant it was probably the most normal thing in the world for Cody to restart the cycle while he was in town. Not only was that not interesting, it was boring. Old. Done.

And yet Nate's chest felt tight and his hand was curling into a fist around his hapless utensil. For a brief glorious-and-yet-horrible moment, the ever-present pain in his ribs subsided as all his attention focused on this news. Or maybe it was because, in that second, he didn't breathe.

Lydia had that breath-stealing effect on him. At least, she'd once had it. From the time he'd discovered girls, Nate had been captivated by Lydia Lipin. She'd been smart, beautiful, kind—well, maybe not kind to him directly, but she was a member of the enemy family, so that was to be expected.

Except Lydia had always seemed as disinterested in the feud as Nate had been. While the other kids had relished the fighting, Nate had despised the glee with which they tormented one another. As for Lydia, she'd mostly stayed out of the fray. It had taken years before Nate had understood why, but her behavior had only fueled his fascination, and getting to know her at last hadn't dampened his interest one bit. Their secret friendship during their final year of high school, and their secret relationship the summer after, had given him some of the best moments of his life.

But that, too, was over and done. He'd moved on from Lydia years ago. Literally, it was why he'd left town. So what he was feeling was nonsense. Nostalgia and nothing more.

Unfortunately, nostalgia didn't explain why he'd developed a bad habit of asking after the Bay Song. Nate knew Lydia had taken over running it, and asking about the hotel was more discreet than directly asking after her. That was his intention anyway, and so far, no one in his family had asked him to explain himself. Given they were all obsessed by the feud, they probably assumed he was digging for gossip.

Lydia and Cody again. Nate twirled his spoon around the bowl, watching his cereal grow soggy.

"You there?" Kelsey asked. "Hello?"

"Sorry, yeah. The puppies are getting up to something."

"Are you sure you don't need help? I know you're always too busy to come home, but . . ."

Nate grimaced, guilt adding to the unpleasant mix of emotions coursing through him. During the off-season, all Nate ever had was time. Many of the guys he worked with used those months to travel or relax if they could afford it. Others worked. Most trained. But the choice for what to do was their own. Nate chose to keep too busy to return home. He volunteered for the Humane Society, and since he had his EMT certification, he picked up work locally with an ambulance crew. He could have returned to Helen; he just hadn't.

It wasn't that he didn't miss his family. His parents might know how to get under his skin, but he loved his siblings, and now that his cousin Josh was living in town, Nate had even more incentive to spend time there. But something kept him away.

Something—he was now wondering if he'd discovered what or who it was.

Maybe it was time to reconsider a visit to his hometown. The tightness in his chest, that ridiculous jealousy he was feeling—there was no excuse for it. Nate had seen Lydia only once in person, from far away, since the summer after high school. Possibly as a result, some part of him was living in the past, remembering things as they'd been back then. That was a problem, and so the solution would be seeing Lydia up close and in person again, making it clear to himself—and every wayward organ—that he no longer had feelings for her.

In an instant, the decision cemented itself in Nate's brain. Going home really was a perfect idea. He couldn't work until his shoulder healed, and there was plenty of time before fire season kicked off. Given how long he'd been neglecting his family, he owed it to them to spend some of that time with them. It would also be good for the puppies to meet his family's huskies as it would help socialize the monsters.

"You're right, Kels," Nate said, pushing away his bowl. "Coming home might not be a bad idea."

Hell, if his plan worked and brought him closure, then trips home in the future would be more appealing too. Nate just hoped he was right. Because even for a guy accustomed to the occasional sixteen-hour day in full PPE while a raging fire loomed, traveling to Alaska with a bum shoulder, sore ribs, and two puppies was going to be an adventure.

3

❧————❧

IT HAD BEEN a long day even before her refrigerator died. Lydia glared at the errant appliance as she refilled her cat's water dish, and water spilled over the sides. Because of course it did.

Cursing to herself, Lydia set the dish down and dried her hands on her flannel pajama pants. Luckily, she wasn't much of a cook, so a dead fridge was more of an inconvenience than a tragedy. The few items she kept in it had been moved to the inn's kitchen, and that was where they'd stay until a new one was delivered. The rest of the day's troubles had been far more annoying, culminating in a section of guests' rooms where the heat had gone out. Luckily, Cody's room had not been one of those affected, which was about the day's only positive. In fact, Lydia hadn't even seen Cody for almost a week, which suited her fine.

As for the guests who *had* been affected, she'd been able to move them into vacant rooms with working heaters. But although they'd been in good spirits about it, such a problem did nothing for the hotel's normally stellar reputation. On top of it, Lydia had to get someone out to fix the issue. The Bay Song was small enough that there was only one dedicated maintenance worker, and he typically contracted out HVAC issues. Since Ralph was out sick, Lydia had to deal with the contractors herself, and they'd treated her call with suspicion. Was she sure the heat wasn't working? Had she just done something silly like forget to bump up the thermostat? After snapping at the man on the phone that having ovaries did not lower someone's IQ, he'd apologized, but still. She had not been in a mood for dealing with a dead fridge after work.

For that, however, there was wine. When Lydia had taken her few staples (mostly cheese) down to the inn kitchen, she'd left a bottle of pinot grigio to chill on the tiny deck outside her door. Living in the apartment above the inn's main building had the occasional drawback— namely, work never really went away—but at times it was awfully convenient as well.

Yawning, she retrieved a wineglass and pondered what to watch on TV while she pretended the day hadn't happened. It had to be mindless and low stress. That made a reality show a good bet.

"What should it be, Merlot?" Lydia called over her shoulder to her cat. "*The Great British Baking Show* or *Queer Eye*?"

Merlot, who was getting up there in age and was no less crabby for it, jumped off his favorite windowsill and took up residence on the sofa. Lydia supposed that was the best answer she could hope for. She loved the tabby dearly, but he'd never been much of a conversationalist.

"You're right," she said to herself. "*The Baking Show*'s

stakes are too high for my blood pressure. *Queer Eye* it is."

Merlot blinked at her, which seemed like proof of agreement.

Lord, she was becoming pathetic. Lydia suspected all people talked to their pets like this, but the fact that Merlot was the only constant male companion in her life was another story. To be fair, he set a high bar. He kept his messes confined to the litter box, didn't hog the blankets, and if he had unwanted opinions about her appearance or homemaking skills, he kept them to himself. She couldn't very well expect the average human male to compete, and she'd pretty much given up hope of finding one who could. Cody might make for an interesting diversion while he was around, but Lydia wasn't overly optimistic about his chances.

She grabbed the giant cardigan she kept by the door before opening it to get the wine. The sweater had belonged to her grandfather, and she'd inherited it along with the apartment. It was old, green, and becoming pocked with holes, but it reminded Lydia of its former owner as well as being soft and warm. During evenings like this, cozy was far more important than stylish.

A cold wind blew her hair back. It was a rare mostly clear night. Complete darkness had fallen hours ago, but moonlight filled the sky, and the inn's lights illuminated the paths below her. During winter's stingy daylight, if she squinted, she might be able to make out the bay and the lines and lines of boats in the harbor. But at night, all she could see were dark trees swaying in the breeze.

She'd left the wine bottle right by the door so she wouldn't have to put on shoes to grab it, but as Lydia reached over, a scuttling sound drew her attention. It was probably a bird or a squirrel in the trees, and Lydia paid it no heed. Merlot, on the other hand, was extremely interested. Before Lydia could shut the door, he shot past her, a streak of orange fur disappearing down the stairwell to the ground.

Shit. Lydia almost screamed out the word in frustration. Merlot getting out was exactly what she needed to end a wonderful day.

"Merlot!" She called after him once, then twice, but didn't bother a third time. It wasn't like he ever came when called. "Damn it."

She knew exactly where the furball had gone. Winding paths threaded through the trees around the inn, and on one of them between the inn and the Tavern was a metal bench. For some reason, Merlot liked to curl up on it after he got bored chasing whatever prey he found. Not that Lydia ever intentionally let him outside, mind. Merlot might fancy himself the big, bad predator, but he was a tiny snack for too many creatures in the area.

Muttering under her breath, she stuck her bare feet in fleece boots, wrapped the cardigan tighter around herself, and trudged out. One downside to her male companion being a cat and not a human was that she'd feel guilty shutting the door on him and locking him out overnight.

The evening air was biting, yet on the warmer side for late January. It got plenty cold in Helen, but the climate was a far cry from places like Fairbanks, where her maternal grandparents lived. She didn't want to be outside long without a coat, but as long as she kept moving, frostbite wasn't an immediate concern.

"Merlot!" Although futile, Lydia couldn't help but continue to call out his name as she traipsed down the steps. At least it was winter and she was unlikely to run into any guests going for an evening stroll around the hotel grounds and seeing her dressed in her frumpy finest.

Lydia picked up her pace, hoping to get to Merlot faster and to ward off the chill. Gravel and dried leaves crunched under her feet, but the path was dry. Remnants of the last snow lingered in the brush, too covered in dirt to glisten in the lamplight. She made the turn through the trees, expecting to find her beloved cat sitting on the bench, probably proud of himself for sneaking out, and found something startling instead—a man, bending over her cat while two dogs chased their tails in circles around his legs.

Not just dogs, actually. Puppies. And not just any breed of puppies. Husky puppies.

Lydia tensed. Huskies were a popular breed, but in Helen, huskies usually meant their owner was a Porter. The joke around town was that all combined, the Porters owned enough huskies to field multiple Iditarod sled teams. Lydia didn't get the obsession, but then Lipins were cat people. Why, she couldn't say any more than she could understand the link between Porters and huskies. Supposedly the feud had something to do with it. If the tales were to be believed, one of her ancestors had tried stealing some Porter's sled dog decades ago. But that sounded like nonsense.

Regardless, happy puppies were not the problem. The problem was that someone, possibly an enemy, was walking his dogs on her property and picking up her cat. And Merlot, the traitor, was allowing it. Lydia wasn't sure which part of this entire adventure was more surprising.

This section of path was dimly lit, and the man's face was cast in shadow as he coaxed Merlot into his arms, but he was broad beneath his coat and tall. Sturdy boots poked out from a pair of weathered jeans, and he wore a knit cap on his head that matched her cardigan in terms of having seen better days. He also appeared to have a sling on his left arm, not that he was letting that get in the way of cat-napping her purring fluffypants.

The puppies had noticed her and were straining toward her in excitement, but the guy ignored their barking while maintaining his hold on the leashes. Lydia couldn't hear him, but she was pretty sure he was whispering to Merlot to get him to behave.

Surprise had rendered Lydia temporarily speechless, but she should say something to the cat whisperer before he absconded with her only male companion. "Hey! That's my cat."

What it lacked in eloquence, it made up for in directness. Nothing more should be expected of a woman wrapped in an old cardigan and wearing pajama pants in subfreezing weather. Especially not when she'd had a long day.

"Oh, good. Then let me hand him back to you. I was afraid he'd run off and freeze out here overnight." The cat-napper-whisperer straightened with Merlot in his arms and turned.

For a second time, surprise left Lydia gaping. "Nate?"

So it *was* a Porter on the hotel property. Lydia hadn't seen Nate up close in over a decade, but some people couldn't be forgotten. In fact, being unable to forget Nate had been a persistent problem in her life. She thought about him way too much and had inevitably compared every guy she dated to him. Or if not to him exactly, then to an idealized memory of him. It was easy to put someone you'd lost contact with on a pedestal, and even easier to use that memory as a way to dismiss others for not living up to an unobtainable standard.

Seeing Nate, however, made it clear that not everything she'd chosen to focus on about him had been idealized. He'd aged, certainly, but in a way that made him only more appealing. Though his heavy coat hid everything below the neck, his jawline had somehow become stronger, and his eyes remained the same smoky blue—a trait shared by most Porters. Teenage Lydia had always thought he was cute, and adult Lydia saw no reason to revise that opinion, although she might choose a different descriptor. *Ruggedly handsome* would do.

Acknowledging this caused a butterfly to flap its wings in her gut, and she didn't like that at all.

"Lydia." Nate's eyes opened wide and he almost dropped her cat. Swearing, he readjusted his grip and winced as the movement probably hurt the arm in the sling.

"Yeah, hi." She pulled her cardigan more tightly around herself. Strangely, she was no longer feeling as cold, but she'd become super aware of her disheveled state. "I'll take him."

"You'll take? Oh." Nate shook himself and placed Merlot in her outstretched arms.

Puppies nipped at her ankles, but Nate's face was so close that Lydia scarcely noticed. There was a day's worth of stubble on his cheeks, and he smelled like . . . Well, she didn't know what, but it was musky and warm, and that damned butterfly was spawning an army of followers. She should have chosen to focus on the puppies instead.

Lydia snuggled Merlot close to her chest, both for warmth and for the way his body covered some of her fashion sins. "Thanks. He used to be such a skittish kitten, but he lost his fear of death a few years ago, and now he loves to escape."

"No problem." Nate took a large step backward, nearly tripping over his dogs. "Feel free to make your own joke about firefighters rescuing cats."

She hadn't forgotten Nate was a firefighter, but recalling it did nothing to quell the butterfly infestation. The demands of his job probably entailed that his coat was hiding a body every bit as appealing as his face.

Lydia smiled, thankful her cheeks already felt flushed from the cold. "Does the job explain your arm?"

Again, Nate seemed startled by her question. "No, actually. Nothing so interesting. That was a car accident."

"Sorry."

He shrugged with one arm. "I got off lightly, all things considered."

Merlot dug a claw into Lydia's chest, and she tried to gently remove it without drawing attention to her boobs. "Are you staying with your parents?"

The question she really wanted to ask was why he was walking his puppies around her hotel, but that seemed confrontational and Lydia was not confrontational. Particularly when her body had abandoned her better sense. She had her cat. She was cold and underdressed. And yet instead of running back to her apartment, she was trying to prolong this conversation.

If she and Nate were two other people reconnecting after years apart, she'd think nothing of exchanging phone numbers and planning to meet up while he was in town. But they were not two other people, and that was undoubtedly why they'd lost touch to begin with. So talking to Nate while she had the chance, even if it was in the cold and dark, was the only sensible opportunity. When they'd gotten together secretly in high school, they'd always had to be sneaky. Nothing had changed since then.

Well, some things had changed. Nate was even more attractive now than he'd been then. That stubble on his jaw had her licking the backs of her teeth, since she couldn't lick *it*.

Lord, she was definitely pathetic. She was literally freezing her fingers off so she could soak up the sight of the man who'd once fueled her fantasies.

The way Nate laughed at her question gave Lydia her answer before he responded. "No, much to my mother's dismay. My family owns those rental cabins down the road. Most are empty for the winter, so I'm staying in one of them. There's only so much family I can take, you know, and my mother stayed with me for the week right after the accident, so it's been a lot already." He shut his mouth abruptly as though shocked by the torrent of words that had poured out.

Lydia bit her lip to keep from laughing. From Nate, it had been quite a speech. "I know those cabins."

Brilliant response. Of course she knew those cabins. That Nate was staying in one of them kind of explained why he might be walking his dogs around the hotel, but not entirely. She'd assume it was because of the path lights. It would be quite dark in the trees—not an ideal location to be walking a couple of energetic puppies.

She started to ask about the dogs, but Merlot chose that moment to dig his other claw into her arm, and the poor cardigan did not provide much armor against that sort of assault. Her cat had to be cold. For that matter, so was she, and Lydia shivered.

"I've kept you," Nate said. "Sorry."

"No, it's okay."

"You're not even wearing a jacket. Here." He pulled

his hat off and fitted it over her head. Once more, his nearness set Lydia's nerves on high alert. His hand was gentle, tugging the hat down over her hair and ears, and Lydia closed her eyes. If she hadn't been holding Merlot, she told herself, she'd have protested. But she was, and Lydia didn't know if she was lying to herself. There was something so familiar about the way Nate wanted to take care of her, but she had to remember this was just Nate. He wanted to take care of everyone he met. It had nothing to do with any residual feelings or attraction he might have to her. And that was for the best.

Still, the heat from Nate's body seemed to wrap around her like a blanket, and the chill resettled under her clothes as he stepped away too quickly. "Thanks again."

Nate smiled. "No problem. Now, get inside before you get any colder. Your cheeks are bright red."

Her nose probably was, too, but Nate was too kind to mention it.

One of the puppies raised its fluffy head at that moment and barked into the trees, and Nate sighed. "I hope I tired these guys out enough that they might let me sleep. Good night, Lydia. It was nice to run into you."

"Yeah, you too." She nuzzled her chin against Merlot's fur as Nate turned to leave.

A few minutes later, Lydia shut her apartment door with little memory of how she got back. An ungrateful Merlot swatted her with his tail before reclaiming his spot on the couch, but she stood by the door a moment longer, clutching the wine but no longer feeling the need to drink any. Her head felt light enough.

"This is absurd." Lydia shook herself, trying to toss off the adrenaline rush. It was only the cold having this effect on her. Once she warmed up, her nerves would settle. She'd realize running into Nate had not been such a significant event, but rather something inevitable, given the size of the town. She'd been flustered from surprise and nothing more.

Which didn't explain why she sniffed his hat when she removed it, hoping to catch a trace of him in its wool fibers.

Fine. She apparently found him attractive. Whatever. He had been attractive then, and he was attractive now. Plenty of men were attractive. That was also not significant.

Light-headed or not, she should probably have that glass of wine anyway.

WELL, SHIT. THAT had not gone the way Nate had imagined it would.

Back at the cabin, he let the monsters off their leashes and took some comfort that the long, late walk seemed to have done the trick where they were concerned. They dashed about the downstairs before collapsing on the rug by the woodstove. It figured that they'd probably sleep tonight while he'd lie awake thinking about Lydia.

He'd been back in town for two days and was still unsure of how to approach her. Running into her while walking his dogs, however, had not been part of any of the plans he'd concocted and dismissed. The idea to walk the puppies around the hotel paths had undoubtedly been because Lydia was on his mind, but the paths were also well lit and so they'd seemed ideal. Since most people didn't go for random nighttime walks in an Alaskan winter, and Lydia wouldn't have dogs to make the behavior less random and more of a necessity, Nate had assumed he wouldn't disturb anyone.

Technically the hotel paths were private property, and Lydia had every right to kick him off them, but Nate hadn't worried about that. And if another staff person saw him, it was unlikely he'd be recognized at this point. He could just play lost and confused, like any number of tourists. He was almost surprised that Lydia *had* recognized him.

She, on the other hand, hadn't changed a bit. Her face had matured, as, presumably, had the rest of her. Though he couldn't tell, he'd no doubt be thinking about it later. Either way, she remained the most beautiful woman he'd ever seen. Her dark hair and eyes had set off the flush of cold on her pale cheeks, turning her into a creature out of a fairy tale as she stood among the trees—equal parts sweet princess and seductive witch. Just the memory of her grateful smile as she took her cat from him had his mouth going dry.

He'd rambled. Actually rambled in front of her. *Christ*.

It was fair to say his plan to get closure by showing himself that he was over Lydia Lipin had been a failure in every conceivable way.

Also, he needed to stop reading those damn paranormal romance novels Kelsey wrote because the stories were obviously affecting his brain.

Nate hung up the leashes on hooks by the door and placed his coat next to them. Reaching for his hat, he recalled that he'd handed it over to Lydia along with the wayward cat. He supposed that gave him an excuse to track her down again, so that was something. He wasn't devious enough to have given it to her on purpose, but he wasn't above using any opportunities that came his way. At the time, though, she'd just looked so cold. He'd have given her his coat, too, if getting it on and off with his sling hadn't been such a pain.

"You're such a dumbass," he muttered to himself, and the confession was punctuated by puppy snores.

While the monsters snoozed, he adjusted his sling and made himself a cup of mint tea in the cabin's tiny kitchen. The tea would warm him up, then he'd go up to the loft, where his bed was, and watch something suitably loud and obnoxious on Netflix. Something that would keep his mind off Lydia.

But he didn't make it past the tea steeping before his thoughts returned to her, because the reminders were everywhere. Even the cabin's dark, wood-paneled walls reminded him of a lean-to on one of the nearby trails. During the summer after graduation, he and Lydia had hiked out there a couple times, since they couldn't hang out together where they'd be seen. She'd liked to sketch the trees, the fallen leaves, the pinecones—anything she could find on the ground. The father of one of Nate's friends had made and sold wood carvings to tourists, and he'd taught Nate enough to make him curious to try it. He'd sit out there next to Lydia, occasionally shaving a tree branch, but mostly watching her.

The way her deft fingers danced over the paper.

The way her brow furrowed in concentration as she struggled to capture something.

The adorable sigh of discontent she made when she became frustrated with her fingers' inability to capture whatever greatness lurked in her head.

Even the so-called worst of her drawings amazed Nate. He'd compliment her skill—and mean it—and he'd show her his abysmal attempts at wood carving, and she'd tell him he simply needed more practice. But he'd never told her that the only reason he bothered was that it gave him something to do while he sneaked glances at her. Because he'd wanted to spend as much time with her that summer before she left for college as possible. Because he'd just won her over after all those years, and he didn't know how to keep her, thanks to circumstances beyond their control.

There had probably been less pine in the woods than there was in his heart.

His chest constricted with the memory, and Nate poked himself in the ribs. They were feeling much better but were still sore enough that the pain could cut through his mental bullshit.

Yup, he'd really done a great job of screwing himself over by coming home, if Memory Lane was the road he was headed down.

Nate dumped his tea bag in the trash and gingerly carried his mug up the creaky steps to the loft. By the stove, Dolly rolled over in her sleep, but the monsters remained conked out. No way would he be so lucky.

It was just nostalgia coupled with a strong physical attraction, he told himself. Their body chemistry hadn't changed, but why would it have? No question everything else about them *had* changed, and that was important to remember. When he got his hat back, those changes would become clearer. He'd make sure of it. He'd grill Lydia on the last ten years if needed. And once he realized how different they'd become and that she was no longer his vision of the perfect girl, the physical attraction would relent.

Past would give way to present, and eventually he'd be able to leave the past behind.

4

THE HVAC GUYS who came to fix the heaters arrived blessedly early, but it meant Lydia had to scurry out of the inn's kitchen, clutching her coffee mug, to deal with them. Fifteen minutes later, she'd showed them where the issues were and had left them to do their thing, but her coffee was cold. Her breakfast would be too. She'd gotten only a single bite in before she'd received word the men had arrived. Today was off to either a terrible start or a great one.

By the time Lydia entered the inn's small dining area, the earliest risers had assembled for the breakfast buffet. A couple of older women were settled at a table by a window, and a man stood by the coffee setup, filling a mug. There was no reason for Lydia to be surprised to see Cody, but she did a double take anyway.

Despite his promise to be in touch, not only had Lydia not actually seen him since, she hadn't heard from him either. She'd been neither surprised nor disappointed. Her feelings toward him were curious at best and indif-

ferent at worst, and surely Cody was extremely busy doing whatever guys like him did once they were already
absurdly successful. In fact, it was fair to say she'd
thought more about Nate in the ten hours since she'd
learned Nate was in town than she'd thought about Cody
since she'd last talked to him.

Acknowledging that, however, proved uncomfortable,
and Lydia rather wished she hadn't.

Coffee. She needed coffee so she could focus on
things other than Nate's arrival.

Cody chose that moment to turn around, and Lydia's
plan to escape quietly into the kitchen failed. His face
broke into a sunny smile that defied the time and the
blackness outside the dining room windows as he called
out her name.

"Good morning." She tried to mimic his cheerful-
ness, but without caffeine, it was an utter failure.

The women by the window glanced over with thin
lips and wary expressions that suggested that even
they—industrious early risers on vacation—did not approve of such a boisterous greeting at this horrific hour.
Cody had the wit to look admonished, and he stepped
closer to Lydia, although she could have heard him fine
at a normal volume from their original distance.

"I'm sorry I haven't had a chance to reach out yet. I've
got some exciting plans in motion, and so I've been bus-
ier than I expected."

Lydia got the sense that Cody was hoping she'd ask
what those plans were, but technology and apps didn't
interest her. On the other hand, the steam rising off his
coffee cup was tantalizing. She'd really like to get in the
kitchen.

How differently she was acting compared to last night

when neither cold nor hole-filled sweaters could prevent her from trying to draw out a conversation.

"What does 'exciting plans' entail?" Lydia asked, not because she cared but to counteract her ridiculous behavior. Even for her, sometimes it was hard to be practical on a January morning pre-coffee, but she had to try.

Cody's grin confirmed her suspicion. "Nothing I can share yet, but I promise you'll be among the first to know. But speaking of that, I was hoping you'd like to be among the first to see what I'm doing with the house. Are you free around noon? I'd love to give you a tour."

Oh Lord. Caffeine would have been really helpful. Lydia's brain struggled with a coherent response, one that was neither rude nor encouraging. "I really can't leave the hotel during the workday. I have maintenance workers here that might need me at any time."

Possibly, she didn't quite hit the mark because Cody seemed strangely encouraged. "What about after work, then? We can grab dinner that way too. It's even better."

"Oh." Lydia's fingers curled around her mug as tension hummed through her. That, of course, was a practical suggestion, and she didn't have a reason why she couldn't accept.

Nor was there a reason why she *shouldn't* accept. Although she didn't want to lead Cody on, she wasn't opposed to keeping an open mind. It would be good for her family and most likely good for her too. And if catching Nate wandering around the inn last night hadn't thrown her off-balance, Lydia suspected that she'd have happily accepted the invitation. She'd have felt flattered even to receive any of Cody's attention.

But Nate had wandered, and she most certainly felt unsteady on her feet. How unfair was it that both men had shown up in her life again at the same time? Lydia felt like she was the butt of some cosmic joke. Or maybe she'd unwittingly wandered into her own reality TV show where sadistic producers ambushed innocent women with all their exes.

Still, all she had to do was say yes to Cody. It was a simple one-syllable word that didn't commit her to anything more. But what came out of her mouth was more like, "Um."

"Yes," said a voice over her shoulder, and Lydia almost dropped her mug in surprise. Taylor had slipped out of the kitchen, and her sister's fingers plucked the mug of cold coffee from her hands. "Whatever you're worried about, I can handle it," Taylor added, turning to Lydia and giving her an encouraging look.

At some point, Cody and Taylor must have reintroduced themselves, because Cody didn't seem at all confused by Taylor's handling of her indecision. "Sounds great," he said.

"Yes, thanks." Lydia somehow formed her lips into a smile. "Sorry. I'm a little slow until I've had my first cup of coffee."

"No worries." Cody winked. "I don't usually make plans until I've had at least two cups myself, but for you, I was willing to make an exception."

"That's very kind," Lydia said. It seemed like the sort of flirty comment that required her to say something. "I'll meet you in the lobby at five? I need to go check on the kitchen."

Taylor raised an eyebrow at that—supervising the kitchen was her domain—but she was smart enough to say nothing, and, given the way they were standing, Cody couldn't see her reaction.

"It's a date!" He raised his mug.

Lydia's smile wobbled. "Actually, it's a house tour, but I'll see you then. Enjoy your coffee."

With a sigh of relief, or perhaps exhaustion, she closed the kitchen door behind her. Heat washed over her; it was a good ten degrees warmer in here than it was in the dining room, and louder too. The air was a delightful cacophony of aromas—coffee, caramelized sugar, and sausages. Marie, who'd been the hotel's head cook since Lydia was a child, was sprinkling powdered sugar on whatever today's breakfast pastry was, while her assistant was stuffing another tray of quiches into the enormous oven. They'd been up and baking since before Lydia had crawled out of bed, and while it looked like chaos in here, Lydia knew Marie had it well under control.

But possibly it only looked like chaos to her, since she wasn't much of a cook. Taylor had stuck to Marie's side as a child, developing a love and talent for cooking that sure didn't run in the family genes.

Trying not to get in anyone's way, Lydia slid into a seat at the wood table where twenty minutes ago she'd been about to enjoy the breakfast Marie insisted on making for her each morning that she worked. Before Lydia could ask Taylor to return her coffee, the reheated mug and quiche landed in front of her.

"So." Taylor sat next to her, sipping her own coffee. Her sister's engagement ring gleamed—a sapphire, because Taylor had insisted she didn't want anything so stodgy or overpriced as a diamond.

"So?" she repeated, digging into the quiche after she'd swallowed several mouthfuls of coffee. Lydia had a fairly good idea what her sister was asking, but she was too hungry to make it easy on her.

Taylor was clearly unamused by her insistence on eating over talking. "Cody. Spill it."

"There's nothing to spill. I think you heard everything."

"What I heard was you hemming and hawing instead of giving the hot, rich guy an enthusiastic 'hell yes.'" Taylor paused to let that sink in while she sipped her own coffee. "I am perplexed."

"You're not the only one." Well, possibly she wasn't as confused as Taylor, since Lydia did have a reason to believe Nate had something to do with it. But the fact remained that Nate *shouldn't* have anything to do with it. Nate's place was supposed to be in her memories— fond memories to be sure, but memories all the same. He wasn't supposed to have any impact on her present, especially since there never could be anything more between them than a damning secret.

"I guess I'm just worried Cody is looking for something that I'm not," Lydia continued, feeling the weight of Taylor's stare. Was it just her, or had it gotten a lot warmer in the kitchen all of a sudden? The temperature differential between it and the dining room must be more like twenty degrees now.

Taylor mulled this over, twirling a stray walnut chunk that had broken free of some of the coffee cake between her fingers. "What are you looking for?"

That was easy—love, stability, the whole damn perfect family life. Something that felt as elusive and miraculous as sunshine in the winter.

"Something that I can't have with Cody," Lydia said, although she had no idea whether it was true. It felt true though. "I don't think we'd be a good match that way."

"You think he just wants a fling while he's in town, and you want more?" Taylor was disturbingly perceptive for such an early hour.

"That's part of it."

"Why not see where it goes? Josh was supposed to be a fling for me, and now . . ." Taylor's gaze darted to the ring on her finger. "You don't know where things will lead."

If she followed her sister's path, things would lead to a mess and that wasn't her style. Her lot in life was to be the one who came around after with a mop to clean up.

Still, Taylor wasn't wrong. After all, giving Cody a chance was what Lydia had been telling herself to do since he'd arrived, and for good reason. "I know. I was just hoping we'd have more of an initial spark. You and Josh did."

Taylor and Josh had sparked, and now they were likely to burn the entire town to the ground, so maybe not sparking was actually better. But Lydia wanted that spark, damn it.

"You and Cody sparked once," Taylor said.

Lydia didn't bother to correct her. When you grew up in a small town, made smaller by the feud, certain things were inevitable. In retrospect, she and Cody had been one of them. They were both nerds, and their families were aligned. If they had truly sparked then, they probably wouldn't have done the whole on-again, off-again dance. Instead, they'd just continuously circled each other because their options were limited.

Until Nate had cut in, that was. He'd disrupted Lydia's ideas of romance with all the blinding force of a lightning bolt's worth of spark.

"Maybe you need time to get back to that place?" Taylor continued, trying to be helpful. "Besides, as you've pointed out, the prospects around here aren't many. Even if it's only the chance for good sex, you might as well take it."

"Not a bad point." Lydia distractedly pushed aside her

empty coffee mug, and a warm brown hand immediately refilled it and pushed it back.

"You obviously need more coffee," Marie said. "Your sister's right. Show a little more enthusiasm!" She grinned knowingly at Taylor, and it dawned on Lydia that this was not the first time she and Cody had been a source of conversation between the two women.

"Oh no." Lydia slid off her chair. "If you're going to start ganging up on me, I'm out of here."

"We would never," Taylor said as she fist-bumped the cook.

Uh-huh. Like she needed the reminder that she was the cautious, stodgy Lipin. Taylor and Marie, who was practically family at this point, would only be trying to nudge her if they thought it was for her own good. But there were pieces of her that neither of them knew, and it was futile to pretend those pieces weren't influencing her decisions.

The caffeine must finally be hitting her bloodstream for her to accept this fact. And in light of such a revelation, there was only one thing to do.

She had to return Nate's hat.

THE MAINTENANCE WORKERS left midmorning to pick up some parts, saying they'd return around noon. That was all the excuse Lydia needed to decide it was a safe time to take a break and do exactly what she'd told Cody she couldn't—leave the hotel.

As she turned her car down the narrow road that led to the rental cabins, the flaw in her plan occurred to her. She didn't know which cabin Nate was staying in, and more than one appeared to have been rented out. Her tires crunched over residual slush as Lydia slowed her car so she could read the license plates of the vehicles in each driveway as she passed. The first was Canadian, so that was a likely no. Same for the second, which was from California. Unfortunately, after the first six cabins, the driveways became longer, making it impossible to see down them. Only one more cabin had smoke visibly rising into the sky through the trees, though, so Lydia pulled down the driveway and crossed her fingers.

She parked behind a car with Alaska plates. Evergreens surrounded the wood cabin, giving the impression that it was more secluded from civilization than it actually was. A single chair sat on the weather-beaten porch out front, and a propane tank lurked around the corner. Whoever was inside the cabin—hopefully Nate—was either not heating it with the propane or was supplementing that heat with wood. The air was thickly scented with fragrant smoke.

Lydia gave Nate's hat a little squeeze. She might have sniffed it one last time in her car, which was silly, but she wasn't sorry as the smoke scent had already driven the memory from her brain.

Familiar barking increased in volume as she crossed the porch, suggesting she had indeed found the correct cabin. That fact was confirmed a moment later, before she could even withdraw her hand from knocking, when Nate opened the door.

Shirtless Nate.

Lydia swallowed. Holy half-naked firefighter calendar model. She'd been absolutely right to assume that the bulky coat Nate had been wearing last night did not do him any favors. Nate had grown up and grown bigger, but that didn't do the form in front of her justice. His broad shoulders sloped down to a powerful chest, which narrowed into a flat stomach that showed off faint ridges of his underlying abs before all that skin disappeared into his sweatpants. It was the body of a man who worked out not for his appearance, but to meet the rigorous demands of his job, and it was a body she desperately wanted to see more of. Looking at Nate, Lydia didn't feel so much of a spark as she did an inferno.

The trail of light brown hair leading down from his chest into his waistband had ensnared her gaze, and she realized she was staring. Blood rushed to her cheeks, and she thrust the hat at him. "Hi. Sorry to interrupt. I was returning this."

Nate's expression was unreadable, seeming to cycle through emotions faster than Lydia could decipher them, but he took the hat. "Thanks. Do you want to come in?"

Nope, she absolutely should not, even though spending time with Nate was precisely the reason she'd come over. But that was before she'd known he was half-naked.

When she faltered for words, Nate adjusted his stance in the doorway. "Not to put pressure on you, but I'm trying to keep the monsters in and it's getting cold."

This time, Lydia was certain his lips had twitched. Lord, she was making a fool of herself. "Sure, thanks. I'd love to meet the monsters."

She hoped *the monsters* referred to the puppies, which were yapping around his feet.

Nate took a step back so she could slip inside the cabin, and Lydia stuffed her hands in her pockets to keep from fidgeting. Or doing something worse—like poking Nate in his chest to see how hard it was.

The cabin was as cozy on the inside as it appeared on the outside. A woodstove to her right formed the centerpiece of a sitting area, behind which was a small kitchen. Directly across from her, stairs led to loft that overlooked the room. All the walls were wood paneled, lending it a rustic but homey vibe, and the business half of Lydia's brain wondered what sort of rate Nate's family rented out the cabins for during the summer.

It was tempting to indulge that boring, logical side because it kept the emotional, hormonal side of her brain under control. But before Lydia could give it a chance, Nate lowered himself to one of the cushy chairs near the stove and scooped up a puppy with one bare arm, and her ovaries might have exploded. At the very least, the butterflies Nate had spawned in her last night were undeniably riled up.

So was the second puppy, who looked almost identical to the first. The husky charged over to her, and Lydia knelt to pet him. Or her. It was all she could do to keep from drooling over the image of a half-naked Nate with a puppy.

Luckily, the new puppy was a blur of black-and-white fur that demanded her attention, so Lydia didn't have to worry about being caught staring again. Cats were really more her style, laid-back and cautious. The contrast between Nate's so-called monster and Merlot couldn't be more stark, but the puppy's excitement was too endearing for her not to be charmed.

No doubt Nate's effect on her emotions had some part in that.

Lydia finally looked up and saw he was watching her with amusement again, and he was no less tempting for it. "What?"

"A Lipin playing with my puppy." Nate shook his head. "Shocking."

"If you haven't heard yet, my sister is marrying your cousin. It's a shocking state of affairs all around here.

But I think it's more fair to say your puppy is playing with me." Lydia dodged as the husky tried licking her face.

"Sparky!" Nate's slightly raised voice startled the dog, who spun around. "Here."

The puppy seemed to consider but Nate repeated the command and he—or she—left Lydia after one more lick.

"Good boy!" Nate heaped praised on the dog, answering one of Lydia's questions, but she couldn't help but note the ginger way Nate moved, as though too much motion caused him pain. She'd forgotten about the sling he'd been wearing the other night, since he didn't have it on now.

Had he hurt his arm or shoulder? She should ask which, but Nate spoke up again before she could.

"This is Dolly," he said, nodding toward the squirming puppy in his arm. "And that's her brother Spark, except I usually call him Sparky so he probably thinks that's his name."

Both huskies' ears perked up at the sound of their names, and Dolly wiggled her way out of Nate's grip, which was probably best for Lydia's state of mind. Gorgeous, half-naked men holding adorable puppies was more temptation than she should be expected to endure.

"Spark sounds right for a firefighter's dog," Lydia said, trying to surreptitiously watch Nate get off the chair. His movements were slow and purposeful, raising her alarm about how injured he was, but it was the way his muscles flexed that she kept focusing on. "What about Dolly?"

Nate flashed her a grin, and headed toward the kitchen counter. With his back to her, he couldn't see the way Lydia's gaze followed him, which was for the best. She'd never appreciated how enticing back muscles could be before.

She had to get herself under control, but the crush she'd once nurtured on Nate threatened to return—matured along with the rest of him. Some part of her had retreated to that spring day around graduation when she'd given in to her dangerous feelings for the quiet, kind Porter boy with the dreamy blue eyes.

"Watch the dogs," Nate said, as though he could feel her gaze on his back. "This is the best magic trick ever."

He turned back around, and Lydia reluctantly switched her attention from him to the puppies. The pair were racing in circles around the living room, a doubleheader of eager puppy energy. Lydia couldn't tell which was which.

"You ready?" Nate asked. He pressed a button on his phone, and music began spilling out of the tiny speakers on the kitchen counter.

Lydia couldn't place the first couple bars of guitar, but then Dolly Parton's familiar voice filled the room with an urgent message for Jolene. For a second, Lydia assumed Nate had become a Dolly fan and named a puppy after her, but that was not the magic. As soon as they heard Dolly singing, the puppies skidded to a halt. Their heads raised. Their ears perked. Their tails wagged. But they sat, and they listened. And one of them—Dolly?—eventually started howling along.

Lydia's jaw dropped. "Did you teach them that?"

Nate shook his head. "Nope. Figured it out pretty fast though. Dolly started it, and I think Spark learned from watching her."

"Dolly's the one singing along?"

"With her namesake." The song came to an end, and

Nate set down his phone. Like they'd come out from under a spell, the puppies started to play again. "Wish she did a better job of holding a tune. My dog, I mean."

"That is the cutest thing." Lydia said a silent apology to Merlot. Much as she loved her grumpy buddy, he'd never once shown an interest in music.

"Careful. You might get disowned for that," Nate said with a smile. "But yeah, they're cute. And feral. My brother trained his puppy recently. I'm hoping he can give me some tips while I'm here."

With the show over, Lydia once more felt self-conscious, and she tucked her hands in her pockets despite the fact that she was overheating. "I'm sure you can convince them that you're the alpha dog."

Dogs weren't humans, but it seemed impossible to her that Nate could walk into any room and not exude an air of being the guy who took charge.

"If not, I'm in trouble." Nate picked up an exercise band from the counter. "Would help if my shoulder wasn't busted."

"Does it hurt a lot? What happened?" Why was she prolonging this conversation when she knew it was a bad idea?

Nate rubbed his face and turned away slightly. "It's not too bad."

Lydia considered telling him he was an awful liar, but she figured it was a manly pride thing. Besides, she was more interested in discerning whether he'd truly tugged on his ear as he'd spoken, or if it had only looked like he did. Nate used to have a tell.

He glossed over the details of the accident in much the same way as he had the pain, downplaying everything, while she listened, horrified. "You could have been killed."

"Wasn't though."

She shook her head, wondering if Nate was minimizing the risk for her sake or his own, or if he was so used to running into danger that he didn't think twice about his own mortality.

"You want anything to drink?" Nate asked, as though he were able to tell her mouth had gone dry with worry for him.

"Um, no. I should probably go."

"You don't have to," Nate said quickly. "If you don't mind me going back to doing my exercises. Tell me what you've been up to."

She really *should* go, but Lydia sat without removing her jacket. She was going to pass out from heat stroke while her ovaries and her brain warred over what to do. It didn't help that Nate had started running through a series of stretches that looked unpleasant for him, but mesmerizing to her.

There was no way this man had that many muscles when they were kids. Not that Nate had been a small guy, even then. Lydia could still remember the way he'd felt, all hard planes under a soft T-shirt that night when she'd finally pressed her fingertips against him.

They'd been at the senior class bonfire. It was the only reason Lipin and Porter students would be hanging out together, and even then, everyone kept to their sides of the fire circle. A smoky crispness had permeated the spring air, along with the scents of hotdogs and burgers. Lydia remembered being nervous and unable to join her friends' and classmates' enthusiasm for the end of high school. All she had left were three months before college, and leaving town and everything she knew made her heart race with dread. She'd wandered away from the fire's heat and the shrill laughs of her friends, cutting through the field while dew-damp grass brushed her ankles, as she searched for her happy face—the mask she hid behind so no one would know what she was really thinking and feeling.

With only weeks until the summer solstice, the sky remained plenty light, and Lydia did her best to disappear into the woods that abutted the field. All she needed was a few minutes. She hadn't realized she'd been followed until Nate stepped on a twig, and she'd turned around with a gasp.

"Are you okay?" he'd asked, stepping closer. "You looked upset."

She'd thought she'd done a good job of slipping away unnoticed, but she'd been learning that Nate noticed a lot more than he let on. "I just needed some time away."

"Do you want me to go?" He immediately backed up.

"No. You can stay." Being with Nate had started feeling a lot like being alone. Not only because he was quiet, but because he was comfortable, like the faded T-shirt under his worn jacket. His presence soothed her, even though the fear of being caught acting friendly with him should have made her run. She desperately wanted to touch the gray fabric of his shirt, which looked so soft.

Nate held out something wrapped in a napkin. "You're missing the s'mores, and they go fast. I brought you one."

"Thanks." She'd reached for it, their hands had touched, and Lydia had thought she might pass out as all the oxygen fled her lungs.

How she'd ended up kissing Nate, she could scarcely recall. Everything surrounding that moment had vanished, wiped out by the nuclear explosion of emotions she'd felt when their lips touched. Nates had tasted sweet, likely from a s'more of his own, and he'd touched her so hesitantly when she'd just wanted to sink against

nore—about her sister returning to town, the work
put into the inn, and people Nate remembered from

laugh knocked something around in him too.
ly his resolve. Lydia, he couldn't help but notice,
iding her attention between him and his dogs as
ke. Every time he glanced her way, her gaze
back to the puppies. Granted, they demanded at-
ut Nate suspected the real reason she kept turn-
was because she didn't want him to see how
ooking at him.

he was also thinking too much about kiss-

ought of it heated his blood, enabling him to
gh the pain holding a dumbbell caused his
He'd so much rather focus on kissing Lydia,
ose troublesome thoughts, he could move his
gain.

for his plan to realize why he shouldn't be
Lydia Lipin. Perhaps he should try a new
find ways to see more of Lydia while he
He might have better success, and he liked
ole lot more.

boring," Lydia assured him. "I've never
tate, unlike some people here. Where are

n." Nate exchanged the ten-pounder he'd
with his good arm for a twenty-five-
ded to keep his blood flowing so it didn't
ard organ. It was a good thing his father
eights he could borrow. "It's about as
ou can get without being in Canada, so
ng either."

his warmth. She'd finally pressed her fingers into his shirt, which had been as soft as it looked, and reveled in the hardness of his stomach underneath. She'd never wanted that kiss to end.

"Lydia?" Present-day Nate snapped her out of the memory.

The scent of woodsmoke from the stove urged her to linger in her thoughts, but playful puppies whacking her with their tails were impossible to ignore any longer. So did the vision of a shirtless Nate, stretching out his good arm. Pectorals and biceps rippled with the movement.

She should have held on to that damn hat, because she was in trouble.

5

◦———◦

LYDIA LOOKED MORE like she was waking up from a dream than someone simply lost in her thoughts. There was a peacefulness that had settled over her face. Nate liked it. It reminded him of the way she used to look when he'd kissed her.

Shit. He shouldn't be reminiscing about the past or thinking about whether she'd look that peaceful again if he kissed her. He was supposed to be coming up with the reasons why he and Lydia had become incompatible.

So far, he had Reason One: Lydia could somehow ignore his puppies long enough to space out, which meant she might not be human.

But that was no reason at all. In fact, Lydia was playing with his puppies at the moment, and it did nothing to make her less attractive. If anything, it made her more so—if for no other reason than that it made it easier for him to do his exercises if he wasn't constantly yelling at the monsters to not chew on his shoes, climb on the table, or knock over a lamp.

"You still need to tell me what you
last few years," Nate said, wishing
jacket. It was making him warm to
very much liked looking at her.

Lydia tucked her hair behind
conscious way, and he couldn't he
ing once done that for her. "Oh,
work at the hotel, I sit on the to
because my father begged me t
evenings in deep philosophical
cat, whom you've met."

Nate laughed and winced
raised his left arm to its maxir
all that high. How was he su
done when even somethin
arm caused him pain? He
weights—a broken shoulde
ing much of anything. But
keep trying. He had to sta
started.

"I'm sure you're mc
said, picking up ten-p
Something was better

"Only when I've ha
is keeping up his side

"That I'd like to

Lydia smiled an
Dolly's reach. The
happened once. I

"I have a hard

She hung he
scarf into Doll
husky lunged.
loose inside h

talk
she'd
schoo
The
Probab
was di
she sp
darted
tention,
ing awa
she was

Like
ing him.

The th
push thro
shoulder.
and in all th
damn arm
So much
interested in
plan—how t
was in town.
this plan a wi

"I'm very
even left this
you living?"

"Washingto
been holding
pounder. He ne
settle in an awk
had these old w
close to here as y
it's not that excit

"But you travel for work, right?"

Nate nodded, preferring not to think about his currently in-limbo job. "And you run a hotel. That can't be so boring. I've seen what tourists get up to."

"True, but it's not like . . ." She trailed off and bent over to play with Dolly.

"Like?"

It might have been the puppy ensnaring her attention, but Nate thought she hesitated a second. "I like running the Bay Song, but it's not like I chose to do it. It was sort of pushed on me. I just do what I'm told."

Now that he thought about it, Nate didn't remember Lydia ever suggesting she wanted to work at the family hotel. At one time, he recalled her talking about being an art teacher. What had happened? "Would you rather do something else?"

"Oh no." She shrugged. "I enjoy it. I just never seriously considered anything else. It was expected of me, and so I did it. You had a goal. I'm boring and did not."

Nate finished his set and put down the dumbbells. Tomorrow, he'd get to meet the local orthopedist, who was probably going to suggest hurting him in all new ways.

"Not sure I see how the two are related. My plans . . ." He caught himself before he rambled again and admitted to how his goal had changed over time.

To his surprise, Lydia laughed. "You still do the thing," she said.

"The thing?"

"You yank on your ear when you're thinking." She mimed tugging her earlobe.

Nate blinked at her. "I do not."

"Do not think, or do not yank on your ear?"

"Either."

"You absolutely do." Lydia paused. "The ear tugging, I mean. I'm pretty sure you do it when you're thinking about things you're not saying."

Christ. Nate rubbed his earlobe self-consciously. Surely if this was common, someone else would have mentioned it. "I used to do this?"

"All the time. I'd forgotten. So what were you thinking about?"

Did she mean this time, or all the supposed times in the past? He'd always thought a lot of things around her that he couldn't say—most of them about how much he wanted to kiss her.

That was something he shouldn't be thinking now, either, but totally was. Watching her, Nate very deliberately stuck his hands in his pockets so they didn't give him away, and smiled. "You'll just have to guess."

It was one thing to hide the truth. It was another to flirt with her, but that was precisely the tone he'd aimed for. He couldn't have made a more boneheaded move if he'd deliberately driven into that tractor trailer. But Lydia had been watching him as much as he'd been staring at her, and the words had slipped out.

Lydia stared back him. But would she play along?

Her phone vibrated, snapping them both out of this dangerous mood. "I need to get back to work," Lydia said, reading the message. "I hadn't intended to stay so long."

"Yeah, of course. We should get together again when I'm not . . ." He gestured vaguely to the dumbbells and the exercise band on his counter.

"Half-naked?" Lydia asked, and color rose on her cheeks.

Nate grinned. "That too. We could grab coffee or lunch?" Normally, he'd suggest a beer, but one of the things Lydia had told him about was the inn's deal with the new brewery in town, and it had come up that she didn't drink much beer herself.

Lydia adjusted her scarf, keeping her eyes toward the ground. "I don't know if we should."

Right. The feud. Nate hadn't forgotten precisely, but he had a harder time caring these days. That was the luxury of not living in town. But Lydia would have to care. With his cousin engaged to a Lipin, Nate had hoped the families would begin to start acting like rational people, but Kelsey—who'd shared that hope—had told him it didn't seem likely.

"We could get together here," Nate said. "Without the family spies being any wiser."

Lydia swallowed, preferring to watch the puppies rather than him. "I mean, maybe."

It was not a very enthusiastic maybe.

Nate turned around, ostensibly to tidy up, but mainly so Lydia couldn't see his disappointment. If it wasn't the feud, what was it? He thought they'd been getting along, and it sure seemed like Lydia was interested. But maybe he was misreading her? He'd been telling himself that he'd changed, and she'd changed, and so there was nothing worth following up on between them. And although it hadn't proved true for him, maybe on Lydia's end it had.

Nate had a hard time believing it. He wasn't vain, and he knew he wasn't much of a charmer, but he'd never struggled with women. At least, not with finding willing partners. Keeping things short and sweet was another story. His friends told him he was too nice, that women misinterpreted his actions. Nate could only assume that most of his gender must be utter assholes if basic human decency and kindness led people to think he wanted more than he was offering. He'd never hidden the fact that he wasn't interested in a relationship. And yet, he'd still ended up with a reputation for being a heartbreaker, which was the last thing he wanted.

So no, finding dates and judging people's interest in him had never been an issue.

Of course, Lydia wasn't like the women he normally hooked up with, because Lydia wasn't like *anyone* else. She was out of his league. It had been true in high school, and it was true now. Smart, beautiful, funny, successful—as far as Nate was concerned, Lydia was out of everyone's league.

But maybe not Cody Miller's. Cody was also smart and successful, and he was obscenely rich, and probably considered attractive by most women.

Was that the reason Lydia was hesitating? Nate hadn't heard more about Cody from his sister, which was no doubt his fault for telling Kelsey he didn't care. But it might be time to suck it up and see if Kels had any more gossip on him and Lydia.

THE ORTHOPEDIST WHO was taking over his care while he was in Helen didn't look any older than him, and that didn't exactly fill Nate with confidence. When had he reached an age where the doctors weren't guaranteed to be older? When he was in his fifties, would doctors all look like kids to him?

Damn, he'd turned thirty-one only a couple of months ago, but he was feeling ancient.

Of course, the pain didn't help with that, nor did his general exhaustion. His ribs were mostly okay these days, but his shoulder remained sore. Dressing was especially painful, and sleeping could be problematic, since he had a tendency to toss and turn. One bad roll over and he was wide awake.

The orthopedist—her name was Dr. Cohen-Liao— shook her youthful head at him. "You shouldn't be doing any exercises that require you to hold dumbbells. In a couple more weeks, you'll be ready to start physical therapy, but for now, you need to be letting that fracture heal."

"I wasn't exercising my shoulder, I was trying to work my legs. Look, I can't not do anything. I need to move."

She rubbed her eyes beneath her glasses, clearly exasperated but doing her best to hide it. "Sometimes the best thing we can do for our bodies is to let them rest. There are weight restrictions on how much you should be holding in your left hand for a reason, regardless of the muscles you want to exercise."

Nate didn't want to argue with her, really. He was certain she was a competent doctor—and his cousin Josh had spoken highly of her—but resting was not him. Getting himself healed, and getting the full use of his arm back, was imperative. As was not letting the rest of his body waste away in the meantime.

"What about my shoulder? Dr. Swan was concerned about my range of motion," Nate said, referring to the original orthopedist who'd patched him back together.

"You have nerve damage that could be contributing to that," Dr. Cohen-Liao said. "But that doesn't make any of this necessarily permanent. Pushing yourself too hard, too soon, on the other hand, doesn't do you any favors in the long run. You could make things worse."

Like rest days at the gym—Nate got that intellectually. You had to give the body time off every few days for the muscles to recover. But emotionally, he hated everything about this. He was stronger than the average person, so if the average person wasn't supposed to hold more than five pounds, he'd figured it wasn't unreasonable for him to hold ten. Maybe it would even help him heal more quickly.

"Healing well is more important than healing quickly," the orthopedist added as though reading his thoughts.

Nate didn't entirely agree. Both mattered a lot to him. His state of mind required knowing that he'd be able to return to work when this was all over. The uncertainty was worse than the pain. Once he'd learned to fall asleep in awkward positions, anxiety had continued to keep him awake.

Firefighting was in his bones. It was all Nate had wanted to do since that shiny red truck had pulled up in front of his elementary school. He didn't know why, and he'd never seen a reason to question that drive too deeply. Helping people, like rescuing animals, was important to him.

If it weren't for that instinct, he might never have had an excuse to get to know Lydia.

Although he'd watched her for years, Nate had never spoken more than two words to her (a particularly memorable *Excuse me* when he'd bumped into her as they'd both rushed through the high school hallway trying to get to class). The feud had made any sort of friendliness impossible, but even if there had been no feud, Nate wasn't sure he'd have approached her. Not then anyway when he'd lacked some confidence. Lydia had been untouchable—an ideal that the less smart, rougher-around-the-edges kid that he'd been could only admire from afar.

That had all changed right before their senior year of high school. He'd been driving back into town from a friend's house and had seen Lydia pulled over on the side of the road, looking like she was struggling with a flat tire. They hadn't been on a main street, and back then cell service had been a lot spottier than it was now. Nate would have stopped and offered his assistance to anyone, but that it was Lydia felt like a sign.

As was typical of the weather around that time of year, a light mist had thickened the air. Lydia must have been outside for a while because rain was running down her face, and her normally flawless hair was wet and sticking to her head. To Nate, she'd never looked more beautiful—or more approachable.

He wasn't sure at first whether she'd accept his help, but Lydia was as pragmatic as ever. "I know how to change a flat." She'd crossed her arms defensively and kicked the offending tire. "But I can't get the lug nuts loosened."

She'd bitten her lip, hard from the looks of it, when he'd managed to do it for her. "They were really tight," Nate said, trying to make her feel better.

He wasn't sure if it worked, but Lydia's shoulders relaxed slightly. "Thanks. I can take it from here."

"I'm sure, but I can hang out in case there's a problem. Like the donut is flat too." It hadn't only been his hormones talking. Leaving her alone to complete the task had seemed like a bad idea.

Working together, it hadn't taken too long, but Nate was soaked through as well by the time they finished. The only other vehicle Nate had seen blew by as they were cleaning up, flinging more water in their direction.

Lydia slammed her trunk shut, glaring at the vanishing taillights. "Asshole."

Nate had attempted to hide his smile, but failed. "I think that was one of your uncles." He'd recognized the bumper stickers.

"I *know* that was one of my uncles. I don't think he even glanced my way."

"Probably for the best, for me anyway."

Lydia made a derisive noise and blew wet strands of hair out of her face. "He'd have no business getting angry that we're talking, considering that you helped me and he didn't."

Nate wiped his dirty hands on his jeans. "I'm not sure logic has any part in the feud."

"No, it doesn't. Which is why it's so frustrating. I mean . . ." Lydia wiped her own hands on her pants, suddenly appearing confused. "Thanks for stopping and helping."

"No problem." He knew he should get in his car and go, that he had no business staying any longer, but he couldn't help himself. "We have to promise no one ever knows about this."

The confusion lines on Lydia's forehead deepened. "I'm not sure who that's protecting—me from appearing pathetic because I couldn't change my own tire, or you for doing something bad and helping?"

"Could be both. Not that you were pathetic. Lug nuts can be a pain in the ass." He'd spoken about them like he'd changed a hundred tires before instead of just one other in his life.

"Trying to protect my ego is very un-Porter-like of you." Lydia cracked a small smile.

Nate shrugged self-consciously. "So was helping you."

"True."

"I thought you might tell me to get lost."

"Seeing as I needed the help, that would have been impractical."

"Anytime." Nate fished his keys out of his pocket. "I'll see you around school next week."

"But pretend not to." She grinned, and his heartbeat quickened.

"This never happened," Nate said. He got in his car and waited for her to pull away before he drove off.

But it had happened, and the secret knowing glances they'd started exchanging during school had happened as a result. And from there, slowly, everything had started changing.

Nate supposed a lesson could be learned from the encounter—helping others helped you too. But while that might be true, it felt kind of cynical, and besides, he'd never needed a reason to help.

Nate tucked his arm back into the sling as the doctor wrapped up their appointment. There were lots of jobs that were all about helping people. Hell, helping people was why he worked as an EMT in the off-season, too, and that was also fulfilling (and also demanded that his shoulder heal properly to continue), but it didn't call to him the same way firefighting did. None of those other jobs did. There was just something about the stakes and the challenge that made it feel larger than life.

But his job had tough physical requirements, and a weak arm or a shoulder with a limited range of motion was going to be disqualifying. Nate was sure he could remain with the Forest Service in another capacity if he wanted to, doing a less physically demanding job. But he didn't want those jobs or any desk job. The boredom would do him in as sure as any backdraft.

So, fine. He was just going to have to be patient so that he didn't make his shoulder worse. He could absolutely do that. Between two puppies, information to dig up on Cody and Lydia, and scheming for ways to see Lydia again, it wasn't like he didn't have plenty to keep him busy.

6

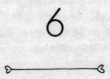

LYDIA WAS EARLY when she arrived at the town hall to meet her friend Jen for lunch, which was unfortunate. She'd have preferred to meet Jen at the restaurant they were going to, but Jen and her husband were currently a one-car family, so Lydia needed to pick her up. That part Lydia didn't mind, but waiting in the town hall lobby meant it was possible she could run into one of those family members she was trying her best to avoid.

The building was relatively new, with open-beam construction and large glass windows overlooking a tiny central square–like area that also contained the post office, the library, and the police station. A few snowflakes floated about on the breeze, almost imperceptible. Like they were for many people, the dark winters could be a struggle for Lydia, but currently bands of blue colored the striated clouds. The midday light was soothing, though not invigorating. She compensated for the early sunsets by drinking too much coffee and leaving the lamps on in her apartment or office at full brightness.

While she waited for Jen, Lydia pulled out her phone and found a new text from Cody. Was wonderful catching up last night. Had lots of fun. Need to do it again soon!

Me too! Sounds great! she typed back. Then, after a pause, she deleted the words.

That was response was all wrong. She'd sounded too excited.

Last night, Cody had referred to their hanging out as a date again, and her subtle attempts to call it something else seemed to be ignored. Lydia wanted to be friendly without being encouraging, which probably meant easing up on the exclamation points. And that was annoying. She tossed around exclamation points like confetti when texting with Taylor and her friends, and she never had to think twice about it.

Sounds good, Lydia tried a second time. But ugh. That just sounded cold. She hated this.

"Lydia! Oh, good, you're here."

Warily, Lydia gave up on her texting struggles and faced her grandmother. With her back turned, hat on, and her nondescript black coat, she'd hoped she would be unrecognizable to the people coming and going through the lobby. But Theresa Lipin could spy a grand-daughter anywhere. "I'm here. I'm waiting to meet a friend."

"Jen Fitz, I assume? She'll be another couple minutes." Theresa wrapped her scarf around her neck, which was a good sign. She didn't intend the conversation to last long if she was preparing to go out. "I have a bunch of things I want to go over with you about the wedding. I would greatly appreciate if you would bring them up with your sister. I think Taylor will be more apt to listen if they come from you."

The lobby was no place to scream, not that Lydia

would have done so in front of her grandmother any-where. But really, she wanted to. Her grandmother had not even filled out her RSVP card yet because Theresa was still threatening not to come to the wedding, as it would—in her words—"give even the appearance that she approved of the marriage."

This, Lydia suspected, was fine with the bride and groom, and no doubt her grandmother wasn't the only person in either family making a stink and claiming they wouldn't show up. In fact, if everyone did plan to attend, Taylor and Josh would be in trouble. They hadn't booked a large enough reception room, having anticipated a boycott, and Taylor had admitted that neither she nor Josh wanted most of the family to attend. They were worried that if they did, things could get messy.

They were probably right. Angry, resentful Lipins and Porters plus alcohol was a disaster waiting to happen.

But that hadn't stopped her grandmother from trying to mother-of-the-bride the whole event. (Thankfully, the real mother of the bride was being quietly supportive of the marriage from afar and only getting involved when asked.) Lydia didn't understand why Theresa thought she should have any influence over a wedding she didn't want to attend, but that was her grandmother. She was used to getting her way. If she couldn't stop the wedding, she could control it.

Or try to.

Lydia took a deep breath and willed Jen to hurry. "I'm not sure I have as much influence over Taylor as you think I do."

"Not as much you should, no." Her grandmother huffed. "None of us have ever had that. If we had, she wouldn't be determined to go through with this farce. But still, you're closer to her than anyone else is."

"And I don't want to ruin that by making her think I'm just a mouthpiece for you." It was as much pushback as Lydia dared to give. She couldn't help Taylor if her grandmother ended up trying to circumvent her.

Her grandmother's lips flattened. "Obviously, but you'll think of something. You're smart and clever. My good, practical grandchild."

Lydia's muscles tensed, and she hoped it didn't show on her face. She knew her grandmother meant it as a compliment, but ever since Taylor had returned to town last year, it was feeling more like a box she'd been shoved into. One that was a touch too small, forcing her to crouch in an awkward position in order to fit.

But the truth was, she *was* the good, practical grandchild, and always had been. She had no reason to feel constrained by the description.

So Lydia said nothing else on the matter, and she raised her hand to wave at Jen, who'd just appeared in the lobby like a frazzled but wonderful escape pod. "We need to leave. Jen only has an hour break."

"Of course." Theresa greeted the other woman and finished bundling up. "I'll send you some things," she said, and Lydia held in a groan.

"Some things?" Jen asked a minute later as they got into Lydia's car. "You didn't seem thrilled about that."

"About Taylor's wedding," Lydia said, rolling her eyes. A delicate layer of white blanketed the windshield, and she turned on the wipers and rear defroster before backing up. "Theresa doesn't want to go, but she wants to plan it."

"That sounds like your grandmother." Jen would know, having worked for the town for the last several years. Besides, everyone in Helen knew Theresa, one way or another.

The drive to the café was short, and they mainly spent it venting about their various work annoyances. Lydia had known Jen her entire life, which was what happened in Helen when someone was the same age as you. They'd been in school together since kindergarten. But over the years, hanging out together had become more infrequent.

Like many of Lydia's friends, Jen had gotten married a few years ago, and having her own family meant she had less time for other people. She and Lydia also had less in common, and she wasn't the only one of Lydia's friends that Lydia was growing apart from. Most of them had children, and that was what they inevitably talked about. Lydia wanted to be supportive, but even as a kid, she hadn't been big on other kids. Mostly, she ended up doing a lot of listening and feigning interest whenever she did see her friends. It wasn't that she didn't care, but she was discovering that parents thought the entire world would find their children's every new tooth or puking session to be of unparalleled fascination. Lydia wasn't sure why. No one besides her cared when her cat coughed up a hairball.

"I need your help with Abby," Jen said as they took their lunches to an open table.

"My help?"

Jen's daughter was seven years old, making her part of that zero-to-eighteen age range that Lydia was generally clueless about. As far as her friends' kids went, however, Lydia had lots of affection for Abby. She was a sweet kid and the spitting image of her mother, with tan skin and large, dark eyes. But she was nonetheless a tiny human whose needs were baffling.

Jen laughed. "Don't look so panicky. It's probably more accurate to say I need your help with Ethan than with Abby."

That might make a bit more sense. Lydia had no experience with husbands, but she'd had plenty with men. They, too, were baffling, but for entirely different reasons. "What's wrong?"

"Our neighbors are the Welds," Jen said. "Which can be uncomfortable sometimes."

The Welds were an offshoot of the Porters from a couple generations back, making them Porters in all but name as far as the feud was concerned. Jen had become a Fitz by marriage, but her family had long been on the side of the Lipins.

It had occurred to Lydia more than once that to live in Helen, you needed to keep genealogical records to survive.

"Anyway, they have a daughter—Julia—who's Abby's age," Jen continued. "I assume they know each other from school. Abby had never shown any interest in playing with her, which was a relief, but . . ."

Her friend trailed off to eat a spoonful of soup, but it wasn't difficult to guess the rest. Lipin and Porter kids did not become friends, not publicly. She and Nate had managed to hide their friendship for a year, and they probably weren't the only ones to pull that off, but if they weren't, those others had done as good a job of hiding things as they had.

"Abby and Julia have started playing together?" Lydia asked, getting the sense that Jen was reluctant to fill in the silence.

"Not yet." Jen grimaced. "But Julia got a puppy, and Abby is obsessed. She watches them running around and playing in the backyard, and she wants to join in so badly. I don't know what to do. Ethan thinks we should let her go over there and ask to meet the dog, but he didn't grow up here so he doesn't get it at that deep level.

Julia's parents don't speak to us, so I don't see Abby getting a warm reception, and frankly, I'm not comfortable with it either."

Lydia absently tore a bit of bread off her sandwich. She wasn't sure what Jen was asking her for. Permission? Or an authoritative no? If she'd already explained the situation to her husband, Lydia didn't want to get brought in as backup, although she was aware that she'd inherited an unofficial role as one of the Lipin heavy guns. It had nothing to do with her personally, and everything to do with being the mayor's daughter and Theresa's granddaughter. Taylor would have the role as well if she hadn't chosen to be the rule-breaking rebel of her immediate family.

So maybe it did have something to do with her personally. She was the "good" Lipin daughter. *Ugh.*

"What about getting Abby a pet of her own?" Lydia suggested. "A kitten or a bunny. Something she can love and that can keep her occupied."

Part of her was tempted to tell Jen to just let her daughter go talk to the other girl. It was the sensible option, after all. But Lydia wasn't sure how Jen would react to that, despite her asking for advice. She also had a fairly good idea that Lydia Lipin suggesting *Let Lipin and Porter children play together* would eventually work its way back to her family, and she had an excellent idea of how *they* would react. Since she needed them trusting her in order to keep them away from Taylor, daring advice was a nonstarter.

Jen's face perked up. "That's a great idea. Abby used to love playing with Max, but we never got a new cat after he passed, and it's been years. A kitten or two might do the trick."

Lydia sank back against the booth, relieved for a

problem she might have been able to solve without getting sucked into someone else's family drama.

"On a more exciting topic," Jen said, "I heard you went out with Cody Miller." She paused. "Again. That's got to be the longest break in your history of dating-not-dating him."

In retrospect, Lydia would have preferred another family problem to solve. She sat upright again, determined to set the record straight. "We're still not dating. We got together because he's in town, but only as old friends."

"He's still cute, and he's now extremely rich." Jen leaned over the table, expectantly.

"But we're still not dating."

In fact, despite her initial overzealous use of exclamation points earlier, her dinner with Cody had been horribly awkward. As she had previously, Lydia had gotten the sense that Cody wanted more from her than being "old friends." It was unbelievably frustrating, since a week ago, Lydia would have been thrilled about that. Even if it had been nothing but a short-term fling, it could have been the boost her ego (and boring life) needed. But although she was keeping her promise to give Cody a chance, she still wasn't feeling any sort of spark. More like the opposite.

Cody had spent most of dinner talking about his work and all the wonderful things his success had brought him. It hadn't sounded like bragging entirely, but it had bored Lydia to distraction. She suspected that was the opposite of its intended effect. On reflection, she was realizing that what had kept her and Cody together throughout high school was that they were on equal footing. He was a friendly academic rival, and he challenged her to work harder. But they weren't competing anymore, and thank goodness for that. In the game of life, she'd lost spectacularly.

What happened next, Lydia wasn't sure, and that was fine. She'd much rather think about the one man who had suggested something a bit more specific.

The feelings Nate had aroused in her when she'd gone to his cabin the other day wouldn't leave her alone. Her Nate problem was basically the opposite of her Cody problem. She was *too* interested in him. But while a fling with Cody would have been acceptable, a fling with Nate was dangerous. She knew she could fall for him again, too easily and too hard.

Honestly, Nate was just too much of everything, and a good, practical woman understood the risks of overindulgence.

7

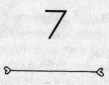

SUNDAY AFTERNOON, NATE pulled his borrowed SUV up to the old warehouse on the west side of town. The building served as a stark reminder of how long it had been since he'd last spent any considerable time in Helen. Nate recognized it, yet didn't. It retained an industrial look, but a lot of work had been put into refreshing the exterior, and the large sign hanging over the entrance declared it to be home of Northern Charm Brewing. The last time he'd been in Helen, Nate's father had been excited to have sold the building to a couple of guys from Florida. Nate had never expected he'd meet the guys.

Come to think of it, he hadn't expected them to have lasted an entire year in Helen either.

He certainly hadn't expected Kelsey would end up dating one of them.

With a deep breath, Nate killed the engine. Time had a funny way of distorting reality, or perhaps it was the other way around. Everything had changed, and yet nothing had.

In the back seat, Dolly and Spark barked excitedly. Nate had been wary of bringing them, but Kelsey had insisted. "Everyone's going to bring their dogs, and it'll be good to socialize them," she'd said.

Nate wasn't sure the puppies were ready for that yet, but if the guys who owned the brewery were okay with him bringing two rambunctious huskies inside, that was on them.

The truth was, the puppies would probably be fine and have a blast. He was less certain about himself. Ostensibly, this gathering was a private beer-tasting for friends. Since he'd never met the brewers and didn't live around here, Nate couldn't shake feeling like an interloper, even though Kelsey had refused to take no for an answer.

Dating Ian was having an interesting effect on his sister. On the one hand, Nate had never seen her so relaxed and happy before. On the other, it was like she'd cranked the very essence of herself up to eleven.

Noticing Kelsey's SUV nearby, Nate got out and went through the ritual of attaching the monsters to their leashes. At least with his sister there, he would know one person. The other vehicles were unfamiliar.

A sign on the door said to come right inside, so Nate did as instructed. The first thing that hit him as he stepped in was the barking. A lot of dogs had been corralled in one half of the large room. Nate recognized two of Kelsey's three huskies, his brother Kevin's one, and three others who might belong to Josh. The instant all the dogs saw his newcomers, they went wild. Naturally, Dolly and Spark did too.

Kelsey rushed over, not so much to greet *him* but to greet the puppies. A tall guy with sandy hair came with her, and he held out a hand and introduced himself as Ian. Kelsey's third husky—Romeo—was at his heels.

Once the dogs had mostly resettled, Nate turned his attention to the quieter, but still chatty, humans. That was when the second revelation hit him.

Lydia was here. She was leaning over the end of a rustic bar, and their eyes met long enough for her to offer him a tentative smile before she purposely dropped her gaze. Her hair was pulled loosely back, and she wore an oversize cream-colored sweater that made her dark eyes stand out more than usual. Nate's chest constricted a little, dulling the ache in his shoulder. If he wasn't careful, he'd do nothing but stare at her.

Hell, he was probably staring at her already.

Aside from Kelsey and Ian, his brother, Kevin, was there with his fiancé, Peter. Ian's business partner, Micah, was also there, of course, and so was his girlfriend, Maggie, who happened to be one of Kelsey's friends. And finally, his cousin Josh was sitting at the bar along with Taylor Lipin—the couple who were indirectly responsible for this most peculiar group.

Of all the changes in Helen since Nate had moved away, Porters and Lipins gathering together was the most unlikely. Josh and Taylor's engagement aside, this kind of thing didn't happen. Nate would be willing to bet the rest of their families had no idea that a small group of them were meeting like this.

"So you're the mysterious other Porter sibling," Ian said, sliding around to the far side of the bar. Romeo followed him like a tail, which amused Nate. His dogs had abandoned him for their own kind immediately.

"I don't think I'm that mysterious." It was warm inside the brewery, and Nate slowly worked his way out of his coat, feeling all eyes on him. Or maybe it was just *her* eyes. He was very consciously not glancing toward Lydia.

"Do you need help?" Kelsey darted over, then stepped back as he glared at her.

"I can manage, Kels. Been managing fine."

She rolled her eyes. "If you say so. Josh, does he look fine to you?"

The expression of his cousin, the doctor, clearly said, *Leave me out of it*, and Josh spun around on the stool to face Ian. "So, beer?"

"Yes, beer." Ian started setting out small glasses. "Now that Nate's here, let's get drinking."

Having successfully removed his coat, Nate stuck his arm back in the sling. "Is anyone else coming?"

"No," Kelsey said, grabbing the end stool near Taylor. "There are a limited number of people in this town who aren't too cowardly to show their faces in a group like this."

"And who you're willing to trust," Ian said, flicking her ponytail.

"That too."

Trust might be here, but it was tentative. Nate could feel an underlying tension in the air, like the hint of smoke from a dying fire. At this point, the flames might appear to be extinguished for good, but an unseen threat could make them erupt into life again. Still, he was increasingly thankful for the invite. Even if he rarely saw most of these people again after he left, being included in this circle made him feel strangely important. This could be the beginning of a new era in town.

With Ian and Micah behind the bar, there were lots of empty stools to choose from. Maggie sat to Lydia's left, and there were two empty seats to her right. Nate chose a stool one over from hers, which was as close as he dared go. Not close enough that he could smell her shampoo or accidentally brush her hand, but close enough that he could count the scattering of moles on her cheek and imagine the softness of her sweater.

He needed a drink immediately.

"What we're testing out," Ian was saying, "are potential summer beer recipes."

"Very important recipes," Micah jumped in. "These are what we'll have available when we officially open to the public at the start of tourist season."

Ian provided a bit of background on the brews he poured. According to Kelsey, he was the brewmaster, or the guy who actually created the recipes. Nate could appreciate the difference between good beer and cheap beer, but the intricacies were lost on him. He enjoyed how into it Ian was, though, and how attentively his sister watched him despite notoriously hating beer herself.

Maggie, Josh, and Taylor were also taking their roles as tasters seriously from the looks of it, but Lydia seemed less certain. Nate continued sneaking glances at her. She appeared to be listening politely, but every now and then she turned his way, too, then their eyes would meet, and a secretive smile would tug at the corners of his lips before he returned to staring at his glass. It felt a lot like being back in high school, just with the addition of beer.

What now? If there really was a truce among this particular group of quasi-friends, would it be okay to act normally with Lydia? Nate had hoped so when he first arrived, but he chose to take his cues from her. She was the one who lived here and thus would have to live with the consequences. But Lydia seemed unsure herself, and she'd chosen to act like they barely knew each other. The

more Nate thought about it, the more frustrated he became. Surely, with Josh and Taylor getting married, no
one would hold their past against them. They might
shock a few people, but they'd get over it.

He wasn't about to say or do anything without Lydia's
consent, however, so Nate kept his mouth shut and his
body distant. The beers he tried were all excellent, but
his mood soured. Only the other day he'd been scheming
for ways to see more of Lydia, but now that she sat right
next to him, it was like nothing had changed. They might
as well have been back in twelfth-grade history class,
pretending to be strangers.

With his exceptionally gregarious twin siblings, plus
Micah, who also proved to be plenty talkative, there was
no shortage of conversations going on around the bar.
Aside from the beer, the dogs, and Micah's determination to open a bagel bakery, the others chatted about the
two upcoming weddings—Kevin and Peter's over the
summer, and Josh and Taylor's in the fall. Lydia contrib-
uted a bit, but Nate mostly nodded along unless directly
asked for his opinion. He was too busy stewing in his
darker feelings. Not, he supposed, that anyone could tell.
The nice thing about being the quiet one was that no one
called you out for acting like yourself.

"How are you really holding up with your shoulder
and those two guys?" Josh asked after Nate and Kevin
had spent a couple minutes chasing down their excited
puppies.

Nate gave him a one-shoulder shrug. "Fine, most of
the time. The trick is to wear them down enough so they
need plenty of naps."

Sensing he was being talked about, Spark came over
and nipped at Nate's boot, trying to get him to play.
When Nate didn't get up quickly enough, the puppy ran

off in favor of someone who moved faster. Kelsey and Maggie did. Nate got up as well, though, as if he could prove to himself and to Josh that a bunch of hyper dogs were nothing he couldn't handle. He hadn't made it more than a step from his stool, though, when Kevin's voice froze him in place.

"Has anyone actually seen Cody Miller yet?" his brother asked. "Or is he too good for the likes of us and is hiding out somewhere?"

"I've seen him." Lydia spun her glass around. She'd been drinking her samples at a much slower pace than the rest of them. "He stays at the Bay Song when he's in town."

Taylor grinned. "She didn't just see him at the hotel. She went out to dinner with him."

Dogs temporarily forgotten, Nate turned to Lydia. His stomach suddenly felt like he'd been swallowing rocks, not beer. "You went out with Cody again?"

Lydia fumbled with her glass and nearly dropped it. "Not went *out* out. Had dinner. We used to be friends."

She kept refusing to look at him for long, so Nate didn't know what to make of her response. Lydia didn't sound defensive, but she also didn't sound thrilled. Was that aimed at him or at Taylor for bringing it up?

He'd have sworn it was easier being around her in high school. But then, in high school, all Porters and Lipins avoided each other as a rule. They'd just needed to follow old habits, which was simple enough.

"I can't believe you guys went to school with Cody-freaking-Miller," Micah said. "The man's a legend."

Nate couldn't hold it in any longer, and he snorted. "A legend in his own mind."

"Cody's nice," Lydia said, and she drank the rest of her beer all at once.

He should keep his mouth shut.

Keep it shut.

Shut up, Nate!

"I know you guys were friends, but Cody was an ass in school."

Lydia shook her head, but she kept her face determinedly fixed on a spot behind the bar. That irritated Nate further. Jealousy punched him in the gut, the same awful, frustrating sort of jealousy he'd carried around with him in high school as he'd watched the easy rapport Lydia had always shared with Cody.

"Oh, do tell." Micah leaned over the bar, and he wasn't the only one to give Nate their rapt attention. Even Josh and Taylor had stopped teasing each other and were waiting.

"Um, well." Damn. This was why he kept his mouth shut. Nate didn't want to anger Lydia by talking shit about her friend, but he couldn't contain himself either. "Just what I already said. Cody always had a very positive opinion about Cody. And look, the guy's smart, but when he wasn't the best at something, he'd cheat to get there."

"On tests?" Taylor asked. "Because if he cheated to beat out Lydia for valedictorian, I'm going to have to punch him the next time I see him."

That caused a smile to finally break across Lydia's face. "Don't risk a lawsuit for something I've gotten over."

"Speak." Kelsey quit playing with the dogs and, with ⌐urious expression, positioned herself next to Nate.

⌐⌐ow how much I love gossip, and you've been

⌐ how much he'd been holding back for

⌐⌐ould kick his ass. She'd be a hypocrite

⌐e wouldn't care. Only a few months ago

Nate had learned Kelsey secretly wrote romance novels for a living. She'd kept plenty of secrets of her own.

Conscious that he was the center of attention, Nate cleared his throat. "I don't know about grades, but we were on the ski team together. Cody cheated on more than one occasion."

Because skiing had been the one activity where Nate could beat him. Cody had better grades, and Cody had Lydia, but Nate could outski the guy. And Cody couldn't stand it.

"He used to go around and smack people in the shins with his skis before a meet," Nate continued. "Our team, another team. Didn't matter. If you were better than him, Cody would *accidentally* whack you." He made air quotes around the *accidentally*.

Kelsey groaned. "I was hoping for something more scandalous. That's the best you got?"

"My shins still feel it."

"They must." His sister raised an eyebrow like she didn't quite believe that was all there was to the story.

Nate vowed to be silent for the rest of afternoon.

That vow was easy enough to keep as everyone started reminiscing about high school. Ian wanted to know if Porter and Lipin kids were required to play different sports so they didn't kill one another, and that led to stories about real and alleged intentional injuries. According to Taylor, her father had once broken one of Nate's relatives' arms during football. Nate believed it, but Ian, Micah, and Peter were appropriately horrified by the families' nasty behaviors.

When Lydia explained that the only sport she ever did was track because she was too uncoordinated for any thing else, however, Nate's lips moved before he co catch himself.

"But you used to draw all the time." The words tumbled out, and he cringed internally. "You can't be uncoordinated and do that as well as you did."

A half second, possibly less, passed in which Nate was positive everyone was staring at him, wondering how he could remember that. He was going to bungle an explanation. Lydia was going to be angry that he spilled their secret. He was going to ruin his second shot at her before he even took it.

Then Taylor jumped in, and Nate breathed again. "Yeah, you were really good. I can't believe you stopped."

Lydia tucked loose hairs behind her ears. "You guys are all too kind. I was okay."

Nate was certain it was actually Lydia who was being too harsh on herself. She'd won a few local competitions, which were no joke. Helen had a thriving arts community, driven by the tourism industry. But Nate managed to keep quiet this time and let Taylor pester her.

The conversation moved on, and the gathering broke up soon after. As much as he'd enjoyed meeting Ian and Micah, and as hopeful as the mixed company made him, Nate drove to his parents' for dinner with a distinctly unsettled feeling. And jealousy. Lots of damn jealousy. Until he could get a better read on Lydia, he suspected neither one was going away.

8

LYDIA SHUT HER apartment door behind her and sagged against the wall. Home, sweet—quiet—home. The beer tasting had been nice, but she'd felt the tension in the air the entire time, pressing down on her shoulders.

She was positive she wasn't the only one. This hadn't been the first occasion where Lipins and Porters had mixed. Taylor and Josh had thrown an engagement party last year, and Ian and Micah had held a New Year's Eve bash. Everyone was being careful to be on their best behavior and make this truce work. Although she was wary, Lydia appreciated that.

Nate's arrival at the beer tasting today hadn't helped her nerves though. Lydia wasn't sure if it was because there was this new tension between them, brought about by her inability to get him out of her head, or if it was the pressure of pretending everything between them was normal around other people. Which was to say, everything between them was nonexistent. Ultimately, it didn't make much difference. Once, hanging out alone with

Nate made her feel better. Now merely seeing him left her confused.

No, not confused. She was very cognizant of her feelings. It was more accurate to say it left her frustrated because she didn't want to feel what she felt, but oh, those feelings were so very good. Her insides had fluttered and danced and generally been relentless since the moment he'd sat next to her, all strong and silent and stubbly in that tight gray henley.

She didn't need dinner; she needed a cold shower.

Merlot meowed about her ankles, snapping Lydia out of daydreams of licking Nate's stubbly chin. Lord, she was a mess, but the least she could do was feed her cat on time.

"What are you complaining about?" she asked as she entered the kitchen. He still had food in his bowl from this morning. "Is that not good enough to tide you over if I'm a little late?"

Merlot meowed again. So clearly the answer was no, old food was not good enough.

Lydia refilled the bowl and watched the tabby settle in with dinner, wishing it were as easy for her to be satisfied. Out with the old, and in with the new? But when it came to Nate and Cody, what was old and what was new?

Lydia retrieved the sandwich she'd bought for herself on the way home and sat down in the living room. Taylor and Josh had invited her over for dinner, but she'd declined despite her sister being an amazing cook. She'd had enough socializing for one day and needed to be alone with her thoughts. It was, after all, much more difficult to think about kissing Nate when she was in company.

Except that wasn't what she was supposed to be thinking about. What she wanted to think about was

Nate's rant about Cody. Not that it was much of a rant, but for Nate, it counted. She'd known they hadn't been friends in school, but that was expected. Their families were on opposite sides of the feud. It sounded as though Nate also took a more personal dislike to Cody as well, and that was a shame. Honestly, she didn't doubt Nate's story about Cody purposely injuring people to gain an advantage at skiing. She just didn't want to hold that against Cody because, regardless of what they were now, they'd been friends at the time.

Besides, she shouldn't care. It wasn't her business. She did wish, though, that she'd participated more in the conversation earlier. It was just hard to think when her insides were having a raucous party, and she was petrified of showing more emotions than was wise.

Lydia took a bite of her sandwich, hoping that would satisfy her stomach for the next hour or so. To keep her mind busy, she'd settle in with some reality TV.

She'd made it through one episode before she got distracted. The show's guest who was receiving a makeover on her screen was an amateur artist, and the show spent a lot of time fussing over her paintings. Lydia set her uneaten half of sandwich aside to better focus on her own critique. They weren't bad, but her mother's were every bit as good. Perhaps better.

It had been a shock last year, learning that her mother used to paint before Taylor was born. Lydia had no memory of it, but after her mother had moved out, her father had brought all of her mother's old paintings out of the attic so she could take them with her. Lydia and Taylor had marveled over them, and in the end, their mother had insisted they each take one or more to decorate their homes.

The one Lydia had kept hung above her sofa—a landscape of Helen in the summer, lines of fishing boats bobbing in the water while the mountains hovered over them. The heavy blue-and-white color scheme clashed with her neutral decor, but she found the image soothing. A lot of her mother's paintings were of winterscapes that left Lydia feeling cold.

She assumed that was a testament to her mother's skill, a skill she didn't think she could match, no matter what Nate had said earlier. But it was funny in way. Taylor had brought up the way she used to draw last summer when they'd discovered the paintings, but Nate had done so unprompted.

She was surprised he remembered, but then, she'd spent a lot of time sketching him. Probably more than he was aware. Nate hadn't liked sitting still long enough to pose—and her portrait work had never been very good—but she'd attempted it anyway. Lydia had vivid memories of Nate leaning over, trying to see what she was drawing, and herself tearing the sketchbook out of his hands.

Then kissing him to distract him, which had resulted in him distracting her. He'd been a good kisser, even then. She hadn't had a lot of experience for comparison, but she'd known what felt good, and Nate's lips had felt amazing. She'd bet he was an even better kisser now.

In need of moving, Lydia rose from the sofa so quickly that Merlot shot across the room in alarm. "Oh, come on," she called after her cat.

Merlot glared at her as she entered the bedroom and riffled through the dusty boxes sitting on top of her bookshelves. All of her sketchbooks were inside. She hadn't opened them since college, but since she'd meticulously dated each one when she'd begun using it, it was easy enough to find what she was looking for. The most recent one was over half-empty.

Lydia took it back to the living room, along with the remains of a charcoal pencil that had seen better days, and stared at Merlot. He'd gotten over his twitchiness and was sitting on his favorite spot on the windowsill. His expression remained surly, but she'd had worse subjects. Really, she didn't even know why she was doing this. She was so out of practice that the only way anyone would know what she was attempting to draw would be if she labeled the sketch *Still Life with Surly Cat*.

Whatever. This had to be better for her than killing more brain cells with reality TV.

Merlot dozed off in another moment, proving he was an ideal subject, and Lydia lost herself for a while as she got back in the groove. She was out of practice—she could see it in her lines. But the more she drew, the more her hand seemed capable of translating what her eyes perceived. It was a like a dormant muscle was stretching before her, creaky but willing to get back in shape if she'd let it.

Eventually her hand started cramping, which was no surprise, given she barely even wrote anything by hand these days. She set the questionable cat sketches aside and noticed she had an email notification on her phone. Self-preservation warned her not to check it until the morning, but she clicked to open it before the brilliance of that plan got through to her fingers.

Her grandmother had sent her list of demands about Taylor's wedding at last. Groaning, Lydia flopped back against the cushions. After a couple days without hearing from Theresa, she'd hoped her grandmother had forgotten. Coming to her senses and realizing she didn't deserve a say in a wedding she refused to condone was asking too much. But forgetting? That had seemed possible.

But apparently it wasn't to be. Lydia didn't have the energy to do more than skim the email, but she could use an outlet to vent about the absurdity of it. Unfortunately, that wasn't a simple thing to come by.

Taylor was the logical choice, but Lydia was trying to protect her sister from the family drama as much as she could. And besides, Taylor would learn soon enough. She didn't need to hear Lydia scream about the situation when it was Lydia's job to be the calm, soothing presence.

Their mother would lend a sympathetic ear, but Lydia didn't want to drag her into it either. She deserved the peace she'd finally sought for herself.

Friends were out, too, because Lipins involved outsiders in family drama only if it were directly feud-related. Had the Porters been messing with the wedding, that would be one thing. But this was a private family matter only tangentially related to the feud.

Lydia vaguely wished she were as close to any of her cousins as Josh and Kelsey were to each other, but that wasn't the case. Her father was the oldest of his brothers, and growing up, all her cousins had been too young for Lydia to ever develop a close bond with any of them. Some of them were still in high school. Besides, the rest of her family was being squirrely about the wedding. Lydia wasn't sure who among them could be trusted.

Come to think of it, outside of the few people who'd gathered at the brewery today, she wasn't sure *anyone* could be trusted with wedding issues.

That gave her pause. One of the people there today had been her confidant years ago. Nate had known exactly what it was like to deal with the feud because he'd had to deal with all of the same nonsense. And like her, he'd never relished the fight, but he'd understood it in a way her other friends couldn't. Back then, when she and Taylor hadn't been close, Nate had been the only person she could talk to when the drama got out of hand.

Nate would still understand; Lydia was certain. She was also certain that reaching out to Nate was the last thing she should do if she wanted to keep any emotional distance, but times were desperate.

Bracing herself for the possibility that she might be making the teensiest bit of a mistake, Lydia picked up her phone again and sent Josh a text asking for Nate's number.

NATE STUCK A fresh log into the woodstove and shut the metal door. It would have been easier on his shoulder to crank up the thermostat, but he liked the scent, crackle, and hiss of the woodsmoke too much. He didn't have such amenities back home, so he might as well take advantage of the stove while he had it, even if it did mean needing to carry in more wood from under the tarp outside.

Yawning, he stood and stretched his back. The monsters watched him with half-closed eyes from the rug. After he'd given all of them dinner, he'd taken the puppies on a long walk, as had become his habit. At least, he'd intended to. They were so worn out from all the excitement earlier that they hadn't lasted long. Nate hoped that meant they'd let him sleep in tomorrow.

The truth was, he was exhausted as well, emotionally. Seeing Lydia, pretending he *didn't* see Lydia, wondering what was going on with Lydia, and worse—wondering what was going on with Lydia and Cody—had done him in for the day. If he were back home, he'd be ready to go out and hit a bar with friends, but all he wanted to hit was his bed.

And Cody. He could hit Cody with his good arm.

Nate shuffled into the kitchen, the wood floor cool despite the heavy wool socks on his feet. He'd make some tea and settle down with a movie or a book. Just not one of Kelsey's books. Nate didn't understand how his sister could stand creating more emotions out of thin air. Life already filled a person with too many feelings. Like right now? He was a damned mess of feelings, and it left him tired at eight o'clock. Ridiculous. He'd pick a movie or a book with lots of action and only minimal emoting.

A text arrived as he set the electric kettle to boil, and Nate's plan for evening entertainment went up in smoke. Just seeing the words Hi, it's Lydia on his screen next to the unknown number had him sizzling and crackling with feelings in a way that could make the woodstove jealous.

On the plus side, seeing her name also woke him up.

I'm having a wedding crisis. Are you available to talk?

Since writing back, *I'm available for whatever you need*, wasn't the best choice, Nate went with the more subtle: Sure. Give me a call.

Only after he hit send did he pause to wonder what a wedding crisis entailed. If she wanted his opinion on flowers or some shit like that, they were both in trouble, although he'd do his best. Honestly, it didn't matter what the reason was. Just the fact that she was reaching out to him after the weirdness this afternoon sent his mood into the clouds.

Feelings were overrated.

No doubt that was why he almost dropped his phone in his excitement to answer when it rang a moment later.

"What's up?" Nate put the phone on speaker so he could talk while pouring the water for his tea.

"I'm sorry to bother you." Lydia sounded as exhausted as he felt.

"You're not bothering me." What had bothered him was the awkwardness this afternoon. This was the opposite of bothering him.

"Thanks." She sighed. "It's just . . . I needed someone who could relate."

Nate dunked the tea bag around, still lost. "To wedding stuff?"

"Wedding family stuff."

Ah, he should have figured it out. Lydia's issue wasn't so much about the wedding as it was the feud. Their final year of high school and that last summer, they'd spent a lot of time commiserating about family crap. Silently, for the most part. There was never much each of them had to say because they'd understood each other perfectly. The details might change, but the essence of their daily lives never did. Nate had never had someone he could wallow in his frustrations with before, and neither had Lydia, apparently. Sometimes it had been enough for them to merely exchange glances, and the other would know. It was weird that such a trivial, inconsequential thing could have made him feel better, but it had. Simply knowing Lydia was out there, tired of the bullshit, too, had made life more bearable.

And then, of course, she'd left.

Nate didn't blame her or resent her for that. Lydia was smart. She'd belonged at college. He'd just planned to be around, waiting for her when she returned, and it hadn't worked out that way.

But he was around now, even if only temporarily. This afternoon's frustrations aside, he had to accept that he would always be around for her if she needed him. It was an unsettling realization that would demand something stronger to drink than mint tea if he thought about it too long.

Nate listened while Lydia explained how her grandmother was simultaneously trying to take control of her sister's wedding and threatening to boycott it, and how she was stuck in between. Part of him wanted to tell her to back away, that it wasn't her responsibility to protect Taylor. He also knew it would be a pointless gesture. In Lydia's place, he would do exactly the same thing, and no one would be able to talk him out of it. It was one more reason to admire her.

"You're a good sister," is what Nate opted to say when Lydia fell silent. "Our families suck."

"Yeah, they do." She sighed again, and he tried very, very hard not to imagine what she was doing or wearing right now. Was she sprawled out in her pajamas? What were her pajamas?

"Tell me your family is being a pain in the ass about it too," Lydia said. "So I feel better."

Nate wished he had something juicy to tell her if it would help, but he'd mostly—luckily—been left out of the chaos. He assumed it was because he lived far away, though Kelsey swore it was because he was the only one of them their father didn't want to argue with.

"My father doesn't talk about it," Nate said, carrying his tea upstairs. "My mother is not happy, obviously, but resigned. Josh isn't her son. I have no idea what Josh's parents think."

"According to Taylor, Josh's mom is happy. She hated the feud, and that's why she left."

"Ah." It was strange. He'd gone almost his entire life thinking he and Lydia were oddballs, but lately he was learning that there were more people out there who were tired of the fighting. So why were they still pretending they didn't know each other?

"Nate?" Lydia asked, and he realized there had been a bit of a pause. "Are you yanking on your ear?"

"What? No." He lowered his hand sheepishly. Still, since he'd been called out, he might as well as bring up the question going through his mind. "Can I ask you something?"

He lay down on the bed, careful not to jostle his shoulder, and stared at the open-beam ceiling. The fan above his head circled, mesmerizing, stirring up the air. These cabins were mostly meant for summer rentals, the ceilings impractical for heating them properly in the winter, even with the fans circulating the rising heat. Nate did not want to be that fan, going around in circles when it came to Lydia. "At the brewery—were we supposed to pretend not to have ever talked before?"

"Oh." It didn't sound like Lydia had expected that to be the question. "I didn't know how we were supposed to act, and you didn't say anything, either, so it seemed wisest to go with that. There's enough drama going on. I'd rather the attention be focused elsewhere."

He hadn't thought about it that way, but Nate couldn't really argue the point. If his and Lydia's past came out, it would be all either of them would hear about for who knew how long. Eventually, the truth probably *would* come out, assuming life around here didn't take a turn for the worse. But he'd rather deal with that then.

"That makes sense," he said. Above, the fan continued to circle and he continued to fixate on it, a sign that there was more he wanted to ask about, but was unwilling to do so. Nate turned onto his unbroken side. "I didn't say anything earlier because you didn't."

"Well, I didn't say anything because *you* didn't. We're both super considerate that way."

"Always have been."

Lydia made a noise of agreement. "Nate? Talk to me about something else. Tell me about firefighting."

Confused by the change in topic, he reached for the tea. "Why do you want to hear about that?"

"Because it's about as far from the feud as anything can be, and I want to think about other things. And it's about you. You never talk about you."

He was about to say it was because he wasn't that interesting, but he'd poked at Lydia for saying the same thing not too long ago. So Nate haltingly explained a little about what he did as part of a crew, and Lydia asked question after question, because he never seemed to give her enough explanation about the people he worked with, the details of the job, or how he spent his off time. Nate didn't think he'd talked this much since his last interview, and he enjoyed the chance to turn the tables on her, bugging her to cough up her favorite TV shows and bands and hand over her social media profiles so he could look her up—something he'd managed to refrain from doing until now and would probably regret later. As it turned out, Lydia's last posted photograph was a throwback to high school, and Nate grinned at it for far too long before he realized the silence had stretched out between them.

"We were such babies then, weren't we?" he finally said, covering up his first inclination, which had been to say that he'd been right—she was even more beautiful than she used to be. "I didn't feel like a baby then, though. Everything between us felt very adult."

"Because we were acting more responsible and mature than our families?"

There was that, but it hadn't been what was on his mind. "I was thinking more about all the kissing."

"Ah." Lydia paused, but when she spoke again, he could hear the smile in her voice. "You were always a very *considerate* kisser."

Nate laughed, his thoughts returning to the questions of what Lydia was doing and where she was. Lying in bed like he was? Imagining that—her stretched out on a bed—sent blood rushing to his groin. "I'm still considerate, you know. And I've gotten better at it."

"Don't sell yourself short. You were always pretty good at it."

"Pretty good?" He moaned like he was hurt.

"Did I bruise your fragile, male ego?"

Nate snorted. "No, because if I was pretty good back then, I promise I'm amazing now."

Lydia laughed. "So much for a fragile ego, then. I'll take your word for that."

"That's one option." Certainly not the one he'd like her to pick.

Nate knew the moment the words were out of his mouth that he'd pushed too hard. It had been so easy to fall back into conversation with Lydia, like the old times.

Yet these were not the old times. They hadn't talked in years, and Lydia had changed; he could sense that. Possibly it was only the awkwardness of their situation that made it obvious, but she'd been quieter today than he remembered her. More reserved. Or she had until this call, which told Nate that the Lydia he'd known back then was still lurking in her somewhere. She'd been coaxed out for a bit, and there was nothing he wanted more than to find her again. That Lydia—once they'd discovered they could be friends—was never awkward or reserved with him. With that Lydia, Cody was no threat, even with all his money.

That was *his* Lydia.

But although Nate couldn't see her through the phone, he knew instinctively that he'd said too much. He could practically feel her retreating from a couple of miles away. He'd screwed up.

Lydia laughed again, but it sounded strained this time. "You're funny, but I need to get going. My day starts early tomorrow."

"Yeah, sure. Good night."

"Good night."

Nate hung up and set the phone beside the mint tea he'd forgotten about. He needed to figure out how to un–screw up. Sure, it was partially selfish, but he really did want to see her face again without the tension in it, wanted to hear her laugh without holding back like she had. Nate didn't know if it was Cody, her sister's wedding, or something else that was weighing on her, but as long as he was in town, he was going to figure it out.

There was nothing like a new plan that was doomed to fail.

9

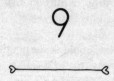

DAWN—OR WHAT passed for it at this time of year—
didn't change Nate's resolve. Every interaction he'd had
with Lydia, culminating in that almost-but-not-quite-
like-old-times phone call last night, had forced him to
realize how much he still cared about her. He could tell
himself all he wanted that it should be impossible to be
head over heels for a woman he'd lost touch with a decade ago, but facts were facts. His physical attraction to
Lydia was as strong as ever, and everything else about
her continued to draw him in like a bonfire at midwinter.
She was a light in the darkness. Warmth in the cold. A
welcoming presence telling him he was home.

Given his screwup last night, Nate wasn't sure how to
go about next steps yet, but he was confident he'd figure
something out. He had Lydia's phone number now, so in
some ways, he was a hundred years ahead of where he'd
been yesterday morning.

After giving the monsters their breakfast, he filled a
thermos with coffee for himself and got dressed. Chang-

ing clothes, like taking his jacket off, was still painful, especially in the morning when his shoulder was
stiffest. Blessedly, his ribs seemed pretty much back to
normal. He'd refrained from attempting any more exercises, since his orthopedist had scolded him, but the in-
activity bugged him almost as much as the pain.

"Ready for a walk?" Nate asked the puppies, and they
charged over. Clearly, they'd learned the word.

It wasn't the only one they'd picked up on, but he was
working on getting them to obey the meanings of those
others.

"Sit." He held their leashes with his left hand and gestured with the right. Spark seemed to contemplate it for
a second, then he barked instead. Dolly wagged her tail.
Nate tried again. "Sit."

It took a few tries and some encouragement, but they
finally sat, and he got the leashes on them both. They
also practiced *stay* while he winced his way into his
coat. That one went over better, surprisingly.

It was a typically crisp early-February morning, and
Nate's SUV didn't have any heat by the time he stopped
in a municipal parking spot near the town's main park.
Kelsey had told him the paths around the perimeter had
been cleared of snow, and so Nate had decided it was
time for a change of scenery.

The sky was looking like it might be a rare clear day,
and the monsters were excited as they bounded out of the
back seat. Nate held carefully to their leashes, making
sure he could hold them and sip his coffee at the same
time. During the summer in particular, the park was always crowded, thick with locals and tourists, but it was
currently almost as barren as the tree limbs. Nate spotted
only a few other people walking their dogs down the
paths.

From where he walked, Nate could see straight down to the harbor where the cruise ships that provided the town with a large chunk of its economy would dock. There were plenty of smaller vessels bobbing on the waves, many covered in the same fine layer of snow as the paths. Fishing and sightseeing were year-round industries, although the latter dropped off significantly during the colder months. Behind him, the town spread out, one- and two-story buildings looking sleepy on a Monday morning as they lined the streets with the yellow glow of their lamps. Behind the buildings were the mountains, stretching toward the sky.

The monsters were oblivious to it all. Snowcapped peaks and gently swaying boats couldn't match whatever interesting smells they discovered on the ground or the joy of meeting new people as their paths crossed. Nate often thought it might be nice to be reincarnated as a well-loved dog. Everything would be exciting then. People would dote on you for simply existing. And hey, no one would care if you licked your balls because you were bored.

As a dog, he might also be unable to pick Cody Miller out of a crowd.

Which may or may not be an advantage.

Nate hadn't expected Cody to be in Helen still, and he definitely hadn't expected to run into Cody at eight A.M. Monday morning in the park. But then, he hadn't expected to run into Lydia outside the Bay Song last week either. Helen was just that kind of small town.

He'd seen Cody approach, but he hadn't recognized him until the other man was about fifteen feet away. Cody was dressed in what looked like some performance running gear, and he'd been making a circuit of the park perimeter from the opposite direction.

Nate sipped his coffee so he wouldn't be tempted to speak or acknowledge Cody's existence. Judging by the way his body reacted to seeing him, however, over the past several days Cody had shifted from *irritating memory* to *active threat* in Nate's head. That was no surprise, but it wasn't a happy feeling either.

Nate was positive he recognized Cody only because his photograph frequently showed up in the news, so he expected Cody to keep running by and ignore him. But Cody slowed and bent down to greet the puppies, who—not knowing any better—returned the greeting with much enthusiasm. He hadn't acknowledged any of the other dogs whose paths he'd crossed, and Nate frowned into his thermos, hoping it was a coincidence.

"Nate. How are you doing?" Cody straightened, his breath coming out in white clouds, his chest rising and falling hard from the run.

So much for a coincidence.

Fine. He'd been doing fine until a minute ago. "Fine. You?"

"Never been better." Cody bent down and gave the monsters more of the attention they were demanding. "You bust up your arm?"

"Shoulder."

"Sucks. I strained my rotator cuff a couple years ago playing tennis. Was not fun."

Nate didn't know what to say to that at first, so he grunted in agreement and drank coffee. "I was working a rescue mission for the Humane Society."

In a roundabout way that was true. It wasn't as impressive as being able to say he'd gotten injured on the job, protecting civilization from the savage onslaught of a forest fire, but it was more noble than playing tennis.

What the hell was going on with him? Why was he

competing with Cody about their injuries? He was completely regressing.

On the other hand, Cody was putting the moves on Lydia.

Competition it was.

Cody didn't seem to notice, or perhaps care, that Nate was currently considering him an adversary. "Humane Society? Cool. It's so great to be back here, you know. I can't believe how much the town's expanded."

Since he'd stopped moving, a chill was creeping under Nate's coat. Subfreezing weather on an empty stomach was a bad combination, but he wasn't about to let it show. In his close-fitting running gear, Cody should have been colder but he didn't appear to be.

"Yeah, it really has," Nate said, sipping more hot coffee.

"You know what hasn't grown? Your vocabulary."

Cody laughed, and Nate let him have the joke, which he considered very magnanimous of himself. Because, yes, he had a decent enough vocabulary; he just opted not to waste it on most people. Saying that felt ruder than he cared to act though. The key to competing with Cody was not giving Cody the satisfaction of knowing Nate considered him *worth* competing with.

"Humane Society?" Cody asked again once he'd finished chuckling. "That's new. Last I remember you were working for the local fire department."

The puppies had lost interest in Cody, and Nate sensed and shared their wish to move on. "I volunteer. I'm still a firefighter, but I left Helen a while ago."

"Really?" For some reason that was what caught Cody's interest at last. "Good for you, man. Getting out of here."

Nate blinked. Good for him? What did that mean?

Yes, there were definite downsides to living in Helen, the feud being among them, but Nate had never disliked the town. In many ways, he still considered this his home. His family was here, his memories and friends too. It might not be as cosmopolitan as wherever Cody lived now, but Helen was a good place to live. A beautiful place.

Besides, why was Cody reputedly building a vacation home here if he hated it? Nate figured there was no reason not to ask, so he did.

"I don't hate this place or anything." Cody tucked his hands under his arms, showing the first signs of being cold. "But, you know, you leave and you realize how unworldly it is. The things that consume people here, like the feud—you realize how small they are once you leave. This place constricts you right down to its size. It's nice to visit, but it would be stifling to live here. I mean, you left. You should get that."

Unfortunately, Nate did, or he had at one time. He emptied his thermos, temporarily confused by his reaction to Cody's words. In those years, when Lydia had left, he had felt not precisely constricted, but stifled.

His thoughts must have shown on his face, because Cody nodded. "See? You know it. You wouldn't have been such good competition back in school if you couldn't feel it too. Everyone who's worthwhile feels it."

"Lydia Lipin never left, and from what I've heard, you find her plenty worthwhile." He should have kept his mouth shut; he'd been doing so well.

Cody grinned and shook his head. "I see the speed of gossip hasn't changed. But yeah, fair point. Lydia is too good for this place. But she *is* good. That's why she lets her family hold her back."

Nate couldn't argue with that exactly. As far as he

was concerned, Lydia was too good for most people, places, and things. And while he wouldn't say her family was holding her back, he was aware that he'd been telling her to step back from them and their drama just last night.

Unwilling to give away his thoughts about Lydia, Nate shrugged. "It's easy for you to say, not being a part of our families."

"Another fair point," Cody conceded. "But that's why I'm hoping to show her there's an alternative to all this mess."

Nate wondered what *an alternative* meant, because if he let it, his imagination could run with possibilities. Most of them not good. "How's that going?"

"Slowly, but the nice thing about being me is that I have lots of time to do whatever I choose with." Cody spread his arms, then quickly tucked his hands back to his side.

Nate bit down a smirk. The cold catching up to Cody pleased him, as did the news that whatever Cody's plans for Lydia were, they weren't progressing quickly. He had time for his own plans—if he ever pulled anything concrete together.

"It's been nice catching up with you." Cody slapped Nate on the good arm, and started jogging in place.

Nate said something vaguely polite back and let the other guy take off toward the road. Once Cody was far enough in the distance, he turned around and started that way too. Unlike Cody, he did not have all the time this morning, and that conversation had effectively prevented him from making it the entire way around the park.

"Next time, guys," Nate said to the monsters as they strained at their leashes, trying and failing to make him move faster. "And when you see that guy again, feel free to bark and jump all over him until he leaves."

TWENTY MINUTES LATER, Nate slid into a booth across the table from his former mentor. Given the size of the town, the Helen Regional Fire Department was small, with only a handful of full-time staff relying on a larger part-time and volunteer crew. When Nate had first expressed interest in firefighting while he was in high school, it was John who had taken him under his wing. Then it was John who had pushed for Nate to earn one of the few paid positions available, and eventually it was John who'd encouraged and helped him with his application to join the Forest Service.

John was now fire chief, and the size of the department had increased commensurate with the growing population in Helen and the surrounding area. Nate visited him every few years when he came home, but this time, he thought John was showing his age more than he ever had before. The lines on his tanned face seemed deeper, and his hair was more salt than pepper. His eyes remained sharp, though, and he showered the monsters with energetic affection.

Nate had questioned the wisdom of bringing the puppies to breakfast, but John had asked specifically to meet them, and the Old Bone diner welcomed dogs as long as they were kept well contained by their owners. They even had a menu just for dog treats. It was, Nate assumed, the only reason anyone ate there, since the human food was mediocre at best, and eating outside (albeit under a tent and with heat lamps) in the winter was an experience. Nate had never seen a place like it outside of Helen.

Cody had called Helen quaint, but the diner suggested quirky might be a better descriptor.

"Aren't they the cutest?" John had already bought a treat for them, and the puppies settled down as they feasted on sausage. If they hadn't already been in love with his former mentor, they were now. "What are you going to do with them when you go back to work?"

Nate grimaced and thanked the server who filled his mug with coffee. The question had been nagging at him for weeks, and since he hadn't come up with a satisfactory answer, he kept trying not to think about it. Getting back to work felt ages away at this point, and it brought its own worries about his shoulder.

"I haven't figured that out yet," Nate said. "Adopting them was a spur-of-the-moment decision, and probably not my wisest."

But how could he have let them go when they clung to him with those little paws and gazed at him with those innocent blue eyes? He didn't regret it, although there was plenty of time for that.

"You'll figure something out," John said, sipping his coffee.

He would have to because he wasn't giving up his career or the monsters.

While Nate warmed up from the brisk walk around the park, they ordered breakfast and caught up. John was well used to Nate's propensity for short answers, and so the conversation at times felt like a rehash of last night's conversation with Lydia, with John asking follow-up question after follow-up until he was satisfied. In return, though, he provided plenty of commentary on the state of the town, the fire department, and every nonfamily or feud-related item that Nate had wanted to know. Nate had mostly finished his pancakes by the time they reached a lull in conversation, and he shared one of his last pieces of bacon with the grateful—and very spoiled—puppies.

"If this keeps up, I expect we'll be able to hire another part-timer in the next year or so," John said, sitting back against the booth. "Town's getting big, and they're still building houses near the highway."

It was probably the statement Nate heard the most every time he came home. Development and growth around here were as hotly debated as ever.

"It's a nice place to live." He was still feeling defensive about Cody's comment.

"It is." John nodded. "Still too boring for you, though, I bet."

Nate paused too long, considering that, and Dolly snatched the entire piece of bacon he'd been intending to split between the dogs, taking it for herself. Nate handed over his second-to-last piece for Spark so as not to have a puppy civil war break out.

Boring, stifled—even *constricted*, like Cody had said—no longer felt accurate, and Nate wasn't sure why. Maybe he'd simply grown up, or possibly the feud no longer seemed as oppressive. Getting together with others at the brewery had been interesting. Life was changing in Helen, and change was rarely boring.

Of course, there was also the possibility that the reason was nothing other than Lydia herself. He couldn't pretend he wasn't a thrill seeker, and the possibility for a second chance with her—even a short one—stirred his blood.

Nate hated sitting still, and back then, staying in Helen, waiting for something that could never be with Lydia, had been torture. As much as the adventure of wildlands firefighting had appealed to him, it was likely the situation with Lydia, rather than the town itself, that had urged him to leave.

But he wouldn't have confessed that to anyone, not even John, who'd been mostly a neutral party with regard to the feud. When Nate had expressed an interest in leaving, *boring* and *stifling* were the words he'd chosen. People understood them intuitively. They didn't need to know that boring and stifling were the symptoms, not the disease. Hell, Nate wasn't sure he'd truly realized it at the time. He'd simply known he couldn't stay when the best thing about staying was out of his grasp.

"I guess my opinion on boring has changed over the years," Nate said. He was going to be grappling with these thoughts for a while before he'd be ready to voice them. And anyway, the Old Bone diner was no place to share confessions, should he ever feel inclined to do so. "It's not so bad, really."

To his surprise, John laughed. "Are you settling down with old age, or is it something else?"

Nate narrowed his eyes. "Who you calling old, Grandpa?" John had proudly showed off photos of his newest grandson during the giant catch-up session. "And what something else?"

"Well, I can't call you Rookie anymore, for sure." John tented his fingers over the remains of his toast. "And I don't know. I always got the feeling that you weren't just chasing more excitement when you left. You were also trying to leave something behind."

Nate took a bite of his last bacon slice before one of the monsters got any ideas. "Maybe. Honestly, I haven't quite figured it out yet."

To listen to himself, he had a lot of shit he had to get together. There was more rookie left in him than he liked to admit.

"Hmm." John picked up his mug and cocked his head to the side. "You've been gone awhile to have not figured it out."

Nate didn't want to lie, so he shrugged sheepishly. Then he winced in pain. By this point, he should have remembered that some gestures were a bad idea, but when his mind was elsewhere, his brain lost track.

The pain made him want to scream. Not because it hurt so badly, but with frustration.

"None of it might make any difference if this shoulder doesn't get better." Nate let the last of the bacon drop to his plate, too discouraged to eat more.

"It'll get better," John said. "You've got to give yourself time. Shit—you're lucky to have gone as long as you have with nothing worse happening to you."

Nate snorted. "That makes me feel better. Thanks."

"I'm just saying, go easy on yourself. Enjoy the time being back here. Things will work out on their own schedule."

"Yeah, I hope so." He didn't know what he'd do if they didn't.

10

IT WAS A relentlessly quiet Monday morning, and the silence was getting on Lydia's nerves. Why couldn't the heaters have broken today? Or better yet—what about a plumbing problem? A fire in the kitchen? Perhaps a delivery truck could have skidded on the ice and slammed into the building. Anything would have been better than being left alone with her thoughts.

But no, she cradled her second mug of coffee and stared at her computer, seeing but not reading the words in her email. The only words that were sticking in her head were the ones Nate had said to her last night. *That's one option.* There'd been no mistaking his flirtatious tone and the invitation it offered.

She supposed that answered one question—the attraction between them was mutual. But that answer posed more questions. Like, was she strong enough to ignore it?

She should never have called him. She'd known it was a mistake since the second she'd heard his voice on the other end of the phone, all sexy and warm and gruff at the same time. Quintessentially Nate.

Talking to him like she used to talk to him was too easy. Falling into old patterns was as well. After Nate had saved her on the side of the road when she'd gotten a flat, noticing him had been unavoidable. As someone who'd done her best to tune out the feud when possible, Lydia had been previously aware of Nate's existence, of course. But there had been a difference between aware and *aware*. Suddenly, Nate had been everywhere she looked, and oh, God help her, she hadn't been able to stop looking.

It wasn't just that Nate had been cute, though he was. And it wasn't just that he'd been unexpectedly kind, although he'd been that too. He'd also seemed to get her, and there was something so comforting and relieving about knowing another person out there understood you. As their friendship had quietly grown over senior year from tentative acknowledgements that the other existed (when no one was watching them) to sneaky conversations about history class, and to commiseration about their families and the feud, Lydia had done her best not to fall for Nate.

Her best had been nowhere near good enough. She'd been too young then to think she had a type, but Nate was in many ways entirely unlike Cody. Cody was loud and sought attention. He was like the cruise ships pulling into the harbor every year—fun, flashy, and impossible to ignore. Nate was more like the year-round fishing vessels—quiet and steady, just getting the job done. Both he and Cody were smart, athletic, and good-looking. But only one had been off-limits, and naturally that was the one Lydia had fallen for hard. It was so not her, and yet with Nate, she'd never felt more like herself.

And here she was, over ten years later, a grown woman who should know better than to toss herself in front of temptation, doing it again. Returning Nate's hat when she didn't have a reason to think he might reciprocate the attraction was one thing. Now that she knew that door was open to her, she needed to exercise some serious self-control so she didn't kick it in.

Because there could be no repeats between her and Nate. Lydia had known the heartbreak of losing him once, and she couldn't go through it a second time. Heading off for college and leaving Nate behind had been so unbearably hard, and that was despite the fact that there had been no future for them together regardless. Nate hadn't wanted to believe it, but Lydia had been as practical then as she was now. Their friendship and relationship had needed to be a secret, and that was no way to live.

Of course, things were changing. Her sister and Josh were proof of it, even though the trail they were blazing might literally yet catch on fire. But what wouldn't change was that Nate's time in Helen was temporary. Lydia knew herself well enough to know that if she got involved with Nate, temporary wouldn't satisfy her. Not if he'd been able to arouse feelings in her that she'd been positive had died away years ago. And besides, Nate's job was dangerous and unpredictable. He lived on the road for months out of every year. She couldn't handle that.

So yes, the only option was to stay unattached to Nate (or no more attached than she already was), and the only way to do that was to not give in to temptation.

Which made calling him last night a mistake she could not afford to repeat.

Pressing her palms flat against her desk, Lydia drew a deep breath. Then she picked up her phone and re-

sponded to the text Cody had sent her this morning—
carefully. She was doing her best to be friendly, not
flirty, but it still seemed to her that whatever she typed,
Cody misinterpreted it. At first, she'd thought it was her
fault. But Lydia had reviewed every text she'd sent and
replayed their conversations in her head, and the more
she thought about it, the more she was convinced that the
problem wasn't her at all. But without being outright
rude and shutting down a friendship, what was she supposed to do?

With the stressful task accomplished, she should get
back to work, but a knock on her office door delayed that.

Taylor poked her head in. "Are you busy?"

"For you? Never." Lydia pushed her chair away from
the desk, relieved for a fresh excuse to keep her mind off
Nate. "What's up?"

Her sister was far too cheerful for a Monday morning.
Waking up next to a guy she was smitten with looked
good on her. "I wanted to . . ." Taylor's voice trailed off,
and she picked up the sketch pad next to Lydia's coffee mug.

Lydia wasn't sure why she'd brought it to her office,
but she'd recalled how she used to doodle back when she
was trying to work through a problem. It hadn't sounded
like a terrible idea to try it again. If nothing else, it might
keep her entertained on boring phone calls.

"Have you started drawing again?" Taylor asked. "I
didn't know."

"I haven't." Lydia's fingers itched to pull the pad away
from her sister, but it wasn't like there was anything too
embarrassing in there. Her Merlot sketches might not be
great, but he was recognizable as a cat. "You guys mentioned it yesterday, and I was thinking about it."

Taylor grinned and flopped onto the chair across the

desk. "I'm so glad. Damn, you were good. Even Nate remembered. How unexpected was that?"

"Yeah." Lydia pressed her lips together. Luckily, the sketchbook she'd retrieved didn't have any drawings of teen Nate in it. She'd never done a lot of them, but she'd done a few, struggling to capture the quiet intensity in his eyes and those lips she'd so desperately wanted to kiss. He'd laugh and turn red whenever he caught her drawing him, and she'd have to stop. But it had made her attempts all the more fun. How far could she get before he realized what she was doing?

If her family had ever found those sketches . . .

Lord, what had she been thinking? In retrospect, drawing Nate seemed incredibly reckless, and Lydia couldn't believe she'd done it. But then, she'd also sneaked out after school and on weekends to hang out with him. What was that if not reckless too?

Lydia chewed this over while Taylor flipped through the pages. She'd spent a lot of time lying to her family and friends that year so she and Nate could be together. The running off into the woods, the snow machining without telling anyone where they were going or what they were doing—all of those behaviors had been risky. Lydia tended to think of Taylor as the rebellious, reckless one in the family, but the truth was that she'd just done a better job of hiding it than her sister. And in the eyes of the Lipins, none of Taylor's teenage shenanigans would have come close to the hell teenage Lydia had been raising.

The incongruity between this realization and the way Lydia normally thought of herself was so strong that she literally fell back in her chair. It was a mystery how she'd managed to bury those memories.

It was one more thing to blame on Nate's return. He was dredging up more than emotions.

She also felt guilty, because the lies of omission about her and Nate grew every time she talked to him. In high school, it had never been a big deal. She and Taylor hadn't been particularly close; they were too different. But since Taylor had returned to Helen last summer, they'd finally started connecting on more than a superficial level. Withholding something like this from Taylor now made Lydia uneasy, but she didn't want to talk about it either. It was better—easier—to wait for Nate to leave and any newly awakened feelings to die back down.

Yes, Nate's return was making her regress in all sorts of ways.

"Have you told Mom you're drawing again?" Taylor's question brought Lydia back to the present with a start.

"I literally just picked up a pencil for the first time again last night, and I'm not sure Mom would care anyway."

Taylor flashed her an *oh, please* look. "Are you kidding? I know I've been talking to her more than you because of wedding stuff, but she's gotten so into her art. She'd love it."

That might be, but Taylor's enthusiasm was enough to up Lydia's feelings of guilt about keeping secrets. Talking more to her mother would make her feel even worse. As it was, Lydia was half considering telling her sister about Nate, but Taylor would probably be encouraging about that, too, and the last thing Lydia needed was encouragement.

"What did you want to talk about?" Lydia asked. Guilt drew her gaze to her computer, and it must have given Taylor the impression that she wanted to get back to work.

"Oh, right. Sorry." Taylor snapped the sketchbook shut and returned it to Lydia's desk. "I wanted to thank you for everything you've been doing for me. I know you're doing your best to keep our family off my back about the wedding, and I really appreciate it."

"That's what big sisters do." It was what any sibling should do—try to protect the ones they loved. But Lydia hadn't done such a great job of it when they were younger, and so she'd been attempting to make up for it lately. Guarding Taylor's secret about Josh when no one else had known about it. Keeping their grandmother and father out of Taylor's business. It was a little late, but it was the least she could do, and she didn't expect thanks for it.

A respite would have been nice though. As evidenced by her mishandling of her grandmother's email last night, Lydia was beginning to crack from the strain. But that wasn't something she'd share with Taylor.

Unsettled by everything swirling through her head, Lydia picked up her coffee mug but it was empty. *Damn it.* Maybe Taylor would be grateful enough to go get her a refill from the kitchen. That was the sort of thank-you she could live with.

"Well, I appreciate it a lot." Taylor retrieved what appeared to be a small notecard from her pocket and set it on the desk. "Which is why I want to give you this, but I'm just going to say it too. Would you be my maid of honor?"

Surprise temporarily stunned Lydia into silence. "Of course! I'd be thrilled. And honored."

And guilty. She'd feel even more guilty about hiding things than she had a moment ago, but Taylor's grin forced Lydia to swallow down the bad feelings and smile back.

"What about Stacy?" Lydia asked, referring to Tay-

"Stacy is definitely going to be a bridesmaid, but she lives so far away that it's going to be difficult. And anyway, I always intended for you to be my maid of honor since Josh and I got engaged. You've been there for me so much since my relationship with Josh began. You've been my right-hand woman in everything."

There was a definite lump in Lydia's throat, and she stood to hug her sister. "I told you—just doing my sisterly job."

"Please." Taylor rolled her eyes as she stepped back. "That means nothing. We both know how messed up families can be."

"True, but we are not."

Taylor pointed her finger at Lydia. "No, we are the levelheaded, rational people. And though we are a small group, we are mighty."

Lydia hoped so. Taylor and Josh's wedding was still some time away, which left plenty of opportunities for trouble. "Who else is in the wedding party?"

"Josh asked Kelsey and a friend of his—Adrian—to be his groomspeople. And we're formally enlisting Nate and Kevin to be our 'wedding guard.'"

"Wedding guard?"

Taylor shrugged. "Josh didn't want to leave them out, and honestly, we might just need such a thing. Once Nate's shoulder heals, I'm sure he'll be more than capable. Even with it busted, he can look intimidating."

Intimidating was not a word Lydia would associate with Nate, but she could see Taylor's point. Nate towered over his younger siblings, and there was no question that the man had muscles.

Lots of finely sculpted, hard, manly muscles.

Crap. She had to stop this. But she'd seen Nate without a shirt, and that image had been seared into her brain.

"Anyway, I'll let you get back to work," Taylor said, "but there's also an invitation in that envelope. You *will* come over for dinner this week. We're hosting the wedding party so people can get to know each other better while Nate's in town."

So she'd have to face Nate again and go through all that awkwardness. Although, pretending not to know Nate in public—while it might make her feel guilty—would make it easier to resist the temptation he posed. He'd agreed to keep up the ruse, after all, and that meant he couldn't flirt with her.

Lydia picked up the envelope and traced a finger around the edge. "You realize the wedding party might be the only guests at this wedding, right?"

Taylor laughed. "Nah, there'll be a few more. Ian and Micah will be there, and Josh and I have a few other friends who don't have their heads up their asses. But honestly, I'm good with tiny. Those who don't like us together don't deserve us."

"That's a good philosophy."

Reckless, too, Lydia wanted to add. Risky. But perhaps she was in less of a position to chide her sister than she'd once believed.

11

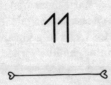

"DINNER IS SERVED." Taylor flourished the announcement with a twirl of her spoon before popping back into the kitchen.

Several cheers erupted from the men present, but Lydia was simply relieved. Eating would give her something to do besides smiling awkwardly and trying not to pay too much attention to Nate.

The group that had assembled in Josh's—now Taylor and Josh's—house was an interesting mix. It wasn't quite the same group from the brewery, but there was a lot of overlap. Lydia felt decidedly outnumbered as the only pure Lipin around besides her sister, although that insecurity was no one's fault but her own. Everyone was being excessively friendly, especially since there was wine and beer. Josh's friend Adrian was here, as were all three of his cousins—Kelsey, Kevin, and of course Nate. Kevin's fiancé was here, too, and at any given moment there were two wedding conversations taking place.

"Pasta bowls over here," Taylor said, pointing. "And

from the left to right, the pots are salmon cheese sauce, spicy cheese sauce, and a more traditional four-cheese blend of mac-and-cheese sauce."

Nate gestured for Lydia to go in front of him in the line that was forming, and he turned to Taylor. "You know, you could have ordered pizza and we would still have liked you."

"I appreciate that, but I like cooking."

Lydia appreciated Nate's comment, too, which was silly. Sure, it was great that everyone was getting along, but it should make no difference to her that Nate would say nice things to her sister. Yet there was no denying that she enjoyed it. What might have been different if everyone had been able to hang out while she was in high school?

"It's a good thing you like cooking," she said aloud to Taylor. "Otherwise I might not have been able to convince you to work with me."

Taylor started to reply, but she was cut off by Kevin, who was sucking some of the spicy cheese sauce off his fork. "Oh my God. This is amazing." He punched Peter in the arm. "Why can't you cook?"

"Why can't you?" his fiancé retaliated.

Kevin opted not to answer that. "Taylor, you're a genius."

"Hey, I helped with that!" Josh yelled from the kitchen.

Dinner passed much the same way as pre-dinner, but eating gave Lydia the respite she needed, especially since fate had stuck her across the table from Nate. He'd pushed his shirtsleeves up, and she couldn't avoid seeing how his forearm muscles flexed when he shifted position, or catching his eyes and noticing the way they slightly crinkled around the edges as he looked back at her—smiling without smiling, like they used to do.

Lydia wondered if they were sharing similar opinions about the group and the conversation the way they once would have too.

Hopefully not. She didn't want to regress any further.

"Having a war plan is smart." Kelsey's voice carried down the table. She was seated next to Josh, while Lydia was at the other end of the table, close to Taylor. "We absolutely can't trust our families to act like normal people. Dark-colored bridesmaid dresses is the way to go."

"I was thinking black," Taylor said. "Keep it simple, and that way everyone can wear them again if they need a formal dress."

Lydia sipped her wine. "Not that I don't appreciate the thought, but I don't have a whole lot of use for a formal dress. Black will hide bloodstains nicely if that's what you're going for, but I wouldn't worry about the rest."

Taylor smiled mischievously. "What about some black-tie function with a certain tech billionaire?"

Across from her, Nate smacked himself in the face with his beer bottle.

Lydia repressed a laugh, lest Nate think it was directed at him when in truth it was caused by her sister's suggestion. "I don't foresee a lot of black-tie functions in my future."

"If Cody ever did invite you somewhere," Kevin said, "he should pay for something nice for you to wear."

"He's got a point," Kelsey added. "What's the cost of a designer gown to someone like Cody? Pocket change. Let the man shower you in gifts."

The twins exchanged satisfied glances, but their older brother looked decidedly unhappy. Did Nate dislike Cody so much that even talking about him put him off his dinner, or . . . Lydia banished the only other thought that came to mind. Nate had never seemed like the jealous type, but he and Cody were both competitive.

No. Ridiculous. She banished the thought more thoroughly. The only thing Nate and Cody had competed over was skiing, and it wasn't as though either one of them had experienced any great success with that. Career-wise, their lives had taken totally different paths. The only other connection between them was her, and that was absurd. At best, she figured she was a diversion for Cody while he was in town, and Nate was . . . Well, she didn't know after that briefly flirtatious phone call, but she couldn't believe he was seriously interested in her again either. Likely she was a diversion for him as well.

If only she could treat him the same way, she might enjoy his stay more.

Lydia came back to the conversation after it had drifted on, and she wasn't sorry for the minor change in topic.

"All I'm saying," Kevin was saying, "is that you don't need this other shit. Don't make such a fuss. We're just going to have a small party at a restaurant."

"That's because you're boring," Kelsey told him. "No offense, Peter."

Kevin's fiancé was shaking with silent laughter. "None taken. Besides, my family is threatening to throw a huge party back home since my grandparents can't make the trip up here. I'm going to be partied out."

"It's going to be a party for the rest of our lives," Kevin said.

Adrian snorted. "You keep telling yourself that. See what you think if you have kids."

"What are you talking about?" Josh asked. "Your wife is at home, watching your kids."

"They're *our* kids, and it's only fair I get a night out

when she goes to her wine-drinking club without me every other week."

"Wine-drinking club?" Lydia said. That sounded like her kind of social scene.

Adrian grabbed his beer with a sheepish face. "She calls it a knitting club, but I know better."

Lydia refrained from a third glass of wine after dinner, seeing as she had to drive home. But once the dishes were cleared away and Josh brought out dessert, she returned to the living room, where Josh's three huskies had gathered. Lydia wasn't sure of their names, but one of them promptly stuck its head on her lap as if demanding to be petted. Rather than stuff herself with more food, she obliged until searching around for a restroom.

"Upstairs," Taylor told her, as the downstairs one was occupied.

The second story was cramped, with a low ceiling and not much more space than a bedroom to the left and the small bathroom to the right, plus the landing. When Lydia emerged, she walked right into Nate, who was standing outside the door.

Despite being startled, she couldn't help but be aware of the way her pulse sped up. His body was so hard, and he smelled so good. "Sorry."

She attempted to step around him, but Nate blocked her way toward the stairs by casually leaning against the wall. Lydia was surprised he didn't hit his head on the ceiling.

"Looks like we're going to be working on this wedding together." Nate raised an eyebrow.

It had been only a couple of days since Taylor had asked her to be maid of honor, and Lydia hadn't given much thought to what that entailed until tonight. Belatedly, she realized Nate was right. Taylor and Josh were doing some stuff traditionally, but not everything. Neither of them wanted a wedding shower, but they did want a joint bachelor-bachelorette party, which was—in Taylor's words—another excuse to have fun. Nate and Kevin might not be groomsmen in the normal sense, but it was clear the bride and groom intended them to be included in planning and decisions. Or, as Kelsey had put it—*scheming and punching.* Whichever the words, there would be no avoiding Nate in the coming months.

That was fine. Surely. Nate would have to do his part remotely soon enough, and once fire season got under way, no one would expect too much from him. He wouldn't be close enough that Lydia could smell him or reach out and touch the softness of his shirt. And they'd agreed to keep their past private, so it wasn't like he'd say anything flirtatious on any group texts. She could handle this.

Except right now Nate was very close.

And she wasn't handling it well.

"Your point?" Lydia asked, curling her treacherous fingers into her palms.

"Don't you think keeping up this ruse might be difficult?"

She swallowed. "We kept it up well as kids. We're smarter now. It should be easier."

Nate stood up straighter. His gaze seemed to be burning holes in her skin. "It doesn't feel easier."

She shook her head because she didn't know what to say.

"It doesn't feel like anything's changed," Nate continued.

But things had changed. She'd changed—hadn't she realized that the other day? Nate must have changed, too, yet she knew what he meant. This connection between them, this need remained the same. She'd been completely wrong to think it had gone away. Every moment in his presence strengthened it again.

Lydia wet her lips, still lost for words.

"Reminds me of the senior class bonfire." Nate smiled. "Remember how you wandered off into the woods?"

"And you brought me a s'more."

The first time they'd kissed. Her eyes were closing, living the memory, wishing she could repeat it. Then Nate's fingers brushed her cheek and lifted her chin.

Oh yes, she was burning up in her clothes, and she needed Nate's mouth to put the fire out. A perfect metaphor if she'd ever heard one. But Nate was a firefighter, which meant Nate was here only temporarily. Nate would leave. Nate could get hurt.

She couldn't have Nate the way she was going to start to crave him if she tasted his lips, so it was better to walk away while she could.

NATE FELT LYDIA'S body stiffen, and not in the same way his was beneath his jeans. *Damn.* He'd told himself not to push her too much, that he'd follow her lead, and he thought he had. Okay, yes, he'd purposely followed her up the stairs so they could have a moment alone, but she'd touched the hem of his shirt first. And there had been no mistaking the way she'd looked at him—not this time and not the time when she'd come by his cabin.

His mouth watered with the urge to kiss her, to say nothing of what was going on farther south in his body. The scent of her shampoo, the softness of her skin beneath his calloused fingers—he was one giant ache of need. He hadn't wanted to touch any woman so badly since, well, her back in the day, and he might as well be his teenage self again the way his balls were throbbing and his blood pumping.

But Lydia, no matter how much part of her obviously wanted the same thing, wasn't ready for it. So Nate dropped his hand from her face and raised his head, and he took a step back to give her air. It didn't ease the tension shooting through his body, but Lydia's shoulders relaxed ever so slightly, even as confusion swept over her face.

"It's not a good idea." Lydia's chin trembled, and she pursed her lips in a stubborn expression. "We can't go back to the way things were between us."

Nate studied her face, hoping he could glean some insight about what was behind those vague words, but they could mean so many things, and staring at her emptied his brain of all deep thoughts rather than filling it. "Things don't have to be exactly like they were. I know they can't. But we can have fun together."

As he said it, Nate wondered if fun would be enough to satisfy him, but he pushed the question away. It would have to be. Maybe fun would even be what he needed to get closure and move on from her. He and Lydia had never actually slept together that summer. If they did now, it could help get this need for her out of his system. Then she could go, be with Cody or whomever else, and he could return to Washington and continue his string of one-night stands who never measured up to the woman in front of him.

Even Nate wasn't buying the shit he was selling himself, but if it was the best he could do, he'd take it. He was like his puppies, damn it. He just wanted to be with her. But Lydia was like her cat—skittish and untrusting.

He was too frustrated to laugh at his own silliness.

A smile must have quirked his lips, though, because

Lydia cocked her head to the side. "What's funny about that?"

"Nothing. I was just thinking how wrong I was to assume I wouldn't want you anymore."

Lydia's cheeks erupted in red. "Oh. Why do you have to say things like that?"

"Did it bother you?" His brow pinched. That was not the reaction he'd been hoping for.

"No. It tempts me."

"And that's bad."

She nodded, back to imitating him with the silent responses. The Lydia of old hadn't been quick to trust him, but she hadn't been this reserved either. Still, being tempted was something, and that would have to be enough to content him for the moment. He'd keep his distance for a while—no texting or calling, no matter how much he wanted to. Then he'd nudge her a little again.

Nate stepped aside so she could go downstairs. "Do you want me to leave you alone?"

As much as he feared yes for an answer, he should probably figure that out. Despite everything he'd run through in his head, if Lydia really didn't want him around, he'd respect that.

Lydia hesitated, and Nate could practically see her at war with herself, conflict raging in her dark eyes. Then she shook her head, and relief had him sagging against the wall.

"No," she said, her foot landing on the top step. "I don't, but I should."

Yeah, they were going to have to agree to disagree on that last statement, and next time he saw her, he'd bring the monsters with him. Lydia might be able to resist him alone, but he had two fluffy reinforcements.

* * *

KELSEY HAD PICKED Nate up for the dinner, and she also drove him home a short time after his stairwell interlude with Lydia. It wasn't a long enough drive for the heat to warm them up, but Kelsey had seat heaters in her SUV. Nate wasn't a fan—they gave him the sensation of having pissed himself—but it was a particularly cold night. The monsters were not getting a long walk when he got back, which no doubt meant they were going to keep him awake.

It was just as well. Thinking of his almost-kiss with Lydia was going to keep him awake too. Even in the cold, his body stirred with heat.

"I thought Ian might be there tonight," Nate said to keep his mind off Lydia.

Kelsey shot him a suspicious glance. "Why? It was supposed to be the wedding party, plus Peter."

"I don't know. Just seemed like he might be." Nate fell silent, watching the dark road bleed into existence through the force of Kelsey's headlights. She hadn't needed to give him a ride, but she'd used his shoulder as an excuse. Nate liked to think that she just wanted to hang out more while he was in town. It was the sort of thing Kelsey would never say. But if it were true, she was being awfully quiet when he needed her at her most boisterous.

"I like Ian," Nate said.

Kelsey didn't take her gaze off the road this time, but her eyes opened wider. "What's wrong with you?"

"Nothing. Why?"

"You're talking a lot."

"I am not." Nate rested his head against the seat, his thoughts continuing to slip away to the imagined softness of Lydia's lips and the very real silkiness of her cheek. Luckily his long coat hid any telltale signs of where his mind was. "I'm trying to say I'm happy for you. I'm not used to seeing you this cheerful."

Kelsey slowed down as they approached a stop sign and waited for another car to go by. "I am happy. It's weird."

"That's profound."

"Thank you." She rolled her eyes and started forward again. "So when are you going to get your shit together?"

It was a fair question. He'd been pondering that since his conversation with John the other day. "I've got my shit together. I like my job. I like my life."

"Don't lie to me. I saw how thoughtful you looked every time the words 'marriage' and 'vows' came up tonight. You didn't give anyone crap about settling down either. Are you honestly going to tell me you haven't gotten sick of banging a new woman every night?"

"I'm not sick of anything. When a woman I'm interested in for more than *banging* comes along, I'll be happy about it."

Her name is Lydia, a voice in his head whispered. *That's been your problem all along.*

Nate turned his attention to look out the side window so Kelsey couldn't see him scowl. That voice might be taking things too far, but it wasn't entirely wrong.

"I'm only pointing out that you're the last chronic relationship avoider in our family," Kelsey said, making the turn onto the road toward his cabin.

"Noted." He hadn't missed the fact that he and Lydia had been the only two people at dinner tonight, or at the beer tasting, who weren't in a relationship. Nate had long joked that people and the media spent too much time trying to pair everyone off—if you weren't in a couple, everyone assumed you must want to be in a couple. And for years, that hadn't been true for him. When he'd been able to put Lydia out of his mind, he'd been happy *banging a new woman every night* as his sister put it in her typical Kelsey exaggeration kind of way.

But Lydia was back in his mind—and likely elsewhere in his body—once more, and if they were the only two people in this friend-and-family group who weren't paired off, that was an interesting coincidence. It was also one he could work with if he wanted to keep seeing more of her.

"It's been good to see everyone while in town," Nate said as they pulled into his driveway. "Once fire season starts, and wedding planning picks up, I'll be out of the loop."

"We'll drag you back in."

"It'll be tough, and not the same over text."

"You could move back, you know." Kelsey stopped her SUV behind his, then she made an exasperated face in his response to his *Not likely* one. "Yeah, yeah, I know. We're too boring for you. You're going to be around for another week? Two?"

"At least." He didn't have a set return date, although it was questionable how long his parents would let him borrow a car or live for free in one of their cabins. "It's nice. It helps me get to know everyone better, since some of them are going to become part of the family."

Kelsey chewed on her lower lip. "It is nice. The more comfortable we are with each other, the more of a united front we put forward for the rest of the family. We're an example."

"Good point. People need to see that." He also needed Kelsey to take the bait and suggest another get-together. It was important any plans not come from him, so Lydia didn't think he'd aimed them at her.

"Maybe I can think of something."

Nate smiled. "You being Miss Sociable?"

"Fight me." She glared at him. "I've decided I'm taking over as the family queen bee. I'm the one who's going to make shit happen."

"You'll be good at it." It was the truth. Nate opened the door, swearing that from this far away he could already hear the monsters barking with excitement over his return. "Night, Kels."

Kelsey snapped out of whatever was running through her head, and she bade him good night. Satisfied that he'd planted the seed of an idea, Nate let himself into the cabin. This kind of deviousness was not his thing, but patience was. He'd patiently waited for Lydia's attention throughout high school, after all.

But this time, Lydia had claimed she both did and did not want to be tempted. He would do his best to give her both, making sure the choice was always hers, but hoping she chose him.

12

LYDIA HURRIED THROUGH the Bay Song, desperately in need of lunch. She'd spent the past forty-five minutes working with Taylor to see if they could find a way to arrange the function room to hold as many people as a potential client wanted to invite to her wedding. The space was rated for that level of occupancy, but figuring out if they could make it work with the appropriate table setup was another matter. The couple was planning for a winter wedding, and since Lydia had plans to increase the number of winter weddings they hosted, she was determined to find a way.

She couldn't help but note with some amusement that weddings were taking over her life. They'd been an important part of the business plan she'd created for the hotel before Taylor returned to Helen, but with her sister getting married in the fall (and Kevin and Peter over the summer), Lydia was spending more time thinking about weddings than she'd ever done before.

Growing up, she had never been one of those girls who'd dreamed about getting married. The idea of it had simply never interested her. She'd figured it would happen, since it did for most people, and that would be that. It was nothing to fuss about. But most people, she was learning, did in fact fuss. Including people like her sister, who as far as Lydia knew, had also never dreamed about her wedding as a girl.

But the result of so much of her attention being given to weddings was that her mind focused on the idea of marriage more than it had before. Not that she'd ever been allowed to forget the concept entirely. Her grandmother—and too many other family members—wouldn't let her. Nor would they stop reminding her that she'd officially been alive for three decades at this point, as though they thought she came with an expiration date. There was no denying that she'd often wished for a reliable, loving male companion in her life (who wasn't her cat), but all the family pressure had simultaneously made her resist.

Possibly it was seeing Taylor so happy, but her resistance was fading and her loneliness was increasing.

Or possibly that was because of Nate's return to her life. It was easy to forget how much you wanted something when that something wasn't constantly dangled in front of you. Out of sight, out of mind, and all that.

But these days, Lydia's mind was focused on weddings and on Nate, and since Taylor and Josh's dinner, her almost-kiss with Nate had combined those two concepts into a holy hell of conflicted emotions.

That kiss. Never mind that it didn't actually happen. Lydia could taste Nate's lips on her own, a little sweet, a little salty. Both rough and gentle. She could feel exactly what it would be like to press her body against the hard planes of his. Her mouth watered with the imagined sensation of taking his tongue inside her.

She might as well have just gone through with it, given that neither her mind nor her body could tell the difference.

Lydia wet her lips and shut her office door, hoping none of these work-inappropriate thoughts showed on her face. That out of the way, she reached into her desk and pulled out a protein bar. She'd promised the interested bride she'd get back to her this afternoon, but her email would be more coherent with something in her stomach.

While she chewed, she checked her messages and discovered an update from Jen about the puppy situation. We got Abby a bunny, and she's in love. Bloodshed avoided! A picture of a cute, reddish-brown rabbit followed.

Lydia smiled at the cuteness. Glad it worked out!

If only all feud-related issues could be handed so easily.

"Hey, Lydia." Shawn's voice came through on the phone. "You've got a package up at the desk labeled 'perishable.' You want me to bring it to your office?"

She hadn't managed to tend to work yet, so there was no sense in Shawn leaving the desk and the phone unattended. "No, I'll be right there." Who was sending her something perishable in the mail?

Taylor was in the lobby, putting out the coffee and cookies right on schedule. Since they'd just left the function room minutes ago, Lydia couldn't figure out how she'd gotten everything set up so quickly. Someone's brain was clearly more focused on work than her own.

Shawn slid a box across the reception desk to her. "A Valentine's present?"

Lydia hadn't entirely forgotten that it was Valentine's Day tomorrow, but the holiday made so little difference to her that she hadn't paid it much heed. "I suppose?"

The return label gave the package's origin as California, but there was no name that Lydia recognized, and her stomach twisted with confusion. There was only one person from California who might send her anything, but she thought she'd been clear to Cody that there was nothing but friendship between them.

Lydia carried the box into her office and found it occupied. Taylor, apparently having overheard the V-word, had dashed ahead and was waiting for her. "A gift from Cody?"

"I don't know."

"Well, open it." Taylor produced a utility knife from her pocket and held it out.

Apprehensive, Lydia sliced open the package. Inside was a smaller box in red gift wrap and a card.

Just thinking of you.

—Cody

It was a cutesy Valentine's Day card, nothing sappy or romantic, but still. Lydia grimaced and unwrapped the box.

"How sweet." Taylor grinned, setting down the card. "Reminds me of the gift Josh sent me when I went back to L.A. for my job interview last year. He misses you."

"You and Josh were dating. Cody has no business missing me after we hung out one time, after not speaking for ten years."

Taylor made a dismissive noise. "So? The guy was busy becoming a tech star, and now he's remembering what he left behind. Cody didn't get where he is by sitting on his ass. He went after it. And now he's going after you."

By her tone, it was obvious that Taylor thought Lydia simply needed reassurance that Cody's interest in her was real. Lydia wasn't ready to explain that reassurance wasn't what she was looking for and that Cody wasn't the man she was obsessing over.

Lydia opened the gift box, which turned out to contain some gourmet-looking chocolate-covered almonds. Laughing, she pushed the box toward her sister. At least she didn't have to worry about feeling guilty for eating Cody's gift when she needed to clarify the status of their relationship. Again.

"Oh dear." Taylor cringed. "He doesn't know you're allergic?"

Lydia's allergy hadn't come on until college, but she was quite certain she'd mentioned it when they were at dinner, and she said as much to Taylor. "I must have been too subtle."

Except she really didn't think so, so why was she continuing to make excuses for Cody? If he forgot, fine. People made mistakes, but this was not her mistake and she shouldn't take responsibility. Just like she shouldn't take responsibility for him reading more into her texts than she'd written. At dinner, Cody had ordered for her—a dish with calamari in it, which Lydia detested. She'd managed to eat around it because she didn't want to create a fuss, but she'd pointed out that she had food allergies—almonds among them—and the inherent unwiseness of ordering food for other people.

So yes, Cody might have made a mistake, but it was more likely that her words had gone in one ear and out the other along with all the other boundaries she'd tried setting.

"It's still sweet," Taylor said.

Lydia pressed her lips together, not wanting to debate the matter with her sister. Sweet would have been Cody listening to her and remembering. Or better yet, at the time, having let her choose her own food.

But not every man could be Nate. Lydia's mind returned to their interlude on the stairwell at Josh's house, and the way Nate questioned her and took nothing about her reaction for granted. He'd wanted her to be comfortable and had let her decide what happened next. She just wished she could have given him a more decisive answer, but she was too torn to know her own mind.

"What?" Taylor asked.

"What?"

"I asked first."

Lydia narrowed her eyes. "I don't know what you asked."

With a sigh, her sister motioned to the almonds, and Lydia nodded. It wasn't like she could eat them herself, and no one loved chocolate more than Taylor.

"Something's bothering you," Taylor said, plucking an almond from the box.

Since a lot of things were bothering her, Lydia could only assume her thoughts about Cody and Nate had shown on her face. She was saved from responding by the sound of her phone and Taylor's buzzing at the same time.

The text was from Kelsey to their group chat. It's time to start planning the next wedding party gathering before Nate leaves town. Open to suggestions.

"Should I be planning these things since I'm the maid of honor?" Lydia asked.

"Kelsey is Josh's best woman, so don't worry. I'm not considering you a slacker." Taylor paused. "Are you okay with everyone getting together? Josh and I talked about it, and we both thought it was a good idea to keep this up. It's hard to unlearn years of bad lessons, but we want to set an example."

It made sense, and although Lydia hadn't gone into meeting with Josh's family without trepidation, the rest of the Porters and Porter friends seemed pleasant enough. "It's a good idea, especially with Nate in town."

And it would give her the chance to live out her ambivalence about what she wanted from him. She could be around him without worrying about doing something she'd regret. Just as long as she didn't end up alone with him again.

"Okay, just checking." Taylor typed a message back to the group. "You seemed a little, I don't know, anxious at dinner."

Great. She really needed to work on her poker face. "I was tired."

Taylor didn't look like she was buying it, but she picked up her phone to read the latest message and her face lit up. Whatever she'd been about to say had vanished.

What about mushing? Nate had written.

Lydia's stomach squirmed. Out in the cold for who knew how long, being pulled around by sled dogs? That did not sound like a good time to her. Damn Porters and their dog obsession. But Taylor's expression suggested that her sister wasn't merely marrying into the Porter family, she'd been won over by the dogs, which was no surprise. Although their family were cat people, Lydia recalled that even as a child, Taylor had fallen in love with dogs and had been fascinated with mushing. And clearly, her sister loved this idea.

And since Lydia loved her sister, she'd suck it up, put on her cold-weather gear, and do this.

Taylor lowered the phone and looked at Lydia hopefully.

"Oh my God. You're making total puppy-dog eyes at me." She had no choice but to laugh.

"You'll do it?" Taylor asked.

"The things I do for you." Lydia shook her head.

"Really?" Taylor looked like she was trying not to bounce on her feet. "Because if you hate the idea, we don't have to. I'll just try talking Josh into it, and we can leave you out. I don't want you to be uncomfortable."

Lydia's cheeks ached from the strain of holding her smile, but truthfully, she did love seeing her sister so happy. And dogsledding wasn't the worst idea in the world. Nate could have suggested karaoke.

Once more Lydia considered confiding in Taylor, and once more she dismissed the idea because she didn't need Taylor encouraging her. "I'm sure it'll be fun, and I swear—I wasn't uncomfortable at dinner. Only tired."

Her sister jumped off the desk and hugged her. "Best maid of honor ever."

"You hold on to that thought when I forget all the important stuff you want me to do."

Taylor waved her hand and grabbed another almond. "I have no important stuff besides having fun and making our families rue their determination to destroy my happiness. But I do appreciate this when I know you're anti-dog."

"I'm not anti-dog. I'm anti–freezing my ass off." She happened to find Nate's puppies unbearably cute.

And a half-naked Nate holding them unbearably sexy.

At least there would be no half-naked anyone while mushing. Frostbite was nothing to mess with.

In fact, the more she thought about it, the better Nate's idea was. There would be no chance for alone time this way, and he'd be fully covered in multiple thick layers. Avoiding temptation ought to be a snap.

13

◦————◦

IT TURNED OUT that Nate had suggested mushing because one of his friends ran a kennel. Also, Lydia had
been wrong to assume this activity wouldn't allow for
alone time with him. Luckily, she was too nervous about
the whole sledding thing to bother with self-reproach.

Adrian had needed to back out at the last minute,
which left them as a group of eight because Kelsey
brought Ian in his place. They'd gathered in the visitor's
cabin at the kennel while Nate's friend, who would also
be one of their guides, went over the basics of what to
expect. Since they were so many, they would need to go
out in two groups for half-hour runs. Their guides
seemed to fear they would be less than happy with the
short time on the snow, but Lydia, already dreading the
chill in her toes, counted it as a win.

After being briefed, Lydia followed the others out back
where the rest of the guides were prepping the dogs and
readying the harnesses, so she and the others could greet
their four-legged hosts. Cat person she might be, but even

Lydia had to admit the dogs' excitement could make her smile as they dashed in the snow and sniffed the newcomers. Unlike her, these dogs had no concerns about the cold as they raced about in their green and orange bootees.

"Go on," one of the guides told her, misinterpreting her reluctance to get as up close and personal as the rest of the group. "They love being petted."

Lydia knelt next to Nate—the only open spot without trudging into calf-deep snow—and rubbed a very enthusiastic tan-and-white dog on the belly.

Nate nudged her with his good arm. "We'll make a dog person out of you yet."

"Why do I have to keep telling people that I have nothing against dogs? Your dogs are adorable."

"I know." Nate looked particularly satisfied by her comment for reasons Lydia couldn't fathom.

"Are these a different breed?" Some of the dogs looked like older versions of Nate's puppies, but most didn't.

"We run Siberian and Alaskan huskies," Nate's friend said, joining the two of them to rub the tan-and-white one on the stomach.

"What's the difference?" Lydia asked.

"Speed. Siberians are traditional sled dogs, but Alaskan huskies make better racing dogs. Most of our dogs are retired racers. They're a little too old to be competitive, but young and healthy enough to pull a sled for fun, and they do love it."

Lydia sat back on her heels, watching the spectacle as the guides got the dogs into their harnesses. Taylor and Ian were asking a lot of questions, and the guides were giving in-depth answers.

"If these are older dogs, your puppies are never going to calm down, are they?" Lydia said to Nate.

He chuckled. "Probably not."

"I'm not anti-dog, but cats are a lot less stressful."

"Are you stressed?"

Lydia pulled her coat higher over her chin, although the wind wasn't too strong in the shadow of the cabin. She was, but it was only partially because of sleds. The rest was all because of the man, despite said man being as bundled up as she was. Nate's face was barely visible between the upturned collar of his coat, the hat on his head, and the sunglasses over his eyes. The most she could make out of him was the scruff on his upper cheeks, and yet she was still intensely aware of him.

"Are you sure you should be doing this with your shoulder?" Lydia asked in way of answering.

"Tom said it would be fine as long as I sat the whole time," Nate said, referring to his friend. "It's been almost four weeks since the accident. I'm ready to ditch this thing," He shook his arm, clearly meaning the sling. "But I asked about you."

"I'm fine. Just wondering why we couldn't choose a calmer activity, say, one that takes place indoors where it's warm."

"You are such a cat lady." Nate smirked.

They both stood as their guides announced that petting time was over. They needed to head back into the cabin so the mushers could make sure everyone was outfitted properly for the cold, teach them basic commands, and decide on who was going first. Nate grabbed Lydia's hand, holding her back as the others filed inside. Although they both wore thick mittens, Lydia's pulse sped up, as though she could sense Nate's skin.

"I thought it was something everyone might have fun with," Nate said.

"Everyone?" She raised an eyebrow that probably got lost under her hat.

"I remember a time when you used to like playing in the snow."

Lydia started to protest, then snapped her jaw shut. Nate kept doing that. Bringing up pieces of her past that she hadn't precisely forgotten about but had pushed aside, deemed no longer relevant. "I don't think I used to be as quick to get cold."

"There's an upside to getting cold, you know. It's called getting warm later."

Lydia was extra grateful for the sunglasses that covered Nate's eyes. She had a feeling his gaze would be burning holes in her otherwise, and it was no coincidence that she was warming up under her heavy down coat.

"Tell you what," Nate said while she fumbled for an adequate rebuttal. "We'll make a bet."

"A bet?"

Nate nodded. "If you hate it, I'll let you choose what we do when we get together next. But if you end up liking it, I get to choose."

It seemed to Lydia that Taylor or Josh should get to choose what the next activity would be, but she decided not to point that out. She would argue that position only if Nate won. "I could lie and claim to hate it, regardless."

"You could." He looked at her thoughtfully. "But I'd know."

Lydia frowned. Was her poker face that bad? Her sister could see through her, but could Nate really? A shiver ran down her spine that was less related to the cold than it was to the heat rising in her blood. Who was she kidding? Nate had already proven how well he still knew her after all this time, and it was both terrifying and electrifying.

After a quick check to make sure everyone was covered in clothes that could withstand the cold and wet, Lydia joined her sister, Josh, and Nate as part of the first group to go. Getting it over with fast was her preference. There would be hot drinks waiting back at the cabin.

"You ready?" her guide asked as Lydia settled into the seated position on the sled.

Ready or not, did it matter?

Then they were off, over the next thirty minutes, racing down well-trod trails through thick trees. Although she was cold at first as the wind whipped at her face and bits of snow slowly coated her body, Lydia soon lost track of the time. Their guide issued commands that the dogs seemed to already know by heart, and trees and snowbanks flew by. Somewhere around the halfway point, they paused so everyone except Nate could switch positions. Lydia had skied before, but seeing the woods this way with only the sound of the sleds cutting a path through the snow and the rhythmic beat of the dogs' feet was wholly new. She could smell the pine in the air and taste the winter on her lips. It made the world feel bigger, wilder, and more peaceful at the same time. Every bit as exhilarating as standing next to Nate.

He was going to win the bet, but fine. As they returned to the cabin faster than she'd have thought possible, Lydia was okay with that. He'd been right after all. She hadn't experienced this much pure joy in years, and watching him as he climbed out of the sled, the urge to kiss him was overwhelming. Why she hadn't taken the opportunity on the stairs last week . . .

Lydia stopped herself, her muscles clenching and

freezing her grin in place. Adrenaline was a dangerous substance. Nate could have his win, but she couldn't let any of this go to her head.

THANKS TO HIS shoulder making everything awkward, Nate was slow to catch a glimpse of Lydia as he got out of the sled. Fortunately, she wasn't even attempting to hide her feelings. A grin split her beautiful face in two, and her cheeks were flushed with excitement as she lowered the zipper on her coat.

Well, maybe they were also flushed with cold, but she practically vibrated with excitement, so he was calling it that.

They all played with the dogs for a couple additional minutes, thanking them for the ride with belly rubs and pets. Then, Nate, Lydia, Taylor, and Josh headed into the cabin. Nate took off his sunglasses and made a point of catching Lydia's eyes as she did the same.

So you had fun? he asked silently.

She answered the question with a half sneer, half smile that said everything.

After his siblings and their partners went out to the sleds, Nate and the others were offered a chance to meet some of the puppies in the kennels while they waited. Taylor couldn't put her jacket on fast enough, but Lydia hovered by the coffee, her hands wrapped around the cup she'd poured herself.

"Coming?" Josh asked Nate.

"Bit of a pain getting my jacket on and off," Nate said. "Besides, I've got enough puppy trouble at home."

Josh had no trouble buying that, and soon Nate and Lydia were alone in the cabin.

She looked at him suspiciously as she sipped her drink. "Go on. Say it."

Her cheeks were pink, and her hair stuck out in damp waves from beneath the knit hat she hadn't removed. Nate's stomach did that weird flippy thing that made it feel like the ground had disappeared beneath him.

"Nah, I don't need to say it. I just get to pick." He hadn't taken a cup of coffee yet, so he walked over to the table with the setup. Conveniently, that put him closer to Lydia.

He noticed that she didn't step away.

Lydia wrinkled her nose. "Shouldn't Taylor and Josh get to pick our next activity?"

Nate dumped a bunch of sugar in his cup. The guys he worked with gave him a lot of shit for not drinking his coffee black, but one of the very few traits he shared with his siblings was a massive sweet tooth. "I never said anything about Taylor and Josh. I meant when *we* got together next. Not the group."

She gaped at him. "But . . ."

"I can't help it if you made assumptions when you took the bet."

"That's cheating." Lydia looked adorable as she shook her head, fighting to suppress a smile. "I didn't agree to that."

Nate ignored her token protest and leaned against one of the chairs in the middle of the room so he could face her. If she really didn't want to spend time with him, he was certain she'd make it known. But between the way she was fighting down her laugh and the fact that she'd practically dared him to try again at Josh and Taylor's dinner, he figured he'd press ahead. Lydia could take an out whenever she chose to.

If she chose to, which he was confident she wouldn't.

"I was thinking we could go snow machining," Nate said.

"More cold?" Lydia's expression turned to horror.

Nate glanced around, but the cabin remained empty except for the two of them. Still, he lowered his voice out of an old habit. "You used to like it."

They'd done it a few times that winter of their senior year. Nate wasn't sure how he'd gotten away with it, but his parents had never asked many questions, and Lydia's had been much the same, from what he remembered. They both had younger siblings who were known troublemakers. When Nate wanted to do something, as long as it wasn't completely outrageous, no one cared. He was the responsible one, a reputation Lydia had shared. Seventeen years of building up parental goodwill bought a lot of freedom, but it all would have been blown to hell if either of the families had ever discovered the truth.

Lydia bit her lip, and he knew she had no rebuttal. "What about your shoulder?"

His damn shoulder was interfering with everything. First his job, now his attempt to resurrect his love life. "My orthopedist thinks it'll be fine."

He hadn't actually asked her yet, but he was allowed to drive, so as far as he was concerned, that was good enough.

"And the puppies?" Lydia asked.

Nate made no effort to hide his grin. He liked winning, and although Lydia didn't believe it yet, this was a win for both of them. "The monsters can come. My parents have a sleigh they use when the dogs are too tired to run alongside. They'll have more fun than you."

"That won't be hard."

He snorted. Sure, it wouldn't.

"I want hot drinks when it's all over," Lydia said.

"It wouldn't be a day in the snow without them." Like he'd turn down more time alone with her? Nate would buy an espresso machine if that was what it took.

And on that note, he should head back into the cold because it was getting way too warm in his body with Lydia so close.

14

⋄—————————⋄

LYDIA HADN'T GONE snow machining in years, and coming off the recent adventure with the sled dogs, she had a startling revelation. She preferred mushing. As a Lipin, she probably shouldn't admit that publicly, but luckily she was hanging out with only Nate and the two adorable creatures he'd dubbed the monsters.

The snow whipping about her face died down as Nate shut off the engine, and blissful silence enveloped the snowscape. Then that, too, vanished as Dolly and Spark began barking in the sleigh behind them.

Lydia waited for Nate to move and was glad that he seemed reluctant. She sat behind him, and at some point during the ride, she'd leaned into him to shelter from the wind. Her arms were partially around his waist, and her face hovered inches from the back of his neck. Of course, there was the face shield on her helmet between them, and her mittens between her hands and his jacket. But it felt cozy and delicious anyway.

Too cozy and delicious. The ride had been short and her adrenaline was flowing, and this time there was no one around to see if she kissed him.

Good thing for the helmets they both wore.

Nate's body shifted in front of her, and she'd swear he leaned back into her on purpose before swinging one of his long legs over the side. "You good?"

Lydia pulled off her helmet and adjusted her hat to better cover her ears. She was too good. Her heart was pounding. When was the last time she'd felt so alive? Something told her it had been the year before she left for college.

"I'm good," she said, standing. The snow here came halfway up her boots. Nate had stopped near some evergreens where the tree cover made the snow not quite as deep. "Are you? That was a short ride."

Nate grimaced, pulling off his helmet. "Yeah, well, as it turned out, my orthopedist was not as cool with the idea of me riding as I'd hoped."

"Wait. You told me your doctor said it was okay!" She was going to kill him. If he'd reinjured himself for . . . For what? She hadn't insisted on riding today. He had.

Because he knew she'd have fun and knew she wouldn't do it on her own. Nate was doing this for her after she'd told him how conflicted she was about spending time with him. He hadn't pressured or pushed, he'd simply dangled an opportunity in front of her, one he knew she'd have a hard time resisting. As if he weren't hard enough to resist on his own.

Lydia's emotions were as wild and uncontrolled as the puppies were acting. Part of her wanted to be angry at herself for being too weak to resist the bait, but that part didn't feel as rational as she thought it should. She was having fun. She wanted to be around Nate. Those things really weren't so terrible. What was so damn practical about refusing to enjoy herself?

"Damn you." She punched him in the chest, which he probably didn't even feel between her lack of arm strength and the thick down in his coat.

"What?" Nate caught her hand. "I kept it short. That's all."

"You did this for me, didn't you?"

He smirked. "You think you're so special that I'd put a lot of effort into persuading you to spend time with me?"

Lydia lowered her sunglasses so she could glare more effectively.

Nate laughed. "I thought you needed to have some fun."

"I know how to have fun." She deeply enjoyed curling up on the couch with takeout, her cat, and Netflix.

"Okay, fine. I thought you needed to have some fun with me. Was I wrong?"

Lydia didn't know how to answer that, so she deflected, as was becoming her habit. "If you reinjured your shoulder, yes."

Nate hadn't let go of her hand and he trudged a step closer through the snow. "My shoulder feels fine. It was worth the risk to see you smiling the way you were."

"Uh-huh. You couldn't see me. I was behind you."

"Eyes in the back of my head. Part of my training. Besides, I know you. I know you were."

She *was* smiling, so all Lydia could do was shake her head, but Nate's words made her tingle again. *I know you.* "Do you know me? Or . . ." She caught herself, wondering if she should say the thought that had popped to mind.

"Or?"

The puppies had jumped out of the sleigh. Lydia could hear them frolicking in the snow, but Nate never took his gaze off her face. It was late enough in the day that they no longer needed sunglasses to prevent the snow from blinding them. The sun hung low and heavy behind the cloud cover. Even if Nate had intended to go for a longer ride today, it wouldn't have been a good idea. A major storm was supposed to be rolling in this evening.

Lydia wet her lips. "Or were we just so compatible that whatever you chose to say or do around me always happened to be the right thing?"

"You know, I like that explanation better."

So did she, and that was why it scared the shit out of her. It meant she and Nate weren't just compatible; they fit together like her hand in her mitten. Like they were made for each other. And if she gave in to the temptation in front of her, she would be completely swept up in that whirlwind of happiness and contentment again.

But would that be so bad, to enjoy a little bit of bliss?

"I thought things must have changed. And you said it, too, so maybe they have." Nate glanced down at the snow for a moment, as though searching for something in the sparkling white, then he turned his intensity back on her. "But I don't think the things that make us compatible have."

No, the pull toward this man had absolutely not. The way he held her hand made her feel grounded. Being in his presence made her feel safe. Being this close to him made her need to kiss him.

Lydia wasn't even aware that she'd leaned forward until Nate's lips touched hers, and her breath caught in her throat. Lord, he tasted good, like freshly fallen snow and the scent of pine needles. The cold nylon shell of his glove pressed against her cheek as Nate pulled her closer, soothing her skin, which was inflamed from the touch of his lips. Her eyes closed, her mouth opened, and she drank him in deeper, hungrier for this one part of him that she could touch when so many heavy layers separated the rest of their bodies.

Kissing Nate was nothing and everything like it had once been. Nothing like it, because they were both more practiced now, and Nate's stubble scraped her chin in a way Lydia found unexpectedly erotic. She wanted to feel that scrape everywhere. And everything like it, because his lips still drove her wild like no one else's had. Every inch of her burned. Her mind was like a feather, floating away on the breeze, while Nate's hands and mouth kept her body steady, so warm and protected that she had no nerves, no anxiety. She wanted to give everything to him.

She would, too, if she kept this up. Not just her time, which was fine. Or her body, which, good Lord, she wished they were somewhere warmer so they could peel off these bulky clothes. But her heart. She was going to lose her heart to him a second time.

That was the answer to the question, What was so damn practical about refusing to enjoy herself? The future and her emotions—those were what. Those were what she'd temporarily forgotten when her excitement got the best of her.

When a moan escaped her lips, the sound shocked Lydia enough to break free. She stepped away from Nate, instantly feeling colder and more alone, though her lips buzzed with his touch.

"We can't." Before Nate could say or do anything else to change her mind, Lydia hurried over to the puppies. They were cuteness that didn't have the same brain-melting and blood-heating effects on her better sense.

* * *

NATE WATCHED LYDIA form a snowball by the sleigh. His head felt sluggish, which was no surprise. Kissing Lydia had left his mind perfectly at peace and all the blood rushing to his cock. Then the moment had shattered abruptly. He was disoriented, and not even the monsters' playful barking was getting through to him.

He didn't think he'd pushed her. In fact, he was pretty damn sure she'd initiated that kiss. Nate had the urge to drop to the snow and roll around in it like Spark was. He needed to cool off.

Instead, he took a hesitant step closer to Lydia and knelt next to his dogs. Their pure joy should have made him smile, but this recovery of his was taking a while.

Lydia tossed the lightly packed snowball at Dolly, who tried to chase it and became extremely confused when it disappeared into the ground. Nate watched her a moment more, until his head was back on straight. Lydia playing with the monsters hadn't helped steady his emotions. It made him happy.

"Why not?" he asked.

Lydia had no trouble recalling what his question was in reference to, even though it seemed to Nate that years had passed since she'd pulled away from him. "I can't get involved with you this way. Not again."

"Why not?" Hadn't he just asked that?

Lydia's lips twisted with something like dismay before Dolly's short legs kicked snow in her face and sent her falling backward with a laugh. She recovered quickly, though, her expression turning serious once more. "Because you're leaving."

"Ah." He might not be the quickest guy on earth, but Nate was starting to put the pieces together. "You're saying I'm too irresistible for you to not get attached."

She blushed but manage to roll her eyes at the same time. "Gee, when you put it that way, is it so hard to understand?"

Nate grinned. Nope. It was easy to understand, because he was utterly attached to her. Apparently, he always had been, but since he'd been so far away, he'd been able to ignore it. So far away and so busy. Just like he'd never been interested in a long-term relationship with anyone, Lydia could be the reason why he'd never been content sitting still either.

He would have to make additional adjustments to his plans, or simply admit he couldn't plan for shit. Where Lydia was concerned, he was a complete opportunist. He'd take any scraps she gave him and run with them, much like the monsters.

But either way, he was going to have to find a way to convince her that his leaving didn't matter. He wanted her too much to cut things off by any specific date. But could he convince Lydia to give a long-distance relationship a try? Nate didn't even know if those really worked, yet he wasn't about to let go without a fight this time. Not like when Lydia had left for college.

No, he'd learned a lesson. Once you fell for Lydia, you never got back up.

Rather than say any of this, Nate picked up some snow and tossed it at Spark. Not scaring off Lydia remained the goal, and he was certain that's what he'd do if she caught wind of how deep his feelings ran.

Spark jumped up, trying to lick the snowflakes as they fell, and Nate realized they weren't only the flakes from the handful of snow he'd tossed in the air. "Looks like that storm in the forecast might be starting early. We should head back."

Lydia nodded and stood. "Thank you for this."

Nate raised an eyebrow. "No problem. We'll chalk it up to part of how irresistible I am."

He thought he heard Lydia mutter, "Uh-huh," as they began herding the puppies back into the sleigh.

The return ride felt like it took half the time of the original. Considering how kissing Lydia had messed with his head, Nate thought he did a fantastic job of getting the four of them back to Helen in record time. Lydia didn't say much on the return trip, but she didn't seem ill at ease from their conversation. Given her silence, Nate was fairly certain she was flailing about internally as much as he was. That they could just exist in that space, however, without feeling uncomfortable, steeled his resolve to convince her they deserved more. A true second chance.

"Do you want to head home?" Nate asked as he approached the intersection where he'd need to turn one way for the Bay Song and another for his cabin. "Or do I still get to make you that boozy hot chocolate you demanded?"

After what had passed on the snow, he wasn't making assumptions, but he hoped she would still choose to stick with the original plan. Always, the choice had to be hers though. He wouldn't push.

Lydia had been watching the monsters doze off in the back seat, and she bit her lip. "I think there's plenty of time before the roads get bad."

Nate tried not to smile at that. He probably owed the puppies extra treats for being so endearing.

Lydia helped him bring more wood inside for the stove, then she played with the monsters while he started water boiling. With their jackets and hats dripping water from the hooks by the door, and flames starting to grow in the woodstove, the first pang of angst Nate felt about leaving rattled in his stomach. Lydia was curled up on the rug, playing a game of tug with Spark, and Dolly rested on her socked feet, keeping them warm. If he could have described his perfect scene of what home should look like, it would be this.

But this cabin was not his house, and the woman was not his . . . something or other. Nate turned his back on the scene and fussed with the mugs so that the sense of longing would go away. *One step at a time*, he told himself.

"Baileys or mint?" he called over his shoulder.

"Baileys."

Nate completed the drinks and topped them both with a mound of whipped cream. Setting Lydia's in front of her on the table, he sat carefully, finally daring to test out his shoulder. It didn't strike him as any worse for the day's activities, but he knew not heeding the orthopedist's warning today had been reckless. Getting his shoulder back in shape so he could return to work was supposed to have been his top priority. Somehow, Lydia had taken over his brain.

Or possibly his dick. Nate didn't doubt that's what his siblings and friends would tell him if they heard what he'd done. What other organ would make a man do such dumbass things? A heart would be the last one they'd guess.

Well, people could claim the two weren't linked all they wanted. In some cases, it was true. God knew Nate had slept with plenty of women whom he would never have risked his shoulder over. But Lydia was different. Watching her play with the monsters or slurp whipped cream off her hot chocolate created a fierce ache in both of those regions of his body. He needed her in every way possible, and now that they were warm by the fire, the urge to kiss her was stronger than ever.

Nate sipped his drink, not sorry it was hot enough to burn his tongue if that would keep it in line. Lydia had put a stop to the kissing, and he wouldn't bring it up again. Not today, anyway.

They kept the conversation light over the next half hour, playing with the puppies and not discussing what had happened on the snow. Nate tried to keep his physical distance. Being too close to Lydia when she smelled like Baileys and he could recall how the snowflakes had melted on her eyelashes was torture. His hands brushed hers as he took Dolly's favorite chew toy from her, and that brief touch was like a vise squeezing his groin. Part of him was relieved when he finally glanced out the window and noticed the snow was coming down heavier. As much as he didn't want her to leave, it might be best for his sanity.

"I should get back," Lydia said, as though she'd read his mind. "I have a few things I need to take care of before it gets late, and it's back to work tomorrow."

"Yeah, of course." Nate got to his feet and carried their empty mugs into the kitchen. He'd picked Lydia up, so she'd need a ride back to the hotel. "How's the driveway?"

There couldn't be more than an inch of snow out there, but if he could avoid putting on his wet boots in favor of less weatherproof ones, that would be nice.

Lydia cracked open the door, then shut it abruptly. "Shit." She opened it again as though questioning whatever she saw.

"What?"

"I don't think I'm going anywhere for a while." She started taking off her coat and gestured toward the door.

Confused, Nate opened it and glanced outside. It had gotten dark over the last hour, but the yellow glow of the porch light illuminated the area well enough, and Lydia was correct. Neither of them was going anywhere.

A moose was napping in the middle of the driveway.

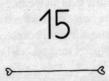

15

LYDIA WAS HANGING her coat back up when the first sign that she might be cracking under the day's emotional toll escaped her throat. It was just a single laugh, more like a snort if she were honest. But it was followed by another, then another, until she was shaking as waves of giggles locked her in place.

She didn't understand. The situation was not funny. She had laundry to do and a cat to feed, and there was a moose outside that did not give two frozen farts how dangerous it was for her to be trapped in Nate Porter's vicinity. No, the moose didn't see how tempting Nate was or understand how badly she wanted to kiss him. How she could still taste him on her lips or feel the warmth of his breath on her face. That moose could be out there for hours, and she'd be stuck inside this cabin with the man she craved more than anything else in the world, and how was she supposed to resist?

Maybe she wasn't.

Lydia didn't believe in signs. If she did, she'd have taken it as one when Cody appeared in her lobby right after wishing for a rich guy to sweep her away. But she did believe that sometimes the universe tossed an opportunity in your path, and you either seized it or ran from it.

Most of the time, she ran. But once, the universe had brought Nate to her when she was stuck on the side of the road, and that had changed her life for the better. Even if only temporarily. Was it too much to want to believe that the universe had tossed a moose in his driveway this time? She could run from this opportunity or seize it. Even if it was also only temporary.

Lord, she didn't know what had gotten into her to be contemplating any of this. The alcohol content in Baileys wasn't high enough to cause this level of clouded thinking, and besides, she'd been feeling completely sober until she'd opened that door, so it couldn't be the alcohol.

She must have just snapped. In some ways, that felt inevitable. She'd been holding herself in and holding herself back for so long. And what was the point when sometimes the universe tossed a fucking moose in your path and there was nothing you could do about it?

"Lydia, are you okay?" Nate sounded seriously concerned.

Lydia supposed that, too, made sense. She was shaking with her back to him, and probably hadn't otherwise moved in a minute.

"Fine, yes. Thanks." Turning around, she wiped away the couple tears that had leaked from her eyes. That seemed to alarm Nate even more, and his expression caused a second fit of laughter to bubble through her.

Even the puppies acted confused as Lydia collapsed

on a chair. They'd grown quiet, and they circled her like she needed to be reined in. Poor monsters. Poor Nate. He wanted to help, and he had no idea how to deal with the woman who'd lost it on him.

"I'm fine. I'm really fine." She took a deep breath. *Inhale. Exhale. Blow out the hysterics.* "I don't know why, but seeing that moose did something to my head."

"Okay." Nate continued to hover over her, like he was afraid he was going to need to apply some of his EMT training.

Not that she'd complain about some more mouth-to-mouth.

Lydia forced down a fresh laugh. "That moose could be there for a while."

Cautiously, Nate sat on the edge of the other chair, facing her. "I had that thought."

"I need to feed my cat." There, that wasn't the sort of concern that made her laugh.

"Ah." Nate reached over and rested a hand on her knee. The gesture seemed more like one meant to comfort than to flirt, and that was disappointing, and yet so perfectly Nate. No wonder she wanted to throw herself at him. "We could wait a couple hours," he said. "The moose could leave anytime."

For all they knew, the moose could have left already, but Lydia had no interest in finding out. She was taking it on faith that the universe had given her a sleeping moose for a reason. It was best not to question her judgment. "By then the roads could be bad."

"Despite evidence to the contrary, I'm not a terrible driver." Nate motioned to his shoulder. "And the hotel isn't far."

"I wouldn't want you to risk it when you're already

injured. You already risked too much today. And the hotel driveway might not be plowed out yet. I know—I
should call Taylor before it gets any later. She's working
today, and she can feed Merlot before she leaves, and I
won't have to worry about it, if . . ."

"If?"

If she ended up staying a lot longer than she'd planned.
Lydia swallowed.

Nate raised an eyebrow. "Are you looking for an excuse to stay?"

Damn it. Nate really could still read her like an open
book.

She opened her mouth to respond and shut it quickly
as the words didn't come. It was one thing to acknowledge her own out-of-character intentions. It was another
to say it.

"Let me text Taylor." Lydia jumped up and retrieved
her phone from her coat pocket.

She was extremely aware that Nate watched her as
she typed back and forth with her sister. Taylor got a
laugh at her dilemma, but a moose causing havoc wasn't
such an uncommon occurrence. Lydia told her she was
stuck at a friend's, and Taylor didn't question it.

Nate picked up the tug-of-war game with Spark as she
put her phone away, but his gaze remained glued to her.
"The cat will not go hungry?"

"He'll be well cared for."

"Good. I wouldn't want you feeling guilty while you
were stuck here." Nate might have smirked ever so
slightly over the word *stuck*.

"Me neither." She bent over to pet Dolly so she didn't
have to meet that knowing gaze. Now that she'd made up
her mind—she was definitely kissing Nate—her giddi-

ness had passed, and she felt like she owed him an explanation for her wild mood swings. She started to offer one, but he held up a hand.

"I'm not certain we can say the same."

Lydia blinked. "What?"

"Fed. I don't have a whole lot of food here. Been mostly eating with family."

"Oh. Are you trying to tell me I should take you up on the offer to leave at the first opportunity?"

"No!" Nate dropped the rope in surprise, and Spark darted away with it. "But I thought it was only fair to warn you."

"The universe wants me to be here. Who am I to deny the powers of the cosmic moose?"

Nate cocked his head to the side. "There was only one shot of Baileys in that hot chocolate."

She kicked his calf. The woodstove was blowing superhot air out, but her feet were chilly from walking on the cold floor beams while she texted Taylor. "I was trying to explain my change of heart to you."

"Is that it? I think your heart's in the same place it's always been in."

Really, she could use him being just a little less insightful. "You know what I mean."

"Yes, that it took a while, but my irresistibility caught up to you."

She kicked him again, a little harder this time, and Nate grabbed her ankle. "How do you know it was you? It could be that I don't want to leave the monsters."

"That's a given. No one wants to leave the monsters. That's how I ended up with them. But you met them before." Slowly, he began massaging her foot, and Lydia sank back into the chair. The motion of Nate's fingers was both relaxing and arousing at once. She wanted him to keep going and to work his hand up her leg.

"That feels good." She closed her eyes, letting the sensation wash over her.

Nate made a noncommittal sound. "I could make you feel even better, but you need to let me know what you want."

"I want you to make me feel even better."

"Lydia?"

At her name, she opened her eyes. Nate stopped with the foot massage, and that was a shame. "Yeah?"

"I need you to be clear, because when we kissed earlier, you seemed to want the opposite."

This was because she hadn't explained herself. Lydia took a deep breath. "The moose . . ." No, that wasn't the correct way to start. "I realized I can't control everything, as the moose makes clear. I can't control the possibility that I'll get too attached to you, but I'm tired of holding back. It's fear, and where has that gotten me? You made me remember how much I like being with you and doing risky things with you. I want to keep enjoying whatever time we have together, even if I can't control the outcome."

Nate remained silent for so long that Lydia began to fear that—despite their earlier kiss—she'd completely misread him. "You want to do something risky and fun?"

"I want *you*."

"Yeah?" He smiled. "Then, come closer, because I've wanted you since I rescued your cat that night."

Lydia's stomach did a few flips. Just speaking of that night reanimated the butterflies she'd felt when Nate had handed her Merlot, although it could also have been the way he looked at her. That was the thing about Nate. He was quiet and serious, even when smiling, and having all of that intensity directed at her could melt a woman's insides. Or spawn a butterfly army.

The chairs by the woodstove were oversize, and Nate slid back on his so she could climb on next to him. Their legs intertwined and he wrapped his good arm around her, pulling her close. In the flickering light, his eyes were more gray than blue, and Lydia could smell that same scent she'd once sniffed on his hat. The butterflies danced, her pulse quickened, and her most sensitive nerve endings went on alert. Simply kissing Nate earlier had been a life-altering experience. Touching him would likely drag her past the point of no return.

She was okay with that.

"Hi." Her face was inches from his, and she had no place to rest her arm except his exceptionally hard stomach. Lord, if he hadn't been wearing at least two layers of shirts, Lydia was certain she'd be able to count his abs through the fabric. Her butterflies were backing down, surrendering to pure arousal.

"Hi." Nate's lips remained slightly upturned, but she could sense his breathing changing, and she suspected if her hand slipped a touch lower, his breathing wouldn't be the only thing she found different.

Nate pulled her closer, then removed his arm from around her shoulders. His fingers brushed hair from her face and caressed her cheek, slowly, almost reverently, and Lydia closed her eyes again.

"You are so beautiful," he murmured. "You've always been so."

She wanted to tell him the same things—he was beautiful, too, not just in body but in heart. He was the most absolutely perfect person she'd ever met. But those callused fingers of his drifted lower, tracing the contours of her lips, and she opened her mouth, impatient to taste him.

Nate inhaled sharply, and she grabbed his hand, afraid he might pull away. When he didn't, Lydia opened her eyes, and the hunger on Nate's face fed her own.

"Closer." He tugged on her again, until she was practically sitting on top of him.

His breath was warm, his clothes were soft, and everything else about him was hard, including the length pressing against her thighs. It was lucky she'd given herself permission to give up control, because maintaining any was becoming impossible.

"Too many layers." Lydia slid a hand beneath his shirts, delighted with how Nate's muscles twitched as she pressed her palm against his skin.

"Patience." He said the word, but she wasn't convinced he really wanted to follow through on it.

"Haven't we waited long enough?"

Nate swallowed. "Yes, but some things deserve to be done right."

"I'm not worried." She leaned over and touched her lips to his, thinking, since she was on top of him, she could take charge of the situation.

Nate must have been surprised, but he recovered quickly and kissed her back, and Lydia admitted defeat. She had no control, no willpower. Nate kissed her, and she succumbed to his every touch. His good-side hand cupped her cheek, holding her in place, and his left one gripped her around the waist, squeezing her through her sweater. Lydia moaned, sinking more deeply onto him, trying to press herself against the hard lump in his pants and give any relief to the ache slowly eating her alive between her legs.

When his left hand slipped beneath her sweater, she came up, gasping for air. "Nate."

"What do you need?" His teeth grazed her throat, and then, oh God, he licked her. Delicious shivers trickled down her back.

She was grinding herself against him, and she didn't care. "Everything."

Nate chuckled. "Could you be more specific?"

"Touch me. Everywhere. I can't get more specific than that. I want it all."

"Then you get it all." He pulled on her sweater. "Take this off."

Lydia tossed the sweater onto the other chair, along with the thermal she'd been wearing underneath. Since she wasn't supposed to have ended up half-naked on Nate's lap, she'd worn a comfy old sports bra, so she tossed that too.

Nate didn't seem to mind. His eyes opened wider, and his body stiffened further beneath her. "Fucking gorgeous."

"Your turn." Her body was nothing special, but she'd already gotten an eyeful of him from the waist up, and that he was not on some sexy firefighter calendar was a missed opportunity.

"I said patience."

She started to protest—how much more patient did she need to be?—then Nate lowered his mouth to her breasts, and she forgot what words were. There was only this, him licking and sucking and squeezing and pinching. And her, lost in sensation, moaning his name as waves of pure pleasure shot straight down to her groin.

One of his hands slipped beneath the waistband of her wool leggings, and Lydia fought the urge to pounce on it, she was so desperate for more. He found her sweet spot soon enough, fingers gliding through her wetness, rubbing her most sensitive skin.

"You need to stop." She did not want him to stop. "I'm going to come."

Nate released her nipple from his lips, which was a damn shame. "Did I misinterpret *everything*?"

"No."

"Then, what's the problem?" His fingers slowed down, which was another shame, but also for the best. She was a breath away from exploding, and although she wanted that—God, yes—not like this.

"I want you to come with me."

Nate shuddered, giving her the impression that it wasn't only her self-control that was close to failing. "What about both? I want to watch you come, Lydia. I want to see the expression on your face. I've been dreaming about it for ages."

She closed her eyes. Looking at him made it too difficult to not do exactly as he asked. All he had to do was move a single finger, and his touch and that hungry gaze would send her over the edge. "Watch me when you're inside me. I want to be with you."

She didn't know why, but it was very important to her that her first time having sex with Nate, the two of them were equals in the give-and-take. Everything else about them had been a strange sort of partnership—in secrecy and in commiseration. It only felt right that this be an equal partnership in pleasure too.

Nate swore, leaning his head back against the chair. "I don't know how to do this, to make it soft and slow and sweet like you deserve. Let me give this to you first."

That was the issue? Soft and slow and sweet might be

nice at some point, but she had years of pent-up sexual need, all caused by the same perfect man, clawing to get out.

Lydia swallowed and kissed him, but held his hand in place so he stopped torturing her. "That is why you are wonderful, but I don't want that. If you want to give me what I need, it's your dick, inside me, now."

Nate swore a second time, and his grip on her tightened. Then he nudged her to climb off him. "Be right back."

He darted past the puppies that had started to snooze on the rug and ran up the stairs to the loft. He'd better be finding condoms somewhere or she was going to lose her mind the rest of the way. On that thought, Lydia yanked down her leggings and underwear while she listened to Nate rummaging around. In spite of the woodstove, it was a lot colder without his warm arms around her.

Nate didn't give her time to regret her decision though. He was back downstairs a second later, and the expression on his face made the brief chill more than worth it. "Jesus, Lydia. The things I want to do to you . . ."

No doubt they were things she'd like. But right now, there was only one thing she needed.

She waited until he stepped onto the rug, then she looped her arms around his neck. "Better hope that moose sticks around for a while."

Nate wrapped his arms around her, and she pressed herself against him and kissed him, all too conscious of how he was completely clothed. His fingers threaded through her hair, destroying the braid she'd worn it back in, and somehow that, too, turned her on. Nate had suggested he couldn't do slow and sweet, but she sensed he was trying anyway. Trying and failing. His kiss was hard and his tongue relentless. The stubble that had lightly scratched her earlier scraped against her skin, and she couldn't help think she'd been a bit of a fool to turn down whatever else he'd been offering if there was the possibility it had meant that stubble between her legs.

But moose or not, she wasn't going anywhere for a while. Like she'd told him, there was time, and she knew what she wanted first.

It began by getting these clothes off him.

Nate's fingers dug into the back of her neck, and he tossed her hair tie aside. "You should wear your hair down more."

"You should take your clothes off more."

He chuckled. "I didn't expect you to be so insistent."

"You make me lose my better sense."

"Really?" He grabbed her ass and kissed her again, and Lord, that was good too.

Too good. His erection was burrowing against her stomach, making her wetter with each passing second, but so was his waistband, minus the wetness. She needed skin.

"Nate." Gathering what was left of her self-control, Lydia stepped back.

He wasn't wearing his sling, she noticed. She hoped that was okay.

"Shirts are still a little slow," Nate said.

"Can I help?"

He raised an eyebrow, teasingly. "Can you be gentle in your current state?"

"Yes." She'd never forgive herself if she hurt him.

Nate removed his right arm from both his shirts, and Lydia helped him pull the left sleeves off so that he could minimize the way he raised that arm. Slightly more satisfied with their situation, she threw his shirts on top of hers and ran her fingers down his chest. Since she'd seen him working out shirtless, she'd been imagining doing just this. The ridges between his pecs, the sprinkling of hair tickling her fingertips, those hard abdominal planes—it was almost too much to absorb.

Her hand caught on the edge of his pants, and he twitched beneath her touch. *Huh.* Now that the playing field had been evened out a bit, she wanted to slow down too. Stroking him beneath the waistband with her thumb, she touched her lips to his chest, licking one side then the other, like he'd done to her.

Nate tensed, but he didn't move. When she glanced up at him, that devouring gaze was locked on her.

Well, then. Lydia kissed her way down his stomach, alternating between brushes of her lips and gentle nips with her teeth. Nate's breathing grew heavier. His muscles quivered. And she was getting wetter, her nipples harder. Slow had been fun for a minute, but she was torturing herself as much as him. At his waistband, she stood to unbutton his pants.

"Did you get your revenge?" Nate asked.

She tossed her hair. "I suppose I did, but don't think it didn't cost me."

"I'm counting on it." He draped one arm across her lower back to tug her against him and kissed her again until she was writhing. Then he finished unzipping and removing his pants. The boxer briefs followed, revealing that her expectation that he was hiding something as large and impressive as the rest of his body in there had not been wrong.

"Nate." She stroked him, unable to help herself. She wasn't going to be happy until she touched and tasted him everywhere.

"Lydia?" His fingers curled around her from behind

and delved into her wetness. She squirmed. "When I thought about this, I imagined stretching you out on my bed, pinning your arms over your head, and pleasuring you in every way possible."

Nate's voice grew thicker as he spoke, and she breathed deeply of his scent, burying her face against the crook of his good shoulder. His words were stripping away the last of her self-control. Lydia bit his collarbone, trying to hold on.

"That's not going to work though," Nate said. "I can't put that kind of pressure on my shoulder."

She didn't care. As glorious as being stretched out on his bed sounded, she'd take him in any position. "Then, forget the bed. Stay right here."

He seemed to have the same idea, and his magic fingers slipped away. "Turn around. One way or another, I'm going to hold you."

Lydia did as asked. With anyone else, turning her back on them while naked would have made her uncomfortable initially, but she trusted Nate to take care of her more than she trusted herself.

"Okay?" He leaned her over the chair.

"If you're quick about this."

That elicited another strained laugh from him, and she looked over her shoulder so she could watch him put on the condom. Then Nate was behind her, one arm wrapped around her and the other nudging her legs apart so he could glide inside of her.

It was too much and not enough. Lydia groaned, glad the chair was of a good height to hold her up because her knees buckled. Nate's one-armed grip on her was strong, too, and she knew he wouldn't let her fall. Nate would hold her, catch her, whatever it took at whatever risk to himself. Because he was Nate.

"Still okay?" Nate asked.

"Almost perfect."

He swept her hair over one shoulder, pressed his mouth to the back of her neck, and started to move. "You have no idea how much I've wanted this. You feel so good."

One of his hands massaged her breast, the other dipped between her legs, fingers slowly circling her clit in time with his thrusting. Lydia whimpered.

"Good?"

"Better." She gasped.

"Good. You are so wet. So perfect." His grip around her tightened.

Lydia tried to respond, to let him know that he was perfect, too, that he felt like magic inside of her, but her words had finally disappeared completely. Leave it to Nate, the guy who rarely spoke normally, to be able to keep up a running commentary during sex. She would laugh if she could, but it was going to end up as one more thing she adored about him.

She hadn't expected it to be a turn-on either, but damn. Nate alternated between whispering in her ear and kissing her throat, and the orgasm built inside her at record speed. "Now. Faster."

His fingers ceased their delicate torture and rubbed her more vigorously, and she came in a strangled cry, bucking against him. The sound seemed to undo him. Nate's teeth dug into her shoulder. He waited for her to finish shuddering and followed suit, hands clenching her painfully but also wonderfully. She'd never felt so satiated or protected during sex before.

Nate continued to hold her another moment, his breath on her face, and the sensation of their sweat mingling on her back. She didn't want him to let go, but she could hear that they'd woken up the puppies, and this couldn't last.

But then, none of this could last. For the moment, she didn't regret her decision to seize this happiness. She hoped it would stay that way.

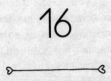

16

MOST MORNINGS SINCE the accident, Nate had woken up with pain in his unbroken shoulder because it hadn't taken kindly to him sleeping on it all night. But this morning was different. He was on his back, and Lydia's arm was splayed across his chest. His head was filled with the scent of her hair, which had fanned out over his arm, and he could feel her breathing where she was pressed against him.

For those reasons alone, nothing could hurt.

Well, except his balls. They were throbbing, and his morning wood was so hard he could probably cut a diamond with his cock. Nate would have thought that after last night, his body would remain sated for a while, but apparently not while the woman he couldn't get enough of was sleeping half on top of him.

He smiled into the cold morning cabin air. Sex with Lydia downstairs had been a dream. Sex twice more with Lydia upstairs had blown his mind. The fantasy he'd been carrying around about laying her down on the bed hadn't needed to come true because he'd discovered something better—Lydia on top of him and being able to watch her pleasure herself with his body.

Recalling that image was in no way calming the storm raging in his nuts, but Nate couldn't bring himself to wake her and ask for morning sex. She was so beautiful, so peaceful where she was. As much as he wanted her back on top of him, he wanted to keep holding her too. Cradling her. She had no idea how precious she was to him, and she deserved to be cherished and adored, not just fucked into oblivion, although he wasn't sorry to discover she liked that.

Sometime during the night, the monsters had come upstairs and fallen asleep on the foot of the bed as well. Nate liked that too. Currently the three most important beings in his life were all crowded into bed with him. He could get used to this, although he shouldn't. He tried to discourage the monsters from sleeping in the bed, but there was no door to close off the loft. As for the woman, Nate wasn't in the habit of sleeping with other people. Sex, yes. Sleepovers, no. He liked his private time kept private and, since he didn't do relationships, postsex sleeping together was more intimate than he was comfortable with.

Lydia was the exception. Lydia was *always* the exception. Only he couldn't get used to sleeping with her, in any sense of the phrase, because even if he could convince her to give them a shot, he was going to leave. She'd been right about that.

And now this perfect moment was ruined because he feared hurting her when that happened. Nate didn't entirely understand why she'd changed her mind last night, and he didn't know how long this new attitude of hers would last. He'd have to take every opportunity she provided to convince her they were perfect for each other, that against all odds, they could make this work.

The thought caused another ache inside him, one slightly higher up than his groin. What would have happened if he'd stayed in town all these years? If he'd waited for her to return from college? Would he have had a second chance to persuade her then?

He supposed it didn't matter because he'd been young and impulsive—and hurting—and had opted to leave. What was done was done. It was Lydia who had chosen to move on when she left for school, after all. Given the situation between their families, Nate understood that she'd thought it was best for both of them, and so he'd agreed, believing it was the right move to make her happy. And maybe it had, but it had left him gutted and restless. He'd even bought her a going-away present that he'd never given her.

Nate could have stayed in bed, counting Lydia's eyelashes and listening to her steady breathing, forever. But by his feet Dolly's ears perked up, and the puppy raised her head. A second later, Nate heard the noise as well—the sound of a motor outside. Gently, he removed Lydia's arm from his chest and sat up, trying not to disturb her.

"Ssh." He put his finger to his lips, not that the monsters would understand the gesture. Now that they were up, though, he'd have to let them out for a potty break. A glance at his phone told him that they'd let him sleep longer than normal. Yet another Lydia-in-the-bed miracle.

Ignoring his aching balls, Nate pulled on sweatpants and a fleece as fast as his shoulder allowed. Let the monsters out, put more wood in the woodstove, start coffee. He could do it all without waking Sleeping Beauty if the dogs cooperated. They were both up, and Lydia hadn't stirred. Nate wondered what it must be like to be so sound a sleeper. He hoped it meant she didn't have the regrets that he did.

"Come on," he whispered, shooing the puppies downstairs. At some point during the time it had taken him to do all of this, the loudest of the noises had stopped. Nate stuffed his feet into his boots, attached the dogs' leashes, and opened the door, braced for however much snow had fallen.

Behind his SUV, the moose had left and someone had parked a pickup with a plow on front. His driveway was mostly clear, but the snow beyond his porch looked to have accumulated a good ten to twelve inches. The monsters wouldn't be venturing far beyond the cabin to do their morning business, which was good because it was damn cold out.

"Heya, Nate." The pickup's owner—or so Nate assumed—walked around from the far side of cab, carrying a shovel. "Doing my rounds this morning, and your dad told me you could use some help with that shoulder."

"Thanks, Jim." Nate didn't recognize the truck, but he did recognize his father's friend. "Appreciate the plowing, but I can shovel off the walk."

Jim waved him off. "It's no problem."

Feeling awkward, Nate had no choice but to step aside so the other man could work his way up to the porch. He couldn't help thinking that he was the one who should be assisting other people this morning. This damn injury wasn't only interfering with his activities, but with his entire self-image. "How much do I owe you?"

"Nothing."

"It's not nothing."

"Take it up with your dad," Jim said. "I do the plowing for all the occupied cabins. The shoveling is a family favor."

Grumbling silently about his helplessness, Nate thanked him and ushered the puppies back inside. The nice thing to do would be to invite Jim in and offer him a mug of coffee, but with Lydia upstairs, that wasn't happening. Jim would surely recognize her, and while Nate might not care if word spread, Lydia had to live with the consequences. Nate would have to figure something out later to repay him.

On that thought, Nate strained to hear if Lydia was moving around yet, but all seemed quiet. Fortunately, the monsters were also quiet in the morning, so he was able to get the fire built up, the dogs fed, and a pot of coffee brewing before he heard movement on the steps.

Lydia came into view a moment later. She'd found one of his sweatshirts—the one actually matching the pants he wore—and was pulling on her wool leggings. Nate couldn't blame her, since the cabin was chilly, but damn. He liked seeing her in his clothes, and he'd especially liked it when she wasn't wearing anything else.

"Hey." He kissed her cheek, breathed in her scent, and reveled in the way she sank into him. His hard-on, which had been effectively destroyed by the cold, slowly returned.

"Hey." She wrapped her arms around his waist. "Oh, thank God you have coffee. I was worried after last night."

Nate laughed. Their pickings for dinner had been slim, though at the time, he'd been more hungry for things that weren't food. It was fair to say that time had passed. His dick might be wide awake again, but so was his stomach, and it was demanding to take precedence. Judging from the sound that came from Lydia's midsection, his wasn't the only one.

"Lucky for you, I also have eggs, sausages, and waffles. What would you like?"

She grinned sleepily. "Everything."

When she looked up at him with such delight on her face like that, he was an absolute goner. "Then you will always get everything."

He just wasn't sure how to make that happen for more than breakfast and sex.

NATE'S PHYSICAL THERAPIST dressed like a gym teacher and sported the heart of a sadist beneath his Seahawks sweatshirt. His first appointment had been disappointing, not because either the guy or the facility had seemed lacking, but because they hadn't done much. The physical therapist had reviewed his chart, assessed him, and sent Nate home with some exercises.

During this second visit, Nate's hopes had improved as they'd gotten down to business—a business that apparently included lots of pain. Nate didn't mind working through pain if that was what it took to repair his shoulder, but he'd expected a medical professional to be more cautious than he would be himself.

Making people comfortable and alleviating their pain was one of those EMT duties that Nate felt strongly about. While some of the people he'd worked with didn't place those things high on the priorities list, Nate considered them paramount as long as a patient didn't have more pressing needs. Helping people meant making sure they weren't suffering.

Physical therapy seemed to take the opposite approach.

"All right," his physical therapist said, stepping back. "I want you to raise your arm as high as it will go."

"Now?" Nate kept his wince entirely internal.

Most days, his shoulder had stabilized at a pain intensity he called *tender*. If he didn't do anything reckless or accidental—like try to carry too much weight, roll onto his shoulder in bed, or make any sudden jerking movements with it—he barely remembered it had been broken. The fracture was healing well, according to his orthopedist. Despite, she insisted, whatever foolish attempts he'd made to screw that up.

But today was not most days. The exercises Nate had been doing at home increased the soreness while he performed them, but the exercises the physical therapist was having him do on-site had made those look like warmups. Which maybe they had been. Regardless, as nervous and excited as Nate was to finally try raising his arm, doing so when his shoulder was already throbbing would not have been his first choice.

Jaime, the gym teacher/sadist/physical therapist, nodded. "If the pain becomes too intense, stop. But see how high you can go first. Slowly."

Slow was the only possible speed. Nate could raise his arm until it was parallel with the floor just fine, and then it was like trying to push his way through a brick wall.

"Pain?" Jaime asked.

No longer able to hide his grimace, Nate shook his head. "It's like something is pushing my arm down as I'm trying to raise it."

"The fracture itself is nice and clean, but you sustained a lot of nerve damage."

Nate had heard this from Dr. Cohen-Liao already. If he was going to suffer from any long-term mobility issues, they were far more likely to have been caused by the nerve damage than the break.

Taking a deep breath, Nate raised his arm another inch. Jaime said something about this being a potentially slow process, and how it was something to work at but not to force, but Nate concentrated on his arm. He thought about the monsters getting bigger and needing more care. About needing to lug fifty pounds or more of equipment around on his back, of dragging ropes and hoses and lifting stretchers.

"I can do it."

"Breathe," Jaime said.

Up a little more. Nate was glad Lydia wasn't around to watch him sweat just from trying to raise his arm. Hell, he could barely raise his left hand high enough yet to twist his fingers around in her hair, and that was a damn shame. Lydia wouldn't care if he couldn't. In fact, Nate trusted that Lydia wouldn't run away from him, no matter the extent of his injuries. She simply might run away for different reasons, and that was what he needed to avoid. He needed to fight for her—for them—and although the fight wouldn't be physical, he would really like a fully functional shoulder back to make it easier on himself.

Nate grunted and looked up at his hand, somewhat in surprise. He'd managed to fully extend his arm, but damn. In the end, it had felt like trying to do a shoulder press with a one-hundred-pound dumbbell in his hand, and he was sweating and shaking like it too.

"Good." Jaime sounded as surprised as Nate felt, and Nate let his arm drop. Raising it had been one long battle. Keeping it up was one he was too exhausted to fight. "How's the pain?"

Nate massaged his upper arm. "Sore."

"Not shrieking?"

"Should it be?"

"Shrieking pain is always bad." Jaime made some

kind of note in the tablet he'd been using to track Nate's progress.

He wanted a nap, but Nate resisted the urge to lie back on one of the room's padded tables. Later, he'd have a beer to celebrate. The thing he'd feared most—never getting full mobility back—hadn't come to pass. Although as he listened to Jaime explain the situation, he was going to need to be diligent about doing his exercises if he wanted the motion to ever get easier.

Nate wasn't concerned about keeping up with that part. Exercise was like breathing for him. Still, this accomplishment felt strangely anticlimactic. With practice, more physical therapy, and another few months of recovery, he'd eventually be able to go back to work. His life would not be upended. He should be walking on the clouds, and yet . . .

Probably he was just tired from today's session, but Nate couldn't shake the idea that somehow Lydia was behind his unexpected mood. Being able to go back to work was great, but going back to work was a reminder that he would be leaving her behind. Sure, he was going to work his ass off to convince her to give them a shot at something long-distance, but last time it was Lydia who'd left. This time it would be him. Something about that realization dug into his gut in a way Nate didn't like.

Instead of driving straight back to the cabin, Nate took a detour and headed toward his parents' house. It was late in the afternoon, and he had no idea if either of them would be home, but he hoped not. An idea had struck him as he pulled out of the physical therapy parking lot—Lydia-related, of course.

Nate couldn't stop thinking about that day when Lydia had told him she thought it was best if they said goodbye for good when she left for college. They weren't even supposed to be friends, after all. Trying to maintain a secret relationship when they were hundreds of miles apart would be daunting.

He'd known she was a nervous wreck about leaving home. Lydia had tried to hide it, but she'd always ended up confiding in him. That was one of the reasons why he hadn't protested her suggestion. If he was one less thing for her to worry about, that was good. Nate didn't want her to get cold feet or feel like she had to spare any energy fretting about him. She had new experiences to look forward to and new people to meet. Part of him was jealous, even though he didn't have any interest in college himself. He had his future planned out, and he'd always known Lydia didn't really fit into it any more than he'd fit into hers.

Still, the less rational part of him had hoped they could see how long they could get away with defying the odds. So when Lydia had made the hard choice and brought up their lack of a future, that less rational part of him had been gutted. He'd bought her a bracelet he'd intended to give her as a going-away present, and he'd been knocked so off-balance that he'd forgotten to give it to her.

Nate needed to find that bracelet. He didn't know why it was suddenly so important to him, but with the realization that he could return to work—that *he'd* be leaving *her* this time—he desperately wanted to hold it again. Lydia had had her moose as a sign from the universe to stay the night at his place; he would have the bracelet as a sign to . . . What, he wasn't sure. Not stay in town. Despite Lydia's comments about him leaving, he didn't even know if she'd really want that. All his hopes to the contrary, the feud hadn't gone away with the news of his cousin and Lydia's sister getting married. Staying, even if he had a job, wouldn't be easy.

Nate's thoughts remained a jumbled mess as he pulled into his parents' driveway. There was no sign anyone was home, no lights on in the house. He let himself in but all was quiet.

Flicking on the hallway light, Nate headed upstairs. Just discovering the bracelet existed would be his sign, he decided. Before he'd left Helen, he'd hidden the bracelet at his parents' house among a lot of other junk. It was entirely possible his parents had tossed it all years ago.

He couldn't have taken the bracelet with him though. Although he'd told everyone, including himself, that he'd joined the Forest Service because it was an adventure, even then, part of him had known he was leaving so he wouldn't have to run into Lydia. Taking the bracelet with him, therefore, would have been like taking her with him as well. Counterproductive. On the other hand, he hadn't been able to bear getting rid of it—and in retrospect, that was surely a big old sign. One that he'd been so naive to have missed.

Still, it was over and done with. The question hurrying his feet was whether his parents still had the box of stuff he'd left at their house sitting in the attic. A rush of cold air swept over him as he opened the attic door, and Nate sneezed at the dust it stirred up. The collar ties holding up the roof hung low, and he crouched, scanning the assorted junk in storage. Lots of unlabeled but unfamiliar boxes, a fake Christmas tree, window fans, camping gear—Nate shoved one of the dusty cartons aside, spying his particular dust-covered one by the eaves.

He brushed a layer of grit off the top and opened the flaps. He hadn't left much behind with his parents, mainly some sentimental items that he'd had no use for but couldn't let go of. His high school yearbook was in here, a couple trophies, one of his sad attempts at wood carving, and there, at the bottom, wrapped in a plastic bag to disguise the contents, the gift box with the bracelet.

The gift box was in terrible shape, so Nate removed the bracelet and stuffed everything else back the way it was. Then he beat a hasty retreat from the chill and the dust.

In the hallway, Nate held the bracelet up to the over-head light, and its glass beads glowed with the colors of the northern lights. Since Helen was a major tourist des-tination in the summer, the town was home to many art-ists and artisans, and the beads had been made and strung by one of them. Nate didn't recall how much he'd paid for it, but he did remember that Lydia had been obsessed with those colors that summer, and though the bracelet had seemed expensive, it had also seemed worth it. And yet he'd never given it to her.

The front door opened downstairs, and Nate shoved the bracelet in his coat pocket.

"Nate, you there?" His father's voice drifted up.

"Yeah." He hurried into the living room, searching for an excuse to explain his unplanned visit. "Thought I'd pop by and share the good news. Looks like I'll have full mobility again in my shoulder."

"Oh, honey, that's fantastic." His mother paused un-loading groceries to give him a lopsided hug.

His father chose to grunt his approval. "Good. Now, when are you going to come visit during deer season so we can put it to use?"

Nate kept his answer to that noncommittal. His fa-ther, like most of the men and many of the women in his family, was an avid hunter. Nate didn't object to hunting as long as people ate what they killed, which his family did. But he'd also never particularly enjoyed the sport of it either. Fortunately for him, fire season and deer season tended to overlap, so he had a ready-made excuse.

On the other hand, if he could convince Lydia to make a go of a relationship, Nate anticipated spending a lot more time in town, and he suspected that was what his family truly wanted.

In his pocket, his fingers toyed with the bracelet. He still wasn't sure why he'd needed to find it, but he couldn't shake the sense that he was one step closer to his goal.

17

❧━━━━━━━━━━❧

"THAT'S FANTASTIC." NINETY percent sure her face
didn't match her tone, Lydia kissed Nate on the cheek to
cover for any sign that she was less than thrilled to learn
about his shoulder.

The truth was, she was happy for him. Nate had confessed his worries about mobility and not being able to
return to work. This was important to him, and so it was
important to her.

But the truth was also that she was not happy for herself. It was selfish, but a Nate who could return to work
was a Nate who would be leaving town, probably at the
earliest opportunity. She'd always known this would be
how it went, and yet some part of her had hoped for another outcome. Not that she wanted that outcome to be
at his expense, but it seemed like the most likely way for
it to happen.

"Thanks." Nate kissed her back, then returned to un-
packing the dinner he'd bought them. "I'd say a weight

was lifted off my shoulders, but that sounds . . ." He cringed.

"Pun-tastic?" Lydia knelt to play with the monsters. They'd been running around in circles at her ankles since she'd arrived. She hadn't meant to ignore them, but Nate's news had distracted her from pretty much everything.

It was best to play with the puppies now. She was growing almost as fond of them as she was of their owner, and they'd soon be gone too.

Lydia swallowed, hoping Nate didn't see the shadow she could feel passing over her face. She had to think of the moose. She was grabbing life by the antlers. The universe had given her an opportunity, she'd taken it, and she would live with the consequences.

When her sister had left for California, Taylor had uttered some cliché about how it was better to regret the things you had done than the things you hadn't. Lydia wasn't sure she agreed, but she was trying.

Really trying, which ought to count for something. After all, she'd known she would get too attached to Nate. That it would be messy and painful when he left. But she'd also known she would regret it if she didn't kiss him. Since she'd been doomed either way, for once Taylor's cliché had made sense.

"Ow!" She'd been lost in her thoughts, and Spark had bitten her wrist.

"No." Nate was suddenly next to her on the floor, staring down the puppy. Spark looked traumatized for a moment, then mildly confused.

Lydia rubbed his head. He hadn't bitten her hard; her skin wasn't broken. "It was my fault. I wasn't paying close enough attention."

"They're at the age when they'll chew on anything, or anybody." Nate sighed and ruffed both dogs' heads. "It's not your fault. They need to learn."

So did she. With Nate so close, smelling so good and looking so cozy in his navy flannel shirt, she kind of wanted to bite him herself. Licking him a little wouldn't be bad either.

Before she knew what she was doing, Lydia leaned over and pressed her mouth to the bare patch of skin just above his collar. He even tasted good on her tongue. Lord, she was becoming somewhat feral, looking at the man next to her and considering turning him into her chew toy.

A naked chew toy. So maybe more like a sex toy.

She inhaled deeply, the faint spicy scent that clung to him going straight to her head. Yup, definitely feral. But Nate had basically confirmed that he'd be leaving soon, so why not take advantage of the situation while she could? It was what Taylor would do. Hell, it was what anyone who wasn't boring would do. In fact, it was the practical choice, and she was a practical woman.

Nate groaned, and Lydia tore herself away from his throat before she turned into a full-on vampire, complete with a horde of furry, biting monsters.

"What were we doing?" Nate blinked those blue-gray eyes at her. He'd grabbed her arm, perhaps to steady himself—she had been rather aggressive—but he didn't let go.

"Biting," Lydia said, wetting her lips. She was so feral she could put the huskies to shame.

"I like it when you bite."

Her cheeks warmed. "I'm not usually much of a biter."

"You bit me last time." Nate grinned. He'd locked one arm around Dolly because she was trying to jump on him, and the other had let go of Lydia's arm and landed on her leg. That felt purposeful.

"I seem to be doing a lot of things around you that I don't normally do."

"Hmm." His hand crept up her thigh. "I don't suppose I can persuade you to do more of those things."

She shouldn't be persuaded. Nate had bought dinner, and it was cooling on his kitchen counter. The monsters would be nipping at their ankles. And the deeper she let herself get involved with Nate, the more it was going to hurt.

Practical Lydia thought the choice was clear. Too bad for her, feral Lydia did, too, and she wasn't without logic.

She so rarely—that was to say, never—tossed caution to the wind and let her inhibitions and anxiety go, but Nate brought out that side of her. Not only should she savor every moment in his company, creating memories to last long after he was gone, she should use this opportunity to live a little. To enjoy the excitement while she could. If she could metaphorically let down her hair, or literally shuck her clothes, that brought her one step closer to being less boring. And damn it, as she'd been thinking lately, she was tired of being boring. Maybe that part of her could stick around after Nate vanished.

So screw dinner sitting out, never mind the pair of hungry puppies who were chewing on the furniture, and forget that the woodstove was just starting to heat up the cabin. She was going to sex up Nate again. Right now.

Nate's hand slipped under her shirt, and Lydia shivered with both delight and the cold air. She leaned over and kissed him, glad he was slacking off in the shaving department. Stubbly Nate was twice as sexy as clean-shaven Nate. But stubble did not keep a woman warm.

Lydia stood, holding his hands. "Consider me persuaded, but the monsters need food, and I need heat or you're not getting me naked."

Nate scratched his neck. "I'll take care of both those things."

While he returned to the kitchen, she took off upstairs. There had to be a happy medium between uninhibited sex and not freezing to death, and she figured she was the ideal sort of person to figure it out.

The cabin's pipes rattled, suggesting Nate had cranked up the heat as well as the blower on the woodstove. Clearly he was taking no chances about the getting-her-naked part. She appreciated that, right down to her chilly toes.

On that thought, Lydia quickly stripped, tossing off everything, including her underwear. She tucked all her clothes neatly beneath the sweatshirt Nate had sitting on a chair so they were hidden, then she climbed under his hefty down comforter and waited. The flannel sheets were cool on her skin, but she warmed herself by imagining him joining her.

After several minutes he clomped upstairs and paused by the side of the bed, looking like he was suppressing a laugh. "I turned up the heat."

"So did I." She raised an eyebrow. She'd been aiming for sultry but feared she'd landed somewhere closer to tepid.

Nate sat on the side of bed, the hint of a smile stuck to him. "I see. So I should climb in here with you until it gets warmer, huh?"

"But first you need to take your clothes off."

"Do I?"

Lydia lifted the blanket, which she'd pulled tight around her neck, giving him a tease of her bare shoulders.

Nate's eyes opened wide. "I see."

"Not until you strip, you don't." She pulled the blanket back up.

He shucked off his clothes with alarming speed, especially considering his shoulder and the fact that she'd wanted to enjoy the show. Lydia couldn't complain, however, when his very hard, very warm body climbed under the covers with her.

"There's a problem with this plan," Nate said, propping himself up on his good side. "Now that I'm here with you, I still can't see."

Lydia inched closer to him and slipped one of her legs between his. "But you can touch." She pressed her hand against his chest, toying with his hair. "And you can kiss." She leaned in and brushed his shoulder with her lips, carefully, because it was the injured one.

He groaned, his body stiffening against her. His hand landed on her hip, and Nate rolled onto his back, pulling her on top of him. It was growing hot under the blankets, and Lydia couldn't tell if it was from body heat or the way her own blood was starting to simmer. She liked this position. That this strong, hard—in every sense—man was lying beneath her, letting her act on whatever dirty thoughts popped into her mind. She licked her lips and wrapped one hand around his length.

The blanket slid an inch down her shoulders, and she was warm enough that she didn't mind. Nor did she mind when Nate pushed it down farther.

"That is a sight I will never get tired of." He reached up and cupped her right breast. Her nipples were already hard from the cold, but his touch stiffened them more and sent jolts of pleasure straight down between her legs. "This position might make breaking my shoulder worthwhile."

Since Nate breaking his shoulder had led to him returning to Helen, it was already worthwhile as far as Lydia was concerned. But Nate's teasing comment struck something deep inside her that she was pretty sure he hadn't intended to hit. For him, this was about sex. Sure, it might also be about rekindling an old friendship, but she shouldn't be looking for or thinking about more than that when it came to him. He'd never given her any reason to. This getting-attached issue was all on her. She and Nate could hang out in secret while he was in town, but his shoulder was healing and soon he'd leave.

She needed to follow his example. Be adventurous. Have fun. Don't overthink it, or perhaps, don't overfeel it. Let feral Lydia rule the day.

She tossed her hair back and smiled, doing her best to bury her anxieties and softer emotions deep down inside. "I'm glad you think so. Now, I think we were discussing me biting you?"

Bending over, she grazed her teeth along his tight stomach, and Nate bucked beneath her. Yes, feral Lydia knew how to have a lot more fun than her normal self. And after another minute of nipping, kissing, and sucking her way across Nate's body, her brain gave up on paying attention to anything but the pleasure.

NATE WOKE UP the next morning like he had the first time Lydia stayed over—with a feeling of utter contentment. And total horniness. Anytime now he should get up and take the monsters outside to do their business, but they were snoozing away, which meant it was either earlier than he thought or he and Lydia had kept them up last night with their noise.

Lydia could be a bit of screamer, a fact Nate enjoyed

immensely because it was not what he would ever have guessed. Poised, perfect Lydia liked letting loose in bed.

No, wait. He didn't enjoy that. He loved it. Like everything about her.

Like just her. Period.

Nate's heart did a weird stutter in his chest, which he chose to ignore. It was better to dwell on how much he enjoyed making her blush when he teased her, or hell, the way she made him grow warm in the cheeks when she teased *him* about dirty talking. Given that he'd never done more than shyly kiss her back when they were teenagers, this past week had been a revelation. Lydia was still his perfect person. Only now, he'd grown up a bit and wasn't too scared to kiss her because of that. In fact, he'd found a whole new way to worship her that involved a lot of time placing his mouth on the most delicious parts of her body.

His cock twitched at the memory, and Nate winced. Since there was no sound of machinery outside this morning, a little sex to start off the day sounded like a great idea, but he wasn't about to wake her up. Lydia got up very early on days when she was working, and so she tended not to stay up too late. And he, selfish, horny man that he was, had kept her up way past her bedtime last night. Nate just hoped he'd made it worth her while. When her eyes had finally closed, she'd been asleep instantly.

So he'd lie here in the silence a bit longer, basking in the peace of Lydia's quiet breathing, the scent she left on his sheets, and the warmth of her skin, despite not being one to normally lounge around in bed. Typically, lying still was like sitting still—Nate couldn't do it. His whole life, he'd gone from craving one adrenaline rush to another—that part about him leaving town hadn't been a lie. When Nate stopped moving, his brain started spinning and all he could think about was what to do next.

But lying here, he didn't want to do anything next. Or well, he did, but he was content to wait. Being around Lydia had that effect on him. When she was there, he didn't need to be anywhere else. If she would always be here, he might not ever feel the need to do anything but spend time with her. He certainly wouldn't feel the push to return to his old job. As much as he loved the rush, the camaraderie of being with his crew, and knowing that he was doing something important, the peace here was every bit as tempting.

If he could do something just as useful *here*, he wouldn't need to leave.

It would be good for the monsters, too, to have him around all the time. He still hadn't decided what the best option was for them when fire season started, and part of him knew that adopting them had been a terrible decision.

But he didn't have a job in Helen that would provide the same satisfaction, and he didn't know if Lydia would even want him to stay, since staying would require them to deal with the feud. There was no way to ask for her thoughts without sounding presumptuous, and he couldn't forget that, until recently, Lydia had been highly skittish about any kind of relationship with him at all. As far as he knew, all she wanted was a good time while he was here. So that was what he'd give her, and he'd save the worries for the future for himself.

He pulled the sheet closer to his nose, hoping to catch more of Lydia's scent on the fabric. His body stirred, and next to him, so did she. *Shit.* As much as he wanted her to be awake so they could fool around before the monsters got up, he didn't want to be the thing that woke her.

Nate attempted to cover her better with the blanket, but it seemed he was too late. Lydia opened one beautiful brown eye and gazed up at him. *Shit again.* The sweet, sleepy expression on her face melted his insides faster than the monsters could.

"Morning," she said.

"Morning. I'm sorry if I woke you."

"S'okay." Lydia yawned and her eyes fluttered shut briefly. "Just don't make me get out of bed."

Nate smoothed her hair back. "One thing you can count on is that I will never make you get out of my bed."

She poked him in the chest, which was probably not supposed to be arousing but absolutely was. "Funny man."

"Beautiful woman. Can't see what's funny about it."

Lydia made a disbelieving noise, then she slid over and draped herself half across him. Soft breasts pressed against his chest, and one alluring leg slipped between his. Nate wrapped an arm around her, lazily letting his hand glide down her back until he rested it over the curve of her backside. It was a wholly wonderful and increasingly unsatisfying position.

"No, I suppose there's nothing funny about this." Lydia squeezed her hand between their bodies and drew her fingers along the length of his cock.

"Definitely not."

"Maybe I should do something about it."

With his other hand, Nate cupped a breast. "First, you should let me do something about these." The feel of her against him was driving him wild.

But who was he fooling? All of this was driving him wild. What was wrong with him, to be willing to give this up if there were even the slightest possibility of waking up with Lydia becoming a regular part of his life?

18

LYDIA PUSHED HER sweater sleeves above her wrists. The Bay Song's fireplace was blowing hot air on her back, but she suspected it wasn't the fire making her overheat. "I just think we . . ." She sipped her coffee and tried again after waiting for the couple grabbing cookies to wander away. "We need to be clear about where we stand."

Cody's brow pinched slightly, but he otherwise seemed totally unconcerned about what she was trying to hint at. Either she wasn't being clear or she'd been misreading him for the past few weeks. Still, even if she'd misread Cody and was about to embarrass herself, she needed to lay everything out. "This is about being friends, because I'm not looking for a relationship right now."

Lie. She was, but with the guy who couldn't give her the happily ever after she wanted.

The pinch disappeared, and Cody nodded. He was leaning back in the overstuffed chair, one leg crossed over the other knee, arms planted casually on the armrests. Though tall, he was shorter than Nate, yet he still managed to make the large chair appear to be the insignificant piece of the visual. If she were to sketch him, Cody would be larger than life. Lydia didn't remember him coming across this way in school, but maybe that's what money and power did to people. They created some sort of aura around a person that screwed with an observer's perspective.

"No relationships right now. Okay." He flashed her one of those photo-worthy grins. "What about sex?"

She almost choked on her coffee. Apparently she had not misread him. He was just smugly confident.

"I prefer for those two things to go together." Lydia's mind returned to her morning of lying in bed with Nate, and confusion heated her blood.

"Fair enough," Cody said. "But do you still want to go flying?"

Cody had gotten a pilot's license and bought a small plane. Because of course he had. It only surprised Lydia to learn that he'd been flying himself into the airfield outside of Helen this whole time. She'd assumed someone with Cody's money would have his own pilot, but she was realizing that was a silly assumption. To Cody, the plane was as much a toy as it was a required way to travel about parts of the state. Naturally he wanted to play with it.

Truthfully, the only thing that should have surprised Lydia about any of this was that she was actually considering letting Cody take her on a flight. She hadn't gotten on a plane—of any size—in years.

Her grandparents in Fairbanks had their own plane, and the last time she'd gone for a ride with them, they'd hit a rough patch of air. She couldn't forget the sensation that the plane had been going one way while she'd been headed in a completely different direction. The shaking, the swooping, the way she'd gripped her seat with her knuckles turning white. Although both her grandparents had logged many hours of flight time, and no one else had been worried, when they'd returned to the ground, Lydia had climbed out of the plane with shaky legs. And she'd vowed never again unless the plane in question was a large commercial jet with a professional crew whisking her off to that tropical vacation that she'd always told herself she'd take.

But for some reason, Cody's offer didn't petrify her.

No, not some reason, like she didn't know what it was.

Because of Nate, Cody's offer didn't petrify her. Because of Nate reminding her how much fun it was to zip through the snow and act on her impulses, the thought of flying over the snowscape sounded at least mildly appealing. There was nothing like looking down on the glaciers from above—endless fields of dazzling white, and blue ice sparkling like crystals over the sapphire water. Remembering it had her itching to pick up her colored pencils again. Lydia's stomach squirmed as it recalled the sensation of dropping out through her feet, but she could overlook it.

"If you're still interested in taking me up," she replied.

"Oh, I'm still interested." Cody leaned forward and set his travel mug on the table between them, never taking his eyes off her. "In everything, that is."

The overconfident, almost predatory way he said that stiffened Lydia's spine. Cody probably wasn't used to being told no by women. On the one hand, that he was interested enough to keep pursuing her despite what she'd told him was kind of flattering. He wasn't a guy who had a lack of options, and she was certainly a step down from the type of glamorous woman he was often seen with in public. On the other hand, it was hard to feel flattered when her heart wasn't into him but someone else.

"First I'll whisk you away on a plane ride, then I'll whisk you away from here all together." Cody's grin was undoubtedly meant to be boyish and charming, but the presumption in it made Lydia reconsider her answer. "It's not like you can want to stay here and run this place forever."

The slight change in his angle caught Lydia off guard. "Why not? I love it here."

"Running your family's hotel?"

Lydia shrugged. It was true that working at the Bay Song had once been something she'd done only out of familial duty, but that had been years ago. Unlike Cody, who'd always wanted to work with computers, or Nate, who'd always wanted to be a firefighter, Lydia had gone off to college without with a specific goal. She'd always known the Bay Song was supposed to be her future, and unlike her sister, she hadn't fought it.

She was glad of it now. A job that had started off as a duty had become something she loved and a legacy she intended to continue. Especially now that Taylor was working here too. This was probably why in all her thoughts about what to do about Nate, the idea of leaving Helen had never occurred to her. Hotels were every-where, but the Bay Song existed only here. She was as much a part of it as the floorboards, and nothing else would do.

Lydia smiled back in what she hoped was a friendly-but-not-too-encouraging way. "I like working here, and I'm not looking to go anywhere else unless it's on a sightseeing trip."

Cody shook his head at her. "That would be a waste, but you can't blame me for hoping otherwise."

Perhaps not. Part of Lydia even hoped he'd be successful at making her fall for him. If she could only develop an interest in Cody, it would lessen the sting of Nate's leaving. And obviously, Cody was the practical choice, which she'd been telling herself all along. This was not a bridge to burn, not for her own sake nor to make her family happy. Whatever adventurous feelings Nate might be rousing in her, they'd likely disappear with him, leaving her doomed to be boring and safe, and there was nothing boring or safe about not hedging her bets with the more eligible guy.

NATE COULDN'T TAKE it anymore. Last night he'd been hanging out with friends, and he'd heard too much for him to ignore. He needed to scream, and there was only one person, who wasn't Lydia, whom he could think of who wouldn't judge him for that. Or, well, she would judge him, but she'd be honest about it and wouldn't tell him to calm down. That was good enough.

"Can you believe this?" Kelsey poured two mugs of coffee for them. "Who does he think he is?"

Nate paced around his sister's living room. The downside to choosing Kelsey for his screaming needs was that he might not get a word in himself. His younger siblings liked to tease Nate about being quiet, but he thought it was closer to the truth that they just never shut up. Prior to birth, he must have agreed to sacrifice his words for their sakes, and in return he got all the height.

Dolly barked at him. He'd brought the monsters to hang out with Kelsey's three huskies while they took an afternoon walk. Now one of Kelsey's dogs was upstairs, hiding from the puppies, and the puppies, who'd been tired out until a minute ago, were getting riled up. They weren't the only ones either. Nate was clearly making the remaining four dogs nervous.

He quit pacing and crossed his arms instead. "Yeah, I heard about the party."

Cody had decided to throw himself a housewarming party, and he'd invited a ton of locals. Some of them, Nate supposed, were probably old friends of his from school, like Lydia. But others were more like old acquaintances, like Nate himself. Either way, Cody had invited Lipins and Porters to the same party, which was just not done.

Among Nate's friends, who were all Porters or Porter-family people, everyone was planning on going to the party anyway. Curiosity overcame everything else, and Nate didn't blame them for that. Even though he was harboring a huge amount of animosity toward Cody, he was curious himself about this compound that Cody was building. And besides, he'd never cared much for the feud.

But other people did, and it took a certain kind of balls to pretend otherwise and invite Lipins and Porters to the same shindig.

"Like, obviously, I'm so over the feud," Kelsey was saying as she pushed a giant mug in Nate's direction. "But come on. The looks I get for daring not to shun Josh over his wedding? The shit all of us are dealing with from our families? And then some rich asshat struts into town and thinks he's better than that—that he's some-how above the feud? It's not like Cody didn't grow up here. He knows. He just has the audacity to think he can ignore it."

"Rich people." Nate snorted into his coffee. "They think rules don't apply to them."

"Rules usually *don't* apply to them. That's the problem. They learn it, and then forget where they came from." Kelsey scowled and plopped on her sofa.

Nate allowed the correction since, in his experience, his cousin wasn't wrong. He watched the puppies trying to get the attention of Kelsey's Juliet. The older husky seemed exasperated, especially since Kelsey's other dog, instead of calming the monsters, had gotten riled up by them.

There was only one way to stop the barking. Nate got out his phone and began streaming Dolly Parton. Both puppies snapped to attention, ears perked. Juliet seemed suspicious of this magic, but Nate just wished he could calm himself as easily. He inhaled the aroma coming off his coffee mug to no avail.

"Everyone's impressed with Cody too," Nate said as the monsters "sang" along. "For what?"

"Well, duh." Kelsey cupped her coffee mug, blowing the rising steam. "He's like a billionaire or something, and famous. That shit tends to impress people."

"Are you impressed?"

Kelsey shrugged. "I wouldn't want to do computer stuff, but I wouldn't mind having that much money. Think of how many dogs I could rescue."

That answer didn't help. What Nate really wanted to know was whether Lydia was impressed, too, but Kelsey had put another worry into his head. Could Lydia turn down a guy with Cody's money? Nate didn't think she was greedy or superficial, but Cody had to be really rich. That kind of financial security wasn't something that could be easily dismissed. He probably wasn't a truly terrible person, either, despite Nate's attempts to present him as one. Lydia wouldn't have been friends with someone who was horrible.

Sure, Nate had secured her interest for the moment, but it was becoming harder and harder to convince himself that Lydia's interest in him extended beyond sex. Particularly when Cody had so much more to offer.

Plus, Cody was still hitting on her. Nate knew this even if it hadn't been explicitly stated last night. One of his friends worked at the airfield, so Nate knew that Cody had given Lydia a ride in his plane the other day. They could have just been hanging out together, friendly-like, but Nate didn't trust that for a second. As far as he was concerned, Cody had made his intentions clear. He'd practically straight out told Nate that Lydia was the only thing in this town he cared about.

"Who would mind having more money?" Nate said, glaring at the ceiling. "That's the problem."

"What's the problem?"

"He took Lydia up in his plane."

Kelsey rolled her eyes. "So? Lots of people have planes."

"I bet his is nicer than lots of peoples'. But you're right. So what?" Kelsey's point made him feel a bit better, and Nate grasped on to it with both hands.

"I'm not following you," Kelsey told him.

"Nothing. I'm just saying, so Cody's rich and has a plane and is building a compound, but so what? I run into fucking wildfires for a living. He's not cooler than me."

Nate knew right away he'd said too much, because Kelsey's eyes opened wide. "Oh my God. This is why you dislike Cody, isn't it?"

Nate swallowed, hiding behind his coffee mug. "Because he's an entitled jackass who cheats at skiing?"

"Do you think I'm oblivious? I write romance, you schmuck. You have a thing for Lydia."

"Did you just call me a schmuck?"

"What? Yes. Ian is rubbing off on me, and Micah's

teaching me the best Yiddish curses. Now, stop trying to distract me." She got off the sofa, practically bouncing in her excitement.

"I'm not . . ." He grumbled into the coffee and turned toward the kitchen, feeling heat creep up his neck. This was why he kept his mouth shut most of the time.

Kelsey swore again, working herself into a fit of giddiness, judging by the way she was moving around. Even the monsters lost interest in the music to stare at her. Nate considered turning up the volume to drown out his sister, but he shut it off entirely instead. Nothing could drown out Kelsey when she got something stuck in her head, so he might as well let her do her thing and get it over with.

"How long?" she asked.

He played clueless. "How long what?"

"Don't even try it. How long have you had a thing for Lydia?"

Nate set his coffee next to her TV and got on the floor. He grabbed the closest puppy, not caring which it was, for moral support. "Awhile."

"Can you be more specific?"

Spark did not do moral support unless licking Nate in the face counted. Possibly from the puppy's point of view it did, but Nate disagreed rather vehemently. "High school," he said wrestling Spark for control of his lap. "We were friends."

"In high school?" She screeched, and Nate couldn't blame her. He'd just turned her world upside down. "Holy shit!"

"How's that in Yiddish?"

"I'll have to ask." Kelsey stamped her foot and repeated the phrase a couple of more times in English. "Does Lydia know?"

Nate had to actually ponder that, so he let the squirming puppy go. "It's complicated." He gave her a quick overview of the last thirteen or so years of his life where Lydia was concerned.

"So you haven't actually tried talking to her about any of this?" Kelsey said when he finished. She seemed calmer, but her energy had all gone back to the dogs, who were running around her downstairs like they were possessed.

"No! I don't want to scare her away." Crap. Saying that made him need puppy support again.

"But you're scared she's going to pick Cody over you." Kelsey raised an eyebrow.

"I'm not scared. I just want to punch him a few times."

"God, I'm surprised you used words to say that and not manly grunts."

Nate flipped her off as he drank more coffee.

"Look." His sister got on the floor with him, and Juliet immediately climbed onto her lap, hiding her tiny frame almost entirely behind fur. "You're leaving at some point. Cody, however, is returning. Think of it from Lydia's perspective. It has nothing to do with how badass you are or how rich Cody is. One of you is making himself available, and the other is making himself scarce. That's the real battle you're fighting."

This time Nate did grunt. All of these points were ones he'd already thought about, but when brought up by Kelsey, they sounded even more ominous. And while his reluctance to talk about his feelings didn't sound cowardly, it also didn't sound wise.

"Talk to her?" He cringed.

"Oh my God. Yes. Use your damn words. What is wrong with men? Do you know how many times I've had to say that to people lately?"

"What if I scare her away by suggesting I want more from her?" Nate asked.

"Then you'll know where you stand."

Oh well, if that was all. He'd know exactly where he was standing when Lydia potentially drove a dagger into his chest and he had to stanch the bleeding without her realizing he was dying before her eyes. No big deal.

Also, he really had to stop reading Kelsey's damn books, if that was where his mind went. This time he meant it.

19

LYDIA TWIRLED HER spoon around her bowl of soup. Potato leek was not her favorite, but it was yesterday's special at the Tavern, and the restaurant's leftovers made a more filling lunch than the protein bar she would have eaten normally. Taylor was having an influence on her— encouraging her to eat better food.

Unfortunately, what was left was getting cold as Lydia typed out a response to the latest photo from her sister. Taylor was off today and tomorrow, and she was staying with their mother in Anchorage, wedding dress shopping. Every so often a new photo would arrive on Lydia's phone as her sister tried on various dresses.

Interspersed with her sister's texts was nonstop chatter from her mother. Apparently Taylor had gone ahead and told her that Lydia had taken up drawing again, and her mother wouldn't stop asking questions until Lydia had promised to take some photos later to show her. The enthusiasm was nice, but Lydia suspected Taylor had oversold her abilities.

Lydia shoved another spoonful in her mouth, trying to decide if reheating would make the soup more appealing or if she simply didn't care for potato leek, when the newest text made the decision for her.

It was from Shawn at the front desk. There's a Nate here asking for you.

Overcome with concern, Lydia dropped the spoon and left everything on the table in the empty dining room. Nate popping by the Bay Song was odd. Not that she minded, but if her grandmother or some other Porter-unfriendly family member was lurking around, they would. And anyway, Nate hadn't called and asked if she wanted to see him. She would have said yes if he had, but the more Lydia thought about the not-texting-her-first thing, the more concerned she got.

She worked herself up on the short walk between the dining room and the lobby, and sure enough, Nate was leaning against the check-in desk with a slight frown on his face. "What's wrong?"

Despite his expression, he seemed surprised by the question. "Nothing exactly. Can we talk?"

Lydia blinked at him. If she hadn't trusted that Nate wouldn't lie to her, she'd have been positive that something was very much wrong. "Sure. My office." She gestured for him to follow her.

As caught off guard as she was, she noticed the obvious change in his appearance only as he unzipped his coat. "Your sling is gone."

"Oh yeah." Nate seemed surprised by this as well. "I still have it if I need it, but I'm supposed to try to go without as much as possible."

"That's great."

"Yeah, probably."

Probably? Something was definitely bothering him if that news rated only a probably. Since Nate wouldn't admit it, though, Lydia tried another tactic. "What did you want to—"

"What'swithyouandCody?" Nate spoke so quickly the words came out garbled.

It took Lydia a moment to parse through the question. "Me and Cody?"

Her office felt even smaller than usual with Nate in it, yet he still found room to pace. "Yes."

"There is no me and Cody. I mean, we're friends. Same as always."

"You weren't always just friends." He pulled his hat off and twisted it around in his hands.

Lydia longed to reach out and put a steadying hand over his to save the hat—she'd liked smelling that hat, darn it—but the implications of what Nate was asking finally hit her. He was jealous? Yes, definitely jealous. But what did *that* mean?

She felt like pieces of her were slowly detaching. Emotions, memories, intentions maybe—Lydia didn't know. But her skin could no longer contain her, and bit by bit she was scattering to the winds until there was going to be nothing left.

"Cody and I are just friends. There's nothing else between us."

"Really?" His eyes searched her, not suspicious but concerned. Hopeful even.

Lydia wanted to be annoyed. She ought to be annoyed. Nate had barged in while she was working (yes, she was taking a lunch break, but he hadn't known that), and he was demanding to know about her personal life. These things were none of his business, because there wasn't anything serious between them. But annoyance was one of those emotions that had broken off and left her already.

Lydia tried to grasp at it anyway and failed. What she actually felt was confused and hopeful. Like Nate's behavior meant something good. "Really. Not that it's any of your business. We don't have that kind of relationship either."

Nate scowled. "What kind of relationship do we have?"

Lord, she was not prepared to have this conversation. "I believe 'something risky and fun' were your words."

They very much weren't hers because they tasted like bile on her tongue. Choosing to sleep with Nate had been reckless, and it was certainly fun, but calling it that and only that felt like a punch in the gut when she wanted so much more. Like she'd known she would.

"Because that's what you wanted," Nate said.

"Because that's all we can have!" Lydia started pacing, too, her fingers winding through her ponytail as though she could take all those errant emotions flying around her and twist them into something orderly and neat, something she could shove back inside before Nate realized what a mess he made of her. "You're leaving soon, and your job scares the hell out of me. Fun is our only option."

Nate raised his hands as though to grab her arms, then he seemed to think better of it. He still looked kind of chagrined for being called out about asking about Cody. Probably he was trying not to antagonize her again or overstep, but she *wanted* his hands on her.

She pretty much always wanted his hands on her.

"My job scares you?" he asked.

"It's super dangerous, so yes."

Nate flinched as though that had never occurred to him before. "I love my job."

"I know. And I would never expect you to quit it for me, but it freaks me out." All of this job talk struck Lydia as completely irrelevant. Nate leaving overrode any other consideration. She'd brought up his job only to convince herself of why keeping things *risky and fun* was the best choice. "Anyway, you're leaving so . . ." She didn't know what else to say, and she wasn't going to have words left if this went on much longer.

Nate scratched his chin, frowning again. "So no matter what, when I leave, things have to stop between us."

Lydia collapsed to her desk with a sigh. "I don't see how it can go on."

"So it's just tawdry sex, then?"

Lydia hadn't thought it possible for a man to sound so bummed out by the prospect of tawdry sex. "I'm not sure how much I'm into tawdry, but . . ."

The words finally vanished. She had nothing left, and she simply stared at him, willing him to explain himself. Willing him to put those hands on her to push all her pieces back together. To put them together in a way that could work out for more and longer than tawdry sex.

THIS WAS NOT the way Nate had envisioned this conversation going. In his wildest hopes, Lydia had confessed to being as infatuated with him as he was with her. In his worst fears, she'd admitted to being attracted to Cody and made it clear that she had no interest in anything serious with him.

But this, this was some nightmare in between. In either of those other scenarios, Lydia was fine with the outcome, but in reality she was clearly not fine. She was looking as distressed as he felt, and it was all his fault. The one thing he'd never wanted to do was hurt Lydia.

"Shit." Nate rubbed his eyes, then realized that was the wrong thing to say because Lydia looked even more distraught. He thought she might cry. "I'm sorry."

"For what?" Her fingers twisted together.

"Upsetting you."

"No, it's fine." Lydia shook her head. "We should have this talk. Clear everything up."

He'd told himself not to touch her because once he touched her, he wouldn't want to stop. "Nothing's cleared up. You told me what you think has to happen. Not what you want."

"What I want is—"

He cut her off by placing a finger over her lips, and even that was enough to send shock waves through his body. "What you want matters. Forget everything else, and answer yes or no. Do you want this to be about more than sex?"

He could feel her body trembling through his finger. He needed to kiss her immediately to make up for distressing her. But if she said no, Nate wasn't sure he could. His own disappointment might be the only thing strong enough to kill his desire for her.

"Yes."

Oh, thank God. He was relieved and immensely happy, and in desperate need of kissing Lydia in a way that would make all of these emotions perfectly clear to her.

That was how he kissed her, like it was an invitation for more, a promise that he could make *more* between them work. And—hopefully—like she would forever be disappointed by a kiss if it didn't come from him.

The latter seemed to have an effect at least. Lydia moaned and grabbed his shirt in her hands. Nate's blood burned hotter as her curves pressed into him, threatening him with a loss of control.

"Nate?"

He wasn't sure what she was asking. For him to stop? For him to confirm that he wanted the same thing? For him *not* to stop? So he blurted out the first words he could conjure. "I want more, too, Lydia. So much more. And I want you. Right now, I need you."

One of those answers must have been the right one, because her hands ripped his shirt from the waistband of his jeans. Soft hands grabbed him around the waist, and her nails dug into his back.

"I need you too," Lydia whispered into his neck. Although her grip on him was firm and steady, her voice wavered. Part of it might have been need, but Nate suspected some of it was also fear. She'd admitted as much. She was afraid of losing him, and he wasn't sure how to erase that fear because he feared losing her too.

But he could—he would—be strong for her, and show her that what they had made it worth working through the fear.

He kissed her throat and the soft skin around her chin. He cupped her breasts through her shirt, delighting in the whimpers she breathed on his face. Nate could swear his dick was ready to break free of his pants, but he ignored it. This was about her, about them, and not just about the way he craved her.

"Trust me." He unbuttoned her pants and slid one hand under the silky fabric of her underwear. He wasn't even sure what he was asking her exactly. Trust him to pleasure her? He would never stop if he could. To find a way to make this work? He had no idea how, but Lydia's admission and her trembling voice rattled around his head.

He couldn't leave her. After all this, all his determination to return to work as soon as possible, he couldn't leave her behind. Not again. Possibly, some part of him had known it was inevitable when he'd gone searching for the bracelet he'd never given her. He'd known it in the way she stilled his mind, and the contentment he'd been feeling about being home. But until she'd said the words, that this was more than sex, he'd refused to consider the possibility of staying.

Now he had to. There was no more reason to leave.

"Nate." Her voice shook again, but not with anything like fear.

The fingers on his right hand delved between her folds, slipping through her wetness as he tugged on her pants with his left. "Yes? Is this okay?" She certainly seemed to be enjoying it, but they were in her office. He wasn't positive the door was completely closed.

In answer, Lydia pushed her pants down the rest of the way. That was all the encouragement Nate needed, but when she tried unzipping his as well he had to put a stop to it. "Not yet, love. Let me do this first."

He dropped to his knees, only half aware that the L-word had fallen off his tongue. He wasn't a terms-of-endearment kind of person, and that one seemed particularly loaded. Mostly because it was true, and he couldn't let himself think about it or how easily that revelation had come to him. And if he did his part correctly, Lydia would be too distracted to notice.

Nate didn't bother gently teasing apart her thighs like he had in the past. Her confession had driven him over the edge. He wanted his tongue on her skin and his dick inside of her, and if he could have had both of those at once, he would have been thrilled. But this, this would do too. He could savor her taste, her moans, the way she threaded her fingers through his hair and grinded against his face.

He knew Lydia still thought of herself as reserved and uptight, but she was completely uninhibited with him, and he loved it like he loved everything about her. Her determination to protect her sister, the way she cuddled her cat and played with his dogs, how she had her shit together so well that she'd been able to take control of the family business when everyone had abandoned her, and made it a success. And yes, the way she tasted, and moaned his name, and how her thighs clenched around his head as she came.

He waited until she stopped shuddering to stand back up. Strands of hair had fallen from her ponytail, and he pushed them out of her face so he could kiss her ears. Unlike every other woman he'd met, Lydia had never pierced them, and he found this oddly enticing too.

"I love taking care of you," Nate whispered. There was that word again. The more he said it, the harder it would be for her to ignore, so he needed to stop. Yet he couldn't seem to control his tongue.

Lydia's breath hitched, and she grazed her teeth over his neck, causing shivers to run down his spine. "Do you think anyone heard that?"

He chuckled. "Possibly not. You'll have to scream louder when I bend you over your desk."

She raised her head, eyes wide. "Is that next?"

"If you want me to." If she didn't, he was going to need to go roll around in the snow without a coat until the cold shriveled his junk back to normal size.

"Yes, but . . ." She reached around him and shut the office door the last inch. Then locked it for good measure. "Now. Please."

Grateful that he'd started carrying a condom around with him, Nate fished it out of his wallet. "Anything you want, you get. Anything, Lydia."

He wrapped his arms around her and kissed the top of her head, too chicken to look at her face and see how she felt about that promise. Instead he concentrated on how soft her arms were as they wrapped around his waist, and her hands sliding beneath his jeans and straining to touch the skin beneath his boxers. When he couldn't take it anymore, he kissed her until he didn't know which of them was squirming more, and he pulled her shirt off.

Nate nudged her to turn around. As much as he liked watching her, he wasn't sure he was ready for her to see the emotions painted across his face. And besides, he wanted to hold her, too, and this way he could. With one arm around her, his hand holding a breast and the other delving into her slick warmth, making sure he was pleasuring her as much as she did him, he was lost. He couldn't have gone slowly or gently if he tried, and luckily, she urged him only for what he could give her. Every thrust drove him close to the edge and was like a vise clamping around his heart. He was in love with her. Helplessly in love. Probably always had been. He buried his face in her hair, drowning in the scent of her shampoo, and came seconds after she did.

Well, she couldn't tease him about talking too much during sex this time. It had been too fast and raw for words. Nate wasn't sure he'd ever find the strength to talk again.

Lydia, too, seemed utterly spent. She sagged against him, the tension drained from her body, and Nate did his best to hold her up with one good arm and one questionable one.

That seemed fitting. He was halfway there. He had her, and he had his mind made up. All he needed to do was figure out a plan. But he would, and when he had one, then he would share his decision with Lydia. There was no sense in making her stressed or more worried before then. They were alike in that way—each determined to make the lives of everyone around them easier, to protect them. The difference was that he did it by taking risks and Lydia did it by playing peacekeeper.

If they were going to make this work, if he was going to stay, that would have to change. Nate was comfortable taking fewer risks because of Lydia, and he hoped she would be comfortable causing a bit of trouble to be with him. Judging by what they'd just done in her office, he figured that was a good sign.

20

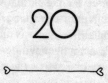

SOMEWHAT AGAINST HIS better judgment, Nate let himself get dragged along to Cody's housewarming party. Like his friends and family, he was curious, and he had to admit that the fear of missing out was real. It was ridiculous, but hey, he was human.

Human—that was also the excuse he was using for why he felt the need to be with Lydia at the party, even if they were still pretending not to know each other in public. Almost a week had gone by since they'd made the jump to more than "tawdry sex." Nate didn't distrust her around Cody, but he sure as hell didn't trust Cody around *her*. A guy who would cheat at skiing and who was used to being fawned over was a guy who might refuse to leave Lydia alone because he felt entitled to her attention. And Lydia, being the gentle peacekeeper that she was, would have a hard time shaking him.

Friday evening rolled around and Nate found himself wandering around the ski lodge–like monstrosity that was to be Cody Miller's vacation home. Between the enormous house and the backyard, where there was an actual ice bar set up for people to drink at and a maze filled with ice sculptures to gawk at, there had to be several hundred people.

Nate left his two younger siblings and their dates by the ice bar and went back into the house, ostensibly to warm up. In truth, he was searching for Lydia. He'd seen her when she first arrived, but she'd been ensnared by a friend. Nate hadn't wanted to appear pushy, so he'd kept his distance until Kelsey and Ian had dragged him outside and he'd lost her. The only upside was that he hadn't seen Cody hovering over her. In fact, he'd seen Cody for an even shorter period of time than Lydia. Presumably he was out there somewhere, making the rounds and showing off his money.

Nate grabbed another appetizer from one of the many tables of food, and pressed his way through the bodies into what appeared to be the main indoor party room. Every few feet he ran into someone else he knew—an old friend from high school, some cousin or other relative, or a Lipin who gave him the stink eye. The endless small talk with people exhausted Nate, but the glares of the Lipins who recognized him kept him too amused to care. If only they knew whom he was looking for and why, some of them would be doing more than glaring. Josh and Taylor, Nate noted, hadn't attended even though they'd been invited too. He was sure they hadn't wanted to deal with the hassle.

The cabin's largest room—the one that made Nate think of a ski or hunting lodge—had floor-to-ceiling windows along one wall, stretching two stories up. The fireplace on the opposite side was enormous, and multiple chandeliers designed to look like barren tree crowns hung from the cathedral ceiling. Nate could probably have fit five of his own rental cabins in just this room alone. For one man, it was ridiculous. Even the air was thick with pine- and cinnamon-scented aromas, as though he'd been transported into a set for *Architectural Digest*.

His height allowed him a decent view of the crowd, but no Lydia. Scowling, Nate popped the last of his appetizer in his mouth and began working his way around the perimeter. The friend he'd seen Lydia talking to earlier was in that direction. It would be a ballsy move to approach a Lipin and ask if they knew where Lydia had gone, but he didn't care. If he was moving back to Helen, everyone was going to have to get used to it.

No, *when* he moved back. He simply hadn't figured out the plan yet. The slipup deepened Nate's scowl and seemed to cause people to move out of his way more quickly.

He stepped into a new, smaller room that was slightly less crowded, but there was still no Lydia in sight. A woman nearby was typing on her phone, and Nate could have smacked himself with the obvious. Of course—he could text her and ask where she was. That was probably what he should have done in the first place rather than go wandering around this not-so-fun house.

"So, Nate."

The familiar voice stopped him cold, and Nate removed his hand from his pocket without his phone. Cody leaned against the wall, holding a beer and wearing a smile that set Nate's teeth on edge.

His host raised a single finger in acknowledgment of a couple of nearby people who called out his name, but he kept his attention on Nate. "I was hoping you'd come."

That seemed hard to believe. "You were?"

"Sure. It's like old times again." Cody raised a hand

as though to slap Nate on the bad shoulder, but he stopped as Nate tensed. "Right. Bum shoulder. Sorry."

The glint in Cody's eye suggested he was neither sorry, nor had he ever actually forgotten that. He'd just wanted to make Nate flinch.

"Healing shoulder," Nate said, allowing himself a smile. He hated this bullshit posturing, but if Cody thought he could outman him or something, that was a joke. As he'd told Kelsey, he ran into forest fires for a living. No pretty-boy tech genius was going to get a rise out of him. "I'm not sure we were ever at the same parties in school."

"True. That whole feud thing." Cody snorted and took a sip of beer. "But I meant the competition. It's fun, right? Gets the blood flowing and all."

Nate stiffened. "What competition?" Sure, *he* knew that he was competing with Cody, but Cody shouldn't know about his relationship with Lydia.

"Lydia."

So much for that. Nate aimed for his best confused expression and let his silence speak for him, as it often did.

Cody rattled on. "I personally dropped off Lydia's invitation to the party, and so I happened to be in her office waiting for her that day. I noticed she had a sketchbook sitting out, and I flipped through it a bit. Turned out, she's sketched you."

Lydia had sketched him on a couple occasions over the past couple of weeks. The monsters too. Nate didn't think he made the most interesting model, but he'd been happy to see her drawing again.

He was not so happy now. "You went through her things?"

"It was sitting on her desk."

Arrogant, prying asshole. The words bounced around inside Nate's skull violently enough to almost override his better judgment. "I don't think Lydia would appreciate that."

"Relax. I'm not going to tell anyone. I know what her family's like." Cody waved off the threat with a flick of his hand before it could even occur to Nate to worry about it.

No, Cody wouldn't tell anyone. Lydia's family would flip out if (when) they learned the truth, and therefore Cody telling them would piss off Lydia. Cody was smart enough to know that would be a sure way to lose her.

"But," Cody continued, "I get why she keeps insisting she's not interested in a relationship. It's because of you, right?"

Nate pressed his lips together, not wanting to give anything away, but mainly not wanting to encourage this bullshit.

"It's all right. You don't have to answer that." Cody took another swig of his beer. "I'm not worried. It can't be anything serious between you, and you'll be leaving eventually. I'll be there to swoop in when you're gone and win her back."

"She's a person. Not something to win." Nate didn't bother to correct Cody's mistaken assumption about him leaving, but if he hadn't already made up his mind to stay for good, this conversation would have done it. He might talk about Lydia not being something to win—and he believed that—but Cody's words had an effect on him anyway. Lydia deserved better than this egotistical jerk, regardless of whether that person was him or someone else.

Cody's smirk suggested he not only felt differently, but he'd decided he was guaranteed to be the winner of this competition. Nate shoved his hands in his pockets, trying to look like he didn't give a shit when in truth, the move simply hid that his hands had balled into fists.

"Good to see you around though, for real," Cody said, dropping some of the arrogance from his tone. "This right here shows me it's possible to bring Porters and Lipins together."

Yes, money and the curiosity that followed it would buy a lot of tolerance, Nate thought as Cody wandered away. But curiosity became satisfied over time, and arrogance would always out itself, and no one liked that. If love couldn't get the two families to stop fighting, it seemed unlikely money would either.

Still doing his best to appear unfazed by the encounter, Nate rambled back into the main room in time to catch a glimpse of Lydia standing by the windows. Finally. He started heading over to her before realizing she appeared to be locked in a heated discussion with another woman with short, gray hair. A woman who Nate was 90 percent sure was her grandmother, the formidable Lipin matriarch.

Whatever it was they were discussing, Lydia's body language clearly indicated distress. Her arms were crossed and she kept shaking her head. Nate was contemplating interrupting the conversation, regardless of the hell it would raise, in order to save Lydia, but before he could decide whether she would appreciate such a move, a third person joined them. Nate didn't have to guess who it was this time—Lydia's father, the mayor. And damn. That made going over to her even riskier.

Instead, he pulled out his phone and sent her a text. Can I help?

Either Lydia didn't hear the text arrive amid the noise, or she chose to ignore the interruption. A moment later, she was urged farther away from Nate by her father, and Cody jumped on a nearby table.

"I want to thank you all for joining me here tonight," he said. He'd abandoned his beer and the smirk, and was in full media-darling mode. Nate suspected Cody practiced his smile in the mirror. "I love my hometown, and I'm excited to be moving back, even if only part-time."

The people around Nate were nodding and smiling happily, but he had to swallow the *Are you kidding me?* that tried escaping from his lips. Unless everything he'd said to Nate a few weeks ago had been a lie, Cody was full of shit. Actually, either way that meant Cody was full of shit, but Nate would bet he'd heard the truth that morning in the park.

"In order to thank the town that gave me my start," Cody was going on, "I'm thrilled to announce that I'm going to be making a gift to our school system so they can upgrade their technology and provide all Helen students with a world-class STEM education."

The room broke into applause, especially as Cody and Lydia's father shook hands. A bunch of people snapped photographs. Nate kept his gaze focused on Lydia, who clapped politely. She was so good at faking, that from afar, Nate couldn't tell if she was genuinely pleased or if she also saw through Cody's charade.

He couldn't blame her if she was touched by the announcement. Regardless of his motives, if Cody actually gave money to the schools, that was at least something decent. In fact, if Cody was determined to show that he could unite Porters and Lipins, there was no better issue. One thing most people could agree on was the importance of educating kids, especially if that improved education didn't take any more taxes out of their pockets.

Nate caught one last glance of Lydia before the crowd

swallowed her, then he headed toward the food, in need of a drink. He couldn't decide on Cody's motive. He could believe that Cody's ego had led him to assume he could mend the feud that had been tearing the town apart for a hundred years. He could also imagine Cody wanted everyone to see him as a benevolent philanthropist, a new Bill Gates in the making. But possibly because of the timing of the announcement, right on the heels of their recent conversation, Nate couldn't shake the idea that this was Cody firing what he assumed would be a winning shot in a competition for Lydia.

If that was so, Nate told himself he didn't have to worry. He was no longer leaving, but returning as well. Even if Lydia didn't know it yet, she'd convinced him. And while he might not have Cody's money to throw around, he had the home court advantage of sorts—he already had Lydia. She was his to lose.

AS WITH HIS decision to return to Helen, Nate opted to keep his conversation with Cody quiet. Lydia already knew Cody was interested in her. She didn't need to know Cody was trying to get under Nate's skin about it. Nate figured that bringing it up would only make him sound whiny and insecure, and it would further stress out Lydia. She had enough to deal with, and besides, he *wasn't* whiny and insecure.

Screw that noise in the back of his head telling him that Lydia's life would be a whole lot easier with Cody than with him.

Lydia had been tense when she'd come over to his cabin tonight, paler than usual and sporting a tightness around her eyes. Unable to forget the heated discussion he had witnessed with her grandmother at the party the other night, Nate had immediately asked if she wanted to talk. He might not be a great role model for that sort of behavior, but he was a good listener. Lydia's response had been to kiss him and demand he sex her into distraction instead. That was even better.

It seemed to have worked, too, because now they rested in his bed, mostly naked under the blankets. Lydia sat between his legs, sketching the monsters, who were curled up on the cushion on the other side of the room. Nate was finger-combing her hair, watching her as she drew, and trying not to let his dick get in the way of what Lydia found soothing, although he was more than ready for round two of orgasming the stress out of her.

Rather unexpectedly, she set down her pen and lowered her head. "Sorry I ignored your texts last night. There was never a good moment for getting away from my family."

"It's fine." As much as he wanted her all to himself, he wasn't the only person in her life, and being open about their relationship in public was not a decision to be made lightly.

"It's not fine though." Lydia rubbed her eyes. "I'm exhausted. They were upset that Taylor and Josh hadn't shown up, then when I pointed out that they would have been upset if Taylor and Josh *did* show up, they got upset about that. Not at me, but at the idea of my sister showing her face, like they hadn't just been wishing her to do it. I can't win with them, and they're getting snippier and snippier with me. I don't know how much longer I can do this."

Nate stopped playing with her hair and wrapped his arms around her. She was so soft and smooth against his skin, and she smelled so good. He longed to press his lips to that sexy hollow around her collarbone, but Lydia clearly needed to talk, even if she'd asked for the more physical option earlier. "So stop. I'm sure your sister doesn't want you to become a punching bag for her. You need to protect yourself too."

"But it's my fault it's getting to be like this. I had it under control until . . ."

Nate could feel her tense. "Until?"

Lydia sighed. "Cody. Their patience, mainly my grandmother's, is getting short with me because I'm not fawning all over the chance to date him. My grandmother's been harping on the fact that I'm not married since I turned twenty-five, and doing everything she can to set me up with the most successful men she can find. And then suddenly, there's Cody. They think he's an answer to a prayer, and I'm blowing it. So now nothing I say or do is given the benefit of the doubt. I used to be the good child who could smooth over any situation. Now I'm the shortsighted and ungrateful one."

Nate was glad she was facing away from him so she couldn't see the grimace on his face. Damn, Cody was messing up everything. It didn't matter that this screwup was probably unintentional.

He began massaging Lydia's shoulders, which had somehow hunched up despite her position. Unfortunately, there was nothing Nate could think of saying or doing himself that wouldn't make it worse for her.

"Well, you know, you could always announce that you're dating me instead," he said, half joking. "That would rip the delusion that you're the good child away, and maybe make them back off."

Although he didn't think she'd do it, Nate wanted her to take the suggestion seriously. But Lydia laughed. "It's tempting, but if I do that, I lose all ability to shield Taylor. And, honestly, I just don't know that I can. I mean, it would be different if you were staying, and then it became something everyone would have to get used to. But it's easier to hide everything otherwise. I'm not brave like you. I was terrified of leaving town to go to college, and you just left and never returned. To fight fires, of all things. I wish I could be bold like that."

Nate swallowed, wishing he was as brave as she thought he was. If that were the case, he'd admit to her that the real reason he left town was because he was scared to see her moving on with her life without him. It had been weakness, not courage.

But because he was scared of her reaction, terrified that these feelings he'd been carrying around for ages would frighten her off, he settled for a half-truth. "I became a firefighter because I wanted to help people. Nothing to do with being brave."

"Something only you would say." She twisted around to give him a wry look.

He snorted and kissed her head.

Across the room, Dolly woke up with a yelp that roused her brother as well. Nate's hope, that he could once again remove Lydia's stress with a little naked exercise, was dashed as the two puppies jumped onto the bed. Spark settled on Lydia's lap, and Dolly nudged her way under his arm with her wet nose.

Lydia grinned, and although it might not have been his hope or his plan, Nate was relieved to see her relax. She pulled her sketch pad out from beneath Spark and rubbed his back. The puppy closed his eyes contentedly, a mood Nate could well relate to.

"Feeling jealous?" she asked the husky.

"Someone is," Nate said drily, eliciting another laugh.

"I will pet you more later."

"I was thinking more about how his head is buried between your legs."

Lydia smacked Nate's knee through the blankets. "There are several layers between us."

"Humph." He leaned over and kissed the back of her neck since it was the best he could do with the new additions to the bed in his way.

All joking aside, Nate didn't mind the break in the tension, and he liked the way Lydia and the monsters had taken to one another. He was less certain how her cat felt about him, but he'd spent a whole lot less time at her place simply because it was easier for them to hide at the cabin. Still, he was confident he could win over the pickiest of cats. Animals loved him.

Now all he had to do was make Lydia love him too. When he was certain he had, maybe he'd find the courage that she was convinced he had to tell her how much he loved her as well.

21

LYDIA CREPT UP the stairs to her apartment in the frigid, dark morning. A light dusting of snow had fallen overnight, softening her footsteps. Below her, the inn stirred as Marie and the kitchen staff finished preparing breakfast and the housekeeping staff got started on the day. But the guest rooms were almost entirely quiet, with no lamplight peeping through cracks in the curtains.

Lydia's breath came out in little white puffs as she unlocked her door. On the nights she stayed over at Nate's, she arrived home tired but happy. Even last night, when she'd thought it would be impossible to shake off her stress, Nate had found ways to comfort and console her. She'd slept well against his side, able to put aside her worries about her family for a few hours.

She needed him to stay, if only for the way he was better at relaxing her than a glass of wine. But she couldn't ask or even hint at it. It was a selfish wish. Nate loved his job, and eventually, he'd go back to work and back to Washington. He hadn't even suggested the possibility of a long-distance relationship, although Lydia wasn't sure how she'd feel about it if he did. Any relationship with him would be better than none, but she'd be left to deal with her family without his touch to ease her mind.

Yanking off her boots and coat, Lydia put these thoughts aside. Her anxieties could—and would—follow her around later. For the moment, she needed to focus on a quick shower and change of clothes so she could meet Taylor in the inn's kitchen for breakfast and to review the day's work plan.

Merlot welcomed her home with a plaintive meow around her ankles. Okay, new plan. First she'd feed and play with her cat, then shower and change.

Lydia knelt down and petted him, and he rolled over, giving her access to his belly. "Oh, you poor thing. You really did miss me. I'm sorry I didn't come home last night."

She rubbed him another minute, then Lydia got out Merlot's breakfast. The tabby darted over to the food bowl, less interested in more love than in his meal. Still, Lydia felt guilty, and she vowed to come home during her lunch break to play with him.

That accomplished, she started toward the bathroom when someone knocked on her door. Frowning, since no one should be knocking, especially at this time of the morning, Lydia opened it and found Taylor shivering on her stoop without a coat.

"What are you doing?"

Taylor pushed by her into the warmth, and Lydia shut the door while her sister removed her boots. "I could ask the same question of you. I saw you walk up the steps a moment ago, and those were the clothes you were wearing yesterday."

Lydia couldn't stop herself from glancing down at her

clothes, despite knowing Taylor was correct. "So they are."

"And I heard from Dad you were dodging Cody at his party, so I guess you weren't overnighting with him."

Good Lord, how had she gone from the child her parents talked to about the *other* child, to the child *being* talked about? Lydia felt her cheeks flush. "Good guess."

"So?" Taylor stood in her way, blocking the hall to the bathroom.

"You're way too chipper for this hour of the morning."

"And you're not getting away that easily."

"Tay."

"Lyd."

Lydia's eyebrows shot up. "You've never called me Lyd before in your life. No one does. It sounds ridiculous."

Taylor snorted. "Hey, you start acting like me, you get your named shortened like me."

"I'm not acting like you." Lydia dodged under her sister's outstretched arm and ran into her bedroom.

"Staying the night at someone else's place? And don't tell me this is the first time; I know it's not. Refusing to talk about it? Running away from your family? Please. You sound exactly like me." Taylor leaned against the doorway. "Which really makes me wonder what you're hiding."

"I . . ." *Damn.* Taylor actually had a point. When she put it that way, Lydia was acting a lot like her more rebellious younger sibling. Factor in that the guy she was secretly seeing was a Porter, and she and Taylor might have traded places.

Taylor's smile was triumphant. "See?"

Lydia swallowed and plopped on her bed. "What's gotten into me? I just thought I'd have a little fun, and suddenly I'm acting . . ." Several less-than-flattering descriptors danced on her tongue, but she was afraid Taylor might feel insulted, even if she didn't mean them negatively, so Lydia stopped herself. "Like you."

"No shit." Taylor sat next to her. "Got to say, this is extremely entertaining. Also, I should rephrase—I suspect I do know what's gotten into you lately. I just don't know who it belongs to."

Lydia shoved her over. Blood rushed from her cheeks to the tips of her ears. She also hadn't laughed like this in a long time. Innuendo aside, the more she thought about it, the more she felt like she had a clue what had happened after all.

She was in love with Nate. Nate had threatened to make her have fun, and he'd ended up driving her absolutely wild. She was acting against all reason. Not just impractical, but daring.

Lost in these revelations, she wasn't ready for Taylor to sit up and shove her in return. Lydia fell over, silently laughing.

"Come on! Tell me," Taylor said. "If you don't, I'll be reduced to sending you eggplant emojis at random times until you crack up inappropriately and really cause a scandal."

"Harsh, Tay."

"It's only because I love you, and I'm nosy. And you forced me to confess to you about Josh before anyone else knew. So?"

Ah, Lydia couldn't argue with that. She'd caught Taylor in a lie when her sister had been trying to hide her relationship with Josh. She supposed turnabout was fair in this case.

Lydia rubbed her face, trying to be serious. "So."

Taylor cleared her throat impatiently.

"I've kind of been seeing Nate."

"Just so we're clear—Nate Porter."

"We're clear." Lydia cringed as the room fell silent.

Then Taylor jumped off the bed and screamed, probably loud enough that she could be heard in the kitchen. "Holy shit! Since when?"

As Lydia filled her in, going all the way back to high school, Taylor danced around the room like a possessed woman, alternately gawking and laughing so hard she looked like she might cry.

"Oh shit." Taylor wheezed and doubled over. "So this is why when I told you about me and Josh, you were way cooler with it than I expected."

Lydia adjusted her shirt, hoping to regain some dignity, then she remembered she still needed to remove it and shower. She was going to be late. Luckily, she was her own boss. "It had something to do with it, yes. It didn't seem fair for me to judge you, and I knew all Porters weren't necessarily demon spawn."

"You always did a good job of hiding it."

"The good kids can get away with murder."

Taylor wrinkled her nose. "True. Whereas I could never get away with anything. But whatever—I can't believe you didn't tell me!"

"I'm sorry! I thought about it many times. But you would have encouraged me, and I didn't want encouragement. I wanted someone to talk me into being sensible, and let's be real. That's not you."

Taylor sucked on her bottom lip as she considered this. "That's fair. You're right. I *would* have encouraged you. You and Nate—I like it."

With an eye on the time, Lydia tugged off her socks. "That's one person."

"You know the rest of the cool-kids club won't either. Josh and I are paving that road for you."

"I do know that. I'm thankful for that." Lydia pulled out her hair tie, catching a glimpse of herself in the mirror. She looked tired, which was unfortunate, but also happy. And she still looked liked herself. She might be acting like her sister, but she didn't see any new spark inside her.

"It's weird," she added, seeing Taylor watching her. "I always assumed that if I acted bold and daring, I'd feel it. But I don't. I'm still scared."

Like she'd told Nate last night—she wasn't brave. Is this what he felt when he insisted he wasn't brave either? That he was just doing what he needed to do, despite his emotions?

"Scared of what?" Taylor asked.

"Of our families finding out, of Nate leaving." Lydia bit her lip. "Of not knowing who I am if I'm not the good child anymore." She made air quotes around *good*, but she figured Taylor understood her anyway.

Taylor handed her the bathrobe. "I don't know if I've ever felt bold or daring. I've just done what I've wanted to do, and to hell with what other people thought. I think it was always more about being stubborn and refusing to let other people define me."

"You always were exceptionally stubborn." Lydia smiled.

"I think you mean just exceptional." Taylor stuck out her tongue. "But honestly, it's pushing through fear that makes you bold. And from the sound of it, this is who you've always been, whatever anyone else has thought. You're not losing who you are; you're finally realizing the truth."

Lydia frowned at her. "Since when does my younger sister get to go around handing out life advice?"

"Please. Since I dated a Porter first, obviously. I'm not only wise, I'm a trendsetter."

"We'll see about that." Lydia shut the bathroom door, so Taylor didn't notice her smile fading. Her sister might be onto something, but her situation with Nate wasn't the same as Taylor's had been with Josh. The younger couple might be smoothing out the Lipin-Porter relationship road—kind of—but Lydia still saw plenty of obstacles standing in her way.

22

IT WAS FLURRYING as Nate pulled his SUV into John's driveway. He'd just finished with PT, and his shoulder was predictably sore, but he was otherwise feeling good. Jaime, the sadist, was pleased with his progress, and overall Nate's moments of pain were growing less frequent. If he hadn't made up his mind about moving home, he'd have been looking forward to returning to work.

But he had decided, and therefore this meeting with John was fortuitous. Nate didn't know why his former mentor had insisted on meeting at his house, but he intended to inquire as to whether John had heard anything about potential positions opening up anywhere nearby. Any job that kept him in Alaska was better than one that had him living in Washington, but it wasn't like Alaska was a small state. Still, the closer to Helen, the better. And Nate didn't need other people discussing rumors about him returning before he told Lydia, so privacy wasn't a bad thing.

Nate parked and got out the monsters. John had been

eager to see them again, too, so Nate had swung by the cabin on his way over and picked them up.

The front door opened before Nate could knock, and John's wife ushered him inside with a hug and a lot of pets for the puppies, who were always pleased to meet someone new. "John's in the den," she said, leading the way.

After five minutes, during which Nate accepted a cup of coffee and watched John play with the monsters, Nate began to wonder if the entire reason John had insisted on meeting at his house had been because he wanted the puppies. Not that Nate could blame him.

Finally John seemed to recall that his coffee was getting cold, and he sat down with a sigh. "I miss Bruno," he said as the monsters sniffed his shoes.

"I'm surprised you haven't gotten a new dog."

"Thought about it. Darla's all for it," he said, referring to his wife. "I think after I officially retire, I will."

Nate blinked. "You're thinking of retiring?"

It shouldn't have surprised him, and yet it did. Even though he saw John every few years and had noticed the gray in his hair, John was still the man Nate had met when he first expressed an interest in firefighting.

John nodded, tapping his fingers against his coffee cup. "I haven't said anything to anyone yet, but that's why I wanted to meet with you here. Someplace where no one's listening in to spill the beans before I make an announcement. You know what this town can be like."

Nate laughed. He did, and it seemed John's reasoning had been similar to his own. "I'm the first to know?"

"The first who's not Darla. We've been talking about this for years. Going to sell the house, buy one of those huge RVs, and drive. She's got family in Philadelphia, if you can believe it. We're going to drive out there to see them." A dreamy look crossed his face as he described their plans.

Nate shook his head, amused but also sad to see John leaving just as he was planning to return. It seemed they were never meant to work together for long. "Now, who's got a fire burning under his feet to get out of this place?"

"It's true," the older man said. "But I've lived around this area most of my life. About time I got to see more of what this continent has to offer. What I'm curious about is you."

His brown eyes were penetrating, and Nate felt unexpectedly exposed. Like John had already seen through him and knew he'd made a decision to move back home. "Me?"

"I got the sense during our last conversation that you were no longer so opposed to spending more time here. That whatever had driven you away was no longer pushing on your soul."

"Hey now, I never admitted to being driven away."

John's "Hmm" suggested he thought otherwise. "But am I wrong?"

"No, you're not wrong about me being less opposed to returning." Returning made him think of Lydia, and thinking of her brought a smile to his lips.

"Thought not." John sipped his coffee. "That's the other reason I wanted to talk to you here. There's going to be a job opening when I leave."

Nate almost dropped his cup, and the noise startled the monsters, who ran over to him in alarm. "Sorry, guys." He rubbed their heads while they licked him and made sure he was okay.

John said nothing until the puppies calmed down, but he raised an eyebrow. "Was that interest?"

That had been the excited response of a drowning

man who'd just been shown a rope, but not yet thrown it. "You could say that."

"Don't be too eager," John said, although Nate's reaction seemed to have pleased him. "I'm going to have to promote from within for my position, but we will need someone new full-time. If you're serious and that interests you, I don't see a good reason why that can't be you."

"Right, obviously." *Don't be too eager* was wise advice. Nate was no longer worried that Lydia was going to run screaming in horror if he announced he planned to move home, but it was still just one step of several in his plan to make her his permanently. He should be cool and casual about telling her. Give her time to react and base his responses on her level of excitement. He should absolutely not do anything like barge into her workplace again to surprise her, because that sort of behavior— although it had worked out well once—was probably not appreciated.

"Sounds great," Nate said.

AN HOUR LATER, he barged into the Bay Song, because he apparently obeyed his own directives as well as the monsters did when they got too excitable. Hell, he felt like a puppy today. Nate had spent another half hour talking to John and learning more about the position and John's road trip plans, but he'd heard only every other word.

He was like Dolly listening to her namesake, but doing all he could to keep his excited howling internal.

He was Spark about to attack a ball of frozen peanut butter and wondering how the universe could be such an amazing and benevolent place.

He was probably going to annoy Lydia, but he couldn't

help himself as excited energy propelled him through the hotel's main doors.

The desk clerk was currently helping someone, which was just as well. Nate remembered to get out his phone, and he sent Lydia a text, telling her he was in the lobby and wanted to talk. She appeared only seconds later from the direction of her office.

"Is this becoming a habit?" she asked. She appeared to be fighting down a smile, a definite improvement over last time when he must have worried her.

Nate finally had the self-awareness to cringe. "Sorry. I know you're working."

"I can't tell if your timing is fantastic or awful." Lydia motioned for him to follow her toward her office. "On one hand, yes, I'm working. On the other, last time you caught me during my lunch break, and this time I'm about fifteen minutes from calling it a day anyway, so I guess it's no big deal."

"Sorry." Feeling a bit more like an ass, Nate rubbed his earlobe. He caught himself almost immediately and dropped his hand before Lydia noticed. "I just, uh . . ."

Lydia shut the door and cut off his train of thought of with a kiss. So much for words. Nate hadn't managed to unzip his coat yet, but screw it. He wrapped his arms around her and pressed her body into his through the layer of down. Her lips tasted like a mix of coffee and sugar, and she wore her hair up in a loose bun. Half of him wanted to pull it apart and entwine his fingers in her hair, and the other half rather liked the idea of doing naughty things to her while she was dressed in a particularly businesslike way.

"So everything's okay?" she asked, pulling away.

"Yeah, shit." He cursed himself for acting so impulsively. Puppies got away with acting like puppies only

because they were tiny and cute, descriptions which did
not apply in his case. "I got some promising news, and
you need to know what I'm doing. But I should probably
have called or made plans to see you."

Some of Lydia's good mood drained from her face.
"Is this about your shoulder? Are you leaving already?"

"No. That's actually what I wanted to tell you. I might
have a job prospect here. Well, I will have one, and it
probably won't start until I'm ready to go back to work."

Rather than looking as thrilled as he felt, Lydia's
brow pinched, and Nate's stomach sank. He'd warned
himself that it was entirely possible that she would not
be happy about him staying. That for all she thought she
wanted to be with him for something beyond this temporary fling, when it became a real possibility, she'd discover her heart wasn't into it. That some wishes were
better off as wishes because reality ruined them. In this
case, reality being the feud.

"I thought you loved your job," Lydia said.

"I do." *But I love you more.* Nate swallowed down the
words since they might only make this more awkward.
"I wouldn't be giving up firefighting. I'd just be doing it
here instead, like I used to. I know you can't just pick up
and move the family business, which is why I never suggested it, but I can move my job."

That was not how he'd intended to tell her any of this,
but he had told himself to let her reaction guide him, so
he was. He might have done a lousy job of not barging
into her hotel, but he could course correct.

"No, I can't," Lydia said. "I could never re-create the
Bay Song's history somewhere else. But it won't be the
same for you either. Nothing here would be as exciting
or as high stakes."

Was Lydia trying to talk him out of it? Nate couldn't

tell if this was concern for him or if she was trying to find a way out of this.

He pressed on. Since he'd interrupted her day, he might as well commit, even if he tempered his enthusiasm a bit. "It's true that I used to want that, or I thought I did. But the truth is, I like doing my job and helping people. Anytime someone's life is threatened, the stakes are plenty high. I don't feel the need to go chasing danger anymore."

There was more he should explain to her, like how she was a large part—if not the main part—of why he'd left in the first place, but until he had confirmation that he wasn't making an ass out of himself, he would hold in the longer story.

Lydia let out a long breath. "Really?"

And there was his confirmation. The way she asked killed off Nate's confusion. There was no mistaking the hope in her tone. "Really. You quiet my mind, and I like it. Besides, being with you is going to be more excitement than we might want."

He took her hands, and Lydia broke into a smile. "When did you decide this?"

Nate started to make a quip about how they were almost in the exact same spots as when he made the decision, but even though that was technically true, it seemed like the decision had been developing in the back of his mind for much longer. Hell, he'd known it was a mistake thinking he could ever leave her again from the very first night they'd run into each other.

"A bit ago," he said. "I didn't want to say anything to you until I figured out a way to make it work."

"A bit?" Lydia sounded incredulous. "You've been leaving me hanging, dreading your leaving for a *bit*?"

Okay, that was not what he'd been going for. Nate

winced. "I thought it might stress you out more if you knew what I was trying to make happen."

Lydia squeezed his hands. "I think you got it backward. It would have made me happy and less stressed."

"Oh." He supposed he could see that in retrospect.

"When did you find out about the job?" Lydia asked.

"Um, like, about forty minutes ago?"

To his surprise, Lydia dropped his hands and stepped back, bumping into her desk. "So you came here immediately?"

Nate raised his arms. "I was doing my best to *not* leave you hanging."

Lydia gaped at him, and confusion once more threatened to overtake Nate. Then Lydia screamed. He told himself it was a happy scream, not a he'd-broken-her scream. He was about to double-check when she threw her arms around him.

Okay, then. Definitely a happy scream.

Nate pressed her closer, wishing he'd been smart enough to use that last couple of minutes to take off his coat so he could feel her better. But something of Lydia was better than nothing of her, and he lowered his face to her head, inhaling the sweet scent of her shampoo and brushing his lips against her soft hair.

Lydia's phone rang, but she ignored it, and Nate was relieved. Nothing, not a phone nor his bulky jacket, was going to force him to release her before they were ready. And now that he was returning, he would never have to release her at all.

NATE WAS MOVING back to Helen? Lydia could barely believe it. In her joy, she was willing to overlook the fact that he'd apparently been considering the move for a while and hadn't given her the slightest hint. No question, part of her wanted to smack him for that. She could have avoided so much needless anxiety. But she could get over it, especially since it sounded like he'd thought he was doing her a favor. Leave it to Nate to err on the side of saying less. Since he would be hanging around and clearly intended to keep her around, too, they might need to have a conversation about communication practices, but she was sure she'd made her own mistakes as well.

Besides, for the moment, all she wanted to do was hold him, this thick coat he was wearing be damned. Oh, and kiss him too. It came to her as an afterthought. She'd been too busy grinning to properly kiss him.

Lydia rectified that situation immediately, stretching up to meet his lips, which didn't require much effort at all. Nate was just as eager, and his mouth was on hers instantly. She melted into him, silently cursing his coat some more because she wanted to feel his body. Kissing him without touching his skin and the hard planes of his muscles was torture.

Nate's hands cupped her head, his fingers delving into her hair. The kiss, which had started hard and hungry, slowed. He pulled back slightly, nibbling on her bottom lip and caressing her mouth with his tongue. Stubble scratched her chin, and Nate's gentler, more deliberate kisses made her want to rub that stubble over every inch of her. It was time to take his coat off and go for round two of sex in her office. They needed to celebrate, and at the moment, she just needed him.

As if reading her mind, Nate trailed a finger down her cheek and pressed it over her lips. Instead of removing his coat, though, he brushed her forehead with his mouth. "I was being serious about the possibility of feud excitement, you know."

Even thinking about their families' inevitable anger couldn't dull Lydia's happiness or the hunger Nate's touch aroused in her. "I'm aware. I've been a firsthand witness to everything my sister's been dealing with."

Nate smiled ruefully. "There's going to be no more saying you're not brave."

She wanted to laugh at that, but it wasn't really funny. "Taylor said something to me the other day about how being bold doesn't mean not caring about consequences. It's about pushing through the fear. I guess I understand you a bit more. I want this too much to let worries stand in my way. I thought I was too practical for that, but maybe I just wasn't sufficiently motivated before."

He grinned, and the way his eyes crinkled was positively breathtaking. "I motivate you, huh?"

"You need to take that coat off so I can punch your hard stomach." Lydia rolled her eyes. "Yes, you've been motivating me to do all kinds of things I never thought I'd do."

"I knew you had it in you."

"And that you would be sufficient motivation to bring out my inner wild child?"

Nate shrugged, not at all modestly. "More like I hoped."

Lydia grabbed his head and kissed him, pleased to make Nate stumble into her with surprise. He grabbed her waist to steady himself. Yup, she was a total wild child. Laughing, she pulled back. "Maybe I got tired of pretending to be the perfect child."

Nate shook his head. "You will always be perfect to me. You always have been."

That kind of line shouldn't have made her blush, except that with Nate, nothing felt like a line. When he spoke, it was only to say something truly important to him. Lydia's cheeks warmed, which was pretty ridiculous under the circumstances.

She reached for him again when her phone rang a second time. With a groan, she retrieved it from her pocket, determined to temporarily shut it off so she could enjoy some private Nate time, then saw it was her father calling.

Nate must have seen the exasperation on her face. "Take it if it's important. Remember—I'm not going anywhere."

Lydia laughed, liking the sound of that. "No idea if it's important, but if he wants to reach me, my dad will keep on calling."

And after all, she might as well get used to family interfering in her relationship with Nate.

That thought was almost enough to wipe away her smile.

"Hi, Dad." Lydia sat on her desk and watched Nate unzip his coat. Finally.

"Hi, sweetheart, I'm sorry to bother you." Wherever her father was, there was a lot of noise in the background, making it difficult to hear. "We've got a bit of a situation. We're calling everyone on the emergency volunteers list, but I wanted to call you myself. Can you come down to the town hall to help out?"

That did manage to wipe away her smile. "Situation?"

"A couple girls have gone missing. One of them is your friend Jen's daughter. Abby."

23

AFTER LYDIA TEXTED Taylor and asked her to feed Merlot, Nate followed her to the town hall. Lydia glanced around for Jen and her husband, but didn't see them among the crowd that had gathered, so she tracked down her father in his office. He was on the phone and hung up soon after she appeared. He didn't look frazzled, but he did seem older. As though his hair had picked up a few more strands of gray over the last hour.

Still, it was a testament to how focused he was on the kids that he didn't make any sign of surprise at seeing Nate on her heels.

"What can I do?" Lydia asked. She was ready and eager to help, for both her friend's sake as well as Abby's, but uncertain as to what she could do. Helen was not a large town and it had a correspondingly small police force, but with a child disappearance, particularly in winter, time was a pressing concern.

Her father tugged at his beard, seeming to look straight

through Nate. "I thought you might be a comfort to Jen. Also, we need someone to stay behind and answer the phone in case someone calls the town number with information after the building closes. Normally, that's Jen's job, but under the circumstances, she needs help and you can do both."

"Yeah, absolutely." Lydia pulled out her bun, for the first time noticing that Nate had nearly destroyed it earlier. "Where are Jen and Ethan?"

"Over at the police department," her father said, "which is where I'm heading. Ethan's trying to convince her to stay behind."

"You're putting together search parties, I assume?" Nate said. "I can help."

Her father glanced at Nate and nodded. Confusion briefly passed over his face, but if he wondered why a Porter had arrived with his daughter, he was concerned enough about the missing girls to overlook it. "We're recruiting volunteers, so if you're able, your help is welcome."

"What happened?" Lydia asked as her father pulled on his coat. "You said there were girls, plural."

"Not clear." Gregory Lipin hurried past both of them on his way toward the lobby. "Jen and Ethan reported Abby missing first. While their information was being taken, their neighbor called to say she couldn't find her daughter either."

Lydia chewed on her lip, recalling that Jen had said that Abby was obsessed with the Porter girl's puppy. She didn't get a chance to mention this, though, because as soon as her father stepped foot into the lobby, he was accosted by the anxious crowd.

"We're putting together search parties next door," her father called out, using his booming voice to best advantage. "If you want to volunteer, head over. Otherwise, I've got nothing to add at the moment."

Nate grabbed Lydia's hand and gave it a reassuring squeeze. "Jen who? She's a friend?"

"Fitz," Lydia said, struggling to remember Jen's non-married name. Nate would have likely known who she was from school, but in her half-panicked state, Lydia's memory couldn't seem to reach that far into the past. "She went to school with us. Abby is her daughter. She's a sweet kid."

"We'll find her."

Nate said it with the same confident assurance as he'd said he wasn't brave. With him around, these were just things that were. Lydia knew that he couldn't be certain, but he made it easy to believe him.

The light flurries from earlier in the day had grown heavier. Fat flakes landed on Lydia's face as they crossed the grounds, and a bitter wind stung her cheeks. Twenty minutes ago, her world had felt warmer and brighter. Now the evening was darker and colder than it had been in a long time.

"Where have people already looked?" Nate asked.

Her father glanced over his shoulder as he opened the police department door. "Got to get that update from Ron," he said, referring to the police chief. "Neighbor across the street says they saw both girls get off the school bus. So far, it sounds like the girls might have wandered off into the woods. That should make it easier to track them, but with the snow coming down . . ."

With snow coming down, and the temperature being what it was—Lydia shivered, stepping into the overly warm building. If it had been crowded at the town hall, it was a circus in here.

Nate bent over and whispered in her ear. "I'm going

to go see who I need to talk to about getting on a search party. Find your friend. We can finish our talk later."

He kissed her head, and Lydia didn't even have the wits to feel nervous about who might have witnessed the act. She felt better that Nate was helping out, and reassured, but also too worried for Abby and her parents, as well as their neighbors.

Despite the size of the department, Lydia was unable to find Jen and Ethan in the densely packed crowd. She stood off in the back for the next ten minutes, breathing in fumes of stale coffee, cigarettes, and stress while the police provided more detailed information to everyone and divided volunteers into search teams.

One thing that heartened Lydia was that there was a good mix of people helping out. Lipins and friends, Porters and friends, as well as the town workers, had gathered and all were eager to put aside differences and find the missing children. It wasn't particularly surprising, but it was nice to see that for the moment, there were concerns that could override any feud-related hatred.

Once the teams began clearing out, Lydia waved goodbye to Nate, her father, and the assorted other people she knew, and she headed toward Jen, who was hunched over on a folding chair near the rear exit. Only a few stragglers remained.

"Hey." She crouched down next to Jen, and her friend raised her head. Dried tears stained her cheeks, and her lips were pale.

Jen grabbed her close and brought her in for an off-balance hug. "Your father told me you were here."

"I'm here. Let's get you across the street where there's more room to spread out and we can handle the phones." Also where the smell of a few dozen stressed-out bodies didn't linger in the air, and Lydia knew where to find a decent stash of coffee and tea.

Jen nodded miserably. "I wanted to go out there with them. Ethan went."

Lydia wasn't sure it had been wise to let Ethan go either. In his distress, he was unlikely to be the most conscientious searcher, but it hadn't been her call. No doubt there was some sexism behind the decisions to let Ethan go but not Jen. This didn't seem like the time to point any of this out though. "You're doing your part by helping me with the phones. I haven't done it in a while, and we need people in both buildings in case someone calls with news."

Jen's frown suggested she didn't quite buy that excuse—and rightly so—but she acquiesced anyway.

Lydia nodded at the police dispatcher, who remained at her desk, and led Jen over to the clerk's office back at the town hall. It was officially after hours now. The building was technically closed, and only a few employees remained.

"Do you want something?" she asked. "Tea?"

Jen tapped her fingers nervously against her jeans and shrugged. "Something sweet maybe. Something with caffeine."

Lydia wasn't sure if caffeine was the best idea, but she understood her friend's need to feel completely alert and focused. There was a Keurig machine in the break room, so she made Jen a cup of half-caff and poured hazelnut creamer into it. Then she brought that and a cup for herself over to her friend's desk.

"Tell me what happened," Lydia said.

She had no idea how to best comfort someone who was going through an ordeal she couldn't even imagine, but she must have asked the right question. Some of the intense haze that had fallen on Jen's face lifted. She seemed relieved to talk.

"They're saying that other girl is missing too," Jen said after reciting the same facts Lydia had already heard between her father and the police. "Julia."

"The girl next door with the puppy."

"Abby was so fascinated with that puppy." Jen sniffed and wiped away a new tear. "I knew it was a bad idea to let them talk."

Lydia sipped her coffee, surprised by that detail. Jen had been insistent that the girls not get friendly. "They talked?"

"A little. I didn't like it, but Ethan thought . . ." Jen grimaced. "Abby knows better than to wander away. She must have followed that Porter girl."

Lydia pressed her lips together, unsure of what to say. New, wild Lydia had the urge to defend the other girl and make it clear that Porters weren't demons sent to lead Jen's daughter astray, but that wouldn't be helpful. Jen needed comfort, and old Lydia wanted her to have it. Somewhere, there had to be a middle ground that let Jen vent without demonizing an entire family, but Lydia was in no state to figure that out.

"We'll get to the bottom of what happened when we find them," she said, pushing Jen's coffee closer to her.

"What if we don't?"

"We will." The woods near where Jen lived were vast and snow was falling, but there were at least thirty people out there searching in the dark. And there would be tracks in the snow, even if faint. And Nate was one of those people tracking the girls. It was totally irrational for Lydia to put so much faith in him, but he'd randomly rescued her back in high school. Saving people was what he did for a living. Irrational it might be, but with him out there, Lydia felt more confident than she had any right to.

Nate just had that effect on her. When he was around, she felt safe. Cared for. Loved. Although, he'd never actually said the L-word. Of course, neither had she. Perhaps she should. If there was one lesson to take away from this ordeal, it might be that she shouldn't take anything for granted. She should tell the people she loved that she loved them while she had the chance. It was heart-wrenching to see what the possibility of losing them might look like. Abby wasn't even her daughter, but Lydia knew she wouldn't sleep tonight if she wasn't found. What Jen and Ethan were feeling was beyond her comprehension.

Perhaps it wasn't being wild or brave, after all, to declare to the world that she wanted to be with Nate. It was simply human to choose to put love first.

"We will find them," Lydia reiterated. "They're two tiny girls. They couldn't have gotten far."

"They got far enough that neither Ethan, nor I, nor Julia's parents could find them." Jen blinked away tears.

"There are a lot more people searching now."

They fell into silence, Lydia sipping coffee her jittery nerves didn't need and Jen mostly staring into space. Lydia tried a couple of times to encourage her to talk, but Jen often trailed away, understandably distracted.

She checked in with Taylor via text and passed the time in a nervous haze until voices in the lobby drew her attention. The building should have been closed, but under the circumstances she wouldn't be surprised if the doors had been left unlocked. Either way, Lydia doubted it was anyone coming in with news. In that case, someone would have called. But the hopeful look on Jen's face tore her up inside as they made their way up front.

"What happened?" A red-haired woman of similar age to Lydia and Jen stood in the lobby, dripping snow-melt onto the floor. She had a young boy with her, who couldn't be more than two or three years old. She turned on Jen the moment Jen and Lydia appeared. "What did you do?"

Lydia recognized the new woman, but she didn't know her name. "I'm sorry. The building is closed."

"I'm not talking to you," the redhead snapped. "That's my niece who's gone missing, and I want answers. Were you supposed to be watching them?"

The question was directed at Jen, whose pale face regained a bit of color. "My Abby was playing in the back-yard. I don't know anything about your niece. Why don't you take it up with her parents?"

"Because her parents are out there in the cold, search-ing, like good parents do." The red-haired woman sneered. "What are you doing—sitting on your ass? This is probably your fault."

"Hey!" Lydia inserted herself between the two women, seeing Jen's fear transform into fury. "Jen is here because she works here, in case anyone calls the town with infor-mation. You need to calm down. If you want to help, the police station is right over there."

That finally got the woman's attention. "You're Lydia Lipin, aren't you? This is none of your business, so stay out of it."

Lydia bristled, because the redhead was partially right. She was neither a town employee nor a family member. But she was on the town's emergency volunteer list, and Abby was important to her. She also wasn't con-frontational, though, so rather than bring that up and get dragged into the fighting, she raised her hands in what was supposed to be a placating gesture. "Look, tensions are high because we're all worried. Let's not make this more stressful for anyone. That's all I'm asking."

"Oh, fuck off, Lipin bitch." The woman spun around and, intentionally or not—Lydia couldn't tell—she smacked Lydia's arm as she stormed out.

Lydia had been holding her half-filled coffee cup, and the contents went flying all over her shirt. She bit down a stream of curses, which was fine, because Jen let them fly in her place. Lydia just grimaced at the sticky, smelly mess she'd become while Jen vented some of her tension at the other woman.

A couple of minutes later, Lydia's phone rang as she was blotting up the worst of the coffee, and she quickly dumped the paper towel into the trash. "Dad?"

"We found them. Ethan's calling Jen. Can you bring her to the hospital?"

Lydia was already racing out of the bathroom so she could grab her coat. "Are they okay?"

"I think so," her father said. "I don't have the details."

Jen was getting off the phone, too, as Lydia entered her office. "I need a ride. They found them."

"On it." Lydia threw her jacket over her damp shirt, ignoring the unpleasant sensation of the wet fabric clinging to her skin. It was a potent reminder that no matter what strides her sister and Josh had made toward healing the Lipin-Porter rift, they were only baby steps. If she was going to be with Nate, the road was going to be rocky.

Rocky, but worth it. It was possibly just the adrenaline high of knowing the girls had been found, but Lydia was more convinced of that than ever.

Lydia dropped Jen off by the entrance to the Helen Regional Hospital ER, then parked her car. There were a couple of reporters from the local papers—two, because a town as small as Helen needed a Lipin-sympathizing one and Porter-sympathizing one—and a couple of cops. Not seeing her father or Nate anywhere, she checked with one of the officers, who told her he didn't know where the mayor was, but a bunch of the volunteers were getting warmed up in the main lobby.

"Thanks." She got out her phone to call one or both of the men, when another man she knew exited the security door of the ER.

Josh saw her right away and headed over. "Were you out searching? I heard they're handing out coffee and hot chocolate in the lobby."

"No, I'm fine. I came to drop off Jen. How are the girls? Do you know what happened?"

Josh was looking a bit disheveled, and his coat and boots were wet. Lydia assumed he'd been out with one of the search parties. "I didn't examine the girls, and I wasn't with the group that found them, but it sounds like they'll be fine. Nothing more serious than some mild hypothermia. They got the puppy, too, so all is right with the world again. I offered to hang around and help, but they've got it covered in there."

Josh was an internist, but he'd had extra training so he could do a weekly stint in the ER, part of the measures the hospital had to go through to keep it staffed twenty-four hours a day.

Lydia let out a breath. That was more information than she'd gotten from her father, and it helped. Now she had to find Nate, have a glass of wine, and they needed to finish what they'd started. "The puppy was lost too?"

"From what I understand, the puppy started it. The one girl was showing the other her puppy, and the puppy ran off. They chased the puppy."

"Dogs." Lydia shook her head, as though Merlot running off hadn't driven her right to Nate. Still, Josh had three huskies, and Lydia considered it her Lipin duty to poke fun at the Porters' dog-collection habits.

As expected, Josh took the comment with a laugh. "Nah, it's forgivable for little kids to let a puppy escape. I think the point we need to focus on is that the girls were playing together, and once they found the puppy, they worked together to stay warm."

"Did they?"

"That's what I heard, and they've been very concerned for each other since. I'm not sure their families can pull their collective heads out of their asses, but the kids are going to be fine."

"Baby steps," Lydia said, mostly to herself.

"Literally." Josh grinned, zipping up his jacket. "I refuse to believe Tay and I are an anomaly. There will be others like us, and every person who refuses to go along with the feud makes it a little more normal to do so."

On impulse, Lydia hugged him, surprising them both. Josh was right, and she owed a debt to him and Taylor. They'd made it possible for her to even have contemplated a real relationship with Nate. In its own way, it was amazing that all the time she'd worried about their future, the feud had never been her top concern. A few years ago, that wouldn't have been the case, no matter how bold she was attempting to be.

Josh recovered quickly and hugged her back. "Take care of yourself. It's been a long night and it's not even eight o'clock. You said you drove, so I take it you don't need a ride home?"

"No, I'm good, thanks. And thanks for your help finding the girls."

Lydia got a text as she waved goodbye to Josh, and

there was her answer to finding Nate. He was in the hospital lobby. Since it wasn't a long walk, rather than respond, she headed over there to meet him.

Josh's information had buoyed her spirits, and the scene she discovered in the crowded lobby did as well. It was a far cry from the scene with Julia's aunt. Lipins and Porters were gathered together, sipping hot drinks from disposable cups, everyone too relieved to give in to old animosities.

As she approached Nate, Ethan came up to him and shook his hand. "I need to get back to Abby, but I wanted to let you know how much Jen and I appreciate your help."

Nate seemed vaguely embarrassed. "It was a team effort, but I'm glad I could be of assistance. And as long as you and Jen are okay with it, I'm happy to bring my puppies by anytime for Abby to meet them."

"Abby will be thrilled." Ethan thanked him again, acknowledged a few more people, then disappeared from Lydia's view, presumably returning to his daughter.

Nate caught Lydia's eye at that moment and made his way toward her. It took all her strength not to beam with as much delight as the girls' parents must be doing right now. Instead, she bit down on her smile and made her way out of the chaos, trusting Nate would follow her.

All the thoughts that had been circling Lydia's head for the past few hours propelled her onto her toes so she could kiss him the moment they had some relative privacy. She didn't care that some family or family friends might see them and not approve. Being together was what was important. Nate kissed her back and pressed his forehead against hers for a moment, as though he, too, was reveling in being close again.

Lydia pulled away. "Did *you* find them?"

Nate shook his head. "More like they found *us* when we got close. But I was the only trained medic with our group, so I was the one assessing their injuries initially. I think I got a little more credit than I deserved."

Lydia wondered about that, knowing Nate would demure regardless. "Josh said you were split up."

"Yeah, there were three groups, with a good mix of people in each one," Nate said as they exited the hospital, heading toward her car. "Your father's a smart man the way he did it."

"You mean a mix of families?" She hadn't paid that much attention to the group assignments, but she could guess.

Nate nodded. "Some people wanted to keep everyone separated, but this needed to be a combined effort. Plus, this way there was someone with medical expertise in all groups." He paused and grinned. "You don't have to tell anyone I said that about your father though."

Lydia pretended to punch him, which reminded her that his coat was wet. "You should get warm."

"Oh, I'm warm."

"And dry." She tugged on her jacket as a proxy for her ruined shirt. "We both should."

"I actually like you best wet," Nate said, climbing into the car next to her. "How about we go to my place and warm up and get wetter and order some dinner, too, because I'm starving after that unplanned trek through the snow."

"Sounds good to me." Lydia started the car, hoping it had retained some heat. "But I need to stop by the Bay Song first. I never shut down my computer before we left, and I need to make sure everything I was working on is backed up. Also, I need a change of clothes."

She gave him a quick rundown of the coffee incident

as she drove. The snow had mostly stopped falling, but the roads were not in the best condition. Lydia suspected the town was a bit behind on clearing the streets because everyone had been preoccupied with the search for the girls. Her father would likely get an earful tomorrow.

At the hotel, she left Nate in the lobby while she dealt with her office then ran up to her apartment to change shirts and give Merlot some affection. Taylor had fed him as promised, so Lydia changed quickly and found Merlot sleeping on her bed. Not wanting to wake him, she left him alone. There had to be a way to introduce her cat to Nate's puppies, so everyone could hang out together. Lydia wasn't sure she wanted the monsters rampaging around her apartment, which was decidedly not puppy-safe, but it was worth considering.

Reentering the inn through the back door by the lobby, Lydia tucked her hat under her arm and looked around. Nate was nowhere to be seen. She checked her office next, then wandered in the opposite direction toward the dining room and kitchen. Voices drifted toward her, easily recognizable as Nate's and Cody's.

Great. Lydia had no idea why Cody might have come by, but keeping him and Nate apart seemed like a wise idea. There was a tiny lounge the inn used as overflow space from the dining room, and Lydia paused in it as Cody's voice caught her attention.

"It doesn't matter what happened tonight," he was saying. "Once the adrenaline wears off, the fighting will restart. And even if it doesn't, do you really think the Lipins are going to tolerate another Porter fucking one of their women?"

"You're out of line," Nate said. He sounded calm, too calm maybe. Lydia had never seen Nate lose his temper, but she'd never seen anything or anyone truly seem to get under his skin before. It was sounding like Cody might be the exception, and given that comment, she couldn't blame him. Only shock had frozen her in place.

"Doesn't matter. Lydia's not her sister. You know it, I know it, and I guarantee she knows it. Why else would you two have been sneaking around all this time? It's probably fun for the moment, but it's not going to be fun as soon as they find out."

Lydia's pulse sped up and she gripped the back of a chair, her knuckles turning white. How dare Cody? She understood why he might think that, but he had no business inserting himself in her and Nate's relationship that way. Maybe Nate had been more right about him than she'd wanted to believe.

"Then, we deal with it," Nate said, calmly as ever.

She closed her eyes. Yes, exactly. As much as she wanted to burst in there, she couldn't make herself move. She had to know what else Cody was going to say. She needed ammunition for when her family ganged up on her for being with Nate.

Cody scoffed. "Yeah, you'll deal with it by breaking up. Come on, man. I never thought you were that stupid, but I know Lydia way better than you do, and she's not going to want to deal with the shit when it hits the fan. You're going to lose, and you might as well cut your losses before you make it more painful for her."

"I'm not losing."

"Oh, you will. Face it—you can't compete, and the feud is just the start."

Compete? Oh Lord, was he seriously turning her into another competition in his rivalry with Nate? A scowl spread over Lydia's features. *Hell no.* She'd heard enough.

"As usual, your ego is getting the best of you," Nate responded to Cody. "I already won. Lydia is going home with me tonight, and you need to back off."

"You already won?" Lydia stopped herself in the doorway. That was absolutely not the retort she had expected Nate to make. Won? Was he thinking of this like a competition too?

Her emotions had been dancing on a knife's edge between joy and panic since Nate showed up at the hotel this afternoon. She'd been ready to crash, but suddenly she felt like she was standing back on the edge of a blade, and a sharp, piercing pain was reawakening every one of her nerves. She needed to scream, and at the moment, she didn't much care who the target was. Both Cody *and* Nate had pissed her off too much for reason.

"Is that what this is?" she demanded. "A competition?"

Both men turned to her, both with guilt plastered on their faces.

"Lydia." Of course, smooth-tongued Cody recovered first. "Let me—"

"Don't." She held up a hand. "You don't know me, Cody. We were friends, or so I thought. But you didn't know me back in school, either, or you would have known that Nate and I were friends then too. And you know me less now."

Cody smartly shut his mouth, which was actually surprising. Nate, however, continued to stare at his feet.

"So, what is this?" she asked again. "Am I another skiing trophy for you to fight over?"

"No." Nate snapped his head up. His calm had vanished. No one else might be able to tell, but she could. Nate had stuffed his hands in his pockets, despite the fact that he must be sweltering in his coat, but it would hide his twitchy fingers. The skin around his mouth was pulled taut, and his eyes looked bluer than normal. They were gorgeous eyes that reminded her of the bay water in winter, but that just infuriated Lydia more at the moment.

She wanted to drown in those eyes, so she gave Nate the chance she hadn't given Cody—to defend himself. He was the only person who might be able to talk her back into rationality.

"Lydia, that's not it at all." Nate closed and opened his eyes, like he was fighting for control. "I came back when I heard Cody had returned to town—"

"You came back because of Cody?" She couldn't believe she was hearing this.

"Kelsey told me he was hitting on you," Nate started again.

Cody laughed. "Seriously?"

"Shut up." Lydia spun toward him, and her words seemed to shock the laughter right out of Cody. "So this *is* a competition?" She turned back to Nate. "I can't believe this."

Nate swore. "That's not what I meant. What I'm trying to say is I hadn't thought about you . . ." He cut himself off this time, saving her the trouble, and swore again then fell silent.

Apparently both men had realized that every time they opened their mouths, they made themselves look worse.

Or maybe it was her grandmother's presence stealing their tongues.

"Lydia?" She didn't know how much Theresa Lipin might have heard, but it had to be enough. "What's going on here?" her grandmother demanded.

Lydia's hat fell from her arm, and she slowly, deliberately lowered herself to the ground to pick it up. She needed to breathe. To be in control. She was a half breath, a heartbeat, from ugly crying and she would not give these two assholes the satisfaction of seeing how much their petty bullshit rivalry had messed her up. She would not let them know that what had been a competition for them had been too real for her.

"Nothing," she told her grandmother. "We were just discussing the evening's events."

"Lydia . . ." Nate trailed off with an anxious glance at Theresa.

It might be for the best that her grandmother was here. Lydia would have been tempted to let Nate fumble his way through excuses if she hadn't been. Excuses that she was in no state to hear or judge the authenticity of. But with Theresa present, Lydia wouldn't risk allowing Nate to stay. There was no sense defying their families when she couldn't be sure he was worth the risk, and at the moment, she wasn't sure of anything except that she was close to breaking.

"Leave," she said, twisting her fingers around the hat's soft wool.

"Lydia." Cody again.

"I said leave." She stood, hating how her voice shook. "Neither of you are guests here, which means you're both trespassing. And that goes for you too," she added, finally looking toward her grandmother. "I'm exhausted. Whatever you need to discuss, we can do it tomorrow."

Not waiting to see whether any of them did what she said, and not wanting to hear any more bullshit, she turned on her heel and walked away, doing her best to feign calmness. Years of suppressing her anger and frustration with her family, of playing the part of the perfect, unflappable daughter, finally paid off. Lydia managed to control her steps all the way back to her apartment door in case either of the men was watching.

The tears didn't start to roll until she was safely ensconced inside.

24

THE WORLD SLOWED down around Nate, leaving everything dark and dizzy, the air sucked out of his lungs. He'd been in a few tight situations due to his job, but the closest experience to come to mind was his car accident. Those achingly long seconds when his entire universe was condensed into a blur that he barely remembered except for one single question—Was this going to be the end?

He'd survived that. The physical damage had been painful, the fear of losing his job had occasionally been overwhelming. But he'd survived. He wasn't sure he'd survive this. Emotional destruction was worse than physical harm in every way.

He'd already known that, having seen the effects of trauma on people he worked with and on the victims of horrific accidents and fires. He'd been fortunate to never experience it himself. Lydia walking away wasn't the same, not by far, but now he thought he understood what before he'd only known.

Nate was vaguely aware of Lydia's grandmother sniffing with disapproval and strutting out of the room. In his pockets, his hands had curled into fists, fingers gripping the glass beads of the bracelet he'd bought for Lydia. He'd stopped by the cabin after leaving John's earlier, both to drop off the monsters and to grab the bracelet. It had seemed cheesy, to give it to her now after so many years, but he'd thought it might signify his intentions in a way nothing else could.

But he'd never gotten the chance to give it to her because of the call from her father, and so it had remained in a zipper pocket in his coat throughout the search for the girls. His thumb rubbed over the beads, pressing the hard glass into a callus. Using the sensation to ground himself. To remind himself of where he was and what he was doing.

Ultimately, however, it was Cody's voice that shocked Nate back into the present. "Good job fucking that up for both us."

Rage slammed into him, knocking away the numbness and confusion. "You're the one who's acting like an asshole. I told you—Lydia isn't some prize."

"Yeah, but you're the one who started it. Only coming here because I did?" Cody shook his head. "Even I didn't see that coming."

"That's not what I was trying to say." *Shit*. He wasn't about to explain himself to Cody. The only person he had to do that for was Lydia, and how the hell did he start? Every time he tried to speak up, he messed it up worse. This was why talking was overrated.

Cody shrugged. Whatever his initial reaction to being called out by Lydia, he seemed to be getting over it far more quickly than Nate. But that wasn't surprising.

Lydia was a prize to him, possibly little more. He probably liked her, sure, but Nate doubted Cody cared much more for her than that. He wanted to see if he could win her over again. For guys like Cody, the world was a series of conquests. People like Lydia deserved so much more.

But honestly, Nate didn't know if he deserved her either. The sad truth was that much of what Cody had been saying before Lydia arrived wasn't wrong. Being with her would make her life more difficult. He couldn't provide her with the kind of security that someone like Cody could. But he'd wanted the chance to try anyway, selfish as it was. And he believed she wanted it too.

Or she had until his bumbling had made it seem like he was treating her the same way Cody was. Nate wouldn't have blamed Lydia for storming away. It had been a stressful day and emotions were running high. But she hadn't stormed out after the initial verbal lashing she'd given them both. She'd walked away so calmly it had sent ice down his spine. He could practically see the Lydia he knew and loved—the brash, defiant woman who was willing to risk everything to be with him—retreat inside her, and the cool, practical Lydia she'd been forced to become return.

He hated that. He hated knowing that she felt forced to be something she didn't want to be because of him. It was bad enough when it had been because of their families.

"Well, cheers." Cody zipped his coat. "I guess we're on equal footing again. For your sake, I hope your apology game is better than your relationship game."

The other man strode out of the room, grim-faced but with more spring in his step than anyone truly cut up inside should have.

Nate took a deep breath, waiting for Cody's footsteps to disappear, then he left too. Although his urge was to run up to Lydia's apartment and bang on her door, he didn't trust himself not to make the situation worse by trying to explain again. Not tonight. After he calmed down and got his thoughts in order, he'd text her.

No, that was also a bad idea. No one wanted to be apologized to over text. That was a shitty move. He would just have to talk to her and hope he didn't bungle everything again. He would fix this. He had to. He'd already made the mistake once of not fighting for them, and he loved her too much to stand aside and let it happen again.

NATE DIDN'T SLEEP. He barely even attempted it. Luckily, when he'd gotten home, the monsters had been in need of a walk and dinner, so Nate had taken them on a long one through the freshly fallen snow. He was personally sick of traipsing through snow, but Dolly and Spark couldn't get enough of it, and for a few minutes, their joy was able to distract him.

But only for a few. After that, he didn't notice the snow much either. Usually exercise could take his mind off anything. It was his primary form of stress relief. But tonight his mind was stuck on the way Lydia had looked at him—the hurt in her eyes, the way her voice had trembled—and his throat kept closing up, making it hard for him to keep up with the energetic puppies.

Nate fed them when they returned home, but he didn't have much of an appetite anymore. Knowing he should eat something, he'd tried to force down a bowl of cereal, but the flakes and nuts stuck to the back of his throat, and everything grew soggy while he stared at his phone. Eventually, he'd dumped the remains.

A text arrived around ten, and Nate had grabbed his phone, hoping it was Lydia, but it was Kelsey, reaching out to him and Josh about the search for the girls as part of their family chat. After that, he'd remembered to bank the coals in the woodstove, and he'd lumbered up to bed. The monsters, sensing that something was wrong, had followed him. They sat on the bed with him, licked his face, and tried to be cute enough to make him smile.

Nate had petted them and played with them, but he couldn't forget how the last time Lydia had been here, they'd climbed onto the bed and snuggled against her. They'd claimed her for their family as much as he had.

But they weren't the ones who'd screwed everything up and lost her.

So he'd lain in bed, staring at the ceiling, wondering if enough time had passed now, then now, or maybe now to call her. But the truth was, he wasn't feeling any less distraught, which meant he wasn't going to be any more coherent than normal, and soon it was after one in the morning. Nate was pretty positive that waking her up would not go over well, assuming she could sleep better than he could.

Around four in the morning, he forced himself out of bed, built up the woodstove fire, and started doing his physical therapy exercises. Without sleep or food following yesterday's rescue mission, he didn't have much in the way of energy. Nate questioned whether going through the motions was actually helping, but it felt like punishment so he kept it up. Physical activity was the one thing he'd always been good at, and for the first time, he wished he'd gotten a bit more of his siblings' gift for gab along with it.

Physical exhaustion mixed with his emotional distress, and the extra cup of coffee Nate made himself only increased his feelings of nausea. There was no putting things off any longer. He knew Lydia was planning on working today, so she'd be up early too. He gave her a call around seven while choking down some toast.

She didn't answer.

He probably should have seen that coming.

Nate paced around the kitchen before dialing again. He didn't want to be a pest, but he hadn't been thinking clearly enough to leave a message last time, and he couldn't shake the hope that maybe she'd just been too busy to answer or hadn't heard her phone. When he got no answer again, he left a message.

"Hi, Lydia. Please call me when you can. I need to talk to you." He kept it simple, to the point. Nothing he could screw up. Belatedly, he wondered if he should have added *I love you* but he'd never said it to her in person yet, so saying it on her voice mail sat poorly with him.

Of course, this morning, everything was sitting poorly. His world felt off-kilter.

Hours went by and she didn't call. He shoveled off his porch with one arm. Took the monsters on another walk. Bought more coffee. When he checked the time, it was just after noon, but it felt like a week had passed.

He should go to her. Lydia had said his timing was good when he came by around lunch, so he should go now. Talking in person was better than over the phone. Body language could only work in his favor, and he could bring her the bracelet and explain everything.

He'd showered, but hadn't shaved, and Nate caught his scruffier-than-usual expression in the rearview mirror as he parked. Lydia liked his scruff. Maybe it was good that he was extra scruffy. Lowering his head to the steering wheel, he tried pulling himself together. On a positive note, he didn't see Cody's car anywhere.

Nate didn't bother texting Lydia when he entered the lobby in case she refused to respond, and he asked the woman working at the check-in counter if she was around instead.

"I think she's having lunch, but I can check." The clerk was young, with tan skin and features that suggested Native ancestry. Nate didn't recognize her, and luckily she didn't seem to recognize him. "Can I have your name?"

"Nate." He leaned against the wall, giving him a good view of the large yet cozy room.

"Hi, is Ms. Lydia Lipin back there?" the clerk asked someone on the phone. "There's a Nate here, asking for her." Nate couldn't hear the response, but the clerk hung up a moment later. "She'll be right out."

"Thanks." He tried to give her a friendly smile, but he feared it came across somewhat broken. He definitely felt broken. His stomach was thrashing around inside his gut, his blood was rushing by his ears, and he hadn't even been this on edge the first time he'd been faced with a real fire on the job.

It was official, then. Lydia meant more to him than his own skin. He'd run into a hundred burning buildings and flee from a hundred raging wildfires rather than lose her.

But when someone walked into the lobby, it was the wrong Lipin. Taylor and her sister bore only a superficial resemblance to each other, but today the expression on Taylor's face was identical to the one her older sister wielded like a weapon. Nate stood straighter, his twisting guts vanishing with the sense that this didn't mean good news. He didn't know Taylor well at all—he'd only really talked to her for the first time on this visit home— but he'd seen her enough to know this purposeful stride and upright posture meant she was channeling Lydia.

"Lydia's busy," Taylor said, pausing a few feet away. "Can I help you?"

Nate swallowed. "Seems unlikely. I need to talk to her."

"She got your message. She'll return it when she's not busy."

"And when do you expect that'll be?"

Something kinder flickered through Taylor's eyes, but it passed so quickly Nate wasn't sure if he saw it or imagined it. "I don't know. If you want, I can give her another message."

It was kindness or—probably more accurately—pity that he'd seen then. Nate debated the offer regardless. The bracelet in his pocket called out to him, but giving it to Lydia without an explanation was no good. And although it might be easier to talk to Taylor than to her sister, he didn't want an intermediary. He just wanted to see Lydia.

With a sigh, Nate shook his head. "Thanks, but I'll try her again later."

Taylor hesitated. "Maybe don't. For a while. Let her heal."

"I don't want her to heal. I want her to . . ." *Shit*. That hadn't come out right either. He didn't want her to get over him was what he meant. Because he loved her. Because they were happy together. Perfect.

His blood pressure was going through the roof. Nate could feel his cheeks growing hot, and he realized he was yanking on his ear. Clearly, he was in no position to talk to Lydia after all. He'd probably make things worse.

"Never mind." He didn't dare look at Taylor before turning and leaving, unwilling to see what she'd made of his comment.

Nate climbed back into his SUV and drove to the cabin before he screwed up anything else.

25

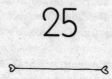

"ARE THERE ANY more men I'm going to need to run off today?" Taylor asked.

Lydia stopped dragging her spoon around a bowl of minestrone soup. She wasn't hungry, and hadn't been so since last night when Nate's words had stomped all over her heart. Besides, she didn't *like* soup. She was only realizing this now after years of forcing herself to eat it. Chunky bits of food in hot liquid was gross.

Well, she was done with forcing herself to do anything she didn't like. *Fuck soup.*

She also wasn't sure she liked males of the human persuasion either. She'd make a few exceptions—Josh, for example—but at the moment she was having a hard time thinking of a single other man who'd earned her approval.

Ian Roth from the brewery maybe? He seemed okay.

Certainly none of the men in her family who were responsible for the feud.

Cody? *Ugh*. She'd thought he'd been all right, but nope.

And Nate. Nate, who'd once been her exception to everything. Her ideal, perfect man—kind, smart, strong, brave. At his core, he was just like Cody. All the people around her wanted to fight with each other. They could call it competition, but what was the difference? She'd thought Nate had been different because he'd never cared for the feud, but so much for that. He got out his aggressive urges in different ways, that was all. And this time she'd been caught in the middle.

In retrospect, she should have realized how much the two men hated each other, but she'd been too caught up in her own dilemma to see the dick-measuring contest going on in front of her.

Taylor plopped down in front of her, shaking both the table and Lydia out of her stupor. "You need to eat."

"I'm not hungry." She shoved the bowl away.

"You didn't eat breakfast." Taylor shoved it back.

"I hate soup."

Her sister frowned. "Since when?"

"Forever, I think."

"I think you just hate everything right now, and that's understandable." Taylor put her hand over Lydia's.

Her sister wasn't entirely wrong, although she was still done pretending to like soup. "I'm not feeling well today."

Lydia wasn't sure when she'd ever feel well again. Falling in love was an awful lot like getting drunk. There was the giddy intoxication and euphoria on the way up. Then there was discovering you'd fallen in love with someone who didn't feel the same, and it all came crashing down, leaving you with an emotional hangover. Food was nauseating. Sleep wasn't restful. Painkillers and coffee could do only so much.

There was a reason Lydia limited her drinks to no more than two on any given evening, and that was only if she was out with friends. The lows weren't worth the highs. Falling in love was no different.

"Are you going to tell me what's wrong?" Taylor asked for what was probably the twentieth time since they'd met at breakfast.

No, she wasn't going to. She didn't want to bring Taylor down. It was bad enough that she'd had her sister running interference on Nate and Cody today so she didn't have to ask the nonfamily staff to lie for her. Taylor claimed she didn't mind and that she owed Lydia for all the times Lydia had stood between her and their grandmother. But Lydia still didn't like it. She was supposed to be the shield. This mess with Nate was a direct result of her forgetting her role in the family.

Since Taylor was out, Lydia had considered calling her mother, but her mother was safely away from Helen and the feud. Lydia hated the thought of bringing her down as well, especially when she wasn't even sure she wanted to mope with an audience in the first place. Some people, like Taylor, preferred hugs when they were upset. Lydia, however, had always been the girl who liked to lick her wounds in private.

"I think it's time I get Merlot a brother or sister," Lydia said. One upside of this disaster was that she'd get to spend more quality time with Mr. Fluffypants. But, her poor kitty deserved a feline friend, too, and anyway, it was never too early to start becoming a lonely old cat lady.

"I think you're dodging my question," Taylor said.

"I would never."

A moment of silence passed in which Taylor ripped open the package of crackers next to the soup and handed them to Lydia. Reluctantly, she ate one. They were salty but dry, and her stomach might be able to keep them down.

"So what did Cody and Nate do?" Taylor asked, getting up. "Obviously it was something bad, seeing as they both showed up here today, and you asked me to run them both off the property. I declined to go into the lobby carrying a shotgun, by the way. There's too much L.A. in me."

Lydia had only suggested it in jest because she knew Taylor wouldn't do it, but her sister's comment managed to elicit a small smile. "They were both being dicks, and I'd rather continue to ignore it. It makes it easier to work."

Taylor crossed her arms. "Look, I know you're the kind of person to repress everything—or is it suppress everything?—whichever. But I'm the kind of person who needs to act when people I care about get hurt. So, do it for me. Tell me who to yell at."

"The last time you got really hurt, you ran away, if I recall."

Her sister frowned. "That was still taking action. I wasn't going through the motions, pretending I'm fine when I won't eat and it looks like I didn't sleep. I polished off half a tray of peanut butter brownies that evening, just so you know."

"Mom's peanut butter brownies?"

"Yup." Taylor's face lit up. "I have the recipe. I can make them for you." She sounded hopeful, like she'd found the secret to getting Lydia to eat. But Lydia wasn't a chocoholic the way Taylor was.

"I think that much richness would make me vomit."

Her sister blew out a disgruntled breath. "How are we related?" She started to say something else and was distracted by a text. "Damn it. Our grandmother wants to talk to me."

Lydia grimaced. "I'm sorry. This is probably my fault. She showed up last night, and I wasn't in the mood to deal with her. Ignore it. I'll respond for you."

Taylor grabbed her hand so she couldn't use her phone. "I can handle it."

"But—"

"No. Look, like I said before, I appreciate you running interference between me and the family. But you've done more than your share, and you're in no state to deal with their crap right now. So thank you for your help, but I got this. Or I will get this, when I feel like responding."

"I want to help."

Taylor squeezed her hand, then released her. "I love you for it. Best maid of honor ever. But I am not letting you stand between me and them for the rest of my life, and I might as well make that clear to everyone now."

Lydia nodded weakly, too worn down to fight her sister. Besides, Taylor had a point. She'd been prepared to be Taylor's shield forever, but it had never been a job she'd been looking forward to, and it was probably best if Taylor confronted everyone head-on. After the recent joint rescue mission, some people might even back off.

Lydia's phone rang, and Cody's name popped up on the screen, bringing her thoughts back to her own dilemma. Lydia glared at it. She had zero interest in talking to him. Although he hadn't hurt her the way Nate had, she was pissed off that he thought he was competing for her, and she couldn't help but wonder—if she hadn't overheard his conversation with Nate, and things had continued between them, would Cody have tried something underhanded, like trying to break them up?

Lydia found she couldn't answer that question with a resounding no, which meant she couldn't trust Cody.

The phone dinged with a voice mail.

"Are you going to listen to that?" Taylor asked.

She wanted to say no, but curiosity would eventually get the better of her. Lydia put it on speaker and pressed play.

"Hi, Lydia, it's me again. I tried to stop by this morning but you were in a meeting. If you get this in the next few minutes, I can swing by again before I go, but I need to leave for a few days. I'm sorry I upset you last night and want to work it out. Give me a call."

Lydia was glad she'd chosen to listen. The suspense of not doing so would have been disproportional to what the message deserved.

"That was a shitty apology," Taylor said, echoing her thinking. "He's sorry he upset you? Not sorry he acted like a dick?"

"That's because Cody doesn't care beyond the superficial." Lydia stuck the phone in her pocket. "You should have told him I didn't want to see him. He'll never realize that being told I'm in a meeting was a brush-off."

"Well, maybe if you told me what he did, I would best know how to channel my avenging-angel persona. But for what it's worth," Taylor said, following her down the hallway, "Cody seemed mildly remorseful this morning."

"I don't care about Cody."

"Okay, fine. But Nate seemed seriously broken. He looked worse than you. I thought he might cry, to be honest, and I didn't think the strong, silent type like Nate even had tear ducts."

Lydia walked right into her office door and stubbed her toes. "Thank you for that." She wasn't sure if it made her feel better or worse, but she was quite sure she couldn't deal with it right now. She hurt too badly even hearing Nate's name. Like she was caught in a vise, and it was squeezing the life out of her.

"Okay." Taylor backed off a few steps. "I'm only reporting facts. It's up to you to decide what to do with them, and I'll be here when you're ready to talk. I've got a wine order being delivered this afternoon, so I'll be well stocked for you."

Lydia let out a strangled laugh. It was the best she could do while being emotionally beaten and squeezed to death at the same time. That, and refusing to eat soup. Somehow, she had to figure her shit out if she wanted to move past this.

"ALL RIGHT, ALL right! I'm coming!" Kelsey's voice was accented by the barking of her three dogs, and a moment later she flung open her door. "What do you want?"

His sister's bark was more potent than her dogs', and if Nate hadn't already been an emotional mess, he might have flinched at her tone. "You weren't answering my texts."

"Because I'm working. That's what most people do during the day." Kelsey looked him up and down, and frowned. "You look like shit. Get in."

Nate let the comment pass as he took off his boots. He was sure she was correct. "I'm sick of people not answering my messages."

"I realize, being a white male, that you think the world exists to jump at your demands, but people have lives outside of yours." Kelsey crossed her arms and hushed the dogs, who were circling Nate and barking with interest.

"I do not think that."

His sister rolled her eyes. "Okay. What do you want, then? What's wrong?"

Nate knelt to pet her huskies, glad that some creatures still showed him affection. Of course, he hadn't screwed everything up with the dogs. Their grasp of English was too poor for that. "I messed up with Lydia."

Sighing, Kelsey took a seat on the sofa and lured her huskies into a quieter state by reminding them of their toys. All but the one Nate was petting wandered away. "Every time one of my male relatives screws up, they come to me. Why?"

"Kevin did?" Nate asked, seizing on the idea that his younger brother might have recovered from whatever mess he'd made with Peter.

"When he was afraid he wasn't good enough or smart enough for Peter, yes." Kelsey tucked her feet under her legs. "Kevin—the boy with an ego the size of this state—required a pep talk before he pushed Peter away with his nonsense. I also had to talk Josh through his screwup with Taylor. Do I look like a therapist? I should start charging you all."

"Josh screwed up too?"

Kelsey narrowed her eyes at him. "You sound gleeful about that."

Rubbing his eyes, Nate dropped the rest of the way to the floor. Kelsey had a point, several actually. She was not the therapist type, and he probably *had* sounded inappropriately gleeful. "I'm not happy about Josh and Kevin, but if they screwed up and recovered, that's a good thing for me. Isn't it?"

"Depends on how you screwed up, I guess." Kelsey glared at him. "Still, I don't see why you all need to make your problems into my problems."

"You write romance." Nate pointed to her excitedly, the realization coming to him at once. "You should know about relationships."

"Neither Kevin nor Josh knew I wrote romance when they dragged their shit to my doorstep."

"Well, I do." Nate shrugged. "That, and you're the only person who knows about me and Lydia. I need help."

"No kidding."

"Brat."

Her glare morphed into an evil grin. "That's not how you get help out of me."

Nate lowered his head to his knees. "What do I do?"

Kelsey groaned. "First, you start by telling me what you did wrong."

He did, haltingly, heat creeping up his neck as he admitted how he'd let Cody goad him and how he'd made everything worse by speaking before thinking. When he finished, his mouth was dry. Chalk it up to another reason why he should keep his lips sealed most of the time. His insides felt dry as well, like he was a withered husk.

How long ago had it been since John had practically handed him the solution to all his troubles? Since he'd thought he could have it all—Lydia and his career? It felt like ages ago. There was no joy left inside of him. Nate hadn't cried, and perhaps this was why. He'd shriveled into nothing.

"All right, admittedly, that sounds bad," Kelsey said, tapping a finger against her lower lip. "But it's not like you dumped her over something asinine, like some guys I've mentioned."

"No, I just made her think I didn't care about her. Only about beating Cody." Nate smacked the floor with his hand, an unexpected burst of anger rising from what a moment ago had been his hollow chest. Even without trying, Cody messed shit up.

But the anger burned off as quickly as it had come, turning to self-recrimination. Nate knew the blame was on him. Cody might have provided the spark, but he'd wasted weeks piling up the dried grass and tinder by not telling Lydia what he felt. If she'd known how much she really meant to him, she'd never have believed he could be using her as some prize in his rivalry with Cody.

"I mean, it's bad," Kelsey said. "But it's not the worst."

"Are you trying to make me feel better or make yourself feel more important?"

Kelsey tossed a throw cushion at him. "Apologize. Use. Your. Words."

Growling, Nate jumped to his feet. "First of all, my words are what got me into this mess. Second of all, Lydia won't respond to my messages."

"Fine." Kelsey mimicked him and stood. "Then try interpretive dance, for all I care. You asked for my advice, right? How long ago did you screw up?"

Nate was too frustrated to bother responding to the interpretive dance suggestion. "Yesterday."

"Yesterday?"

"Yesterday."

"God, no wonder." She pretended to slap him. "She's still pissed off. Give her space."

Nate took a step back and almost tripped over a

husky. Puck glanced up at him, unimpressed. "That's what Taylor said too. But I feel awful."

"Yeah, you're supposed to when you screw up. Congratulations for not being a total asshole."

"Thanks, Kels." Nate sighed and rested his head against a wall. He was completely out of ideas.

"Look." Her tone softened just a bit. "You said yourself that not talking to her enough about what you feel is what got you into this mess. That means that talking is going to be what gets you out."

There was logic to that. Nate hated to admit it, but it was there. "But I suck at talking. If this was one of your books, you'd have the clueless hero do some big gesture to show he's trying to atone, but . . ."

"But?" Kelsey asked.

"I don't think Lydia would like anything big. Believe me, skywriting already occurred to me. I do better with words if I can write them out first."

"Skywriting?" Kelsey raised her eyebrows. "I like that. Might need to steal it. But you're right that anything you do needs to be tailored to what Lydia will appreciate. And regardless of whatever else you do, you need to talk to her. Maybe the strong, silent thing worked well enough to get you laid for years, but in an actual relationship, communication is important."

It was true that silence had worked well enough, but Nate had already acknowledged that it hadn't worked well with Lydia. If he'd spoken up more when she was leaving for college, she might have broken off their relationship anyway, but maybe not. He'd never know because he hadn't tried.

Well, he'd learned one lesson from all those years ago, and it was that he was done running away from Lydia when things got rough.

After returning home, Nate looked up the job information John had sent him and got to work gathering
everything he'd need to apply. He had no idea how to
communicate better with Lydia, or what he'd say, or even
how to get her to listen, but he wouldn't be going anywhere, so he would have time to try.

26

"YOUR GRANDMOTHER AND your father are here," Shawn said. "I told them I wasn't sure where you were, so they said they would wait in the dining room."

Lydia swore silently. "Thank you for the warning and the lie."

"No problem. They, uh, didn't look happy."

Theresa Lipin never did when she came by the hotel, and after Lydia had brushed her off the other night, she was probably especially unhappy. What concerned Lydia was that she'd brought her father with her. She was being ganged up on.

Lydia thanked Shawn again and made a mental note to check whether she could swing a slightly larger-than-anticipated raise for him on the anniversary of his hiring date next month. Assuming she wasn't locked up for murdering family by then, that was. Good help might be hard to find, but help that was more loyal to her than they were to her intimidating family was almost impossible.

That was what she got for cultivating a reputation as the peacekeeper Lipin.

Unfortunately, Lydia had no meetings or excuses for not dealing with her family immediately and every reason to get it over with while Taylor was occupied elsewhere. Still, she refused to rush as she saved the contract she was reviewing. She pulled a portable mirror from her desk drawer, fixed her hair, and applied a touch of lipstick. She hadn't been sleeping well since the Nate-and-Cody incident, but there was no way she was going into whatever this was without her mask in place. Besides Taylor, her family had no idea how torn up she was inside, and Lydia intended to keep it that way. With Nate, their wrath would have been bearable. Without him, she had no wish to face it, and no reason to.

Most likely, this was about Taylor's wedding, and in that case, Lydia was once again prepared to stand between the rest of her family and her sister, regardless of what her sister had said. To appease Taylor, Lydia wouldn't jump between her sister and their grandmother anymore. But if the family had sought her out, then she felt it was fair to make this her fight.

Unable to put it off any longer, Lydia crossed the strongly scented lobby, which currently looked like a florist's shop had exploded in it. Every surface was covered in extravagant bouquets, and so were parts of the floor. She'd hosted weddings that contained fewer roses, but Lydia didn't stop to appreciate them,

Her father was seated at the largest table in the dining room, drinking the hotel's complimentary coffee. Her grandmother, however, was pacing the room, and Lydia wished she'd grabbed a couple glasses of wine from the lobby to bring with her—one for each of them, or perhaps better yet, two for herself.

Lydia hadn't quite reached the two-fisted-drinking stage over the past few days, but there were times when she'd wished for that kind of emotional oblivion. Unlike her sister, though, her stomach seemed to reject food and drink when she was upset.

"To what do I owe this unexpected visit?" she asked, purposefully sitting down at the head of the table.

"What in God's name happened in the lobby?" her father asked.

Lydia folded her hands together primly. "Cody Miller."

Gregory Lipin seemed bemused. "There must be a hundred dollars' worth of flowers in there."

"Closer to a thousand, if I had to guess," said her grandmother. Theresa knew a lot more about flowers than any of her progeny, although even Lydia could have told her father that it must have been a long time since he'd bought roses.

Outwardly, she merely shrugged. Cody could probably riffle through his sofa cushions and find a spare grand lying around. Lydia was neither impressed nor moved by such a generic attempt at an apology. Besides, she hadn't been interested in Cody in the first place, and obviously her attempts to make that clear had been brushed off. As such, she felt nothing was wrong with brushing off his rose garden.

"It's very sweet of him," her grandmother continued. "They're lovely arrangements."

Lydia blinked. That might have been only the third or fourth time she'd heard her grandmother utter the word *sweet* in her life, and the first time she'd done so not in relation to complaining about food. It was beginning to occur to her that this meeting might not be about Taylor.

With great force of will, Lydia clasped her hands more tightly to keep her fidgeting in check. "They're quite nice."

"He cares about you," her father said.

Lydia pressed her lips together, but the moment of silence following her father's comment got to her. "I'm sure you didn't come here to talk about Cody."

Please, let them not have come here to talk about Cody.

"Actually, we did," said Theresa.

Shit. Lydia smiled. "That seems unnecessary."

"I understand the two of you had a fight?" Her grandmother refused to sit, but at last she'd stopped pacing.

Lydia realized she'd started fidgeting again, but she couldn't quit twisting her fingers around. How much had her grandmother overheard of her argument with Nate and Cody? She hadn't shown up until the end, which suggested not much. The only person Lydia had told about it was Taylor, and Taylor and Theresa were not speaking at the moment. As for her father, Lydia was just as positive that Taylor wouldn't have told him either. Which could mean only one thing, and her restless fingers ceased their movement as her pulse quickened.

"Did Cody tell you that?" she asked.

"He's most upset," her grandmother said, clearly not recognizing the warning tone in her granddaughter's voice.

"I wasn't aware that you two were so friendly." Her cool, unflappable air was cracking. Lydia leaned back in her chair, trying desperately to reclaim her emotions, but it wasn't working. Wild Lydia had been awakened from her post-Nate depression.

"We got to talking to him," her father said, "because of him wanting to be involved in the town when he moves back. He's a nice guy. Always was, if I recall. You used to like him."

"I did." Her jaw was starting to ache from the effort of keeping her face placid. "But I don't see how this is your business."

Her grandmother let out an enormous sigh. So that was one of them who wasn't bothering to suppress their emotions. "He is a perfect match for you—smart, handsome, wealthy. It is impossible to do better."

"I don't know. I kind of think love would be better." Wild Lydia spat out the words while the rest of her—her better sense—recoiled. Yes, love had worked out so well for her. She'd fallen for the guy who was only trying to win her over to spite Cody.

"You used to like him," her father said a second time. He seemed overall less invested in the pro-Cody argument than her grandmother, like maybe he actually wanted her to be happy. But then, her parents had split only about eight months ago. Was it too much to ask that he'd learned something about relationships?

"There's no reason you can't learn to love him," Theresa said. "He's smitten with you."

Lydia rather doubted that. Determined to have her—sure. Cody wasn't used to being denied, and it probably irked him that she hadn't fallen at his feet. She'd yet to see any evidence of more intense feelings than that. "I suppose he told you that?"

"On a few occasions," her grandmother said, and Lydia had to shake herself to be sure she'd heard correctly. She'd assumed her family was reacting to the argument, but this was sounding like they'd had more than one conversation about her.

"He'd mentioned you seemed reluctant to get involved with him," Theresa continued, "but I assured him you were just hesitant about relationships in general. You never wanted to date the men I introduced you to either."

Because the men her grandmother introduced her to were men her grandmother thought were appropriate, not people who were chosen because anyone thought Lydia might actually be interested in them. But that was beside the point. She couldn't take this any longer.

"You encouraged him?" The ruse was over. Lydia stood, and she gripped the edge of the table as though it were a stress ball she could knead until her blood pressure lowered.

"Naturally."

"He's a good guy," her father added. "You just need to spend more time with him, remember what fun you had together. We didn't want you rushing to judgment."

Her grandmother crossed her arms. "It was for your own good. We assumed you might find him intimidating these days. You're so quiet and sturdy; all of his wealth and fame might overwhelm you. But I had full confidence that you would come around and make the right choice."

"The right choice?" She screeched. Actually screeched as she jumped to her feet. "The right choice is my choice. It's what *I* want. Not you. I am so sick of being expected to do what makes everyone else in this family happy."

The words burst from her mouth, a truth bomb dropping in the middle of the room. Lydia's pulse pounded and yet some of the tension in her chest vanished. It had been a weight, sitting on her for years, decades maybe, and she'd tossed it off.

Her father and grandmother stared at her. She'd shocked them into silence. The quiet and sturdy one didn't yell. She didn't push back. She did the practical thing—the right thing—and dated the man who could bring wealth and power to the family. Even if she didn't end up with Cody long-term, Lydia understood the angle. Her dating Cody was a win for the Lipins. There was prestige to be had. Cody moved among powerful circles, and he dated the "beautiful people." She'd have been one of them by association, which meant her family was too. Her happiness, her wants, were secondary, because to be the good Lipin was to put family first.

And she was sick of it. So damned tired. Taylor was right. She'd been shoving herself into this little box, always driven by some need to be perfect when she wasn't.

"You." Lydia pointed at her father. "When you got tired of running the hotel, you left it to me and Mom. I never got to pick what I wanted to do with my career. You're lucky that I loved this place enough to suck it up, and that I loved it *so* much that I was able to beg Taylor to move up here and help me run it when Mom left. I stepped up for the family and never asked for anything in return.

"And you." Lydia turned to her grandmother. "I tolerated you meddling in my love life when you were just pushing me to date men that you approved of, wealthy guys who bored the hell out of me, because that's what made everyone happy. Everyone except me. But you need to stop.

"And both of you—no, all of you, including the ones who aren't here—need to back the hell off about Taylor's wedding. Come and be happy and gracious that you were invited, or shut up because no one involved wants your opinions or advice about how miserable Taylor is going to be if she marries Josh. Taylor is happy, Josh is wonderful, and if you can't approve of that, it's revolting.

"And finally, stop talking to Cody about me behind my back. I know what I want, and it isn't him. And what he wants?" Lydia gestured in the direction of the lobby. "It's not me or he wouldn't be sending anything as cliché and generic as a bunch of roses. He'd put some damn thought into it."

Finally, she paused to catch her breath, waiting to be overtaken by the horror of having just vented not only her spleen but likely every other organ in her body. Instead she felt relief. The weight on her chest remained gone. Her pulse was slowing back to normal. The pain, ugly and terrible, about Nate quickly spread to fill the gaps left in her emotional repertoire, but that was something else entirely. Lydia hated that pain, but for the first time since that fateful evening, she thought she might be in a place to confront it.

Across the table, her father had the decency to look upset about his role in her outburst, but her grandmother was inscrutable. Lydia didn't know what that boded for the future, but she knew an opening when she saw one. She spun on her heel and left the room.

27

⊶———⊷

"I UNDERSTAND THAT you need catharsis," Taylor said, lifting her end of the inn's metal firepit. "But couldn't you have come up with a plan that didn't involve so much cold?"

Lydia didn't respond as they carried the firepit into the center of the patio. It was a cloudy but snow-free night. Cold, but not unbearably so, dressed as she was in thermals and her down coat. In fact, she was dressed much the same way as she'd been when the wedding party had gone mushing, which struck her as somehow symbolic. That was the day Nate had tricked her into spending more time with him.

Well, he'd tricked her only in the sense that she'd been willing to be tricked, but still. It should count, since everything was feeling a bit like a trick.

Only, that wasn't entirely true, either, or she didn't think so anymore. Since the blowout with her family, Lydia had been doing a lot of thinking, but she'd reached no firm conclusions. Hence the need for the firepit.

"It won't be cold once we get the fire going," she said, satisfied with the pit's placement. "Fire's symbolic."

"Because Nate's a firefighter?" Taylor raised an eyebrow. "You're starting fires to prove to yourself that you're over a firefighter. Okay, I get it. Well done."

Actually, Lydia had been thinking more about how fire was supposed to be purifying, and she was in need of a fresh start, but she didn't bother to correct her sister. She needed Taylor's help, and anyway, she wasn't ready to admit out loud that she wasn't over Nate. That she would never be over Nate. She knew from experience.

It took another ten minutes to get a reasonable fire going, during which time Lydia began to wonder if this had been a mistake. After all, the inn's lobby had a perfectly serviceable fireplace. But that wouldn't have been as private. Not that the back patio was especially private, come to think of it, but it gave her the illusion of privacy. On a winter's Thursday night, the hotel wasn't crowded. From where she stood, warming her hands over the flames, Lydia could see only a few guest rooms lit up, and the hotel itself was only at about a quarter occupancy.

"Would s'mores be too much?" Taylor asked, joining her over the fire. "I could swing by the house and grab some marshmallows."

Lydia shot her a not-amused face. "I have other things to tend to first."

A fresh start meant letting go of the past as it related to Nate, and she had a whole box of crap sitting in her apartment. Some of it was recent, like her sketches of him and the puppies, and some of it was stuff she'd found from high school. Items she didn't remember saving, but that were tucked away in a box in her closet.

There were sketches of a younger Nate and souvenirs from their daring days of sneaking out—an old fortune from a cookie, a pinecone she had no clue why she'd kept, a flyer advertising a band they'd seen together (yet not together) over the summer.

She took a deep breath of the smoke-tinged air. As she'd expected, the fire didn't stave off the chill entirely, but it was warm enough and the air smelled fragrant with pine. It was kind of relaxing really, just standing beneath the indigo sky and listening to the fire crackle and hiss. She'd get the box down soon.

Taylor cleared her throat. "So what are you intending? Because my butt's getting cold, and I have no marshmallows."

Lydia snapped out of her daze. The flames sent shadows flickering over her sister's face. She'd spaced out for several minutes, but rather than wanting to move forward, all she felt was reluctance to move at all. Getting her box brought her one step closer to destroying everything, and that filled her with sadness, not excitement.

It turned out—maybe?—she didn't want to burn away all these memories. She'd only been in need of something to do, an activity to appease the anxiety pumping through her veins.

Unbidden, a whimper escaped Lydia's lips. "I don't know if I can do it."

"Do what?"

"Burn stuff." Lydia closed her eyes, but the fire left an orange glow behind her eyelids. It was taunting her, telling her she couldn't even follow through with something this simple. "I thought it was a good idea to get rid of my memories of Nate. Start fresh. New me, bold and brave."

The sort of woman who had no problem standing up to her overbearing family.

"But I don't think I have the guts after all." Lydia sighed. "No matter how hard I try, I'm still me."

Taylor squinted at her through the firelight. "Of course you're still you. We had this conversation. And you are finally acting like the badass I always knew you were."

"Shouldn't being bold and brave mean I can toss off the shackles of . . ." The fact that she couldn't figure out what word to use there was probably a clue. It wasn't like she was burdened with Nate. The only shackles she was dragging around were her own bad decisions. Hence, the anxiety.

Ever since she'd stormed out of that conversation with her father and grandmother, her brain had been free to focus on Nate and nothing but Nate. And what Lydia had begun to think put some of the blame, perhaps most of the blame, for that fateful evening on her own shoulders.

She'd overreacted. All of the tension and pressure she'd been carrying around—from protecting Taylor and hiding her relationship—she'd needed an outlet for it, and so she'd created one at the first opportunity. She should have let Nate explain, again and again if he had to. He'd been under pressure, too, and angry, and in retrospect she should have known it wasn't in Nate's character to do what she'd accused him of. Nate would never use her, or anyone, for that matter. She'd vented at him and Cody, but it had never been about him. It had been about how she felt used by her own family.

But she'd told him to go away and leave her alone, and after his initial attempts to set the record straight, he had.

Lydia couldn't blame him. Nate had always been the kindest, gentlest person she'd ever known—a sweetheart wrapped in a six-foot frame of solid muscle.

"Being bold just means you followed your heart," Taylor said. "That you were willing to risk it and live with the consequences. It doesn't make it any easier to get over heartbreak."

Lydia scowled and tossed a few more of the sticks she'd gathered onto the firepit. "What if the heartbreak is my own fault?"

"How could this be your fault?" Taylor asked. Her sister sounded suspicious and ready to leap to her defense.

Lydia appreciated that loyalty, although she wasn't sure she deserved it. She'd stopped being her sister's shield the moment she'd lashed out at their grandmother. Of course, Taylor claimed she didn't care. She only wished she'd been around to see it. Lydia feared she'd regret that later.

The fire no longer felt as warm as it had a minute ago as Lydia regaled her sister with her recent epiphany. They took turns tossing on more sticks, but they were rapidly running out. She would need to either burn her stuff soon or toss another log onto the coals. Or admit defeat and go back inside—that was also an option.

"Your reaction was understandable," Taylor said when Lydia finished speaking.

"You don't have to defend me."

"I know I don't have to." Even in the dim light, Taylor's face spoke volumes. "I'm saying what you heard didn't sound good."

"But Nate tried to explain later and I didn't let him."

Taylor wrapped her arms around herself for warmth. "True, but you were angry."

"And now I've lost him." The words were sticky in her throat.

"Did he refuse to talk to you?"

Lydia huddled closer to the fire. "I texted him this morning, and he didn't respond."

It had only been a simple *Hi* to see what sort of reaction she'd get. The answer had been none at all. Clearly he was treating her the way she'd been treating him. It was fair but painful.

Lydia almost wanted to believe it meant she was wrong. That she hadn't misinterpreted Nate's comments, and he had been competing with Cody the whole time. That would make her angry, and it was easier to feel bold and brave when angry. Who knew whom she'd end up snapping at next? In this town, with her family, the possibilities were endless.

"Did you text him a second time?" Taylor asked.

"I didn't want to be annoying. The first text wasn't going anywhere."

"So practical, as always."

Lydia snorted. "No, practical would have meant accepting Cody's apology and trying to date him."

"Exactly." Taylor tried snapping her fingers, which wasn't possible with gloves on. "You're being bold, admitting you made a mistake and working to correct it. Although, one text is kind of weak. On the other hand, jumping straight into burning things is kind of extreme. I'm not sure how to score you here."

Lydia held up a hand. "Please, no references to scoring. Metaphors that have anything to do with competition are dead to me."

Taylor made some sort of noncommittal reply and abruptly stepped away. "Well, if you're not burning anything, we might as well toast some marshmallows and get use out of this fire."

Confused by the change in her sister's tone, Lydia motioned behind her toward the hotel. "You don't need to go home. I think there are some in the inn's kitchen."

She was getting cold and feeling sillier by the minute, but if Taylor wanted to toast marshmallows, she might as well hang out and eat gooey, gross blobs of sugar. Lord knew she hadn't been eating much of anything for the past few days, and friendly company was definitely preferable to returning to her apartment alone.

No offense to Merlot, but he really wasn't a great conversationalist, and he wouldn't stop her from sending tipsy texts to Nate about what a jerk she'd been. Although, to be fair, Merlot had snuggled with her when she'd cried herself to sleep the first few nights. He also didn't share Nate's habit of stealing the food on her plate. So he had that going for him too.

Crap. Suddenly she was on the verge of tears again, remembering the times she and Nate had sat around in his little cabin kitchen, sharing food or trying to cook food when neither of them was particularly good at it. She should have known the tears would come back. First she'd cried because she'd been hurt by what she'd assumed was betrayal. Then last night she'd cried because she realized she'd ruined everything. The only thing that had kept her from crying today, when her phone had been hauntingly silent, was work.

But now was a terrible time for the tears to return. They'd freeze to her face and likely prompt her to do something regrettable, like try Nate's number again.

As Taylor dashed into the hotel, Lydia danced from foot to foot for warmth and to keep herself too occupied to reach for her phone. Still, her gloved fingers curled around it. She should at least check if Nate had responded. Better late than never.

Lydia was pulling her phone out of her pocket when barking startled her out of her bad decision, and she spun around. Nate was standing on the edge of the patio along with the monsters.

28

THE PUPPIES STRAINED against their leashes as soon as Lydia turned around, excited to see her again. So was Nate, but he held them in check, just as he held himself in check. If he couldn't run over and beg for her affection, then, damn it, neither could they. Especially since they were more likely to get it than he was.

Lydia stood in the shadow of the fire's glow, but Nate could recognize the shock on her face, and he swallowed. Probably showing up without warning like this was rude, and he should have responded to her text. But he hadn't known how. After her silence for the last few days, the simple *Hi* had confounded him.

If it were possible to butt-text someone like you could butt-dial, he'd have assumed that's what this was. The odds of butt-texting *Hi*, however, seemed low. So Nate had assumed Lydia was ready to talk to him again, only as usual he didn't know what to say. He was more tongue-tied and word-shy around her now than he'd ever been in his life. His mouth had betrayed him once. He could not blow a second chance.

And yet, the more Nate thought about it, the more he came to accept that Kelsey was right. Maybe not with the interpretive dance exactly, but he needed something to get Lydia's attention and make her realize he was serious. Something that he couldn't screw up. And then he needed to talk to her and explain himself. Unfortunately, he'd lost the confidence to do it. It would be so much easier if life were like the movies. Then he could run into a burning building and rescue Lydia (and her cat), and he'd understand in that moment how much he loved her.

But life was not a movie, he didn't actually want her motel to burn down, and there was something pathetic about being a grown man who would rather run into a burning building than express his feelings.

Lydia's text had given him hope, and he knew he couldn't sit around and not approach her, whether in person or by phone. He'd spent most of the day trying to think of some gesture, some action he could do to prove his intentions to her without involving burning anything. Ironic, then, that after he'd made a plan, he'd arrived at her staircase only to find her hanging around a fire. It was in a pit rather than raging out of control, but it left Nate off-balance, which was not cool considering he was already hopping around on one leg mentally.

Dolly and Spark barked. Nate swallowed. Lydia stepped closer, and he lost more of her to the shadows. The flames behind her cast her in silhouette, but he could see her breath rising from her mouth in little clouds. He wanted to press his mouth against hers so badly, to steal those white puffs from the cold, uncaring sky. His chest ached with it.

"Nate?" She'd been bouncing on her feet a moment ago, likely for warmth, but surprise had stilled her.

"Sorry I interrupted." He didn't understand why she might have been standing around a fire on a winter's night with Taylor, but she must have had plans.

"It's okay." Lydia took another hesitant step forward. "Did you get my text?"

He wouldn't have rushed over here if he hadn't, although from her perspective, she might not have seen this as a rush. But Nate had intended to come up with some quietly romantic idea—not interpretive dance—to get Lydia to listen. Now that he had some assurance that she might, he'd rushed into Plan Two, which was neither quiet nor well thought out, and only dubiously romantic.

"Yeah, I did. I didn't want to respond and . . ." Nate glanced around the dimly lit patio, finding it wholly inadequate for his plan.

"Oh." Her tone conveyed what he couldn't see on her face.

Nate swore out loud. "That came out badly. I wasn't done talking. Just . . . Fuck." And to think, he used to get annoyed at himself for babbling around her. What he wouldn't give for a little verbal oversharing.

"I had a plan," he said, reaching into his coat pocket and pulling out his phone. The speakers would be crappy, but he didn't need it for long. "I wasn't sure if you'd run away if I came by to talk to you again, so I thought I might need to go to extremes to get your attention with this."

"With what?"

He already had the song queued up to the right spot, and Nate hit play. The chorus of Dolly Parton's "I Will Always Love You" sounded awful coming out of his phone's speakers, but the monsters recognized it instantly. In seconds, the courtyard filled with the sound of their "singing."

Nate hit pause as soon as the chorus ended, fearing hotel guests might start throwing rotting vegetables their way, but Lydia had covered her face with her gloves. She was shaking, and he couldn't tell if it was with laughter or something worse.

"They're kind of hard to ignore when they do that," he said, kneeling down to pet the huskies, who seemed upset that their idol had gone silent so quickly. "I thought it might make you hear me out, or at worst—make you acknowledge me long enough to yell at me to leave."

Lydia spread her fingers so that her eyes became visible from behind her gloves. "Isn't that song about someone leaving?"

Nate winced. "Yeah, but that's why I only played the chorus. Because that's the deal, Lydia. I'm *not* leaving. Not giving up. Not again. I did leave last time because I thought you deserved a shot at a life without me, and it was going to break me to see you having it. But I can't give up without a fight this time. I love you, and I think I never stopped loving you. And yes, I came back here when I heard Cody was in town, because I was jealous, even if I couldn't admit it to myself. If you want to know why I never liked Cody, you're the reason. You were close to him, you cared about him, and all I could do for so long was to watch you from far away."

"You never stopped?"

He could barely hear her whisper, but Lydia's question knocked him off course. How could she sound surprised by that?

"How could anyone not be in love with you?" Nate swallowed. "You are all I've ever wanted. And here's the thing—the time we had together back then was amazing, but the time we've been having now is even more so. So yeah, I competed with Cody then, and if I had to compete with him now, then I did. But it was never a game. You were never a prize. You are everything. I love you, and this time I'm not leaving. Even if you don't want me back, I'm coming home, and I will be here in case you ever need me."

Oh well, the babbling was back. He'd have been embarrassed if he weren't so panicked about Lydia's reaction. He was overheating in his coat.

"Lydia?" Nate's throat was dry.

She'd frozen as he'd vomited words all over the place, but she let out a whimper. He didn't know if that was good or bad, but before he could ask again, she was next to him. Crouching on the cold, damp stones, she'd wrapped one arm around him and enveloped the extremely happy monsters in the other. They jumped up around and licked her face, and Nate wasn't sure if they were doggy kisses on her cheeks or tears.

A drop slid from her eye, so tears.

"I'm sorry." He hadn't wanted her to cry.

"So am I."

Nate hadn't a clue what she might be sorry about, but any concern that it was bad news for him evaporated as she smashed her mouth against his. He couldn't breathe or think. Lydia's body pressed against his through two layers of coats, so he couldn't feel her, either, and he was desperate to. But he could taste her, and she was warm and sweet, summer on a cold winter's night. She even smelled like warmth, like smoke. The skin of her cheeks, the only parts that weren't covered, was soft. Nate inhaled those white breaths, hungry for every part of her he'd feared he'd lost, letting her very essence warm him to the core.

"You're still crying." The one hand he'd used on his phone was free of its glove, and he wiped the tears off her beautiful rosy cheeks.

"It happens." Without any success, she attempted to clean her face with her jacket.

"I'm sorry I made you cry." The monsters were running in circles around them, and Nate had the thought of picking up where they left off. Kissing all the tearstains from Lydia's face. Then kissing the rest of her too—her chin, her throat, worshipping her body the way she deserved. The cold barely even registered. His blood ran hot for her, but it wasn't merely desire raising the temperature. She truly was his bonfire at midwinter, the light in his darkness.

She was home, and he was never leaving again.

LYDIA SNIFFED, HATING that she probably looked and sounded gross, but something told her Nate didn't mind. The way he gazed at her . . . Lord, despite the cold, she could melt into a puddle. She didn't know how her knees hadn't given out during his speech, and she hadn't wanted to stop kissing him. No one had ever said things like that to her, and coming from Nate, she could tell that none of it had been preplanned. He'd emptied his guts into the air, and this time, she'd let him. If only she hadn't thrown a fit the other night, maybe she would have known he'd been working up to say those words then. Days had been lost.

But for that reason, she had things she needed to say to him, too, before she kissed him some more. "I'm sorry I freaked out on you."

"You don't need to apologize. I know what it sounded like." Her face was inches from his, and his breath brushed her nose every time he spoke.

"I do though." Lydia closed her eyes, pushing down more tears. She was happy, she was upset with herself, and the emotional overload was making her dizzy. She grabbed Nate's arm. "Let's go inside?"

"I thought you'd never invite me." He kissed her again, less greedily and more with the strong confidence she'd grown to expect from him. Possessive but gentle. The Nate who was her perfect rock was back with her. "The monsters though?"

They'd never been in her apartment.

"If you're not going anywhere, it's time for them and Merlot to get acquainted."

Nate stood, untangling leashes from around their legs. "I like this next step in our relationship, but I'm a little concerned about what Merlot will think."

"I think Merlot will adjust better than our families will."

Lydia checked on the fire, but it had grown low in the cold without constant tending. Left alone for another hour, it would probably burn itself out entirely, leaving a mess for her to clean up in the morning, unless the grounds staff got to it first, which she'd try to prevent. It was her personal mess, not the hotel's.

Another thought occurred to her, overriding the need to warm her toes inside. "Where's Taylor? She was coming right back. I need to let her know I'm going in."

Nate's smile was charmingly unsure. "I, uh, think she left for good when she saw me arrive."

So that explained her sister's unexpected dash for marshmallows.

Lydia brought out an old towel to wipe off the monsters' feet and hung up her and Nate's coats. Merlot watched the puppies from his windowsill, ears perked with curiosity. His tail remained unmoving, however, so he wasn't upset, and when Lydia petted him, he closed his eyes like the long-suffering companion he was. After a couple minutes, Dolly and Spark lost their interest in their new friend who refused to join them on the floor, and they took off exploring the living room and kitchen. Nate had wisely closed the other doors so they couldn't get into trouble without being seen.

Nate rummaged through his coat pockets. "I have something for you."

He had something for her? She hadn't even had a chance to apologize yet, and Lydia rushed over and placed her hands on his arms. Just that much touching, not even skin to skin, made her heartbeat catch. His gray sweater was soft, and it clung to his muscles. Total Nate—soft and hard at once, strong but gentle. Lydia didn't want to talk anymore; she wanted to wrap her arms around him and kiss until their clothes fell away, and give in to the ability they'd always had to simply exist blissfully wordlessly around each other.

"I bought this for you," he said, removing one of her hands so he could show her what he was holding in his.

Nate opened his palm to reveal a bracelet of beautiful green and blue glass beads, held together with a silver clasp in the shape of a star. The colors shimmered like the aurora.

"I was going to give it to you before you left for college, but after . . ." Nate trailed off, but she knew what he'd been about to say and tears reformed behind her eyes. "Anyway, I couldn't get rid of it, but I couldn't hold on to it, either, so I hid it at my parents' house when I left town. I dug it out a few weeks ago, and I'd been meaning to give it to you. To show you I never gave up completely, but it never worked out right. It has to work out now."

Nate put the bracelet around her wrist and a fresh tear

rolled down her cheek. "I never got over you," Lydia whispered. "I thought I could, but I was always comparing every guy I met to you, and none came close."

"Even Cody?" His lips quirked, letting her know it was a joke.

"He's not even in the same league. Oh, crap." Somehow, through her tears, she snorted a laugh. "I'd told Taylor no more competition metaphors, and that has to count."

She reached up and kissed him, sinking against his body, which was so much nicer without the heavy coats between them. She could feel the heat over every inch of him, and she was melting once more.

Nate raised one hand to her cheek. "You are so beautiful. I love you so much."

He might as well have been kissing her still, given the effect those words had on her body.

"You know, you should speak up more often. When you do, I fall more in love with you."

A mischievous smile broke across Nate's face that did nothing to cool her blood. "Good to know."

"Also it makes me want to rip your clothes off."

"Even better to know." He tilted her head up for another kiss, forcing Lydia to gather all her willpower and step away.

She had to be strong and not give in to the desire coursing through her. "I still need to talk."

Nate's smile drooped. "You have nothing to apologize for. I'm not upset. You had a right to be angry."

"Maybe, maybe not. But I overreacted, and I took out all of my frustrations on you. That wasn't fair of me. I thought I was being brave and bold by letting everything out, but I should have let you finish. You weren't the one I was angry at, not really. I was upset, but I just . . ."

To her surprise, Nate laughed ruefully. "I held back what I was feeling and thinking because I thought it was best, and you've been holding back everything with your family for the same reason. It backfired on us both. That's all."

She sucked on her lip, not having thought about it that way before. Nate kept pointing out all the ways they were similar, things she would never have considered. First it was their protective streaks, now this.

Scuffling noise behind her temporarily interrupted her thoughts. The monsters had found her slippers under the table, and the next couple of minutes were given over to getting them free and on Lydia's feet while Nate lectured the puppies about their shoe fetish, using words they surely didn't understand but a tone they probably did. Grumpy at being caught, they settled next to the radiator by the window where Merlot was hanging out. Lydia's cat took one glance down at them and went back to sleep with what could only be considered a kitty-style eye-roll.

When the drama subsided, Lydia wrapped her fingers around the hem of Nate's sweater. "What if I keep screwing up as I try to be less stodgy and more fun?"

Nate took her hands, and shivers trickled through her as he ran his thumbs across them. "Then we both screw up again, and we figure it out again. But you don't need to change for me or anyone, Lydia. Just do what comes naturally. You're perfect as you are."

She swallowed, her skin sizzling under his touch. "So are you. Only I want you to talk more because it turns me on."

He chuckled. "In that case, let me get practicing."

Epilogue

THE WEDDING HAD been simple, sweet, and short, officiated by a justice of the peace while only close family and a few mutual friends looked on. Now the group of about thirty was packed into the back of a restaurant where the music was supplied via a streaming playlist and the food was serve-yourself. No matter how different they were in background, the two grooms shared a common distaste for formality and an unwavering belief that a taco bar was the height of celebration food.

Nate wasn't about to argue with any of that. Tacos were excellent, and seeing his younger brother practically glow with happiness and be the life of the party was worth being crowded into a room that he was pretty sure was packed beyond its occupancy rating. He didn't start his new position with the Helen Regional Fire Department for another few weeks yet, though, so he pretended not to notice.

The far more likely source of danger here was with his parents being in the same room as Josh, Taylor, and

Lydia, but they were wisely sticking to chatting with Peter's parents. Although his mother had been polite and perhaps something like friendly to the Lipin women earlier. Nate chose to believe the best. It seemed rude to assume anything else at a wedding, and besides, he was too happy to want to do anything else.

In fact, since Nate had announced he was moving home and that he was officially dating Lydia, it was as though a spell had been cast over the town. The animosity remained, but muted. At times, Nate could feel it in his bones, like an electrical charge in a storm. But people kept their mouths shut and sometimes seemed embarrassed when they talked to him, as though they knew they'd been behaving badly. Plus, he'd been welcomed at the homes of Lydia's friends, or his dogs had, and he'd seen the two neighbor girls playing together himself. Even the shit Josh and Taylor had been dealing with had died down. Nate wasn't sure some of the town's ice would ever thaw, but warmer winds had started blowing.

Josh talked about it like they were containing a virus, an immune response was kicking in. Kelsey went on about how they were setting an example that couldn't be ignored. Lydia joked that everyone just looked up to Nate and felt intimidated by him, which made him laugh. If anyone was intimidating, it was her—his successful, beautiful, poised Lydia. She'd been speaking her mind more often, and no one could ignore it when she did.

Speaking of her, Lydia slipped her arms around him from behind and kissed his neck. Desire stirred inside of him, and he forced it down. This was not the place. But she was wearing a dress, and his mind had been roaming all day with thoughts of how he could take advantage of this rare opportunity. Mostly, though, he was having a hard time keeping his hands to himself when he wanted to push up the fabric and start touching her.

Nate was pretty sure she knew it, too, because she kept torturing him. Like now, her breath tickled his ear and the soft curve of her breasts pushed against his arms. "Your brother and Peter are adorable."

"I don't know how you can say that after spending so much time staring at Kevin's face."

Once his siblings had seen some of Lydia's sketches of Nate and the monsters, they'd been intrigued, and Lydia hadn't been able to resist taking their requests. Her wedding gift to the grooms was a portrait of Kevin and Peter.

"After spending so much time staring at your brother's face, I have no trouble seeing the family resemblance," Lydia said. "So stop that."

"There's no resemblance. Kevin's a pain in the ass. He's just a happy pain in the ass at the moment."

"Brothers clearly have a different dynamic than sisters." She stepped around beside him and took his arm.

More torture of a different sort. This position gave him a better view of her lovely face and the swath of skin below her neck. The dress had a drooping cowl neckline that exposed a hint of cleavage, and he was surely a caveman because dragging his gaze away was painful.

"What? You and Taylor never beat the snot out of each other as kids?" Nate asked.

"Can't say it occurred to us, no."

"Huh. Guess I'm glad I never hurt him too badly."

Lydia poked him in the ribs, and frankly, that was more torture. "But you're here for him now, and from what I understand, that made a difference in *them* being here." She nodded toward his parents.

"I don't know about that, but I wouldn't miss this."

A cheer went up as the wedding cake was rolled into the room. It was a monstrosity, way too big for the group gathered, but that was not surprising. Kevin had inherited the Porter family sweet tooth with the rest of them, and the one thing no Porter wedding would go without was an excess of cake.

"If they do that cake-smashing thing . . ." Lydia shook her head.

"My brother would never waste cake. My family has limits."

She poked him again. "At one time, those limits included never dating a Lipin."

Nate let go of her arm and pulled her closer so that she was in front of him and he could hold her while they watched Kevin and Peter do the cake-cutting ceremony. It was both a wonderful and a terrible idea, as whatever scent she was wearing filled his head, and the curve of her ass swayed against his groin as she moved lightly to the music. Although, at least with her positioned this way, no one could see what that did to his lower body.

"Every generation improves on the one before," Nate said. "Isn't that the hope?"

"I think it is." Lydia clapped along with the group as the guys fed each other cake. It wasn't exactly a civilized feeding, but it wasn't smashing either. "Your father keeps glancing at us, by the way."

"Good." He resolutely did not look in his father's direction. It was going to take time, but Wallace Porter would have to get used to this, along with everyone else.

The cake was wheeled away to be cut for everyone, and Kevin and Peter raised their hands together as "We Are Family" started playing.

Nate grinned. "Good choice. I think this song should become a wedding tradition."

"Ooh, yes." Lydia shimmied in his arms, and he just about died from the sensation. "I'll suggest it to Tay. It will have quite the effect at their wedding."

Nate leaned forward and kissed her temple. "And at every other Porter-Lipin wedding that follows."

"Every other?"

He couldn't see Lydia's face, but he could hear in her tone the way her eyebrows had raised. Nate hated teasing her, but he had *some* manners, and he wasn't about to propose at his brother's wedding. "You don't think there will be more?"

Lydia spun around and planted a kiss on his cheek. "I think we need to talk later."

It was one talk—and one future—he was very much looking forward to.

ACKNOWLEDGMENTS

I can't believe the Hearts of Alaska series is over with this book. After spending so much time with these two stubborn and ridiculous families—and their more level-headed and loving members—it's a little hard to let them go. If you're reading this, I hope you've enjoyed their journeys.

I come from a couple of generations of people who married without family approval (or, at least, without enthusiastic family support), so maybe it was inevitable that I'd end up writing about fictional couples who do the same. My maternal grandparents actually had to elope. While I was lucky enough to have my grandfather in my life for many years, unfortunately my grandmother died when I was very young. I wish I remembered her better, but all the memories I do have are ones that warm me with a sense of love. Naming a fictional town after her, where love wins in the end, seemed like the perfect way to honor the memory of her and my grandfather.

As always, many thanks go to my wonderful agent,

Rebecca Strauss, who was the first to believe in these characters and without whom these books wouldn't exist. You are the best! Also thank you to my amazing editor, Sarah Blumenstock, for all her super-helpful notes, her enthusiasm, and for forcing me to up my pun game. More thanks go to Natalie Sellers, Stephanie Felty, and the entire Berkley team working behind the scenes who bring these books to life.

I would be a wreck without my writing groups—the Purgies, the Y-Nots, and the Berkletes. A special thank-you also to Bethany Bennet for answering my weird questions (Is it really "snow machining" and not "snow-mobiling"? What about sneakers versus tennis shoes?). Any regional word choice or other details that I got wrong in this series are my own fault.

Finally, thank you to my family for their support, and to Al, who is still waiting for me to write a sci-fi series for him. One day.

Don't miss

HEART ON A LEASH

Available now from Jove!

IN RETROSPECT, TAYLOR Lipin would consider the termite chilling on her toothbrush to be an omen. At six thirty in the morning, however, it was simply disgusting. She screamed, flung the toothbrush into the trash, and retrieved the spare she'd had the foresight to stash in her bathroom cabinet. Five minutes later, standing under the hot shower spray, she took heart in the knowledge that her day was unlikely to get any worse.

By the time she stopped at the coffee shop near her office to meet her best friend, she'd mostly put the termite out of her head. Stacy had texted to say she was running late, so Taylor ordered for both of them and stepped aside as she waited for their prework caffeine infusions to be prepared. The shop smelled wonderful, a blend of coffee, sugar, and vanilla that set Taylor up for disappointment each weekday morning. In a city filled with coffee shops, she'd yet to find one that could make her favorite drink as well as the place in her hometown. Likely it had nothing to do with the quality of the beans or the baristas and everything to do with nostalgia, but that was life.

A new text arrived before either Stacy or the coffee, and Taylor read it, expecting a second update from her friend. Instead it was from her sister, and that was when Taylor recalled both the termite and that old saying about what happens when you make assumptions.

Emergency. About Mom. Call me soon.

The chaotic chatter of dozens of voices, the hiss of the espresso machine, the barely audible beat from whatever song was being pumped through the shop's speakers—it all dissolved beneath the thudding of Taylor's heart as she read the message a second time. Cool, unflappable Lydia was not prone to hysterics.

Was it a heart attack? Cancer? A bad fall?

"Taylor L.?" The barista calling her name snapped her out of the endless stream of morose questions.

Taylor took a deep, steadying breath. If her mother was in imminent danger, surely Lydia would have called. That would be sensible, and her older sister was nothing if not sensible and dutiful. Therefore, Taylor wouldn't panic, and she'd take a sip of her coffee before calling. God knew, she'd probably need the caffeine.

Since there was still no sign of Stacy, Taylor carried the drinks over to a slightly quieter corner near the entrance and dialed Lydia.

Her sister picked up on the second ring, leaving the caffeine with no time to work its magic. "Taylor?"

For someone who'd sent a text declaring an emergency only a minute ago, her sister seemed awfully surprised to hear from her. But Taylor was too concerned to point that out. "What happened?"

"You actually called. I was hoping to catch you before work, but I didn't expect that."

Lydia's incredulity required her to take another sip of her drink. "You said it's an emergency. Of course I called. What's wrong?"

Lydia seemed to collect herself, and her voice returned to normal. "Mom took off."

"What do you mean *took off*? That's not a euphemism, is it?"

"What? No. She got in the car and drove. To Anchorage, I think. They're getting divorced."

For a second, Taylor thought she must have heard her sister incorrectly. Mom and Dad divorced—no, it didn't make sense. Then her sister's words sank in, and confusion warred with relief. So her mother was fine, but her mother was also clearly not fine because a fine mother wouldn't be asking for a divorce. Taylor felt like the universe had slapped her. "They've been married for almost thirty-five years. This is impossible. They're so happy."

She'd thought they were anyway. Lydia's tone, hinting at her lack of calls home, wasn't entirely unwarranted, but her parents had always seemed happy when she did call or during the one or two times a year when she visited.

She wasn't the only one confused, though, which made Taylor feel better. "I know. I'm blindsided."

Taylor glanced toward the door as a fresh wave of people entered the shop, but still no Stacy. "How's Dad handling it?"

Lydia made a strangled noise. "He's acting indifferent. He's more worried about how this will affect his reelection."

That made as little sense to Taylor as any of this news did. Sure, her father was as poised and reserved as Lydia, but he should show some emotion. Worrying about his next election had to be a way to deflect the pain. Divorce hadn't been a scandalous sort of thing in decades, and everyone in her hometown knew her dad. Their opinions were unlikely to be swayed at this point. "Maybe he's in shock."

"Maybe, but this was two days ago."

"Hold on. This happened two days ago and you waited to tell me until now?"

"I wasn't sure how you'd take it." Lydia didn't sound the least bit apologetic.

"So you were concerned about my reaction, and therefore decided to send me a vague and alarming text at eight in the morning? Two days!"

That finally put her sister on the defensive. "Well, if you came home for more than just Christmas, I might assume you cared more. When Mom first left, I figured everything would eventually blow over so there was no point in worrying you. You could go on being blissfully ignorant of our lives."

"That's low." Taylor squeezed her coffee cup so hard the plastic lid popped off, and her restless fingers fumbled as she set it on the table. "I don't get a lot of vacation time."

Lydia sighed. "I'm sorry. I'm just stressed out. Can you come home for a week or two? I could use some help."

Taylor was sympathetic. Part of her wanted nothing more than to do exactly that. Run home, hug her dad, and fret over every detail with Lydia while they consumed questionable quantities of chocolate and wine. She wanted family and security, but home for her was currently Los Angeles, and the rosy haze of her childhood memories had been ripped away with this call. Changing the state she was in wouldn't change the facts.

"Remember the part about me not getting a lot of vacation time?" Taylor ran a distracted hand through her hair. "My company was bought out last week, and things are unstable at the moment. I'm not sure I could get the time off approved. I'll call Mom and Dad and offer my support, and we can talk more later."

"*They* don't need your support. They seem to be doing just fine. *I* need your support, but I need it here. To help out with the inn."

The Bay Song Inn was the boutique hotel her grandparents had opened back when their small town was first becoming a tourist destination in the late seventies. When her grandparents had decided to retire twenty years later, her parents took over the inn, but her father had mostly left running it to her mother and Lydia as he became more involved in town management.

"You expect me to abandon my job to help with yours?" She understood her sister was in a bind, and the family business was obviously important, but Lydia was being completely unreasonable. Or so Taylor's only partially caffeinated brain was telling her.

"Look, I wouldn't ask if it wasn't serious. When Mom left, I thought it was simply to find a lawyer, but it's been two days, and she's returning my calls with one-line texts telling me not to worry. As if that's possible. I checked her closet and she must have packed at least a week's worth of clothes. I can't handle the business side of the inn and the hospitality side at the same time. I don't care what kind of midlife crisis she's having; Mom's timing is awful. Tourist season has begun. We're booked solid every week through August, and with weddings most weekends."

"That's . . . wow. That's amazing. Grandmother must be thrilled."

"She is, but that's assuming everything doesn't go to hell because I can't handle the work by myself. Since *Travel and Leisure* named us one of the ten best places to get married in Alaska last year, it's been unbelievable. And I will not be the person who lets the inn get run into the ground."

That honor was almost solely due to Lydia's efforts, Taylor was certain, and she didn't doubt her sister's commitment to the business. "Can't you hire someone?"

"I would have if I'd known Mom was going to go AWOL, but like I said, tourist season has already begun. No one's available, especially no one who knows the job like you do. Even if I could beg someone I trust to help out part-time, I'd have to train them. Tay, I need you."

Taylor grimaced. Now she understood the real "emergency" from Lydia's text. She did have a pretty good idea of what the job entailed, and it was precisely what she'd never wanted to do.

Ever since she was little, Taylor had been determined that—in her six-year-old self's words—she was going to be a "business lady." Little Taylor had devoted countless hours to making her Barbie dolls into perfect "business ladies," which had mainly meant they wore stylish clothes, worked in tall buildings, and bossed people around. Her understanding had expanded as she grew older, but her desire to leave home and work someplace with tall buildings and stylish clothes had not. Taylor had taken off to Southern California for college and never turned back.

It was true that sometimes she wondered if she was still chasing an ephemeral ideal, because working in marketing had not lived up to her childhood expectations. And it was also true that sometimes, more frequently in recent years, she'd started wondering if she should have left childhood ideals in childhood and chosen a field that didn't make her feel like her soul was being crushed on a daily basis.

But it was just as true that returning home and working at the inn remained on her list of Things to Consider Only before Selling Off Internal Organs. But even then, it might depend on which organ. No one needed two kidneys.

Lydia was still speaking, and Taylor caught the end of her last sentence. ". . . to help shut down the gossip too."

"What gossip?"

"The usual. Mostly people speculating about affairs and garbage like that. All instigated by the Porters, I'm sure."

Taylor snorted. Possibly living so long in L.A. had changed her perception about such things. "Can anyone back home actually have an affair without everyone else knowing about it?"

"Dan Fidel, the high school principal, carried on with a third-grade teacher for two years before his wife found out. So yes. But that's not the point. The Porters are spreading lies, and rumor is Wallace is considering running against Dad for mayor. They've been looking for ways to cut us down since the article. We can't afford to let them see us struggle. This is about family, however fractured we currently are."

With her free hand, Taylor poked at the foam on her coffee. Sure, it was only eight in the morning, but she might need something stronger to drink if this was turning into a Lipin-Porter battle on top of a regular family disaster. Unfortunately, she could easily believe the Porters would try to take advantage of her family's situation. After the Bay Song's write-up, they'd started a whisper campaign that the hotel had only gotten such a glowing recommendation because her family had bribed the writer. Or, depending on which Porter was talking, because Lydia had slept with the guy.

It was easy for Taylor to roll her eyes from the California coast, but back home, the nastiness was something her family had to deal with on a daily basis. It was also another reason Taylor had been eager to leave.

The coffee shop's door opened, and this time Stacy entered, along with a whiff of exhaust from the delivery truck idling outside. Her friend waved and began worming her way through the crowd.

"We can talk more about this later," Taylor said. "I need to go."

"Fine. Will you think about what I said? Please."

"Promise." It was an easy one to make. Taylor doubted she could do anything else.

"Are you all right?" Stacy asked. "Sorry I was late. My alarm didn't go off, but you look more stressed than I feel."

"My parents are getting divorced." Taylor filled Stacy in, leaving out the part about her sister's gossip worries, her father's election concerns, and why the Porters would make everything worse. Explaining the ridiculous century-old feud would take more energy than she had.

As soon as they stepped outside, Taylor regretted not getting an iced coffee. On a day when the temperature threatened to hit the nineties, there was a lot she missed about living three thousand miles to the north, not that she would ever admit it.

Her hometown was hardly the frozen wasteland conjured up by most people's visions of Alaska, but even though temperatures could creep into the seventies in the summer, it rarely got as hot as L.A. was half the time, and there was always a salty breeze blowing off the bay. On days like these, she missed that scent, which had been replaced by the stench of exhaust and smoldering concrete. She also missed the harbor and watching the boats as they bobbed on the water, and she missed looking out her window and stretching her neck to see to the tops of mountain peaks that seemed to vanish into the sky. She didn't miss tourist season, when the town swelled to bursting like an overripe grape, but L.A. was a tourist town year-round. The city had its own charms, and palm trees were pretty, but it was a world away from Helen, Alaska.

"You should go home and help her," Stacy said. "Even if it's only for the emotional support. Family is family. Lizzy Fernandez worked remotely when she had to go to Phoenix for her grandmother's funeral. You should ask. I mean, assuming you can work from Alaska as easily as here. Can you?"

Desperate for the air-conditioning, Taylor breezed past her to head inside. "Depends on what exactly my sister expects me to do."

"I just meant, like, will you have an internet connection?"

Taylor blinked at her and then, despite everything, burst out laughing. "Um, yes. We have the internet in Helen. It's not as speedy as it is here, but it's sufficient. We also have this newfangled electricity stuff and running water. It's pretty civilized. Even the bears sometimes wander into town to check their voice mail."

Stacy's cheeks turned pink, and she laughed too. "Shut up! I wasn't sure. But wait, do bears really wander into town a lot?" Her eyes grew as round as cartoon orbs.

Yes, bears did occasionally wander into town, but not as often as Stacy seemed to be thinking. Since her friend's reaction amused her, and goodness knew she needed the laugh, Taylor opted to merely smile and let Stacy wonder.

She wondered too—about whether working remotely was feasible. Trying to balance her regular job with helping out Lydia sounded like hell. More to the point, since the merger, she wasn't sure that would be an option, but she supposed she could look into it.

Taylor's smile lasted approximately ten minutes longer, at which point the ominous termite on her toothbrush and her phone call with her sister collided in a perfect storm that would have had her laughing hysterically if panic hadn't seemed like the smarter choice.

The storm arrived in two emails. The first came from the large, impersonal management corporation that had bought out her apartment building last year. They'd been making tons of updates to the building since, and while that was nice in theory, Taylor often felt like she was living in a construction zone with all the resultant noise. But the email did not contain a notice about more repairs. Rather, this was a notice that the builders had found massive termite damage. An exterminator had been contacted, and they'd be fumigating soon. She had to leave for a minimum of three days.

Super. That seemed like a good reason to ask about working remotely. But then the second email arrived, this one from her boss, who was calling a division-wide, mandatory meeting. Taylor knew that couldn't bode well, and sure enough, when she left the meeting twenty minutes later, working remotely was an issue she no longer needed to worry about.

The company's new owners had just laid off her entire division.

Taylor walked out of the meeting, clutching the coffee that was a poor imitation of her hometown's finest, and sat on the edge of her desk. She was dazed from one too many blows in a short period, concerned about her bank count, and really ruing her morning optimism about

termite on her toothbrush.

"As an upside, I guess you can go help your sister,"

cy said, smiling glumly.

"I suppose so." She raised her coffee cup. "To unem-

oyment."

Stacy tapped Taylor's cup with her own. "To days

nting for jobs while lying on the beach."

That sounded a whole lot better than what Taylor an-

ipated. Lydia would be thrilled, but no matter what

e tried telling herself about nicer weather, sisterly

nding, or her favorite coffee, Taylor couldn't help but

el like she was planning to leave behind a perfect

orm for a category five hometown hurricane.